2/09

This book was

purchased in

memory of

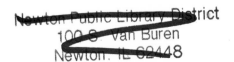

Also by Dorothy Koomson

My Best Friend's Girl

MARSHMALLOWS FOR BREAKFAST

◆ ◆ ◆

DOROTHY KOOMSON

DELTA TRADE PAPERBACKS

MARSHMALLOWS FOR BREAKFAST

First published in Great Britain as a paperback original in 2007 by Sphere

Published by Bantam Dell
A Division of Random House, Inc.
New York, New York

ISBN 978-1-60751-700-9

Printed in the United States of America

For Tess,
who inspired this story

ERM, EXCUSE ME . . .

Publicly expressing gratitude is one of the best things about being a writer. Please indulge me, I love doing this, so here goes . . .

My fantastically fabulous family: Samuel, Agnes, Sameer, Kathy, David, Maryam, Dawood, Maraam, Muneerah, Yusuf, Ahmad, Muhammad, Ameerah, Liah, Skye, Aysah, Habiba, David, Jade. All of you are so special to me, not least of all for your support.

My astounding agents: Antony Harwood (aka GAM), "above and beyond the call of duty" should be your middle name—thank you for *everything*. James Macdonald Lockhart, you're, like, the calmest man alive and I adore you for it.

My perfect publisher peeps: Jo Dickinson (aka MGE), every writer should be as lucky to have you as their editor—thank you, especially for staying in touch during your maternity leave. Louise Davies, bless you for being so patient and understanding. Jennifer Richards—really do love ya work. Kirsteen Astor—love ya work, too. Plus Kerry Chapple and Emma Stonex—thanks for keeping me in gossip and books.

My brilliant British-side buddies: Richard Atkinson (thanks for being the first to read the "new Dorothy

Koomson"); Emiliy Partridge; Andy Baker (thanks for being the only one to visit me in Oz); Rhian Clugston; Sharon Wright and David Jacobson and Luc; Marian, Gordon, Jonathan and Rachel Ndumbe; Stella Eleftheriades; Jean Jollands; Emma Hibbs; Bibi Lynch; Adam Gold; Rob Haynes; Janet Cost-Chretien; Tasha Harrison; Denise Ryan; Sarah Ball; Martin, Sachiko and Connor O'Neill; Tanya Smale (thanks for being my Kamryn); Colette Harris; Nuala Farrell; Maria Owen; Sharon Percival.

My amazing Aussie-side amigos: Lucy and Olivia Tumanow-West; Lindsay Curtis; Rebecca Buttrose; Rebecca Carman; Jen, Danny, Dylan, Isabella, Sunny, Jolie, Gemma and Violet (aka the Adcocks); Erin Kisby.

And, to all the people who were so gracious in telling me their stories that went into this book, a deep, heartfelt thank-you for your honesty and bravery.

PROLOGUE

This is like the moment between heartbeats. The space where nothing happens. Where the blood slows in your veins, your breath catches and your mind spins out into that huge blank space of unreality.

I'm talking to him on the phone.

It's him. It's really him.

"We need to talk about our baby," he says.

I would throw down the phone if I could move. If his voice hadn't snaked its way through my body and caused all my muscles to petrify.

"Kendra?" he asks. "Can you hear me?"

The line crackles slightly because calling from a mobile, a phone is ringing somewhere across my otherwise empty office but I can hear him. Of course I can hear him. Every word is clear and precise, his low voice as deep and smooth as a vat of warm syrup. I can hear him and the memory of him flashes through my mind.

———

His large, muscular hand reaches out to stop me from stumbling; his steel-like grip encases my throat. His mouth smiles as he says he'll do anything for me; his breath is against my ear as he promises to kill me.

———

"Kendra, can you hear me?" he repeats to my silence.

"Yes." I push out the words. "Yes, I can hear you."

"We need to talk about our child . . . You need to tell me about him or her." He pauses, sucks in a breath. "I don't even know if it's a boy or a girl. That's not fair. I have a right to know. I have a right . . . Kendra, you have to talk to me. You owe me that much at least."

I say nothing.

"I'll meet you," he says. "After you've finished work. I'm outside your building now but I'll wait. What time do you finish?"

Like a nest of disturbed bats, panic rises up inside and becomes a blanket of thick, black leathery wings, dampening all other sensations. He's outside? He's outside—now?

"I'm busy tonight," I reply, trying to sound normal. Trying not to let my voice expose my fear.

"I don't care if you're busy," he hisses. "Nothing is more important than this. We have to talk."

"I, um, I, erm . . ." I falter. I have to take back control of this situation. He can't do this to me.

"I know where you work, how long do you think it'll be before I find out where you live? I'll show up at your house. I'll come to your work every day and then go to your home. I won't leave you alone until you talk to me. You can avoid all that if you meet me now."

He means it. I know he means it. I know what he does when he doesn't get what he wants.

"I'll meet you outside at quarter to five," I say. "I can give you half an hour."

"Good girl," he purrs, his tone soft, reasonable and calm. "I knew you'd do the right thing. I can't wait—"

"Bye," I blurt out and cut the line, almost throwing the white handset back into its cradle.

Five minutes ago I never thought he'd find me. Five minutes ago it never occurred to me he was looking for me. Five minutes ago the most pressing thing on my mind was about which supermarket to visit for the shopping.

And now this.

———

His hand crushes my throat; his honey voice crawls in my ear.

———

He's really going to kill me this time, isn't he?

CORNFLAKES, ONE TEASPOON SUGAR & ICE-COLD MILK

◆ ◆ ◆

CHAPTER 1

*Y*ou're black."

Surprisingly, I didn't scream, yelp or collapse into a quivering heap when I was confronted by an intruder in my home. I reeled back as my heart lurched to a stop; I stared at her with wide, shocked eyes, but I didn't scream.

It was early on a Saturday morning. I'd just stepped out of the shower and had been about to dash across my flat to the bedroom to get dressed when I'd found the intruder—intruders, actually—standing in the area outside the bathroom, staring at me. The intruder who spoke to me was about three feet tall, six years old with green eyes that were as dark and glossy as eucalyptus leaves, and shoulder-length black hair—one side bunched with a red elastic band, the other falling in waves to her shoulder. Beside her stood her male mirror image—he had shorter dark hair but was the same height, the same age and had the same green eyes.

The pair of them weren't dressed so much as "ensembled." Her pink skirt with ruffles at the bottom she wore over striped blue and white tights, and with a white, long-sleeved T-shirt under a faded orange vest. She had yellow socks bunched like legwarmers around her ankles, while red shoes with big yellow flowers on the front adorned her feet. He wore long blue trousers, one leg of which was tucked into one of his green socks. His white T-shirt was decorated with avant-garde artwork of felt-tip pen marks and grubby fingerprint streaks; one collar of his blue fleece zip-up jacket was folded inwards, hugging his shoulder.

Both of them wore clothes that were crumpled and creased, as though they'd slept in them.

As well as the dishevelled clothes, the twins also shared grey-white complexions with dark, blue-purple circles smoothed like smudges of dirt under their eyes. They looked like a pair of street urchins, battered and worn by the February cold, who'd wandered into the warmth of my flat. But they weren't street kids, I was pretty certain of that. They were my landlord's children. I'd only just moved into this flat and had yet to meet my landlord and his family because they'd been away overseas when I'd arrived from Australia. Obviously they were back.

The children openly explored me with their eyes, took in the clear plastic shower cap that covered my black hair, my cleansed and moisturized face, my damp neck and shoulders, the towel I'd wrapped around my torso and was currently clutching closed in a death grip, my knees peeking out from beneath my towel, and my water-spotted calves. Their gazes lingered on my feet, probably fascinated by my fluffy white slippers.

"You're black," the girl stated again, her voice clear and firm; she spoke with the honesty of a child and the confidence of an adult. She knew how to address people no matter how old they were. In her arms she carried a blue, floppy toy rabbit.

"So I'm told," I replied.

"I'm Summer," she said, confirming she was my landlord's daughter. She jerked a thumb at the boy. "He's Jaxon. We're twins." She looked me over again—from my shower cap to my feet—then whipped her eyes up to mine. Our gazes locked. She had me hypnotized, had my undivided attention for as long as she wanted. Her face, framed in that unusual way by her hair, was innocent and open, yet wise and private. A million insignificant and profound thoughts went on behind that face.

Summer shrugged her small, bony shoulders, breaking eye contact as she gave a slight nod of her head. "You're quite pretty," she said.

"Erm . . . Thank you, I think," I said.

Jaxon leaned across to Summer, cupped his hand around his mouth and began whispering in her ear. He talked for a few seconds and when he stopped, she nodded. Jaxon straightened up. "You're not as pretty as my mumma," Summer informed me.

Guessing this was his contribution, I glanced at Jaxon. He stared defiantly back at me, daring me to argue. He obviously wasn't much of a talker, but he knew how to get his point across. "Oh, OK," I said.

"Summer! Jaxon!" a male adult voice shouted from the bottom of the stairs, near the front door of my flat, causing my heart to lurch again.

"What are you doing up there?" the voice continued as footsteps began up the stairs. This was probably my landlord, Kyle Gadsborough, running up to join his children as they watched me with no clothes on. Before I could plan an escape, could work out if I'd be able to fling myself back into the bathroom, Mr. Gadsborough appeared.

He took up the area at the top of the stairs because he was a tall man, over six foot at a guess. He was slightly older than me, thirty-six, maybe thirty-seven, with a solid but trim body. He was dressed in loose, navy-blue jeans and a creased white T-shirt under a gun-metal-grey jacket. His black hair was cropped close to his head; his eyes were as large as his children's but brown. He had a shadow of stubble on his face and, like his children, he was the kind of pale that looked like he was fighting off sleep.

My landlord came to a halt at the top of the stairs, heaved a sigh and rolled his eyes at his children. "I told you," he said, "she's not here—probably out shopping or something." When they didn't respond to him and instead continued to stare at me, he obviously wondered what they were looking at and glanced in the direction they were focused on. He gave me a brief "hello" nod before turning back to the kids. He stopped. I saw the moment his brain registered that he'd seen a person in that quick glance to his right. He turned back towards me, surprise and confusion on his face. "Oh, you are here," he said. "Sorry, we—" His voice halted as he realized he was in the presence of a virtually naked woman. One who wasn't his wife. His grey-white, sleep-deprived face exploded with color and two bright stripes of red burned a scarlet trail across his face.

"Oh-h-h," he stammered. "Oh, um, I, um . . ." He started to back away, forgot he was standing at the top of the stairs, missed the top step, and slip-tripped backwards. For a moment, a fraction of a second, Mr. Gadsborough seemed to hover midair, then his body began its fall down the wooden staircase. My already racing heart went to my throat as I watched him, waited for him to tumble out of sight, but at the last moment his hand snapped out and caught hold of the white banister railing and managed to keep himself upright. Once steady on his feet, he ran down a few more steps until all we could see from where we stood were the soft bristles that sat in uneven swirls on the top of his head. He faced the wall so he wasn't even vaguely looking in my direction.

"Come on, kids, we've got to go," he said to the wall. "Now. NOW!" And his footsteps pelted down the rest of the stairs and out the door as though the devil was on his heels.

Summer, who, like Jaxon and I, had been watching Mr.

Gadsborough, turned back to me. "We've got to go," she said seriously, her tone adding, *But we'll be back.*

"OK," I replied to both the spoken and the unspoken statements.

Summer started down the stairs first; through the gaps in the banisters I saw her move carefully down each step until she disappeared from view. Jaxon started down after her, but before putting his foot onto the second step, he stopped, turned and threw a look at me. *You don't fool me,* that look said. *I can see right through you.*

I drew back a little at its intensity.

Only one other person had looked at me like that in all my life. And that was an age ago. The look had unsettled me then, but now it almost knocked me over. How could a six-year-old boy look at me as if I were an open book?

I blinked at him, wondering if he was going to say something. But no. His work done, his look thrown, Jaxon turned and trooped down the stairs after his sister and father.

OK, I thought, as the door clicked shut behind Jaxon, *I have to get out of here. Right now.*

CHAPTER 2

*B*efore I did anything else, I propped a dining chair under the handle of the bedroom door.

I was taking no risks with this: if I was going to take my towel off to get dressed, then I wanted a several-minute warning in the event of anyone from the Gadsborough family showing up again.

Double-checking that the chair was secure before I dropped the towel, I picked up the bottle of body lotion sitting on the bedside table and squeezed a large creamy-white dollop into the palm of my hand. I moisturized my body in record time—thirty seconds, tops—then grabbed my black bra from the bed and fastened it on. I shoved my legs into my knickers and pulled them on, then I tugged on my white, long-sleeved T-shirt and buttoned on my jeans. It took me less than two minutes to get dressed, and as I did so, I kept my eyes fixed on the doorway, just in case.

Seven days ago I was in Australia.

That still spun me out a little, made me look around checking my surroundings like a mole seeing the light aboveground for the first time. I'd be constantly reminding myself that the bare trees, the cool temperature, the fresh bracing air meant I was in Britain. I was back in the land of my birth. Back home. Seven days ago I was living a very different life in Sydney. I had an apartment near the city center, and I was communications officer for a large media company.

Five days ago, cramped, exhausted and buzzing slightly from the sugar high, a twenty-four-hour sweets binge, I'd wandered out of immigration and customs at Heathrow airport and into the arrivals area. Ignoring the people who ran into each other's arms, reunited and happy, returned and being collected, I'd made my way out to the taxi queue. No one was meeting me because few people knew I was back. My parents lived in Ghana, my sister lived in Italy and my two brothers lived in Spain and Canada. My family was scattered across the world and I couldn't impose on any friends to come pick me up.

I had all my carryable worldly goods in a backpack and two suitcases. My papers I'd posted to myself the day before I left so they'd arrive at some point. I'd queued up for a taxi at the airport and asked for an address in Brockingham on the Kent-London borders.

As the taxi cruised along the motorway, heading for the knot of traffic that was London, I knew the Gadsboroughs, my new landlords, wouldn't be there. Kyle Gadsborough had told me that his family needed to go to New York, and while it wasn't ideal that they wouldn't be there to greet me, there was nothing either of us could do—they needed to be in America, I needed to be in England.

To pick up the keys I had to go to the next-door neighbor's house. She'd opened the door to me and I'd drawn back a little. She had hair that sat like a brown meringue on her head, violently plucked eyebrows and a mouth so wrinkled with fault lines it looked as though it was on the verge of caving in on itself.

She hadn't wanted to hand over the keys. She'd asked to see my passport and a copy of the rental agreement. Once I'd complied she'd asked to see another form of ID. I'd shown her my British credit card. Knowing she couldn't delay any longer, she'd said she'd put her shoes on and come over with me. That'd been it for me. After twenty-four hours on a flight and spending £150 on a taxi, my patience, which had already been stretched, was now paper thin. I'd held out my hand for the keys. Reluctantly she'd dropped them into my palm.

The entrance to my flat, Mr. Gadsborough had told me, was on the right of the house behind high, ornate iron gates. After unlocking the gate, I'd wheeled my luggage along the stone path and the side of the white house. The back opened up to a large, grass courtyard surrounded by large, slate-grey flagstones. Opposite the main house stood my flat.

Mr. Gadsborough was an architect and had designed and rebuilt the flat that sat above a former garage as a self-contained studio for his wife. It was white on the outside, with a row of six large picture windows that looked over the courtyard and three skylights embedded in the slanted roof. At the center of the building, where the entrance to the garage had been, was the blue front door.

As I'd approached it, it had felt like my flat, even though I'd only seen the pictures that Mr. Gadsborough had e-mailed me. It felt like the place where I could start again. Leaving Sydney had been a decision made in haste. I had no idea where I was going to live, no family in England I could impose upon, so I'd spent hours trawling the Net until I'd seen the ad for this place. After a few conversations with the owner, when we'd gone through the process of couriering contracts back and forth, and transferring money, it was mine. All mine. I'd felt a calmness flow through me when Mr. Gadsborough told me I could rent the flat. I had somewhere to live, somewhere to hide.

I'd wheeled my metal-grey suitcases around the grey flagstone path to my flat. The navy-blue front door had a brass knocker. Behind the door would be stairs that led up to what would become my space.

The chill of the place had come rushing down the stairs to greet me as I'd swung open the door. It was cool outside, but colder inside—the absence of someone in the house had left its mark.

I'd stared up at the wooden stairs with a gentle turn at the top—there was no way I'd make it up in one go. Leaving my suitcases on the doorstep, I'd climbed the stairs.

I'd shed my rucksack and bag, then pelted back down and bumped one of my suitcases up the stairs, pelted back and bumped up the other one. After shutting the door behind me I'd stopped. It seemed to be the first time in weeks I'd done that, stopped. I'd stopped and allowed the stillness that came from a place that hadn't been inhabited for a while to descend upon me. I'd closed my eyes, inhaled the sensation of motionlessness deep into my lungs, then exhaled it. Pushed it out to join the quiet around me. This was what tranquillity felt like. This was what I wanted when I'd boarded the plane for home.

I'd opened my eyes and for the first time properly took in the room. The entire flat was about forty feet long, most of it open plan. To my right was the living area with a sofa, the television and a coffee table. Beside the sofa was the door-way that led to the bedroom. To my left was the small and round dining table with three chairs. Beyond that, at the far end was the kitchen with a whole wall of glass that let light flood in. Beside it, the door that led to the bathroom. The entire flat, apart from the bathroom, had stripped wood floorboards, topped with brightly colored rugs that sat like islands at equally spaced points along the floor.

On the dining table stood a box of chocolates tied up in a pink bow, a piece of white card propped up against it. I'd picked up the note.

Welcome to your new home, Kendra.
From the Gadsborough family.

A sweet and unexpected gesture that told me they were good people. Normal, kind. I'd felt that every time I'd spoken to Mr. Gadsborough. They were decent and friendly.

Friendly. That had caused a trickle of anxiety to run through me. *Their potential friendliness could be a problem,* I'd thought, as I'd put down the note and stared at the chocolates. I needed to be left alone for a while. I felt like a fugitive, running away from Australia, and I needed solitude now that I was home. A place where I could spend time on my own, licking the wounds that had made me leave Sydney; get myself together. Get stronger as I eased myself back into being around people again.

My biggest fear as I'd fingered the cellophane covering of the chocolates was that they wouldn't leave me alone long enough for me to start rebuilding my life. That they wouldn't leave me alone, full stop.

I paced the bedroom floor, wringing my hands, fretting. An irrational terror was growing bigger and more real with every passing minute. The kids had probably gone back over to the house and told Mrs. Gadsborough what had happened. "She's quite pretty," Summer would say casually.

"She had no clothes on, did she, Dad?" Jaxon would blithely add.

Any moment now Mrs. Gadsborough would be marching over here, frying pan in hand, to read me the riot act. To tell me to keep my clothes on, even in the shower. *Especially* in the shower.

Even if she didn't come over here for that confrontation, it would hardly endear me to her. It'd put a seed of doubt in her mind about me, make her wonder if I had an eye on her husband and make her decide to keep an eye on me.

With that thought crystallized in my head, I pulled on a V-neck jumper, struggled into a black cardigan and put on my long black coat. Quickly, I wrapped a stripy, multicolored scarf around my neck, grabbed my bag and made for the door. I'd go visit a few estate agents, get the train into central London and spend the day there. I'd be back as late as possible, by which time they'd be asleep. I could keep doing that—staying out till late—until I found somewhere else to live.

Before I stepped out of the flat, I eased open the front door a sizeable crack and peeked out, checking that it was all clear. Across the courtyard stood the house, large, white and imposing. From where I was, I could see the large kitchen window. The wooden slatted blinds were up and I could make out Mr. Gadsborough standing at the kitchen table, gesticulating wildly at the two children who sat at the table, both of them engrossed by what he was saying. Mrs. Gadsborough was nowhere in sight. This was my chance to escape.

I stepped over the threshold and eased the door shut. Just as carefully, I slipped the key into the dead bolt, gently turning it. Then, I slid the key into the Yale lock, turned that just as soundlessly to double lock it.

Biting my lower lip and tensed to move stealthily across the courtyard towards the gate, I turned—and found Mr. Gadsborough, box of Weetabix in one hand, right behind me.

"JESUS CHRIST!" I screeched, leaping back and clutching at my heart. "DON'T DO THAT!" What was it with this family and its talent for appearing from nowhere?

All at once my landlord looked stricken, as though he couldn't believe he'd done that to me. "Oh, God, I'm sorry," he said, reaching out to me with his free hand. I flinched back, pressing my body flat against the door to stop him from touching me. We'd already crossed far too many barriers in the last half hour, we didn't need to trample down any more.

He drew back his hand, stepped away from me, gave me room. I moved a little away from the door, now that he was at a safe distance.

"Miss Tamale, I'm sorry, I didn't mean to scare you," he said.

"Call me Kendra," I said cautiously, my heart still racing.

"I'm sorry, Kendra, I didn't mean to startle you. That's the last thing I wanted to do."

"It's OK, Mr. Gadsborough, I'm fine. Really. I'm just a bit jumpy."

"Call me Kyle," he said.

"OK, Kyle."

"I was giving the kids their breakfast," he said, pointing to the kitchen behind him, "and I saw you. I wanted to catch you before you left to apologize. I didn't know what time you'd be back and we're probably going to go straight to sleep after breakfast. Jet lag. But I want to apologize for before. You know . . . *Before* . . ." His voice trailed away and he flushed a gentle carmine as the memory obviously refreshed itself in his mind.

"It's fine," I dismissed automatically, although it wasn't. It hadn't been intentional, which made it a little fine.

"It most certainly isn't fine," he interrupted. "I've just spent the better part of half an hour explaining to the kids why it's not fine. I'm so sorry." His voice was smooth and gentle, a hint of an accent, northern maybe, overlaid his words.

"It's OK, really."

"It's not. I just want to assure you it won't happen again. It's the kids, you see. I don't know if you've ever had kids?" His eyes trailed down my body, as though he could assess whether I'd had kids from examining the curves of my form, then his face bloomed red again as he obviously remembered seeing these same curves in a towel.

"I know of kids," I said, a touch of sarcasm to my tone. If I had kids would I have moved into his house without them?

"Well, my two, when they get an idea in their heads, they won't let up. When I told them I'd rented the place to you they wanted to know everything all at once. They wanted to meet you straight away. Wanted a picture. Wanted to find out where you were right then. Wanted to fly over to Sydney. They couldn't understand why we couldn't go to Sydney on the way to New York because, you know, there's a plane ride involved in both of them. But, when we got to New York, nothing. Didn't bring it up at all. I thought they'd forgotten, but on the way back from the airport just now, Jaxon, I think it was, remembered all of a sudden, reminded Summer and off they went. I couldn't get them to stop until I let them in to prove you weren't there, which of course you were."

The strong silent type Kyle was not. All the while he talked his eyes, which were the deep maroon of mahogany, danced. Close up, he was an attractive man. Ignore the exhaustion, the paling of his skin and the semicircles of darkness under his eyes and you had a handsome soul. Rugged physique, soft lines at his jaw, strong but striking features, an air of natural inquisitiveness his daughter had inherited. Woven into his height, his body, his persona, was a gentleness that would put most people at ease—when he wasn't creeping up behind them.

"We did knock," Kyle said to end his explanation.

"I was probably in the shower," I said, with a deadpan face just to see him redden again, which he did, right on cue. When Kyle blushed, dipped his head a little, he became a bashful boy who had been caught looking through his mother's underwear catalogue; he became the adult version of Jaxon.

"It won't happen again," he promised. "Look, if you want to take the spare keys back and give them to someone else, feel free."

"No, I'd rather someone nearby had them, you know, just in case I slip in the shower and can't get up."

He didn't blush this time; instead he tilted his head to one side and his lips slid up into a smile. He had a nice smile, warm, sweet, inviting. "You're going to keep on making shower jokes for the rest of my natural life, aren't you?" he asked.

"Yup, pretty much."

"As long as we haven't scared you off. I hope you weren't going out to find a new flat. Because it absolutely will not happen again. I'm going to learn to keep the kids under better control. That's my mission."

"Oh, they're fine. Just spooked me a bit, that's all."

"Yeah, you say that, but you don't know how often they run rings around me. I'm new to all this, you see."

"Oh," I said. Weren't they his kids after all? Where was his wife?

"My wife and I are separated," he said in answer to my silent query. "Very recently. Well, a few weeks. That's why I'm renting out that space—it was her work studio," he said with a nod towards the flat. "We've just been to New York, that's where she's thinking of moving to. Without us. We're getting divorced. I thought the trip was a reconciliation, but on our last night we're lying on the huge hotel bed, the kids are asleep between us, and she whispers, 'I want a divorce, Kyle. We can't make it work so I want a divorce.' Nice huh? We slept in the same bed the whole two weeks. All four of us, just like old times, and that's how she ends it. I hadn't even known we'd been trying to make it work."

With every word my toes had been curling under, clenching themselves in my trainers while every muscle in my body strained with the effort of not turning around and running away from him. I knew all about divorce. I'd just fled from divorce. I did not need to run straight into another one.

Kyle stopped talking and we stood, unmoving and silent. His act of emotional bloodletting that had dragged me into the deepest recesses of his family vault stood between us, an unexpected horror. Neither of us knew what to say and an uncomfortable, stifling quiet flowed over us.

"You're going to move out in the middle of the night, aren't you?" he said sadly. He shook his head, ran a hand over his cropped hair. "I'm sorry, this must be the world's worst introduction for you—first the stuff in the flat, and now a brief history of my failed marriage. I'm sorry."

He hadn't been like this on the phone. Admittedly we'd been discussing business but he'd seemed quiet, as though many thoughts went on in his head but few made it out. Maybe it was the jet lag combined with the sudden realization that he was going to be a single father that had loosened his tongue. Either way, I didn't know what to say.

From the Gadsborough house, loud and shrill, the phone started ringing. The knots of tension twisting my shoulders and stomach relaxed and my toes unclenched themselves. I didn't have to say anything, he'd go answer the phone and I could get as far away from him as possible. He stared at me as though waiting for an answer to something. I stared at him waiting for him to answer his phone. The ringing continued in the background.

"Do you want to get that?" I said, pointing to the house.

Surprise sprung onto his face as he glanced behind him. "Oh, right," he said, turning back to me. He still made no move towards his house. He gave me a small, bashful smile, then glanced down at his feet before raising his head a little to me. "Would you . . . I don't suppose you'd want to come in? Have breakfast with us and meet the kids properly?" He shrugged. "They'll only keep on at me until they do meet you. Well, Summer will keep on, Jaxon will give her backup. Silent backup, but just as effective . . . Look, I promise I'll shut up if you come for breakfast. If you want to?"

If I was honest, truly honest, I didn't want to have breakfast with them. It was nothing personal. The Gadsboroughs seemed very nice, but I'd only been around them for an hour or so and life seemed to have become a tangle of embarrassment, anxiety and complications. Mrs. Gadsborough had left, which was why I had a place to live. I'd literally flown halfway across the world only to end up back where I started—on the front line of a divorce; now I would witness everything I tried to run from. I'd see firsthand how brutal, ugly and vicious a permanent separation became. And then there were the kids. Being around children was a form of torture for me. It tore me up inside, reminded me of missed opportunities, made me feel a deep, searing pain. Living near them would be fine, engaging with them would not.

I should not have moved in here, I realized as I stared at my landlord, the phone still ringing in the background.

"Please?" Kyle asked.

"OK," I said. I really had no way out.

CHAPTER 3

*I*n the kitchen, Jaxon and Summer sat in silence at the wooden dining table.

Summer was at the head of the table and was making her blue floppy bunny hop around her place mat—occasionally the bunny would jump high in the air, then would make a kamikaze dive into the empty white cereal bowl in front of her, only to leap out again, unscathed. Jaxon, who sat to Summer's right, had his elbow on the table, resting his face on his hand, and was staring down into his bowl as though divining the secrets of the universe.

The table was ready for breakfast: on it sat a box of corn-flakes, spoons, a white ceramic bowl heaped with sugar, glasses, a carton of milk and an unopened carton of fresh orange juice. Kyle deposited the box of Weetabix on the table as he dashed past to answer the phone.

I hesitated before I stepped into the doorway. The kids, who watched their father run out of the kitchen without saying a word to them, both turned in my direction.

Summer's face lit up when she saw me. She beamed, then raised a hand and waved at me. Jaxon looked from me to Summer, then scrunched his mouth, frowned and glared at his sister as though she had betrayed him.

"Hi," I said cautiously, scared to move from the doorway. Scared to enter the room and be with them when their father wasn't there as well. Neither of them spoke, even though Summer's beam grew across her face.

"Your dad asked me to stay for breakfast," I explained. "Is that OK with you?" Summer glanced at Jaxon, as if asking his permission. Jaxon stared back at her, a sliver of an expression flitting across his eyes before he lowered them to the table again. It didn't take a mind reader to know he wasn't happy about this. He really didn't want me there. Summer grinned at him, then turned to me.

"You have to get a bowl," she stated and pointed to one of the white cupboards on the wall.

"OK," I said and dumped my bag beside the chair to Summer's left, opposite Jaxon. I shed my coat, but kept on my cardigan. I followed Summer's pointing finger and went to the cupboard, found a bowl that matched the ones on the table. I took it back to the table and went to sit down. "And you have to get a glass for juice," Summer said, just as my bum had touched the wooden seat.

I followed her pointing finger to the cupboard next to the bowl-and-plate cupboard, and from inside its depths I retrieved a straight, smooth drinking glass. "Anything else?" I asked. Summer shook her head and treated me to one of her smiles. Jaxon, who had been studying me, raised his hand and pointed to the drawer beside the cupboard I was leaning against.

"Oh, yeah, a spoon," I said.

Jaxon nodded and a hint of a smile crossed his face before he cast his eyes down to his cereal bowl again.

In the background, through the doorway, Kyle paced the corridor, the white cordless phone pressed to his ear, an expression of intense displeasure soaked into his face.

He was talking to his wife. His soon-to-be-ex-wife. Only someone you loved could make you wear that kind of expression. Someone who had once loved you knew how to get to the part of you where pain lived. They knew where you kept that softest, most tender part of your heart; they knew which words and looks and actions would slice deep into you at that spot; they knew which cuts would take an eternity to heal.

I watched Kyle pace. He hadn't mentioned that he and his wife were separated during our phone calls and e-mails. Not once. I didn't realize as I'd signed the tenancy agreement that it would just be him and the children living over here. But then, how do you mention that? How do you explain to a perfect stranger that your life had an "under deconstruction" label on it? Now I understood why they had to go to New York. Now I understood why he looked so tired. It wasn't just jet lag, it was life lag. Kyle was playing catch-up with the events of the past few weeks.

He'd been knocked out by his marriage going wrong. He hadn't expected any of it, I suspected. He hadn't even thought it a possibility until it was happening. Did anyone think divorce was a possibility, though? Did you say your vows and think for even a fleeting moment it was going to end with your spouse living a seven-hour flight away while you stared down the double barrels of an irretrievable breakdown?

Kyle's face closed down in a scowl at something the person on the other end of the line said. He took the phone away from his ear, threw his gaze up to the ceiling, raised his hands as if asking the Lord for strength, then returned the phone to his ear. If anyone did think divorce was a possibility as they said "I do," Kyle certainly wasn't one of them. And having been floored by the derailment of his marriage, Kyle was obviously still reeling, hadn't worked out how to steady himself. In fact, he was probably still trying to clamber up to his feet.

Knowing that the conversation had probably begun with Mrs. Gadsborough ringing to check they'd gotten back OK, despite it being the middle of the night over there, I stopped watching Kyle pace and scowl, returned to the table and took my seat. "What's your name?" Summer asked as I clattered the spoon into my bowl.

"Erm, Kendra," I replied. "But most people call me Kennie."

"Kendie," Summer said. "Kendie." Summer nodded. "I like Kendie. It's a nice name."

Kendie. I smiled to myself at that, a private joke. I didn't bother to correct her, either, because it'd do no good—even if I did she was going to call me Kendie. That's what children did with names. If they decided to rename you, it was pretty much a done deal.

"My name is Summer," she said. "That's a season. Did you know that?"

I nodded. "I did know that. I like your name, Summer."

"He's called Jaxon," she said, pointing to her brother. "That's not a season. It's just a boy's name. My mumma chose the name." Summer elongated the word *mum* before she added the "a." I hadn't heard anyone say it like she did.

"I like Jaxon's name as well," I said and smiled at him.

He glanced up for a moment, then glanced down again, a ghost of a smile on his face.

Silence came to us. I wasn't sure how long we should wait for Kyle. *If* we should wait for Kyle at all or just get on with breakfast so I could leave, and this could end. "What's your rabbit called?" I asked, for something to say.

Summer looked down at the blue toy in her hand, shook it a little. "Hoppy," she replied. "She hops." She showed me how her bunny hopped around the table, and how the toy managed to survive a few death dives into the smooth white depths of her bowl.

I smiled at her. "That's nice," I said. "Is she your best friend?"

Summer stopped Hoppy midhop, raised her navy-green

eyes to me as she used her free hand to push the non-bunched part of her hair out of her face. She seemed surprised by the question and frowned a little at me. Then she pointed at her brother. "My best friend is Jaxon. He's my brother. And he's my best friend."

"Oh, I see," I said, feeling suitably stupid. "So, does Hoppy like to eat carrots?" I asked to redeem myself.

The little girl's eyes narrowed slightly as she stared at me, then she pressed her pink lips together in genuine concern. She put down her bunny, reached out and patted the back of my hand in a comforting gesture. "Hoppy isn't a real bunny rabbit," she said quietly and gently, as though worried what revealing this news might do to me. "She's only pretend. She doesn't eat anything." Pat, pat went Summer's hand on mine. I bit my inner lip so I wouldn't laugh at her serious tone. She was genuinely concerned for me; her face was knitted with the worry that I was an idiot. I stared at her small, white hand as it patted mine and sadness unfurled itself in my chest. It was followed by the familiar kick of pain, the agony from connecting with another child.

"NO! YOU LISTEN TO ME!" Kyle shouted suddenly, causing all of us to jump a little in our seats and our eyes to dart to the doorway. His body was rigid with anger, his face filled with red rage, his eyes on fire. "YOU LEFT ME, ASHLYN! NOT THE OTHER WAY AROUND! YOU LEFT ME! SO YOU'VE GOT NO RIGHT TO SAY—"

I shoved back my chair, leapt out of my seat, strode over to the kitchen door. As my fingers closed around the doorknob, Kyle saw me, suddenly remembered where he was, who was listening. His voice stopped shouting and our eyes met. He raised a hand of apology, his face grimacing in regret, but I broke eye contact and shut the door in his face. I didn't want his apology. He shouldn't have done it in the first place. Not with his kids in hearing range.

Kyle's silence continued on the other side of the door, and almost immediately his footsteps were on the stairs. Then a door somewhere upstairs shut, sealing him away from us.

I spun back to face Jaxon and Summer. They were still fixated on the doorway, their mouths pressed flat with worry, their eyes brimmed with dread.

A spike of pain twisted inside me as I remembered being in Sydney: *A phone ringing. The awful silence afterwards. That voice* . . . I snapped back to the present. I'd left all that behind and I had to live in the present. The present where two children were terrified by their father's anger. Wondering if he was OK. If that anger would be directed at them.

"Right, so, about breakfast," I said, trying to put a little jolliness into my voice.

The pair of them watched me with trepidation. Summer's sadness, her unhappiness at her family situation, was painted across her pale little face in broad strokes; Jaxon's fear, the worry of what would happen with his parents, was pressed onto every inch of his face. Neither of their parents seemed to have remembered the pair of them in all of this. Their mum had taken off for New York; their dad was shouting at their mother. Summer and Jaxon were sitting at a table waiting for breakfast.

I had to do something. Anything. They needed to have their minds taken off their parents. My eyes scanned the room, looking over the sleek lines of the units, the expensive gadgets, for something to entertain and distract them. "You know what I really love for breakfast on a Saturday?" I asked. My eyes settled on my coat, a spray of crinkled cellophane peeking out of its pocket. I'd worn the coat on the plane home, and had been mainlining sugar for most of the journey. The bag in my pocket was the last packet of sweets that I'd opened as we came in to land.

They said nothing to my question.

"Well, looks like I'll have to tell you, seeing as you're both so interested," I said with a smile. "No, no," I raised my hands to ward off their nonexistent protests, "don't pretend you don't care. I can tell you're both desperate to know but you're just too shy to ask." I widened my smile as I looked from one twin's face to the other. They were so similar, the same mouth, same eyes, same small nose.

"I love to have marshmallows," I explained as I sat at the table. "You know what marshmallows are?" I knew I wouldn't get an answer—they'd both retreated into their shells and it'd take more than a little joviality to coax them out again. "They're those little squashy sugary things. They're usually pink and white. And sometimes, I eat them for breakfast. But only on a Saturday and only on very, very special occasions. Although that's my little secret." I nodded at them. "I've only told you two about that." I could have taken the scrunched-up bag of marshmallows out of my pocket to show them, but I didn't want to give them sweets for breakfast.

The pair of them continued to stare at the babbling fool at their table. "Anyways, so most Saturdays what I do have for breakfast is cereal. Just like this one." I pointed to the box of Weetabix. "But I like to make it special, because breakfast on a Saturday has to be special, don't you think? Monday to Friday can be special if you want, but Saturday always has to be special. Otherwise, what's the point of having a weekend?

"To make it special, you have to do this. You have matching bowls, like we've got. Then you have to pick up your bag of wishes, which is always sitting beside you. You pick up your bag of wishes and dip your fingers into it like this." I reached into my invisible bag and took a pinch of its contents. I sprinkled it into the empty cereal bowl in front of me. "The first dose of wishes is always love," I informed them. I reached into the bag again, took another pinch. "Now this second dose is always happiness. Because that makes you smile in your tummy." They weren't saying anything but they were paying attention. I took another pinch. "And this dose is sunshine to warm you up inside." I took another dose. "Do you know what dose this is?" I asked, then waited. I had to wait. I had their attention, but I had to engage them to make sure they put their dad's row behind them, even for a little while. I carried on waiting. Time ticked past. I was starting to feel stupid, holding the next dose of invisible wishes, but I had to wait them out.

"Magic," a small voice said. Reluctant, but offered.

I grinned at Jaxon, pleased that he'd spoken. That he was paying attention, and was engaging. "You're so right, Jaxon," I said, still grinning. I sprinkled it in the bowl then took another dose. "And what's this one, Summer?"

"Fun," she said and grinned.

"That's right!" I said and added it to the bowl. "OK, now that we've put in the wishes, we can add the cereal." I dropped in a couple of Weetabix. "It can be any cereal but this is my favorite. And once it's in the bowl, we add another wish. This is the most extra, extra special. Because what we sprinkle on top is a secret wish that we don't tell anyone. You can wish for anything. Absolutely anything. So, do you want to give it a try?"

Summer moved first. She put down Hoppy and looked down at her bag of wishes. She dipped into her bag and began sprinkling her wishes in the bowl. "Love," she said after the first one. "Happiness." Jaxon picked up his bag of wishes. He didn't speak out his wishes, he did them silently, and soon all three of us had a bowl of cereal in front of us—them cornflakes, me Weetabix.

"Now it's time for the extra, extra special secret wish," I

said. I picked up my handful and waited for them to do the same.

Summer closed her eyes, said something that moved her pink lips slightly and then opened her eyes to sprinkle on her wish. Jaxon went next. His face became a picture of concentration as he held his secret wish in his hand, looked briefly but longingly at the door and then sprinkled his wish on his cereal.

I took my sprinkle in my hand, closed my eyes and allowed the wish to form in my mind and then to solidify. Suddenly I realized I actually believed in this. I'd started this as a way to get two children's minds off their father, but now I was believing it a little. Believing if I wished hard enough for what I wanted, it might come true.

My wish was to make things right. For everything I'd left behind to right itself and for no one else to get hurt. And for those who had been hurt to survive. Survive. I just wanted to make things right. I opened my eyes, smiled at the kids as I coated my cereal in the wish. Even if it didn't work, at least I was thinking it. Hoping for it. *Trying.*

I poured milk on the cereal in our bowls, poured orange juice into glasses and unintentionally we all took the first mouthful of our cereal together.

"This tastes nice," Summer said as she chewed, showing us the orange mush of cornflakes.

Jaxon nodded as he chewed.

"It tastes like marshmallows," Summer said, revealing that she had yet to taste marshmallows.

Jaxon nodded.

"A little bit," I said, not wanting to contradict her. For all I knew, cornflakes would taste like marshmallows to Summer.

"I like this special Saturday breakfast," Summer informed me through another mouthful of masticated cereal.

Silent Jaxon nodded again.

"I like it, too," I said.

"You're nice," Summer said.

Jaxon didn't nod. He just stared down at his food, as though he hadn't heard.

"Thank you," I said to Summer.

Summer looked at Jaxon until he raised his gaze to her. They stared at each other for a few seconds, communicating through some sort of secret, silent sibling code. Summer turned to me. "Jaxon thinks you're nice, too. He can't talk," she explained.

"I heard him talk earlier," I replied.

"He can't talk much," she amended.

"Oh, I see."

The door opened and Kyle wandered into the kitchen. His complexion was the color of whey, his eyes were dulled and troubled, every muscle and sinew tensed by anger. He stopped, looked momentarily surprised to see me. "You're still here," he said.

"Yeah, course," I said with a slight scoff, trying to lighten the moment. "We're having breakfast."

"Special Saturday breakfast," Summer added.

"Right, right," he said distractedly. He hadn't heard what either of us had said. He went to the kettle, flicked it on. Started running his hand over the bristles of his hair as he stared at the kettle. He opened a cupboard door, took out a mug. Opened another cupboard and took out a jar of fair-trade coffee, spooned two heaped teaspoons of the brown granules into the mug and doused them in boiling water. Without turning around, he started to sip his strong black coffee. Scratching his hair, Kyle walked out of the room. It must have been a vicious row to have him so ensnared in his misery that he only noticed us as ornaments in his kitchen, not living breathing human beings who wanted to be communicated with.

Jaxon started to rapidly spoon cereal into his mouth. He was eating as though he meant it, as though if he ate all his cereal his wish would come true.

"My mumma isn't very nice to Dad," Summer informed me.

"Oh, I see," I replied.

I'd guessed her mumma wasn't very nice to Dad, that Dad probably wasn't very nice to her mumma.

I also suspected that if I wasn't very careful, I'd become involved in this mess of not very niceness.

CHAPTER 4

The neighborhood was alive with children.

The sounds of them came fluttering into my flat from everywhere. Playing, screaming, laughing, fighting, making up, splashing about in paddling pools, running towards the jolly tinkling of ice cream vans. Every one of them enjoying the gift of an unexpectedly warm, sunny Sunday in late February. Everyone except the Gadsboroughs. The court-yard that separated our two buildings was conspicuously quiet. Still. Dead. It was the type of silence that held no peace; it was the unnerving hush of a graveyard at night. The still after a bereavement. A deep, penetrating silence that made anything potentially happy—even the air—wither as it passed over the garden.

It had been bothering me all day.

When I'd been cleaning and vacuuming with a CD play-ing loudly, I heard the silence. When I was watching televi-sion I felt it. When I was flicking through newspapers it haunted me.

I glanced out of the window beside the sofa that over-looked the main house's upper floors and dark slate roof. As I stared, subconsciously searching for any signs of life in the upstairs windows, a thousand little scenarios of what the si-lence might mean played across my mind.

I didn't want to get involved with them, with anyone, but there were children involved. Did my resolution extend to that? To ignoring them and what was potentially happening to them? Yesterday, Kyle had forgotten them at breakfast. He'd actually, genuinely forgotten.

After we'd finished breakfast, Summer and Jaxon both wanted to go to bed. They didn't say anything—to me or to each other—they simply seemed to come to the same decision at the same time that this was what they were going to do next. Summer moved first, climbed down from her chair. Jaxon did the same. They were both paler than they had been when they were in my flat, and the dark shadows under their eyes had become purple-red bruises. God knows how long they'd been awake. They'd just returned from another country, it was a miracle they were still standing. Jaxon came around to Summer's side of the table and she turned to me. Close up I could see that a ring of mahogany outlined her navy-green eyes.

"Good night, Kendie," she'd said. She was going to bed, so even though it was light outside, it was night in her mind. Jaxon didn't say anything; he looked at me, studied me in that way he had in my flat for a few seconds, then his gaze fell away. Despite what Summer had said, he wasn't sure if he liked me or not, so was reserving judgment for the moment.

"Good night, guys," I'd replied. "Thanks for breakfast."

"Kiss?" Summer had asked and presented the smooth white curve of her right cheek to me.

I'd hesitated. I didn't know this girl very well but she was determined to push this relationship into closeness. It was only a kiss, though, it wouldn't hurt. I'd leaned down and pressed a good-night kiss against her cheek. Jaxon's eyes were still lowered, but, surprisingly, he'd presented his face to me as well. I'd dropped a kiss on his cheek. I'd watched as they walked out of the kitchen and disappeared into the heart of the house. *How could anyone not pay attention to these two?* I'd wondered as they'd rounded the banister of the stairs, Summer in front. *How could anyone not think they're the most important things on the earth and spend every spare second staring at them?*

Before leaving I'd cleared the table, washed up the breakfast things, wiped over the surfaces with the pink sponge. I'd also flipped the latch on the kitchen door, took one last look around at the smart, stylish kitchen before leaving them to it.

I hadn't seen Kyle again. He'd clearly abandoned them at breakfast. Had he abandoned them today as well? I hadn't heard anything from them or from the house after I left . . . More scenarios danced across my mind.

I stood up, marched across my flat to the top of the stairs, ready to run down, throw open the door and march across the courtyard to the house to double-check that things were as they should be. That the children had eaten, had been bathed, had been communicated with. It was my duty as a neighbor, as a human being. You heard it all the time after a tragedy—people saying they had a feeling that things didn't seem right but had ignored the feeling, and things had ended in a hospitalization or worse.

I paused at the top of the stairs. *They're not your children,* I reminded myself. *It's nothing to do with you. You. Are. The lodger.*

Besides, Kyle didn't seem the type to hurt his children. Whatever the "type" was. He seemed to care about them. He'd been nice to me. The look of horror at frightening me crossed my mind. *He doesn't seem the type.* And there was a huge gulf between abusive neglect and neglecting a child because you're struggling to cope. They may well be two dif-

ferent points along the same continuum, but it was a continuum I hadn't ever struggled along so how could I know
how easy it would be to ignore your children when it was all
too much? Maybe Saturday was just a bad day. Maybe they
were sleeping today. *Maybe you should mind your own business.*

With that final thought, I forced my body to go back to
the sofa, pick up the remote and turn up the sound on the
television to drown out the deadening silence.

My worry about the Gadsboroughs was probably fueled
by procrastination, if I was honest. I had something I had to
do and I didn't want to do it. I had a letter to write. I should
have written it a month or so ago, but in the panic of leaving
Sydney, finishing up at work and training my replacement,
there hadn't been time.

Now I had time on my hands and I had to do it. And I
couldn't. The paper, which sat on the coffee table in front of
me, seemed vast and wide. Appropriate since I had an immense amount to say. Yet, so far I'd managed a small blue
dot on the top right-hand corner of the page. That was
where I'd pressed the nib of the pen when I started to write
the date, then decided against it in case I didn't finish the
letter for a while. I'd taken the pen away, and stared at the
sheet knowing I couldn't write my address because he might
track me down. That was the sort of thing he would do.
Find out where I was, try to tell me he didn't blame me or—
worse—that he loved me. That no matter what, he loved
me. I couldn't face that. I felt guilty enough without knowing he didn't hold me responsible for ruining his life.

So, no date and no address later, I'd hit another stumbling block. I wasn't sure if I should go for "dear," which felt
too formal, or "hi," which felt too casual. And then I'd
thought of just writing his name and I'd frozen. I couldn't
do it. I'd been petrified by the thought of committing to

paper the fact I had a relationship with him so close I could use his first name in any context. It was something most of us took for granted, using someone's first name. But it was an implied intimacy, a closeness that at moments like this said so much. At that point I'd tossed aside the notepaper and pen and went back to worrying about the family across the courtyard.

And now, I didn't know what to do with myself.

In frustration, I stood up. I stretched my five-foot four-inch body, enjoying the pull in the muscles of my back, stomach, arms and legs. My shoulder-length hair swung loose as I threw my head back. I was momentarily free. As though I was stretched beyond the confines of my physical body. All that existed of me were molecules that could reach up and touch the sky, that could push down into the center of the earth.

I picked up the remote, flicked through the channels. Finding nothing that grabbed my attention, I walked over and switched off the television.

Bed. I'll go to bed. Sleep this off.

I was probably still a bit jet-lagged. It'd only been a week since I got back, and I'd been working right up until two days before I left Sydney. And since I'd gotten back I'd been exploring Brockingham, had been acquainting myself with its transport system, winding side streets and little shops. I'd traveled to where I used to live in west London to have my plaits taken out and have my hair straightened. I'd also been into work for a couple of hours on Thursday and Friday. All of it—not easing myself into things—was probably adding to my ennui, my tension, my frustration. I hadn't slept a whole night through in weeks and tomorrow was the first day of my first full week back being a recruitment consultant. A good few hours in bed, listening to music, would be soothing.

I lay on the bed, flat on my back, spreading out, turning myself into a human starfish under the white duvet, trying to fill as much of the bed as I could. Peter Gabriel's low, husky voice enveloped the room as "In Your Eyes" started. It was 5:30 p.m. and darkness had already bled into the sky, inking out the world beyond my blinds.

Closing my eyes I started to float on the words of the song: *emptiness. Running away. Going back to the place where you started.*

The memories started as frozen frames, images that imprinted themselves on my mind like clicks of a camera.

Click. The feel of that soft patch of skin at the nape of his neck.
Click. The warmth of his body under my fingertips.
Click. The intensity of his eyes.

I snapped open my eyes, thinking that would stop them, that would be the way to fight off the memories, return them to the darkness where they belonged. They kept coming. Slowly turning from frames to moving images.

Click. The brush of his lips on the well at the base of my throat.
Click. The curve of his mouth as he said, "I could be with you forever."
Click. His hands as they tugged my top over my head.
Click. His slight gasp as his eyes ran over my seminaked body.

I stopped fighting it, allowed the clicks of memories to keep flashing up behind my eyes. Memories of him. Memories of us. Memories of who I was when I was with him.

I surrendered myself to the remembering. It was easier

than fighting. And, right now, I had very little fight left in me.

I woke up with a start, with a scream at the back of my throat and terror branded onto my heart.

There was someone in my room. I could feel it.

Or maybe someone had touched me. Either way, there was definitely someone there. My eyes snapped open when I was already half upright. It was still dark in my room so I had no idea what time it was. My heart raced as I reached for the bedside lamp to shed light into the room, to chase away the darkness and reassure myself there was no one there.

The light came on and I jumped all over again, a strangled cry of shock escaping from my mouth. There was someone in my room. Someones.

Summer. Jaxon.

They stood about two feet away from the bed, near the open door.

They were only recently out of bed, I realized as I stared at them: Summer was wearing an old-fashioned nightdress— greyed white flannel with frilly collar and cuffs and vines of tiny pink flowers crawling over it—and her hair was a sleep-mussed mass of black on her head. Jaxon was wearing blue and red Spider-Man pajamas that stopped a few inches shy of his wrists and ankles, his hair stood on end and his face was still puffed up with sleep.

Twice in three days they'd broken into my flat. Twice they had scared the life out of me. I had definitely locked the front door—I'd triple-checked, like I always did. Moving the key in the lock again and turning the knob of the Yale lock to ensure that they were in place. That I was safe. That any danger was outside. Sometimes, like last night, I'd wake up, worried that I'd forgotten to check, and would go to quadruple-check that the door was locked and the windows were secure. All so that this wouldn't happen. I wouldn't wake up, terrified because uninvited guests had decided to drop by. My heart took its time slowing down to a steady canter. I raised my knees to my chest and blinked my eyes clear, tightly weaving together my fingers over my knees as I waited patiently for this scenario to play itself out. If things ran true to form, Kyle would come racing up the stairs and into the bedroom any moment now to herd out his children like a shepherd recapturing two stray sheep. Then he'd offer me a genuine and heartfelt apology that was essentially meaningless. Yes, he was sorry, but it'd happened again: his children were inside my home. I was of the mind that woven into the letters of *sorry* was the meaning: "it won't happen again." If it did happen again, you probably weren't *that* sorry.

Maybe I will ask him for the spare keys to my flat back, I thought, *because any more of these little "visits" and my life expectancy is going to be severed in half.*

A minute passed. And another. No Kyle.

I glanced beyond the children, into what I could see of the living room, just in case he was lurking in there, too embarrassed to cross the threshold of my room. Nothing. It was empty.

I refocused on the children. Jaxon had stuck his thumb in his mouth. I'd never seen a six-year-old boy do that. His other hand worried at the bottom of his Spider-Man pajama top, twisting it around and around his forefinger, as though trying to burrow into the thin stretch-jersey material. His navy-green eyes, ringed with shades of brown, were glazed over and were staring fixedly at a point near my feet.

Summer had Hoppy, her blue bunny, in her hands and was twisting at Hoppy's left ear. Twisting it forwards, twisting it backwards, forwards, backwards, forwards, backwards, as though trying to wring something out of it. She was facing me but her eyes weren't seeing me. They were staring through me, focused on the headboard behind me. Her cheeks were marked by thin, shiny tracks of tears.

Oh.

In that instant I knew I should be throwing back the covers, spinning my legs over the side of the bed and stepping down onto the rug beside the bed, standing up, pulling on clothes, going over to the main house.

I knew what I should be doing, but I couldn't. This was how nightmares began. How I became immersed in a horror I couldn't stop. A moment when the sense of disaster began whispering in my ear, writing across my chest. If I moved, it might become a reality. If I didn't move, I could be wrong. Kids were always being woken up by bad dreams that made them cry. Dreams that drove them out of their beds and into their parents' rooms. I could be wrong about this.

"What's the matter?" I asked.

Summer rubbed at her eye with the palm of her hand. She was so pale the dark green and blue veins that branched out from her neck and curved over her jaw line stood out like jagged, badly penned tattoos. Jaxon continued to suck at his thumb, his line of sight never straying from my feet.

Even as I willed her to say "I had a bad dream" my heart rate began to gallop. Speeding in my chest, faster than it had when I turned on the light a few minutes ago. It battered in my ears, pounded in my head, drummed in my throat. *Please say bad dream, please say bad dream.*

"You have to come to our house," Summer said, her voice

so weary it sounded as though it was about to collapse under the weight of its troubles.

"Why?" I asked.

Her eyes persisted in staring through me, as her small rosebud lips opened. "You have to come to our house," Summer repeated. "My daddy won't wake up."

CHAPTER 5

Will he be blue?
Lying on the sofa? On the floor? Was it his heart? Did someone get in the house and do something to him? Did he decide it was all too much and end it all? Will he be cold? How long has he been gone? These thoughts circled my head like a flock of bloodthirsty vultures as I walked across the courtyard. I'd never seen a dead body before. Why did this have to be the first?

With gentle verbal prodding and coaxing, I'd managed to get an explanation from Summer as to what had happened. Jaxon had stayed shrouded in his silence, his thumb still in his mouth, although he closely monitored my reaction to their story. Summer had heard a noise downstairs when she woke up. She went to her dad's room to ask him what the noise was but found his bed empty. So she'd gone to get Jaxon and, together, they'd gone to investigate. The noise was the television. Their dad was lying on the sofa and the television was on. Summer had shaken him, tried to wake him up to tell him he'd left the television on. But nothing. Jaxon tried. They shook him. They called his name, but nothing. They'd sat down on the floor, waiting for him to wake up, had gone back to sleep beside him, but he hadn't woken up. In the end they'd decided to come and get me. To see if I could wake him up. They'd used a chair to stand on to open and unlock the back door, then had come over to my flat. Used the spare keys—they knew where they were kept—to get in.

Once I'd heard the story, all the while feeling ice-cold fear trickling in a thin, steady stream down my spine, I'd asked the kids to wait for me in my living area, flicked on the television, found some early morning cartoons for them and went to change. I could have worn the jogging bottoms, T-shirt and black fleece that I slept in, but I'd decided to get dressed to give myself time to prepare. To steady myself. With trembling hands I'd pulled on underwear, jeans, T-shirt and a black V-neck sweater. All the while, *You should have done something, you should have done something. You should have done something* was the thought being screamed over and over in my ears.

If I'd just gone over yesterday, talked to him, talked to them, maybe this wouldn't have happened.

Dressed but no less terrified, I'd returned to the living room. The first thing that hit me was the scent of alcohol. It wasn't strong or overpowering, simply a waft of the slightly stale, acidic smell that caught my nose. I hadn't had a drink since I'd moved in, there was no alcohol in the flat, so why did the living room smell of booze? Beer. Yes, beer. I'd glanced at the kids, but they hadn't moved, were sitting in the same position, staring blank-eyed at the television.

I'd sniffed again and it was gone.

After I told their blank faces to wait for me in the flat and that I'd be back soon, I'd started my trip across the courtyard. It was only a few meters, but in reality it was the journey of a lifetime. A journey that would change my life forever. Once I'd seen Kyle's body—a dead body—that would be it. There'd be no going back to the person I was before. That moment would be one of those indelible marks on my soul. Another scar that would never quite heal. God knows what it had already done to the two six-year-olds waiting in the flat.

As I approached, I saw their maple wood back door was

still ajar from where they'd left and I gently pushed it open, taking a deep breath. The house was still as I stepped over the threshold, my heart racing in my ears, a loud drumbeat that drowned out everything. I was holding my breath, I realized as I crossed the wooden-floored kitchen, moving to the far door, the door that led to the corridor. I stopped, forced myself to exhale, forced myself to start breathing. A ragged, shallow in-and-out that resided in the upper part of my chest, it was the best I could do, but at least it was breathing. The stripped wood flooring continued out of the kitchen into the corridor, pointing me towards Kyle. At the end of the corridor was the front door with the chain slung across as security. It didn't look as if someone had broken in. A few steps in front of the front door was the staircase, and in the space between the staircase and front door was another door, which was shut. Closer to where I was, to my left there was another door that was open. I guessed that was where he was. I couldn't imagine the kids shutting the door behind them as they left to get me.

As I moved closer to the open door it occurred to me that I should call the police. But the need to know was stronger than going through the formalities. Once I knew, had confirmed what the three of us suspected, I'd know how to treat the children. I'd think of something to say, some way to protect them until this part was over. I didn't want a police officer, a complete stranger, to tell them. I was a virtual stranger, but not a total stranger.

At the doorway I hesitated, wondering if I should think again. Go call the police. They were trained to do this sort of thing, I wasn't. I was trained to recruit people, not deal with . . .

Summer and Jaxon's emptied faces came to mind. The hollowness of their stares, the hopelessness smoothed over their expressions. They'd already done this. They had no choice in the matter. *If they can do it, so can you,* I scolded myself.

The living room was incredibly large. It used to be two rooms—a domed archway marking the wall that had been removed to create one bright airy space. There was a dining area at the back, in the living area there were two sofas and two armchairs, all in a soft-looking burnt-butter leather, arranged in a square facing the television, which was squawking noisily by the window.

I saw the soles of his feet first. On the sofa nearest the door, his feet were facing towards the door, one slightly crossed over the other, the left foot on top. My heart all but froze as I looked at the network of small lines on his feet. I opened my mouth, started breathing heavily, trying to calm myself and at the same time not pitch forwards into hyperventilating. I was on that knife-edge between pure calm and total hysteria. And then it happened. It clicked in. I lost all feeling in my body as I decided to leave. I went to that place, that little corner where I was always safe. Always calm. Always protected. Protected from every nasty little thing in the world.

None of this was difficult anymore because I wasn't scared. I could do this. I had to, so I was going to. I stepped forwards, one foot in front of the other, aware with every step, every move forwards, of the overpowering smell of alcohol that saturated the air.

I continued to take more steps right towards the center of the room until I was closer to the sofa. And, oh, my, God. Oh my *God!*

The area around the sofa was crammed with bottles and bottles of alcohol. Bottles and cans of alcohol. Small green flasks of gin, large clear bottles of vodka, amber bottles of whiskey, brown bottles of beer, a few green bottles of white wine, a couple of dark bottles of red wine. A smattering of cans. Mainly spirits, though. They were like a moat around the sofa. That was why my flat smelled of it—the scent had clung to Summer and Jaxon, hitched a ride on their clothes, twisted itself into the strands of their hair and the pores of their skin. Amongst the sea of booze bottles and cans I could make out the two crescent shapes the kids had made so they could lie down beside their father. Lie down and wait for their father—who had quite clearly and purposefully drunk himself to death—to wake up.

If I hadn't been around they might have stayed like that, curled up beside their dead father for hours, if not days.

My attention moved to Kyle.

He was motionless, frozen in the last position he'd been in before the final gulp that ended his life took effect.

His body was stretched out on the sofa, his back flat against the seat, his head almost tipped upright and to one side against the armrest. One of his arms lay at his side, the other trailed down off the sofa, hanging down amongst the detritus from the night before.

His clothes were rumpled, his light blue shirt tugged out of his sand-colored trousers from, I presumed, where Summer and Jaxon had tried to shake him awake. His skin was the pale grey of clouds before a storm, but not blue. I'd expected him to be blue if he'd been *gone* for a while, but I couldn't know for sure. I stared hard at his chest, watching to see if it rose or not. I stared and stared, but nothing. He didn't seem to be breathing. And there was an unnerving stillness about him. A stillness that was like a smooth, silky sheet of lifelessness that lay over him and the room.

The only way to tell for sure if he was . . . *gone* would be to touch him. To check for a pulse. I stepped forwards, and unbidden, my mouth flooded with saline. Even though my mind was elsewhere, my body was still reacting as it would in this situation if I was behaving consciously. The smell of alcohol was stirring up a nauseating brew with fear in the pit of my stomach. I had to force myself not to heave. Once I'd done this, once I'd checked, I could move on. Get on with things. Think what to say to the kids, call the police.

Picking a path through the bottles, I went towards him, stopped within touching distance.

Deep breath.

Do it. Do it now. Do it and get it over with.

My hand shook uncontrollably as I reached out for him, aiming for the grey area of exposed skin just above the neck of his blue shirt. I forced myself to look, to make sure I was touching the right place, and I held my breath even though breathing was the only thing that stopped bile spilling out of my mouth. My fingers made contact with his flesh. Surprisingly, it was warm. But I tried not to think too much about it. A body didn't just go cold, it must cool down slowly as the blood that was warming it up, the chemical reactions that kept its heat constant, stopped. I slid my fingers up, aiming for the point under his jaw.

"Nuugh!" Kyle murmured suddenly, shrugging off my hand, as though swatting away a fly.

"JESUS CHRIST!" I screamed inside and stumbled backwards, crashing into a few bottles, knocking over a couple of half-drunk cans and spilling their pale liquid onto the carpet. I kept stumbling until, clear of the debris, I lost my fight for balance and fell, landing hard on my backside.

I sat, chest heaving, staring at him, waiting for him to react to the sound of clashing bottles, to open his eyes, to sit up, to acknowledge he'd just taken another ten years off my life. Nothing. Having scared me half to death, having scared his kids half to death, the bastard continued to peacefully float his way through his pissed up, passed out dreamland.

♦

I sat watching Kyle sleep. His body was like a long muscular thread stretched out on the burnt-butter leather sofa.

In all the time that had elapsed since I found out he was alive—pissed, but alive—he hadn't moved. I'd been back to the flat to tell the children that he was OK. I'd explained to them at length their father was only sleeping. He was very, very tired, a grown-up type of tired that meant it took a lot to wake up. I'd also explained he'd wake up on his own soon, but until then we'd go back to their house and get on with our Monday. They'd watched me with impassive eyes, didn't ask questions, didn't—if truth be told—seem to need my long-winded explanation. They'd only seemed to need to know that he was OK and that they could go home. As they'd moved towards the stairs, I'd hung behind to turn off the television and a glint of green glass peeking out from behind a sofa cushion had caught my eye. Curious, I'd moved towards it, picked up the cushion and found an empty bottle of beer, lying on its side, nestled in the crease between the sofa back and the sofa seat. I'd snatched away the next cushion and found another one. And another one under the third cushion.

From the corner of my eye I'd watched Summer and Jaxon, saw their eyes were round circles of alarm and their cheeks had been hollowed out with fear. No wonder my flat smelled of alcohol. No wonder they weren't surprised when I said their dad was a special kind of tired. They'd seen it all before. Had been through it all before.

They were used to their father doing this and were probably used to hiding the evidence. In the house only a couple of the cans of beer had been opened. Other than that, there were no other empties to be seen. They'd carefully secreted away evidence that their father had been drinking, had just left the full ones. Those poor kids. What they must have been through . . . My insides melted at the thought of it. *My mumma isn't very nice to Dad,* Summer's voice repeated in my head. Now I had a pretty good idea why.

As I'd continued to watch them from the corner of my eye, the lines of horror on their young faces deepened. I knew their secret now and they were terrified. What was I going to do? Would I get their dad into trouble? Would I blame them?

Still uncertain of what my reaction should be, I'd replaced the cushions over the bottles, pretended I hadn't seen what I had seen, didn't know what I knew. It probably wasn't healthy to pretend that this hadn't happened, that I hadn't been disturbed by what they'd done, but they'd been through enough already. They didn't need my questioning. If anyone should be shamed and exposed, it was their father.

In silence we'd wandered back to their house, and they'd gone upstairs to get changed. I'd called work and told my boss there'd been an emergency so I probably wouldn't be coming in today. Then I'd made us all toast with butter and jam for breakfast. It was all I could find. He obviously hadn't been shopping since they returned from their holiday nor, it seemed, before their holiday, so the cupboards were bare, even of cereal. There'd been a half-full box of cornflakes on Saturday and at least eight Weetabix, so that was obviously all they'd eaten over the weekend. The fridge was even emptier—the butter, the strawberry jam, an onion in the vegetable crisper, a bottle of tomato sauce, a bottle of soy sauce, the dregs of a carton of orange juice, a canister of expensive real coffee and half a carton of curdled milk. The freezer had yielded a loaf of granary bread and I'd made as much toast as I could and we'd drunk water. Afterwards, they'd willingly gone out to play while I had cleared up the breakfast things.

All through breakfast I'd been hoping Kyle would come round, would see what he'd done and would feel awful enough to come rushing in to apologize to his kids. My hoping had been in vain. He hadn't moved.

And now, I was sitting on the arm of the armchair opposite the sofa upon which he lay, watching him.

Chewing on the knuckle of my thumb, I listened to the occasional murmur of a drunken snore escaping his full lips. More minutes passed and Kyle didn't stir. He resided in his place of drunken oblivion, protected from the reality of life. And that was very nice for him. We all needed oblivion sometimes, but his was about to come to an end.

I got up from the armchair, went to him and reached down to where his stomach, covered in dark hair, was exposed, took a piece of his flesh between my thumb and forefinger then twisted. As hard as I could. Then I grabbed a few of the dark hairs and yanked at them, pulling three or four free.

"*Ow!*" Kyle yelped, coming straight out of his oblivion into a world of pain as he sat up. "What the—?" His hand went to his stomach, rubbed at the pain. He glared up at me. "What—?"

I greeted him with a look of disdain and a fractionally hitched eyebrow. "I think we need to have a chat, don't you?" I said.

CHAPTER 6

*M*y head feels—" Kyle began as he staggered into the kitchen about half an hour later.

I held up my hand, a stop sign to his words. "I don't want to hear it." This wasn't college or the best of our single years. I hadn't been out drinking with him and wanted to share his pain, or laugh conspiratorially at how much we'd put away. "We've all got our problems. And I don't want to hear it." I indicated to the seat in front of the part of the table where I'd made him a pot of real coffee and had put two painkillers and a glass of water. "Sit."

A frown creased Kyle's thirty-something face, furrowing the space between his eyebrows and hairline, cascading down over his smooth features. His frown pursed his mouth and for a moment he was going to argue, object to my tone of voice and attitude by reminding me it was his house. But his hangover won out and he pulled out the chair, sat down. While he took the painkillers, knocked them back with a couple of jerks of his head, I poured coffee into a mug, added sugar. I slid it across the table to him.

"Thanks," he mumbled. He dipped his head, took a couple of sips of coffee. He'd been in the shower and still smelled of warm water, sandalwood shower gel and clean clothes. He'd had a shave so his chin, cheeks and the skin around his mouth were soft and pink. His hair was a shiny black, the short hairs curled backwards and still wet.

Outside the children were playing. Summer was on her

pink bike, riding around the flagstones. Jaxon worked on building a giant fort out of the large, multicolored blocks in the middle of the green. There wasn't a sound from them. And Kyle didn't seem to notice. I hadn't heard him clearing up the living room and he wasn't wearing a single shred of shame. It wasn't important that I'd seen the state of his living room, that I'd seen him unconscious, nor that his children had seen him that way.

I watched his bowed head. Kyle was a big man. He was lean, with long limbs and wiry muscle making up his frame, but he was large in the sense that there was a lot going on inside him. In his mind, in his heart, in his soul. It was too much for his body and spilled out. Like Saturday when he'd enlightened me about his life in three minutes. It was probably the reason he'd decided to drink so much last night. Trying to control the hugeness of what was stirring inside him.

"I think you should let her have them," I said to him. I'd been thinking it over, all through breakfast, all through watching him sleep, all through waiting for him to appear from the shower. It was the obvious solution to this. He wasn't coping; the enormity of what was going on inside him was making everyone in his immediate vicinity suffer, was making life hell for his children.

"Excuse me?" Kyle said, stopping his mug's journey to his mouth.

"You clearly can't cope with them, so let your wife have them."

"*Excuse me?*" He was incredulous, outraged, *angry* as any man would be.

"I assume that's what you and your wife were fighting about on Saturday on the phone. She obviously wants them. It'd be easier all round to just give them up. Stop using them as a bargaining tool and give them to her."

Kyle slammed his cup onto the table with such force I was surprised it didn't crack then shatter. The thick black liquid sploshed out onto the wooden table top. He shook his hand dry, his angry eyes drilling into me. He was on the verge of shouting at me, but held back. "Who the *hell* do you think you are?" he snarled, his body seeming to double threateningly in size as he leant towards me.

"No, who the *hell* do you think you are, Mr. Gadsborough?" I spat back.

He paused, surprised at how quickly, decisively and venomously I'd reacted. His attack hadn't been met with a defense, but a stronger offense.

"Your children thought you were dead," I continued in a low, angry voice. "Dead. They were terrified. Finding you lying on the sofa, amongst an ocean of alcohol and then having to come to a virtual stranger for help. They had to get a chair to unlock your back door, come over to my place, unlock my door and then come upstairs to my room. And then tell me that you wouldn't wake up.

"The trauma in their eyes, the look on their faces . . ." My voice faltered as I remembered their looks. "Do you have any idea how that feels? Because for me, an adult, who's lived a bit, I was terrified as I walked over here. I didn't know how I was going to go through with looking at a dead body, but for them? They lay down on the floor beside you and waited for you to wake up. And why? You were *drunk*. I don't know how long it's going to take those two to get over it. So don't give me all that outraged bullshit because you are so far in the wrong there's no way you can find your way back to being right at this moment."

The rage drained out of Kyle's eyes and before he lowered his head to stare down at the mess he'd made with his coffee on the table, I saw shame and regret enter his expression. Slowly he raised his forefinger, traced a pattern in the coffee.

I curled my fingers into the palms of my hands, digging my fingernails into the soft fleshy pads to hide the trembling. No one would know, having listened to my outburst, that I didn't lose my temper very often. I couldn't remember the last time I'd done that.

Like most young girls I was taught to be polite, that people didn't like you if you caused a fuss and drew attention to yourself. Speaking up for yourself made people not like you. I rarely did it, but when it came to speaking up for others, I could. I did. (My boss used to call me Soapbox Kennie.) Especially when the people I was speaking for were two children who thought their dad had died in the night. Now that I had voiced my anger and disgust, though, I was shaken and shaking.

"I had another row with Ashlyn," Kyle said eventually, his face still cast downwards.

"Don't care" was my instant reply.

His head snapped up, his expression surprised, his eyes saying he thought I was hard-faced.

I inhaled deeply and silently, breathing calm onto my raging sensibilities. I fashioned a rudimentary look of sympathy for my face. "I didn't mean that," I said quietly. "I do care. I care very much." I paused, calmed myself some more, enough to raise my eyes to meet his. Kyle held my gaze. A moment of intimacy passed between us—we understood each other. It normally took years to develop that sort of understanding, but my little rant had fast-forwarded our relationship: he'd done something wrong and I was capable of being a complete bitch about it. "You just pissed me off."

"I'm getting that idea," Kyle said ruefully, then sipped his coffee again.

"Tell me what happened," I said softly, trying to understand where he was coming from. It wasn't fair for me to jump to conclusions, to make judgments when I wasn't living his life; I hadn't been floored by a divorce.

"Same old nonsense," he said with a shake of his head. "She wants the kids with her, but as far as I'm concerned, if she wants them back, she's got to come home."

"Why?" I asked.

His eyes flew up to look at me, as though I'd asked the most stupid question on earth. "Because this is their home."

"But, Kyle . . ." I stopped. It seemed wrong somehow to be having this conversation with him. My landlord. I sighed deeply, stirred my cold, undrunk cup of coffee, wondered how I got here. Why I was involved in this.

" 'But, Kyle' what?" he asked.

I sighed again. "You're not coping. Why not give Ashlyn the children?"

"Give up my children, just like that? They're not items. I can't simply hand them over and find new ones to replace them." He shook his head, hardened his voice. "You've *obviously* never had kids."

That stung, and from the expression on his face, the angry gleam in his eye, it was meant to. "You're wrong, actually," I snapped. "I do have kids. I have two kids called Summer and Jaxon. They became my kids the day I had to make up some breakfast ritual because their father was so wrapped up in shouting at their mother that he didn't even acknowledge their existence. I knew that day I had a responsibility to them. Once you bond yourself to a child, you can't just walk away."

Kyle stared at me but didn't argue.

"I do have kids because when they hid three empty beer bottles in my flat, I didn't ask them about it."

"They did what?" Kyle asked, visibly shaken.

"They hid the bottles that you'd drunk because they were scared of you being found out. They sorted through that embarrassment of alcohol to hide your secret."

Distraught, Kyle ran his hand over his hair, then scratched absently at a point on top of his head as a million tiny, unnameable thoughts danced across his face while he struggled with his conscience. His eyes darted outside to the children, watching them as more emotions bloomed on his face.

"What were you doing with all that alcohol?" I asked. I had to know. There was so much of it, had he really set out to drink it all, to kill himself, but passed out before it worked? "Were you seriously going to drink it all?"

From distraught, his expression segued smoothly into contempt. "That's none of your business," he stated and went back to glaring into the black depths of his cup. We sat in silence, all good feeling had been quashed. He didn't like me, and I wasn't exactly wild about him.

"Be honest, Kyle," I said eventually to break the silence. "You don't want the kids, do you?"

His face went to protest, to argue.

"Be honest, it won't go any further," I prodded.

He said nothing, sat back in his chair, stared down at his coffee cup with his lips slightly twisted together.

"You don't do you? You're just keeping them because you think it'll make her come back."

Kyle glanced away, back out of the window, watching his children play. I spun a little in my chair to watch them, too. They should be at school, but I'd had to ring and say they were ill. Jaxon's fort was pretty high, the colored bricks vivid in the February sunshine. Summer had abandoned her bike at the part of the path nearest my flat and was on the grass beside Jaxon, making her rabbit jump around his fort. They were both still subdued. How often was what happened earlier replaying itself in their minds? How deeply had it scarred them? How many times had it happened before? How scared were they that it'd happen again?

"I'm not saying you don't love them, but you're using them, aren't you?"

Kyle looked away from his kids, his line of sight moving up towards my flat. "It's not that simple," he said.

"I know it's not that simple. And to be honest, Kyle, if I was in your situation, I can't put my hand on my heart and say I wouldn't be doing the same thing. But you can't use them as weapons without hurting them."

"You make it sound as though she's the perfect one, that she loves the children and I don't. She didn't just walk out on me, she left them as well. I woke up one morning and she was gone. She's the reason why Jaxon doesn't talk, you know that? He saw her leaving and she told him not to say anything, and he took her literally. Stopped talking. He only speaks to Summer now, really. A couple of sentences every now and again to me, but other than that, nothing. His mother did that to him. You think I'm going to send them back to that?

"And that ridiculous family holiday we went on . . . 'Oh, Kyle, let's still go on the holiday.' It was her idea. And you know why? Because I'd already paid for the flights and hotel so she thought she'd use it to go for an interview she had set up over there. And she's staying there. I, meanwhile, am thinking . . . So they must be thinking . . . But no. She wants rid of me for good. 'Oh, and by the way, could you take the kids home while I sort out my new life over here and then when I'm ready, I'd like to take the kids away too.' "

Anything I said now would sound trite, as though I was dismissing what he'd gone through. Truth be told, I didn't understand. It must be hell. It must shred at his insides. And his wife . . . She obviously had her reasons for doing what she did, but what they both seemed to have forgotten is that Jaxon and Summer didn't ask for this. They didn't ask to be born, especially not to two screwed-up people. They had been. Nothing could change that. It was Kyle and his wife's duty now to spare them as much pain as possible.

"I'm not saying Ashlyn is perfect. I don't know her. But you have to be as close to perfect as you can get. Don't your kids deserve that? And if you can't do that, then give them to someone else who will at least try to be." Oh that sounded pathetic. As though I was on a TV show where everything would be tied up nicely at the end of fifty minutes. Where, after listening to my bons mots, Kyle would pick up the phone, call his wife and when she answered, the first thing he'd say would be, "Let's talk . . ." and they'd work out some arrangement that would benefit everyone.

The truth was, whatever I said, no matter how much he listened now, his hurt, anger and pride would seep back in over the following hours, he'd want to hurt her as much as she'd hurt him and that would mean using the only weapons he had: Jaxon and Summer. Summer and Jaxon. The two people in this who probably wanted nothing more than to have their parents reunited, to have their ripped-apart family sewn back together again.

"To be honest, Kendra, you know nothing about it," Kyle replied. Maybe it wouldn't take that long for his anger to seep back in.

"No, I don't," I admitted.

"But thank you for coming when the kids came to you."

"That's fine. I'll always come. But I can't promise not to call social services if it happens again."

Kyle's face did a double-take, hardened into a state of

shock, his eyes slightly rounded, his lips pressed firmly together, his jaw rippling as he ground his teeth together. Inside I drew back a little. This was his real anger. This was when he'd really turn on me.

The back door flew open and Summer dashed in, Jaxon bringing up the rear. "Can we have ice cream? From the ice cream shop?" she asked, racing to a stop in front of her father. He ignored her because he was glaring at me. "Dad," Summer insisted, tugging at the hem of his T-shirt. "Can we have ice cream?" she asked again.

Kyle's eyes burnt into me.

"*Dad!*" Summer shouted at the top of her lungs, needing to be heard.

"Yes?" he asked, finally turning to focus on his daughter.

"Can we have ice cream?" she asked. "From the ice cream shop?"

"Um," Kyle began, "yes. Why not? Let me go put on my shoes and get my jacket and wallet and phone."

Jaxon came to me, slipped his hand into mine. His hand was warm, the skin soft. I hadn't held a child's hand in nearly three years—since I last saw my nieces and nephews in Italy. A sense of calmness came over me, followed by the kick of sadness. I had to concentrate on the tiny little lines in his skin, his square, neat nails, to stop myself from tearing up. To stop the sadness welling up and over. Summer watched him, then said, "Jaxon wants to know if Kendie can come, too?"

"I think she's busy," Kyle said, pointedly. He really didn't want me around. Funnily enough, I didn't want to be around him, either.

"I am busy," I agreed. "I should probably go to work."

Jaxon's short, fat fingers tightened around my palm, as though urging, pleading with me, to come with them.

"You have to come," Summer said.

Jaxon's fingers continued to cling to my hand.

"You can't force her to come," Kyle said. A rivulet of a threat ran through his voice, warning me off. I'd crossed the line by threatening his family unit and he wasn't going to put up with it. Which was fine. More than fine. The man needed a rocket underneath him. A fire that would make him pay attention to his children, fight for them. Not against his wife. But against himself. He needed to see that the problem here wasn't his wife, but him. His indifference, his anger, his resentment that these children were with him—that was the biggest threat in their lives.

"No, really, I have something to do," I said.

Jaxon's face began to close down, like dominoes falling. His expression went from hoping I'd do something as normal as have an ice cream with his family to anxiety that I was going to abandon them.

"Actually," I said, "I think I need an ice cream. I think we all deserve it."

Two hours later, Kyle and I sat watching the children playing in a small park with swings and roundabouts. Summer, clutching Hoppy under one arm, was climbing over the roundabout. She'd dressed herself in an orange pinafore dress over a blue T-shirt and under a pink cardigan and her blue puffa jacket along with red tights, pink socks and yellow shoes. Her hair, which glittered like fine shards of jet on her head, was tucked behind her ears.

Jaxon, who had dressed himself more soberly in sand-colored trousers, a white T-shirt, black jumper and his blue-fleece jacket, was repeatedly going up and down the slide.

The four of us had spent the past couple of hours wandering around the center of Brockingham, had an ice cream in a café and then looked in a few shops before we went to the park. Kyle had managed to avoid talking directly to me the whole time. While we spooned ice cream into our mouths, he'd ignored me. When we walked down the road, in and out of shops, Summer holding his hand and Jaxon holding my hand, he acted as though I wasn't there. He avoided looking at me, except in those quiet moments when I was concentrating on something else and I would feel the weight of his gaze upon me. Scanning me, wondering if I was telling the truth. If I would follow through with my threat. I could feel his gaze, but refused to look up at him because I was scared, too. I was scared because I hadn't really thought it through when I'd said it. It came tumbling out and now I really would have to do it. I couldn't say it and not mean it. Isn't that one of the golden rules of good, consistent parenting? Say what you mean; make a statement and then go through with the promised consequences if the undesirable behavior reared its head again.

Ten minutes of silence passed as we sat on the bench. A tense silence that was starting to slip under my skin, putting me on edge. I wanted to say something. Anything to breach the divide. I wanted him to say something, even if it was to threaten me to keep my nose out of his business. This silence, it was suffocating me. In the chilly fresh air of this sunny day, I was slowly having the air smothered out of me.

"Did you mean what you said about reporting me to social services?" Kyle asked. I was so grateful to hear his voice I exhaled in relief and didn't really hear his words. Then I replayed what he said: "Did you mean what you said about reporting me to social services?" He wasn't looking at me, and that was taking all his strength. His rigid posture showed he wanted to glare at me so was making sure he kept his line of sight fixed on the children.

Now I was in a difficult position. I couldn't say yes, couldn't say no, and "maybe" wasn't an option. "I try not to say things I don't mean," I eventually said without looking at him. It was the best answer I had.

CHAPTER 7

*T*uesday morning, just shy of 6:30 a.m., I arrived at work. I was early to make up for the day before. Monday was our busiest day, especially for me—it was the day most temps were booked for the week, and other temps who'd ended their assignments would be calling in for work. Although Gabrielle, my boss, had been fine about me not coming in, I'd felt awful. She'd had to cover for me and I'd only just come back.

Gabrielle had started her own "boutique" recruitment agency but had managed to convince Office Wonders, an international recruitment agency, to finance it. If it worked, they would consider selling franchises for boutique—small, more personalized—branches. Her entrepreneurship had come at the perfect time for me. My love affair with Sydney had turned sour a day or so earlier and I was desperate to come home. Out of the blue, Gabrielle had e-mailed me and asked if I would consider coming home to take up the second-in-command position in her company. "I caught my current head of temp recruitment doing lines of coke and a potential candidate on my desk one night. I need someone I can trust," she'd written.

I thanked God and the universe. I had an escape route home. I'd told her I was more than interested and could start in a month. With her going out of her way like that, I'd felt extremely guilty having to call in to say I wasn't coming in yesterday.

I'd also slept very badly. After saying good-bye to the Gadsboroughs, I'd decided to go to the cinema. I'd had to sit in the dark, surrounded by strangers with something else to focus on so I wouldn't obsess about the kids and what was going to become of them. Absent mother, potentially alcoholic father. Nothing I could do about it. Except sit in the dark feeling angry. I'd been tempted to have another chat with Mr. Gadsborough. Get some assurances he'd pull himself together and pay attention to his children. So many people would kill to be in this position—to be a parent—and he seemed to be throwing it away. He couldn't see the blessings in his life.

When I arrived back from the cinema their car was gone. I heard them return a few hours later and from my flat could see the light on in their kitchen. Hopefully he'd been shopping for food. Hopefully what I'd said had been the rocket he'd needed. I'd then spent most of the night lying awake in bed worrying about them.

I climbed the stairs to Office Wonders *Lite,* which was on the high street in Brockingham, and as I raised a hand to push open the frosted glass door I experienced a sudden, unsettling feeling of déjà vu. It could be ten years ago, when I'd first started working with Gabrielle in recruitment. The same feelings I'd had way back then came over me as my hand connected with the door and I wondered briefly if I should be doing something else. Not something better, just something else.

When I'd gone to college the first time around and studied English lit and media, I was meant to grow up to be the next Lois Lane. One half of the female Woodward and Bernstein. A hotshot reporter who would hunt out corruption and write about it. Politicians and fat cats of big corporations would quake in their expensive suits at what I was going to do with a keyboard.

Then, everything changed. At some point everything became too difficult. Focusing on studying was a struggle. I worked hard, often pulled all-nighters to get essays done, but my grades kept falling from their usual average in the low seventies. Fell and fell, and no matter how hard I worked, I couldn't get them up again. I didn't have the confidence to argue a point in class. I knew I certainly wouldn't be able to hold my own in the media, not against a group of driven, ambitious people who were hell-bent on getting to the top. It was hard enough clawing my way out of bed of a morning let alone contemplating spending a few years clawing my way to the top of the press pack. My friends and lecturers became worried about me and I was press-ganged into going to the doctor. I sat opposite him in his small, sparsely decorated office while he told me that I was obviously depressed, that it was probably a result of being under too much pressure at college and that I should try to relax. I should drink less alcohol and eat more fresh fruit and vegetables. "Take up exercise, as well, young lady. Looking better will make you feel better."

I'd nodded at him and left, realizing I had to hide my feelings better. I had to buck up my ideas. My plans to become a journalist might have evaporated but I still had to perform for my parents, my friends, my lecturers. I still had to prove to the outside world I wasn't a complete failure, that I was normal. I pushed myself hard, to the limit and then beyond. Pretended I was OK so I could get through college. It was such a struggle, long nights revising and reading and forcing myself not to give up. I finished with a first, a degree better than anyone had anticipated.

My parents, lecturers and anyone else who cared were overjoyed with my results, not realizing what it had taken. And, after that, I was spent. Couldn't do any more than I had done. I took up temping to pay my bills, and—I told my parents—so I could go on to do a master's degree. And, because it was easier than working out what career I wanted to begin, I applied for courses in media and ended up getting on one in south London. I didn't make any real friends there—people tried, but I wasn't interested because I was just there to keep my folks off my back. And once I finished, I ended up as a recruitment consultant because I met Gabrielle Traveno.

———

I was fresh out of college for the second time and wanted temp work to tide me over while I looked for a job. I'd decided to try an office on Oxford Street in central London that I'd walked past a few times. It was behind a glass door and under a square purple sign that read Office Wonders. I pushed open the door, climbed the narrow staircase and opened the door at the top of the stairs.

It was a large, open-plan room with desks and computers and filing cabinets at the end where the window looked out onto Oxford Street. At the other end of the room was the waiting area with comfy purple chairs for temps and other employment candidates pushed back against three of the pale purple walls. Almost all the chairs were taken up by smartly dressed young women. Each of them in a dark skirt suit with a white blouse or shirt underneath. And each of them carried some variation on a bag that looked like a shiny black briefcase. I was the only one in a burgundy trouser suit and I had my scuffed black slouch bag slung across my body. When I saw them, my confidence in getting a job wavered. Is this how temps are dressing nowadays? I asked myself as I unhooked my bag and stood up straight, wishing I'd thought to wear makeup.

At the business end of the office only one woman was run-

ning things. She had a young woman sitting in front of her, whom she'd probably been in the process of interviewing, but she was on the phone with someone, trying to be professional and polite, while a look of harassment tugged at her eyes.

Her blue-black hair was cut into a sharp side bob that ended at her chin. She was statuesque, her frame curvy, dressed in a navy-blue suit. As soon as she put down the phone, it rang again and irritation flickered across her face before she picked it up. Another phone on another desk started to ring. And then a third. Instead of joining the row of women who'd obviously come for an interview, something in me knew that if I didn't answer the phone I'd snap. It'd been a long day, even though it was only noon and I knew there'd be a "Temp Murders Seven over Unanswered Phone" type headline splashed across the papers in the morning if I didn't answer it. Without really thinking, I went to the desk, picked up the phone, answered the call, took a message. I'd worked a similar phone system before, so once I'd taken the message, I hit **8 and picked up another call. And another one. And another until I'd answered about seven calls and the harassed woman had finished her phone conversation.

Ignoring the woman in front of her, she came striding over to me. She was tall, quite imposing.

"You must be my new trainee recruitment consultant," she said.

"Erm, no, I'm just here about getting some long-term temping work," I replied, suddenly aware that the other people in the office were all staring daggers into my back.

"You misunderstand me, you MUST be my new trainee recruitment consultant," she said. I noticed how smooth and glowy, creamy white her skin was, on her face, on her neck, across her chest. Up close she was beautiful; the kind of woman you would always look at twice. Striking.

"*I just want to temp,*" *I repeated. I didn't want a full-time job with commitment and responsibility and having to think about it after I left work. I wanted to walk out at the end of the day and not worry about it until I walked into the office the next morning.*

"*Fine,*" *the woman said.* "*Do it for six months, If something better comes along I'll let you leave with a week's notice, no questions asked.*"

"*Erm . . .*"

"*The pay is better than temping, plus you get benefits. And bonuses if you get us more clients.*" *She was talking in a language and using words that didn't interest me. I wanted less commitment, not more of it. I wanted to be free, not shackle myself.*

The black phone on the desk beside us started ringing and automatically my hand reached for it. "*Don't touch that phone unless you mean it,*" *the woman warned.* Don't tell me I can have something if you're going to snatch it away, *her look said.* I can't handle it.

It was the look on her face. The desperation. The desolation. Years later, I realized it was something else as well. It was the quiet torment buried in her clear blue eyes—I'd seen it several times before when I'd looked more than fleetingly in the mirror.

She raised her eyebrows questioningly at me and I picked up the receiver, effectively sealing my fate. Without even telling the woman my name, or finding out what her name was, I'd got myself a job. While I was on the phone I heard the woman tell the others the position had recently been filled—the candidate in question demonstrated an impressive amount of initiative.

Something better hadn't come along. Not in six and a bit years. Not until I decided I needed to move to Australia.

———

Gabrielle was always the first in.

In all the years I'd worked with her, no matter how hard I tried, nor how early I arrived at the other office we'd worked in, every morning she'd be there, behind her desk, cup of coffee half drunk, croissant crumbs on a grease-soaked paper bag, typing away. I was yet to disprove the theory that she actually slept in the office.

She'd once told me that she was a compulsive early starter. In the way some people are always late, she couldn't help herself being early. I must have just caught her arriving because she was in the process of uncapping her cup of coffee.

"Blimey," she said, her hands paused on the top of the white plastic lid, while her eyes went to the clock on the wall above the candidate waiting area. "Thought it was just me who couldn't stay in bed in the mornings."

"I'm trying to catch you out," I joked. "And I wanted to make up for yesterday."

"Emergency all sorted?" she asked as she watched me shed my coat and unwrap my multicolored scarf.

"As far as it can be," I said. I didn't want to tell her everything, but I had to talk to someone, had to share my concerns. "My landlord's two kids were worried because they couldn't wake up their dad. And they were so scared that I couldn't leave them on their own. Not even when we knew he was OK."

"Where's the mother?"

"America, apparently. Although she might be back, I don't know. Not at home, basically, which is why the kids came to get me."

"Is he hot?"

"Who?"

"The flaky father."

I shrugged. "I don't know, I guess. Haven't really thought

about it. So much has happened since I met him and we aren't exactly on the best of terms. That taints how you see someone."

"I'll take that as a yes."

"Take it how you want, sweetheart. I'm more worried about his children."

"What, he's abusing them?" Gabrielle asked, concerned.

"No. No." The two crescent shapes carved out in the bottles of alcohol flashed through my mind. "Nothing like that. He's being, like you said, flaky. They're going through a divorce, he's struggling. I'm just being a bit dramatic. It's fine."

The words sounded hollow in my ears. It wasn't fine. It was far from fine. But if I said it enough times, I might just start to believe it.

Knowing when to leave well enough alone, Gabrielle listened to my too-many reassurances and then smartly changed the subject. "So, how about you get a cuppa and we'll have a catch-up."

Throwing myself into work was the way forward. That was the way to temporarily set aside the sallow, hollow faces of Summer and Jaxon that were scored into my mind.

They were sitting on the lip of my doorstep when I arrived back that evening.

I'd stayed late at the office to catch up on work, so it was dark and cold by the time I'd wandered down the pathway from the front of the house to my flat. In the pool of orange-yellow light thrown out from their kitchen, they sat. Around their shoulders were tartan blankets, across their laps was a duvet.

Jeez, you'd think he'd wait a few days to neglect them again, I thought as I approached them.

Both their faces lit up, although Jaxon quickly hid his delight by looking down. "We've been waiting for you," Summer said, still grinning. She fizzed when she smiled; her smiles came from the joy deep inside her heart and she had no worries about showing it.

"I can see that," I said, crouching down in front of them. "Is something wrong?"

"No," Summer replied. Jaxon shook his head.

"Oh, right. So you're sat here because . . . ?"

"We've been waiting for you," Summer repeated, as though I was somehow slow.

I nodded, and rubbed the bridge of my nose. My eyes were burning, my head was throbbing and my neck was a knot of tension from too much time in front of the computer and too little time asleep last night.

Jaxon nudged Summer as if to remind her why they were there. "Dad said we had to come and say thank you," she explained.

"He did, huh?"

"He said we had to say thank you for you looking after us on Saturday and yesterday. He said we had to draw you a picture." From the space between them under the duvet Jaxon pulled out a slightly rumpled sheet of A4 paper. It was stiff from where the paint he'd used had dried. He'd painted me a steam engine. A lime-green body and funnel with navy-blue swirls for wheels. In the corner he'd written "Ken."

"Thank you." I smiled in surprise as I took it.

"And this is my picture." Summer brandished her picture, again taken from under the duvet. She'd drawn a picture of a lady in a purple skirt and orange top. The woman had a blond ponytail and big brown eyes with long black lashes, red lips, dainty nose. She carried a pink handbag on her arm. Summer had used pencils to color it in and had pressed hard so each color lay thick and shiny on the surface of the paper. "Thank you" she'd printed in her uneven handwriting across the top of the page.

"Thank you to you as well."

"Do you like them?" Summer asked.

"I love them," I admitted. I loved them particularly because it meant Kyle had spent time with his children doing this. He'd gotten himself together and had put them before himself. That made these pictures all the more beautiful. "I'll put them on my fridge so I can see them every day. Is that OK?"

They both nodded.

"Dad said we had to buy you a present as well," Summer said. Jaxon pulled out a bag of marshmallows.

"Jaxon told Dad we have to get you marshmallows because you eat them for your breakfast," Summer explained.

"You don't like chocolate," Jaxon mumbled into his chest.

I did, actually. But clearly my talk of marshmallows had negated all other sweet things in his mind.

"Dad said every woman in the whole country kingdom universe likes chocolate, but he still bought it. Do you like it?"

Taking them from Jaxon, I held them in my hands. The pack had been warmed by its time beside their bodies under the duvet. Its cellophane packaging crackled in my hands, the pink and white cylinders of sugar giving easily under my fingers.

"I like them very much. I love them, in fact. Thank you for being so thoughtful."

"It's OK. You're our friend," Summer replied.

Jaxon nodded in agreement. I'd made great leaps with him without even trying. I wasn't simply someone whose hand he wanted to hold in the street, I was his friend. He liked me, even though he tried to hide it.

"Right, so you're off to bed now, aren't you?" I said, standing up to the tune of cracking knee joints.

Jaxon's shoulders fell; Summer rolled her eyes. "Can't we watch television in your house?" she asked. "Only for a little bit."

"Five minutes," Jaxon echoed.

I knew when I was being hustled. Their dad had probably told them they could stay up until they said thank you. Now they were trying to outstay their bedtime. "Much as I'd love to, I have to say no. You've got school tomorrow."

"Five minutes," Summer begged.

"Why don't you ask your dad if you can watch television for five minutes in your house?" I said. "Come on." I picked up their duvet, folded it over in my arms.

Reluctantly, they got up, clinging onto the blankets around their shoulders. As I turned I saw their dad standing in front of the window. He'd clearly been keeping an eye on them all the time they were outside. Well good. He was capable of behaving responsibly. The weekend was probably just a hitch. Of course it was. They didn't look abused. He was just struggling.

He moved to the door, opened it fully, ready to receive his children back.

"She loved it, Dad," Summer said, stepping around him into the house. "Kendie said we can watch television for five minutes." She led the way across the kitchen with Jaxon following.

"I never said that exactly," I said to Kyle. Didn't want him to think I was trying to be a parent to his children, was disrespecting his role.

"I didn't think you had," he said.

"I said they could ask you if they could watch TV for five minutes," I added. In the background the sound of the television went up a few notches.

"I know you did."

"Oh, here," I said, handing over the duvet.

He took it and folded it over in his arms, using it as a shield almost.

We stood in silence for a few moments. So much had happened between us in these past four days and both of us wanted to say something to acknowledge it and then lay it to rest. He was going to do better next time, I was sure of it.

"OK, I'll see you," I said when it became clear neither of us could find the right words.

He nodded.

I turned to leave. As I was walking across the grass I could feel his eyes on me. It felt as though he was watching over me; just like he'd been making sure the children were safe while they were sitting on my doorstep, he was ensuring I made it the short distance into my flat. He actually cared.

As I opened the door, he called my name. I turned back to him.

He tipped his chin up in a nod. *Clean slate?* he was asking.

I nodded back. *Clean slate.*

PANCAKES & BACON
SMOTHERED IN MAPLE SYRUP

◆ ◆ ◆

Ohhh, look, Kendra, a letter from Australia," Janene called across the office while waving a white rectangular envelope in the air as though trying to flag down a car with a handkerchief.

Everyone in the office—even the two young potential temps who'd walked in without an appointment and were filling out forms and waiting to be interviewed—stopped and stared.

Four of us worked in Office Wonders *Lite:* Gabrielle, me, Teri, who was a forty-year-old mother of four who worked two and a half days a week as a senior recruitment consultant, and Janene, our office assistant.

Janene was a twenty-four-year-old mean girl. And she made no secret of the fact that she didn't like me. Not me per se, so much as Kendra Tamale, head of temp recruitment. She thought that should have been her position, even though she'd only worked with Gabrielle for three months and hadn't had any training in recruitment. It galled her that someone else had been practically airlifted in to do the job and she'd told Gabrielle that she was disappointed in her for not at least giving her an interview. As a result, in the three weeks I'd been here, she obsessively concentrated on the minutiae of her job to derive some kind of satisfaction from gaining the upper hand on me.

It was something I'd experienced the world over: someone who had no power in their lives—be it at work or at home—took control over the tiniest things and became obsessed with carrying them out to the letter. For Janene it was ruling with a rod of iron her admin duties. Including—actually, *especially*—handing out the mail.

She would go through the post and open anything that she thought was interesting or juicy or would help her know what was going on in the business, then claim she thought they were invoices that needed reconciling. It was pathetic that she got such pleasure from opening other people's mail, but I still wasn't going to put up with it. I'd reminded her it was illegal to open anyone else's post without their express permission and asked her not to open any more of mine, no matter what she thought it was. In response, she did this, called out where the post came from. If it had a return address, she would call that out, too.

"Forwarded from your old office, over there, I think," she continued, examining the letter as though trying to read what was inside. Had she been alone in the office she would no doubt be in the kitchen, hunched over the kettle, trying to steam it open.

"Thanks, Janene," I said mildly as my heart began jittering in panic—there was only one person who would take the time to write me a letter and ask my former employers to forward it.

Clearly this was not the response Janene wanted. She came across the office from her desk, pointedly placed it on my desk between my phone and my keyboard and stood, arms folded, in front of me waiting for me to open it.

I didn't even acknowledge it. Instead, I glanced up at the two temps who'd gone back to writing on their pads. The white girl with her hair severely pulled back in a bun still had her head down, poring over her clipboard. The other girl, who had flawless mahogany skin, huge chocolate-brown eyes and shoulder-length, straightened black hair was looking up, smiling. She'd obviously finished the spelling test.

Pretending I wasn't desperate to see if I was right about the letter, and at the same time terrified to see if I was right about the letter, I got up. "Are you done?" I asked the temp. She nodded.

Brushing past Janene, whose frustration at me not playing along pulsed outwards from her, I went towards the candidate. As I took the clipboard I knew my hands were shaking. *It's from him, I know it is.* Scanning the clipboard, I smiled. "Wow, Kathleen, you've got 100 percent on the spelling test. I think that's a first. If you follow me, I'll set you a computer test. It's not difficult; we just need to get an idea of what programs you're familiar with." I led her through the archway down the corridor into the computer room, chatting all the way.

I busied myself with the two candidates for the next hour and a half. Talking to them, testing them, interviewing them and then seeing if I had anything suitable for them. All the while, I was actively ignoring the letter that was burning a hole beside my phone on my desk.

A couple of hours later I was alone in the office. The other three had gone out to lunch and I was covering the phones. I finally picked up the letter. Stared at it. The original address had been pasted over with a white sticker, but "Kendra Tamale" was in the original handwriting. It was his handwriting. Thin but full lettering. *Breathe,* I told myself. *Inhale, exhale. Breathe.*

The door rattled as it was opened inwards and my heart leapt to my throat. Gabrielle came almost bounding in. I snatched the letter out of sight, under the desk, into the darkness where it belonged.

"There's a guilty look if I ever saw one," Gabrielle said, shedding her green coat and sitting down behind her desk.

"You're probably right," I replied. "I was brought up Catholic so guilt is embroidered into the very fabric of my soul." I ducked under the desk, pressed the letter into the pages of my diary, gently shut it.

"Who was your letter from?" Gabrielle asked, uncapping the plastic top of her soup. It was a vivid red; the pungent aroma of tomatoes and onions filled the office.

"I haven't opened it so I can't rightly tell you," I replied.

She swirled her spoon in her soup, stirring up the smells. "Why did you leave Australia?" Gabrielle asked.

I glanced out of the window behind her head, stared at the sky. It was beautiful out. Beautiful and blue, stroked gently with white clouds. When I was a little girl, I used to want to live in the clouds. I wanted to skip from cloud to cloud, to feel myself sinking into the softness, feel its soothing embrace. I was such a daydreamer. "Why do you ask?" I replied.

"When I e-mailed you and asked if you'd come back, I thought you'd tell me to get lost. Five weeks later, you're back. I'm glad to have you, don't get me wrong, but you know, why did you come back from Australia?"

A current of tension ran up my neck, settled at the base of my skull, pummelled at the soft, tender space to the left. It shot forwards, pooled thickly behind my right eye.

I moved my head to the left, to the right, trying to stretch out the tendons. Trying to pull myself together. "To be honest, Gabrielle, I don't want to talk about it," I said. "It's enough that I'm back, isn't it?"

She scooped soup into her mouth with the deep plastic spoon, swallowed. "What's his name?" she asked.

I pressed the palm of my hand onto my eye, trying to

push back the pounding in my head. I pulled my head from side to side. I wanted relief. I needed relief from this agony.

"What part of 'I don't want to talk about it' don't you understand?" I said quietly at Gabrielle.

"Pretty much all of it, I guess," Gabrielle said, then lowered her head and concentrated on her soup.

To Gabrielle, I was being obstructive. Reticent. For no good reason. We were friends, right? Had known each other ten years. Why wouldn't I tell her my secrets? Share the truths about my departure from antipodean shores. She didn't realize that I couldn't tell her because it'd make her hate me. She'd think so much less of me and I didn't need that in a person I saw every day.

I didn't need to see the look of disgust, nor to hear the lecture on how stupid I'd been. I knew it, I knew it all. But feelings aren't like thoughts, they can't be changed at will. I'd tried. I'd tried so hard, so many times. And it still happened. I still felt it. In the deepest part of my heart, in my soul, when I woke up in the mornings, when I went to sleep at night I was still doing it. I was still in love with a married man.

"Here, take this," Gabrielle said, scrawling on a yellow stickie. She held it out over her desk and I got up, went over to collect it, then perched myself on the edge of her desk while I read it. "Mick Stein," his number and his address, which was in Rochester on the other side of Kent, were scrawled on the small yellow square.

"Who is Mick Stein and why are you giving me his number?"

She pointed at my head. "The way you've been rolling your shoulders, moving your head, blinking lots, I'm guessing you've got a pain in your neck." She let a beat pass and both of us avoided looking at Janene's desk. "He's a chiropractor. He'll be able to knock your neck back into the right position. And believe me, you'll feel a whole lot better after seeing him. He'll cure whatever ails you."

A chiropractor wasn't going to cure what ailed me. I doubted anyone could do that.

Gabrielle watched me in that way she did. She, like Jaxon, had a way of staring at you, making you think they knew everything that was working its way through your head; that your heart and mind were transparent and everything you had painstakingly buried was written in huge letters. "Just go. If you don't like him, you can go to someone else."

"There's a chiropractor down the road—why would I go to the other side of Kent to see this one?"

"Mention my name and he'll give you a discount."

"Really?"

"No! Just go to the damn chiropractor, Kennie. I don't want you to be in pain when you don't have to be."

"More like you don't want me to have you up for health and safety."

"That, too. And to show you what a great boss I am, I'll let you have the afternoon off to go see the most gorgeous chiropractor in the U.K."

———

Evangeline, a friend, had just had her script accepted by a film company and was celebrating with drinks in the center of Sydney.

We'd known each other for years in England before she returned home to Sydney and I wanted to support her, so had forced myself to go—even though I'd only know Evangeline, Evangeline's husband and one other person.

I plucked up my courage as I walked up the stairs of the bar, pulled back my shoulders, plastered a smile on my face and entered the room. Mild anxiety fluttered in the space between my heart and stomach, my palms were sweating slightly as I scanned the darkened room, seeking out Carrie, the only other woman I knew. I saw her, sitting on the bank of sofas, surrounded by people. I went past the bodies drinking in the bar and made my way over to her. She smiled a hello, but was in midconversation so just scooted up so I could sit down. That action of moving her bum a little to her right instead of to the left was a moment that changed my life. I didn't realize it, of course. I just sat down and waited for her to finish her conversation.

To my right, a knot of people sat, tight in conversation. The man sitting beside me was mentally hovering on the edge of the conversation, his body turned slightly towards them, but his eyes were focused elsewhere. He wasn't there. "You have no idea what they're talking about, do you?" I said to him.

He blinked, turned to me. "Is it that obvious?" he asked. He was British, had a strong, clear London accent. For a moment I was transported home, back to the other side of the world.

"Yup, and I'm so telling on you." This was unusual for me. I was usually so shy, especially with people I didn't know. But I'd decided that, to avoid slinking home feeling like a failure, I had to speak to someone. And since Carrie was otherwise engaged, this man would have to do.

"I'm Will," he said and held out his hand. "I think you should know my name before you destroy my reputation."

I took his hand, smiled and shook. "Kendra," I replied. "Most people call me Kennie, but since I'm about to out you, you'll probably have some other choice things to call me."

"No, no, I won't resort to name-calling. I'll take my punishment like a man."

"What, rant about it, retreat into your shell and then go pick on someone smaller than you to make yourself feel better?"

He laughed out loud, and his deep laugh, which moved his

chest and lit up his brown eyes, made me laugh, too. We spent the next few hours talking, laughing, mercilessly taking the piss out of each other—and nothing. Not a flutter, not a stomach dip, not a thought at all in "that" direction. When he left—he lived quite far outside of Sydney—he said good-bye to the people in the group we'd virtually ignored, and then turned to me and said, "I really appreciate you not turning me in, Kendie. I'll never forget it."

"Not a worry, Willie. I'll see ya."

"I'll see ya."

And that was it. He was gone. We didn't exchange numbers, we hadn't bought each other drinks and we certainly hadn't flirted. I didn't even remember what he looked like until the next time I saw him. I talked to three other people and I went home feeling elated that I'd managed to chat to people. The night I met Will he didn't even stay that long in my mind after he was gone.

I didn't realize that's how it worked sometimes when you met the person you were going to fall in love with.

———

With Gabrielle listening, I rang and made an appointment with her chiropractor for later that afternoon. He'd had a cancellation, the receptionist said, so he could fit me in. And still under the watchful eye of Gabrielle, I got up at three o'clock, put on my coat and left.

"Say hi from me," she called as I stomped rather bad-temperedly down the stairs.

CHAPTER 9

I didn't go to the chiropractor. Of course I didn't. I waited until I got to the end of Brockingham High Street and called to cancel the appointment.

He'd probably worked wonders with Gabrielle's spine—she had great posture—and she was probably right about him being gorgeous, but neither of those things was going to erase the past two years of my life. He wasn't going to take away the guilt and regret I felt when I was awake and when I was asleep. He wasn't going to adjust my spine and allow me some peace; unhook every memory of Will that was fused into my body.

Instead, I decided to use the time wisely. I walked the forty-five minutes home, hoping the exercise would loosen up the muscles in my back. Once I got in, I was going to take a hot bath, fill my hot-water bottle for a heat pack, down a couple of painkillers and then take to my bed.

As I neared number thirty-four, I saw her.

Her, Mrs. Eyebrows, with the unfriendly eyes, mean little mouth and abused eyebrows. The one who'd—eventually—given me the keys to the flat when I'd first moved in. She was standing in front of her glossy blue front door, turning the keys of her various locks. She might be coming my way. And if she was, there was no way for me to avoid her. I'd have to acknowledge her, say hello. Things like that set me on edge. Even if it was just a nod of the head, I didn't want to get into it. It might lead to a conversation. The horror of that, with someone who hadn't been that friendly in the first place, made me break out in a cold sweat. It was a wonder I did the job I did. I had to go out and hunt out business, place people, interview people. All of that, fine. More than fine. I could focus on the purpose of the conversation with work. With small talk, with talking to people I didn't know, especially ones who made it clear they didn't particularly like me . . . The space under my arms started to tingle, I was about to start seriously sweating.

"NO! I WON'T DO IT!" exploded into the air as I passed the front window of the Gadsborough house, erasing all thoughts and worries about engaging with Mrs. Eyebrows. Alarmed at the volume and severity of the shout, I stared at the window.

Mrs. Eyebrows, who had also heard the shout, waddled past me, glanced at the house, turned to me, raised an over-plucked eyebrow and shook her head as she twisted her face into an "it wasn't this bad until you arrived" look.

Hijacked, I didn't have time to give her an "it's not my fault" look in return. I tried, turned my head and craned my neck, but she was too far away and didn't turn around.

"YOU CAN'T MAKE ME!" Summer screeched through the window. Neighbor-lady yanked her handbag farther up her shoulder and shook her head even more firmly.

It's nothing to do with me! I almost screamed after Mrs. Eyebrows.

Great. She was going to bad-mouth me now. I could just see her—big meringue hair wobbling, wrinkled mouth quivering, cruel little eyes widened by disgust—as she stood in the local shop regaling them of how out of control the kids had become since their mother had left and that lodger moved in. "That colored girl had a British passport, but you never know these days, do you?" she'd probably add, eliciting nods from her coven. "It said in the paper the other day that these girls are coming over here and getting passports and then getting work as au pairs. I'm sure that poor Kyle wouldn't know any better. She was so cagey when I asked her where she'd come from and where she worked. She probably can't even speak English. Those poor children."

Damn this timing. This was what I got for skipping work and not going to the chiropractor. In the past two weeks I'd successfully avoided the family to give them breathing space, let them reassimilate to life without their mother. Since the children hadn't been in my flat and hadn't called even though I'd given them my number to do so if they ever needed me—all I'd had was a note pushed through the door saying they were going away last weekend—I had assumed things were going well. Assimilation was working, life was normalizing for them. But now my reputation was under attack. And worse, I knew my reputation was under attack. If I didn't know Mrs. Eyebrows was more than likely spreading rumors about me, I'd carry on as I was, oblivious. But now . . . I marched up the front path and pressed the doorbell.

The bell ding-donged through the house.

"DON'T ANSWER IT DADDY!" Summer yelled. "I SAID DON'T ANSWER IT!" she continued to scream as Kyle's tall, sleek shape crinkled towards me in the mottled colored glass of the front door. He flung open the door, caught it with one hand to stop it swinging back on its hinges.

His line of sight settled on me, then he sighed a little as he said, "Hi." Not pleased, not irritated. If anything, he was indifferent to see me. He clearly had bigger things on his mind.

"Hi," I replied. "I was passing and . . . Is everything all right?" I asked, suddenly realizing that me doing this could be seen as me criticizing Kyle's parenting skills again. That I was looking down my nose at him.

"Oh, fine. Just the usual Summer meltdown hour," he said casually. His body language was anything but casual. Every sinew in his muscular arms, exposed in his blue T-shirt, was flexed as he held open the door, making the bar code tattoos engraved on the upper parts of each of his biceps seem to stand away from the skin. His neck muscles were also tensed and a nerve in his temple was pumping rapidly. His skin was pale and clammy, the ghost of a frown puckering his forehead and the area around his eyes. He looked worse than he had when he'd been hungover. "She won't eat her dinner, wants to play with her toys, won't listen to a word I say, has a fit when I ask her to clear up the toys. Like I say, the usual."

"Do you want me to try? A third person might take the drama out of the situation." My voice was low and contrite, didn't want to throw petrol on this flaming situation.

He rested his head against the door frame as his body sighed in resignation. "Seeing as I'm seconds away from locking myself in the bathroom and punching the walls, at this moment, Kendra, I'll try anything. So . . ." He stepped aside, swept his hand before him, indicating the room on the other side of the staircase, the one I hadn't been in yet. "Be my guest."

I stepped in and went towards the door of the other front room. My eyes fell first on Jaxon, who was in the far left-hand corner of the room half sitting, half lying on the blue carpeted floor. Around him was the large oval of a train track, and he was moving a five-carriage train behind a burgundy, gold-edged steam engine. He was wearing Superman pajamas that fitted him a lot better than his Spider-Man ones. A bubble of calm surrounded him, protecting him from the rest of the room, which was in a terrifying state of chaos. Chaos ruled by Summer Gadsborough.

She was in the middle of the room. Her legs, covered in

blue jogging bottoms under pink shorts, were planted wide apart. Her arms, the color of dark opal, were exposed in her red T-shirt with a yellow unicorn on the front, and her hands were bunched into fists that rested on her hips. Atop her head, sitting like a tiara, was a padded, silky eye mask in a Pucci-style swirl of red, blue, yellow, green and orange. Her face was filled with red rage, her eyes wide and determined, her teeth gritted behind her pinched-together mouth. It was a look she must have inherited or copied from an adult. She had it down pat, had adapted it and refined it for her purposes. And her current purpose was to terrorize the playroom.

Her realm had been haphazardly but determinedly created. On a normal day the back wall had, about one foot above the floor, a low row of seats constructed from a light-colored wood with a navy-blue leather padded top. Inset into the frame was a set of wooden drawers to store the kids' toys.

Today was not a normal day. Each and every drawer was open, some hanging precariously on the edge of their wooden frames, others completely removed and sitting up-turned on the floor. Every drawer had been emptied and toys—electronic handheld games, stuffed toys, board games, books, pens, papers, drawings, brightly colored wooden toys, jigsaw puzzles, clothes from her dress-up box, makeup, spangly bits of material, trains, building blocks, cars and balls—were everywhere across the room. Nothing looked as though it had been placed in that position; it all had most likely been thrown or dropped or kicked.

"Hi, guys," I said cautiously.

Jaxon glanced up from his train's progress, fixed his large navy-green eyes on me, treated me to a small, shy smile that opened his mouth enough to expose his missing lower front tooth. It was definitely the largest smile he'd aimed my way since we'd met. It warmed me through from the top of my head to the soles of my feet, lifted my heart. I grinned back, pleased he was showing in the tiniest way that he liked me. I scared him, it was too much, too soon, and he ducked his head and returned to moving his train around its track.

In contrast, his sister didn't say anything, didn't respond. When she saw me, her expression wobbled for a fraction of a second: she wanted to smile, to say hello, to slip into our friendship, but she was committed to being a terror, she was ensconced in the tantrum and wasn't giving that up for anyone. I heard Kyle close the front door and then he stepped into the room behind me. This movement was a red flag to the six-year-old and the mist of rage descended again upon her eyes, upon her face, upon her entire body. Her dad was obviously the source and focus of her rage. He'd done her wrong and she was taking a stand.

"Summer," Kyle said through gritted teeth, his voice so forcibly calm it was transparent how close to the edge he was. Sparks flew between them; this was all-out war. "Please tidy this room up. Or come and finish your dinner. One or the other. *Please.*"

"*Noooooo!*" she screamed, her whole body folding forwards so she could force the word out with a volume that made Jaxon, Kyle and me all draw back a little.

"Tidy. The. Room. Up."

Jaxon stopped his train's progress around its track and made to get up. "No, Jaxon, you're not to do it," Kyle said, clearly spotting his son's attempt to put an end to this conflict. "Summer made the mess, Summer can tidy it up." Jaxon sat down again, went back to his train. He wasn't big enough yet to use his diplomacy skills.

That would be my job, since I'd invited myself into it. "Come on, Summer, listen to your dad," I cajoled.

Dangerous and slow, her head swung towards me; her

flaming eyes threw a poisonous look at me. "You can't tell me what to do, you're not my mumma," she said, triumph coating her words. This was a child's ultimate weapon against an outsider—reminding me that I didn't belong. Had she been a teenager, she would have told me to go do something sexually unpleasant with myself or an inanimate object.

The air thickened; Jaxon and Kyle both watched me, wondering how deeply her words had hurt me, how I'd react.

My reaction was to lock eyes with Summer. And then to drag up a smile. A tiny grin of recognition. I knew this. She was only six, but I knew what was going on and how to deal with it. Summer needed understanding. Not someone to shout at her or to fight with her, but to communicate with her from a place of understanding. I understood her.

"You're right, I'm not your mumma," I replied calmly. "And in about eight minutes, you're going to wish more than anything that I was."

Behind her beautiful navy-green eyes I could see the cogs whirring, wondering what I meant. "I'll be right back," I said and turned on my heels. Dropping my bag on the bottom step, I made my way down the corridor and into the kitchen, and began opening cupboards and drawers until I found what I was looking for. And then I went back to the play-room, reentered with my hands behind my back, hiding what I'd found.

"So, Summer, do you want to know why you're going to wish I was your mumma in just under eight minutes?"

She stared at me, defiant, but curious: her eyes asked why even though her mouth wouldn't.

"Because, in about three minutes, I am going to use these." I brandished my kitchen find—a roll of large black binliners. "You see, I know lots of kids who'd love these things," I said, indicating the sea of toys and playthings at her feet. "They don't have toys, and even if they do, their toys aren't half as nice as these things.

"Now, if I was your mumma, I wouldn't think of giving all this stuff away because I would have spent hours and hours at work, earning the money to pay for them. She'd remember how much everything cost. She'd also remember how much you loved playing with that set of wooden dolls." I pointed at the brightly painted set of Russian dolls that lay separated on the floor by her foot. "And your mumma would remember how you used to sleep with that rag doll, and how sweet you used to look, all cuddled up with her." I pointed at the battered green and pink doll with black wool hair and a missing eye that lay splayed under the window. "And your mumma would know how much you loved to read that book before you went upstairs for your bath, even though you'd both pretended you were too old for it and she was the one who wanted to hear it." I pointed at the book of childhood rhymes that had obviously been flung at the wall beside the door and bounced back, open, onto the floor. "Since I'm not your mumma, I don't know all these things. These toys mean nothing to me and I don't know what they mean to you. I don't know and don't care how much they cost, all I know is that they're a nice bunch of things that several other kids would appreciate. And would probably keep very tidy.

"So, Summer, I've taken two minutes to explain all this, so in about a minute—that's the time it takes to count up to sixty—I'm going to get down on my hands and knees and start packing this stuff up. Obviously, if they're all tidied up and put away, I won't be able to do that. But, as you said, I'm not your mumma, I can't tell you what to do, so I'm not going to ask you to tidy up. I'm just going to count to sixty and then start putting things in my bags. Either way, I reckon that in under six minutes, this floor is going to be clear of toys."

As I'd been talking, Summer's eyes had been growing wider and wider. She wasn't sure if I was pulling her leg, trying another way to upset her, or if I was serious.

"And, don't worry, I'm not going to count out loud or check my watch, I don't want to stress you out. I'm just going to count in my head and then start packing, OK?"

Summer looked to her father. He stood by the door, leaning on the door frame, and obviously wasn't going to intervene. Her gaze darted to her brother, who was also watching the unfolding scene.

"They're Jaxon's toys, too," she informed me.

"I know." I shrugged. "Your mumma would care about that. Your mumma would worry that Jaxon would be cross with you because you got all his toys taken away, but not me—I'm not like your mumma." I unrolled the black binliners in my hand and snapped one off at the perforations, the sound ricocheting off the tense silence in the room.

In response, Summer threw herself onto her knees, started gathering up her toys, clinging to all she could in one arm, while trying to right the drawer nearest to her. Once it was upright, she threw stuff into it. She moved at lightning speed, her eye mask wobbling on her head as she worked, her face a picture of anxiety. She scooped and threw and tidied with a fervent energy that was exhausting to watch. Within the predicted eight minutes the floor was clear and Summer was out of breath. She clambered onto her feet, her eye mask askew on her head, her face taken over by a grin.

I smiled back at her. "Well done, Summer, I'm really proud of you," I said. "You tidied up perfectly, you're a really good girl." I opened my arms. "Do I get a hug to show we're still friends?" She moved towards me, threw her arms around me and squeezed. Hard and tight. All the gratitude she was feeling expressed in that hug. She was thanking me for talking her down without a shouting match. She and her father had reached an impasse: neither of them could exit that power play without losing face. She was the type of girl who wanted to win, would do almost anything to win, but wanted people to like her, too. She wanted to do the right thing, but it was hard. I straightened her eye mask, then bent and kissed the top of her head.

"Are you going to eat your dinner?" I asked her. Without hesitation she nodded her head against my solar plexus. "Go on then."

She broke away and then wandered off to the kitchen. Jaxon got up and followed her. I hijacked him on the way out the door, hugged him and gave him a kiss on top of the head, too. Once they'd gone, I exhaled, tension draining out of my muscles like sand running through an hourglass. In seconds I was almost weak with relief. Every minute I'd been waiting for World War IV to start: for her to throw a toy at my head and a tantrum on the floor; I'd been prepared for bloodshed.

I turned to Kyle, who was looking at me with a mixture of admiration and surprise. "Taking on Summer," he said and whistled. "You're a braver person than me."

"She's terrifying," I replied. I put my hand over my racing heart to slow it down. "I kept waiting for her to completely lose it. I don't know what I would have done then. I take it your wife used to deal with this?"

Kyle's eyes flickered with sudden fury and, for some reason, shame. He gave a noncommittal half-shrug and then said darkly, "Something like that."

That was a stupid thing to say, wasn't it, Kendra? I thought. *Every time he speaks to his wife it ends in a row he's drunk himself comatose because of her. So what do you do? Talk about her.*

"Summer wasn't always like this," he said, still mired in whatever hell had descended upon their lives since Mrs. Gadsborough had walked out. "Well, not with me. And not every day. She was lively, but not . . ." He ended the sentence there. He had no words for what Summer had become. "And Jaxon wasn't so quiet, so meek. He was like any other boy his age. Always running around, playing games, talking. Now all he does is . . . Not much."

"Oh," I said. Either separation from their mother had done this to them or—as was quite possible—Kyle hadn't been around enough to know what his children were always like. He probably only saw them before bed or before school or on weekends. He probably wasn't here for that crazy hour, nor to experience his son retreating into his own world. It was possible—actually probable—that Kyle didn't know what his children were like at all.

"Do you fancy staying for dinner?" he asked. "There's plenty left. It's only pasta and salad but, despite Summer's behavior, it is edible."

I smiled at Kyle. "Love to, thanks," I said. Yes, I had intended to keep my distance, but they needed help. It'd shown in the forlorn, desperate way Summer had hugged me, the welcoming look in Jaxon's eyes as he managed a slightly larger smile at me, the twist of bewilderment that had taken over Kyle's voice. I wasn't sure if I was the person to give that help to them, but I at least had to try.

CHAPTER 10

*T*here are many things that make me uneasy: people who are nice 100 percent of the time (a sign of repressed rage); those who believe that cucumbers don't taste of anything (they do, actually, and they're the work of the devil); people who use the term *politically correct* as though it means something; my phone ringing after midnight and before 7 a.m.

When the flat's phone started ringing just as I was leaving for work, my eyes went to the clock on the wall in the kitchen area: 6:30 a.m.

I knew instantly it was the kids. *Oh God, what's happened now?* I'd given them my phone number to call me if they ever had any problems or if their dad had . . . I fell on the phone, almost ripped it from its cradle and asked a frightened, desperate, "Hello?" into the receiver.

"It's Jaxon," he said, his voice hesitant and small.

"What's the matter?" I asked, instead of saying a reassuring "Hi."

"Nothing."

"Oh," I said. "Well, it's nice of you to call me. How are you?"

"Fine," he said. And then paused. Waiting for me to say something.

"That's good. And how's your sister?"

"Fine," he replied.

"OK, that's good. And how's your dad?"

"Fine."

"That's good."

"You didn't ask about Garvo," Jaxon said, an accusatory and disappointed tone to his voice. *Garvo?* I hadn't heard of Garvo before. They had no pets. They had no friends I'd met nor whom they'd mentioned.

"Oh, sorry, how is Garvo?"

"He's fine. He didn't like his breakfast—Dad made toast." Garvo was around for breakfast? Curiouser and curiouser. "He doesn't like Dad's toast. It's always burnt on the edges. Mumma's toast is nice. Garvo likes it best." Four whole, un-coaxed sentences from Jaxon. Four. I was so stunned I didn't know what to say. "Summer wants to talk to you," he said. I glanced at the clock again. If I didn't leave in the next five minutes, I'd miss the bus. And then get caught up in rush-hour traffic. I wouldn't be late for work, but I wouldn't be on time by my standards, either. The day would start at a rush, trying to get my little routines—checking e-mails, going through the want ads in the papers and online—done before the calls started. Before the temps arrived to wait and see if there were any last-minute bookings. I started jiggling from one foot to the other. I really needed to get going.

He handed over the receiver. "Hi, Kendie," she said, bright as a button that had taken advantage of all the sleep allotted to them.

"Hi, Summer," I replied.

"I'm ringing to ask you a favor," she said. "It's not a big favor, but it's quite big."

"What's that then?"

"Will you get us from school tomorrow?"

All thoughts of being late left my mind. "Pardon?" I asked.

"Dad has to go to work tomorrow for the afternoon. And he said we can go to Gra'ma Naomi's house or wait in the car. But I said you would pick us up. At Gra'ma Naomi's house you can't do anything. She always says, 'Sit down, dear' 'Don't play with that, dear, it's 'spensive.' So you have to get us."

I do? "Thing is, I've got to work, too. I don't finish until after six, so it won't really be possible."

There was silence on the other end. A yawning, unimpressed silence that resonated with the patheticness of my explanation. "After school tomorrow I've got gymnastics and Jaxon's got football. So we finish at . . . Dad, what time do we finish? . . . It's on the fridge! Yes it is! . . . Next to the picture of the train . . . *Dad!* . . . Oh, OK, we finish at four-thirty. So you can come get us then," Summer said, as though I hadn't just explained to her why it wasn't possible; why her dad having to work shouldn't impact upon me.

If you need anything, anytime, call me. I'll be there. Hadn't I promised them that? Hadn't those noble words come out of my mouth when I had clipped on my cloak of the rescuer, folded my arms across my righteous chest and looked down my nose at their unsuitable father? Did I want to become an adult who lied to two children with an absent mother and a father who was barely coping?

"I'll see if my boss will let me leave early so I can come get you. But if she says no, then you'll have to go to Grandma Naomi's house."

"She won't say no," Summer reassured me. "You need to bring us a picture, Dad says."

"A picture?"

"Talk to Dad, he'll explain it. Bye."

Twenty minutes later I was on the way to work, having given the Gadsboroughs a photo of myself for the school records so Kyle could sign a piece of paper adding me to the list of people who could collect Jaxon and Summer. After a bit of argy-bargy of "No, I couldn't possiblies" and "No, you musts," Kyle had handed over the keys to his wife's car so I could drive the kids home. A silver Mercedes that was at least ten years old, with two booster seats in the back for the kids. It sat under a green plastic cover outside Kyle's house, unused, unloved, unnoticed since she'd left them behind. It was creepy holding the keys to the car of a woman who wasn't here anymore. It was almost like being asked to step into a dead woman's shoes, take her place in the family.

Especially when I didn't understand why she'd left it behind. If she'd left in the middle of the night, as Kyle said she did, then wouldn't she need to take her car? To help with the getaway and to have something to sell if she needed money? If I hadn't known that they'd been away together, and if I hadn't been there while Kyle had spoken to her on the phone that first day, I'd wonder if he'd done away with her. Had buried her somewhere. Instead, I was wondering what had happened to make her so desperate and determined to get away and start over on her own. What was the terrible thing that had happened that made her so desperate and determined to flee that she left her children behind?

I'd said we'd be OK on the bus, but Kyle had been firm: if I was going to pick them up, then I'd either have to drive them or get a taxi. Drive it was. In a vanished woman's car.

Gabrielle sat back in her chair, stretching out her curvaceous body.

I'd just asked her if it was OK if I finished early the next day and told her why. Now, she was sitting back, contemplating me in a quiet, faintly disturbed manner. Eventually she said, "Let me get this straight: you haven't got children of your own, but you've got to leave early to pick them up?"

"That's about it, yes," I replied, knowing how it sounded. Had I been on the other end of that conversation my reaction would have been identical. Something along the lines of *"Are you taking the piss?"* "I'll come in early tomorrow and work back on Wednesday."

"Just wondering, as one does, what he did before you so conveniently moved into his backyard."

"Gabs, I'm not living in his garden shed. And I don't know what he did," I replied. "But I said I'd ask so I'm asking. I'll totally understand if it's not possible."

My boss shrugged her shoulders. "Kennie, for as long as you've worked with me, you've put in the hours, so you can leave early if you wish, but . . . Ah, never mind."

"What?" I asked.

She shook her head. "Never mind."

"No, tell me."

"Don't let him take you for a mug."

"He's not. It was Summer's idea. She asked if I'd pick them up."

"I'm sure she did, but he's a man on his own with two children, probably for the first time. He'll always take the easy way out. And, I'm sure your mother told you this, you don't want to get a reputation for being easy."

Gabrielle's words had the vein of truth trickling through them. Kyle was struggling and, rather than pull himself together and find a way to meet this challenge, at the moment he was still wallowing in the loss of his wife. He was getting drunk; he was rowing with his wife then slinking into a depression that meant he ignored his children; he was having stand-up rows with his daughter. I wasn't surprised Jaxon rationed his speech, was quietly defiant; I wasn't shocked Summer had worked out that the quickest, most foolproof way to get her father's undivided attention was to throw a tantrum. They were twin behaviors, two sides to the same silent, desperate cry: NOTICE ME!

It'd be easy, possibly even wise for me to leave them alone. Let Kyle work it out and reorder his family life himself. Life isn't easy. And, as I'd said to Kyle that day I found him drunk and virtually lifeless on his sofa, "Once you bond yourself to a child, you can't just walk away."

I had bonded myself to them, I couldn't walk away. I couldn't let Kyle alone to work it out, his kids stumbling around in his wake, scrabbling around for as much attention and overt love as they could get from him. If I could do something then I had to.

I was about to explain this to Gabrielle when the door swung open and Janene, resplendent in her ankle-length, caramel-colored suede coat, carrying a Louis Vuitton bag and wearing Gucci sunglasses, entered. Despite her job title and low pay packet, most of her outfits cost more than six months' rent for me.

"Hi," she drawled and swept over to her desk.

Her arrival ended our conversation. Gabrielle glanced down at her watch, then up at Janene. "Thanks for dropping in, Janene, it's always nice to see you." Gabrielle had explained to her at length that if she wanted to be trained as a consultant, she had to prove she was up to the job and to start putting in the hours. To her, this meant turning up at nine o'clock. To me, when I was being trained, it meant arriving at 7:30 a.m.

A wash of embarrassment pinked up Janene's face but she decided to brazen it out. "Anyone for coffee?" she asked and smiled brightly.

We both shook our heads.

"OK," she said. She shed her coat like a snake leaving its old skin behind, then wandered off to the kitchen at the end of the corridor through the doorway beside my desk.

"That," Gabrielle said, pointing a maroon, manicured finger in Janene's wake, "is what happens when people believe you're there to make their lives easier."

I ducked my head. Gabrielle was right. But if she saw the

looks on Summer and Jaxon's faces the day they thought their father was dead, felt Summer's hug when she had her tantrum, saw the anxious way Jaxon looked at his father . . . Whether Kyle was taking advantage or not, I couldn't walk away.

STRAWBERRIES, BLUEBERRIES, SLICES OF APPLE, SLICES OF PEAR & A DOLLOP OF YOGURT

♦ ♦ ♦

CHAPTER 11

Supermarket shopping became a whole new experience in the weeks following my collecting Jaxon and Summer from school.

Now I had two personal shoppers (three if you counted Garvo, Jaxon's imaginary golden retriever with one brown leg, whom we weren't allowed to leave outside the shop with all the other dogs).

I was a novelty who paid them attention, so every spare second they could, they spent with me. I'd come home from work and they'd be sitting on the steps outside waiting for me. They'd often ring and ask if I would be able to pick them up from school because their dad was working. They rifled through my things and took whatever they liked. If I couldn't find something I could lay odds on one of them having it. It wasn't petty theft, not in their minds; it was simply an extension of our friendship. My antique silver and turquoise ring I'd bought in Sydney that I constantly wore, for example, Summer had seen lying on my dining table and had taken because it reminded her of me. She wore it on her thumb in her house and was very careful not to let it leave her sight. She never, for example, took it to school. Jaxon had taken possession of the mobile phone I'd used in Australia because Garvo (who spoke in barks only Jaxon could understand) had told him he could call Australia with it.

And if the children saw me leaving the flat after we'd had

breakfast on a Saturday, they'd run out, besiege me, ask me if I would take them with me. I invariably said yes, mainly because I hadn't worked out how to say no to them.

"Do your mumma and dad live in the same house?" Summer asked me one day while we were doing my weekly shopping.

"Yes, they do," I replied as I dropped a tin of chickpeas into my trolley. "Which is a miracle to me and all my siblings. My brothers and sister, I mean."

"Why?" Jaxon asked.

"Because they argue. Boy, do they argue."

"Like Mumma and Dad," Summer stated. It was a statement with the weight of the world on its shoulders.

"I suppose," I said.

"Why didn't your mumma go away?" she asked.

Because they enjoy torturing each other too much, was the flip answer I'd normally give. *Because they got together when marriage was for life and they'd had to work it out,* was the more considered reply. Whatever reason, after witnessing and living with all their rows and torturous silences it was reasonable to wonder the same thing that Summer was asking.

"I don't know," I replied, the most honest answer I could give without them taking it the wrong way. An adult would be able to detect the nuances of my family's story and understand why one size doesn't fit all—a child would just take it and fit it over her experiences like she would slip a shop-bought, mass-produced dress on her mass-produced doll.

Summer and Jaxon both stared at me, my three-word answer clearly not good or illuminating enough.

"During all the arguments, we all knew that our parents loved us. Even if they didn't like each other all the time, they loved us all the time." As an adult I could stand back and see that. Back then, I knew no such thing. All I knew—

all my brothers and sister knew—was that my parents *hated* each other. That they wanted to do as much as possible to make each other miserable and they didn't seem to notice how it affected us. All we knew was that we could never predict what day would be the start of another marathon argument. Years later, having been through many experiences, I knew that even if you were consumed by arguing with the person you once upon a time supposedly loved, you still had room in your heart for your children. You still loved your children, even if you forgot to show it. I wished my parents had told us that, had shown us that, but they hadn't, so I was trying to do that for Summer and Jaxon now.

Summer put her head to one side, regarded me with her languid inquisitiveness. "You mean Mumma and Dad love us even if they always tell each other off all the time?" she asked.

I'd wanted to sound profound, to have the message I was conveying to settle gently into their psyches like the soft falling of snow, to slowly melt into their minds so they knew without knowing that no matter what happened they'd always come first in their parents' minds. Instead, Summer had cut the bull and stated outright what I had been trying to diffuse. I really should stop watching those trite shows where everything was neatly wrapped up in fifty minutes. The way they resolved everything by saying "you love each other" really didn't work in the real world, not even on a six-year-old. I nodded at Summer. "Pretty much."

"When Mumma used to get sick Dad would tell her off," Summer said.

I had been about to place a packet of kidney beans into the wire belly of my trolley, but the statement stopped me, and I turned my attention to them. "Your mum used to get sick?"

In unison Summer and Jaxon nodded. "All the time. If she didn't take her medicine she'd be even more sicker." Summer explained. "It used to make Dad even more cross."

"When Mumma was sick he'd shout and then go upstairs to his room for a time-out and do his work," Jaxon said quietly, his eyes not focused on the present of a busy Saturday afternoon in a supermarket, but back in the past. Obviously it still played on his mind. His father shouting at his mother, his father's angry footsteps on the stairs.

"Sometimes, when Mumma was really, really sick he'd take us in his car for ages and ages," Summer added.

"And Mumma would cry. She said we didn't love her because we left her. We didn't want to leave her."

"Dad said we had to," Summer concluded.

My eyes went from one to the other, a disturbed feeling growing inside me. When my parents rowed we'd hide in our rooms, waiting for their tempers to subside or for dinner, whichever came first. But, in all of it, my parents never did this. My dad wouldn't bundle us out of the house to punish my mum; my mum wouldn't sob and wail and claim we didn't love her. They'd create a hell we had to reside in, but I didn't remember them using us as weapons—they found far too many things wrong with each other to bother.

"Your mum's sick, you say?" I asked.

They nodded in unison.

"What's wrong with her?"

Their eyes darted to each other in unison, communicating in their secret way, the way identical twins were mythically supposed to, the way Summer and Jaxon did even though they were fraternal twins. They turned back to me, shrugged in unison and mumbled, "Don't know."

"Don't know," they said, but it felt more like, *"We're not allowed to tell."* Cutting off further questioning, Summer wandered a few feet down the aisle, picked up a liter packet of liquid stock. "Do you want this?" she called out, hefting it up with both hands. I'd bought it last week and she'd obviously remembered.

"Yes, please," I called back. Rather than bringing it over, Summer stood and read the ingredients list. Her head bowed and slightly to one side, her forehead furrowed in concentration, her lips pursed. *That is me,* I realized with a start. In just a few weeks she'd gotten an impression of me food shopping down to an art. Jaxon, meanwhile, stood on tiptoes on the metal wheel bar of the trolley, my shopping list in one hand as he leaned into the trolley, rifling through the fruit and veg I'd put in there, looking at the list and then looking at the goods, like I usually did before we went to the checkout. They had cut me off by unintentionally pretending to be me.

Being so expertly cut off by them was isolating and bewildering. Whatever it was that caused them to do that must be a huge secret. Something so huge and scary it'd made them shut down and shut off.

Since I'd become a bigger part of their lives I'd learned a fair bit about Mrs. Gadsborough from the kids.

I'd learned that she called every other day to speak to her children and after each phone call the pair of them would be quiet and sullen, would often go to their rooms for a while to deal with their loss in their own way.

I'd found out that she couldn't speak to her husband without rowing with him.

I'd discovered she was beautifully photogenic. Long waves of caramel hair tumbled around her face, cascading down onto her shoulders; her eyes were the same deep, mesmerizing navy-green as her children's but an altogether different shape; her mouth was shaped like her children's, her small nose was not. The pictures of her with the twins were always vibrant, alive with her energy. Her head was always raised, her eyes overbrimming with joy, her cheeks glowing, her arms wrapped around Jaxon and Summer, cradling them as though they were the most precious things in her life. With Kyle beside her in pictures she was more subdued but no less passionate. In the photos that were still on display in the children's rooms, she'd often be looking at him a mix of awe and tenderness smoothing out her features, molding the grin on her face and teasing out the sparkle in her eyes. Kyle would usually be looking at the camera, his head dipped sideways towards his adoring spouse, the bashful grin of a man in love on his face.

All the pictures of the pair of them had been taken down from the living room, from the hallway, from the kitchen. Faint outlines of where the large glass frames had been were still evident on the walls and he'd left the twenty-by-sixteens of her and the kids up for them, but the others, the reminders of their times together, he had rehoused in the cupboard under the stairs. Summer had taken them out and shown me once, almost as though trying to show me the life they used to have. While we'd been flicking through the pictures, Jaxon had stood near us, eyes wide with anxiety, moving from foot to foot and wringing his hands like an old woman sending her only child off to war, so terrified was he that his father would walk in and catch us.

I was told that she was a graphic designer and freelanced on various advertising projects. I was also told she and Summer would dance in the living room, she and Jaxon would dig up the garden. The three of them would sometimes ride their bikes in the park when the weather was fine. She'd read them stories in bed, make up games to play in the bath.

Another thing I discovered was that she didn't take very much with her. One time, when Kyle was on site and I picked the kids up from school, they'd taken me upstairs to show me the rest of the house. We'd been up to the attic, to Kyle's neat, orderly office—which took up the whole of the top floor of the house. Each of his surfaces—of which there were many—displayed his models and drawings and brightly colored computer-generated printouts of virtual buildings, but the leather chair in the corner beside his radio was surrounded by chaos. Newspapers and architecture magazines were stacked haphazardly by the chair, pictures of the kids were tacked onto the walls. The room smelled of him, felt of him. One part quiet, reserved man, one part barely restrained bedlam.

We'd also been into the kids' bedrooms, then the master bedroom. I'd been uncomfortable crossing that threshold—hadn't wanted to look at these elements of Kyle and his wife's life together—and had hesitated. But Summer had no such problem and dragged me in and over to the walk-in closet. Almost one side of the closest had been emptied, the hangers still clung onto the rail like the bare branches of a tree in winter, but the floor was stacked with boxes. The labels, in Kyle's writing, said the boxes were full of clothes, shoes, bags, makeup, books, magazines, photos. Summer regularly went through the boxes. It was where she found the eye mask she wore like a tiara—it reminded her of her mother, she'd told me. She'd also given Jaxon their mother's sunglasses, which he kept on the shelf by his bed. I didn't understand why Kyle would go to the trouble of carefully boxing then labeling her belongings, nor why she had left so much behind. Maybe because she'd left in the night and couldn't take much with her had been one explanation, but it felt much more as if she had been determined to leave as much as possible of this life behind. To shed this life and never look back.

Now the illness. Another piece in the jigsaw puzzle that was her disappearance from their lives.

What's wrong with Mrs. Gadsborough? I wondered as we started down the aisle again. *And how do I find out without it seeming as if I'm prying?*

CHAPTER 12

*K*endie wouldn't let us get a burger," Summer informed her father as she marched into the kitchen.

She trawled across the wood floor, dropping her bag, her sweater, PE bag and homework pouch on the way behind her, heading for the biscuit jar on the counter. I followed in her wake, picking up the discarded elements of her school day. She got onto tiptoes, grabbed the terra-cotta jar, cradled it in one arm and took off the lid with a faint pop. Her little hand reached in and scooped out two biscuits.

Kyle looked from his shiny silver laptop at me, then at his daughter.

"We wanted a Smiley Smiler meal with a toy. It's a pink watch. Jaxon wanted the racing car. Kendie said we weren't allowed to get one."

"Why not?" he asked her.

"She's idiotically opposed to them," Summer said and shoved one of the digestives in her mouth, biting down. Golden crumbs rained down the front of her blue school shirt.

Kyle curled his lips into his mouth so he could laugh quietly.

"Ideologically opposed," I corrected, feeling rather stupid.

Her head cranked around towards me, a sour look on her face—it'd been there for most of the journey home, along with folded arms. Had she been able to raise a condescending eyebrow at me, she would have done. "That's what I said," she replied in a voice that told us: *I know what I said and it's what I meant.*

"I'm going to give Jaxon his biscuit," she said on the crest of a huff.

"Lid," Kyle reminded before she'd gotten too far across the room.

She heaved a sigh to let the world know how unjust her life was, turned and replaced the lid, then swept out of the room.

"Are you really opposed to fast food?" Kyle asked.

I placed Summer's belongings on her chair at the head of the table. "Not fast food per se, although I probably should be. No, I love junk food, I simply won't go into certain establishments," I explained.

"Why?" he asked, taking off his computer glasses, putting them to one side. "Life's hard enough without adding to it with things like that."

"Thing is, Kyle, I have this problem—I believe in too many things. I have all these things that I won't do on principle and it's hard for me to let them go even for an easy life. Even before I got to university I went on protest marches and stood on picket lines. It's part of who I am. Give me a good cause, I'll back it. And, hey, don't tell me about any company that's doing people wrong because that's it, I'll stop buying their stuff and will hate myself for having bought it in the past."

From deep in the house, the television went on, blaring out a cartoon. And then it went quiet before the squeaks, bells and noises of a computer game exploded into the atmosphere.

"I think it started with being brainwashed about veal when I was in middle school. My teacher told us at length how veal was produced and, well, that was it. I just couldn't. Me and my sister both. I haven't even tasted it. And I think my beliefs grew from there." I was aware that I was explaining far too much about myself to Kyle. Usually when I dropped the kids off it was literally to check that they were safely ensconced in the house and then I'd be on my way back to work.

Kyle put his head to one side, looking me up and down as though seeing me for the first time as someone other than the interfering, pain-in-his-arse lodger. The person he played tag with over the children. The person he had to eat dinner with once or twice a week and who gave his children breakfast on Saturday mornings while he slept in. "I used to believe in all sorts of things before I had kids," he said. "That's when I learned how hard life can be and how much easier things are if you stop fighting all the time."

"Ah nah, you see," I said, stroking my hand over the back of Summer's chair, "one of the things I'd want is for my kids to have strong beliefs. Even if they're not the same as my own, I want them to be aware of something other than their immediate worlds. That they don't have to sit back and accept stuff because it's easy, that they have the ability and right to effect change.

"If I had a girl, I'd want her to know that she can be anything she wants and that she doesn't have to rely on her looks or clothes or hair or makeup to define who she is or to get respect from other people. I'd want her to know she has a right to be respected or noticed because she was born. I'm not talking about all that girl-power nonsense, I'm talking about my girl growing up knowing she has the right to be treated decently simply because she was born." I was on a roll now.

"And if I had a boy, I'd bring him up to know that being a man is all about feeling good about who you are. Not all that macho bullshit, but feeling so comfortable you don't have to disrespect other people, or put them down to feel good. You don't have to follow the crowd to be a man. He can believe in whatever he wants, think whatever he wants, be whatever he wants without worrying about his masculinity.

"And I'd make sure that whether my child's a boy or a girl they'd know that they don't ever have to put up with being treated badly. Not ever. Nor have to do something because their friends are all doing it.

"If we're going to change the world for the better, kids need to know that they can by feeling good about who they are and helping others."

An indulgent, vaguely patronizing smile crept onto Kyle's face. "You're not a parent, you don't know" that smile was telling me. He just about made it through the day bringing up his kids without trying to fill them up with oodles of self-esteem and save the world on top of it.

He cocked his eyebrow at me and asked, "So, because you want to change the world, you're seriously not going to feed your children fast food from certain outlets?"

The question was like a punch to the softest, most tender part of my stomach and it forced all the air out of my body. I glanced down at the chair I was standing behind, rubbed my forefinger over the smooth knots and waves in the oak. "Absolutely not," I said with firm, quiet certainty.

"OK," he scoffed. He was clearly thinking I'd change my mind the second I was on a road trip somewhere with two screaming kids in the back and no other food outlet for miles.

I looked up at him again. "I'm not going to have children," I said. "I'd love to, but I can't. Physically, I mean. I can't physically have children." I'd never said that before; those words hadn't left my mouth and stained the air. Saying it made it a little more solid. Permanent. *Real*. I'd never wanted it to be real so I'd never said it out loud.

Shock boomeranged from one end of Kyle's face to the other, erasing all smugness in its path. Suddenly he looked uncomfortable. Now he knew how it felt to be on the receiving end of too much personal information from a virtual stranger. "Oh," he said. The pale olive skin on his forehead crinkled as he frowned and I could see his eyes trying not to stray down to my "baby-growing" area. "Why can't you have kids?" he eventually plucked up the courage to ask.

"Because I was really stupid this one time. Trusted someone I shouldn't have. Ended up with pelvic inflammatory disease, then was told that because it wasn't treated in time . . . Well, basically, I can't have kids."

"*Scarring*," "*irreversible damage*," "*nothing we can do at this present time*." The words began to swim through my mind. They were the only words I remember from talking to the surgeon after the keyhole surgery that confirmed my fate. I remember his eyes, dark and heavy under his green paper surgeon's hat, and those words. Nothing else.

Pity was ingrained on Kyle's face, smudged into his crow's feet, into the creases around his mouth, into the black pupils of his mahogany eyes. *Urgh.* I did not need to see his pity nor to experience it.

"So there, you're renting a flat to a freak of nature," I said, trying to make light of it. "Don't worry. I'm not contagious or anything." As I spoke I was moving towards the door. Trying to distance myself from Kyle's pity and this conversation. "It's all sorted," I continued as I reached the door. "I'd better get back to work," I added then fled. "Bye, kids, I'll see you soon," I called as I dashed down the corridor, snatched open the front door and escaped down the path.

Kyle caught up with me as I swung open the car door. "Kendra," he said, holding onto the top of the door, stopping me from getting in and, essentially, impeding my escape. "Do you want to come over for dinner later on to-night?"

I stared down at his hands, which were gripped onto the door of the car. He had big hands with long fingers; they reminded me of the kids' hands but instead of being stained with paint and pen, his had badly bitten nails and split cuticles.

"I'll give the kids their dinner and wait until you get back so we can have ours after they have gone to bed. Afterwards we can watch television, talk or listen to music. Do you like Sarah McLachlan?"

I nodded cautiously, still not looking at him—didn't want to see that pity.

"I've got all her albums, but I hardly ever play them. Ashlyn didn't get it, and the kids used to look at me like I was torturing them or something. And you don't go around telling other men you like chick music. So, what do you say? I'll even throw in a coffee or two."

It was tempting, but was he asking me this because he felt sorry for me of the barren womb? I raised my line of sight but didn't look at him; I stared instead down the neat row of houses snaking into the distance of Tennant Road.

"You'll be doing me a favor," he reassured. "It'll be great to have some adult conversation that doesn't involve, 'Yes, there is a way to fit that two-hundred-foot extension into your ten-foot backyard for two pounds fifty.' "

Over Kyle's shoulder I spotted Mrs. Eyebrows. Her sparse eyebrows nearly shot off her face in surprise at how close Kyle and I were standing by the car, then her mouth twisted into an "I knew it!" expression before she hitched up her handbag onto the brow of her shoulder and scurried off down the road. No doubt she'd be dropping in at the local shop to let them know how much I was turning that nice

Kyle's head. And him a recently separated man, as well. And didn't she say she knew I was trouble from the moment she laid eyes on me?

"OK," I said to Kyle, finally meeting his gaze, "I'll come over."

His face curled up into a sweet, pleasant smile and I almost didn't mind that he'd probably asked out of pity. "Now I'd better get back before Gabrielle blows her stack."

"Cool," said Kyle and stepped back to release me.

As I drove off, I glanced into the rearview mirror and saw Kyle standing on the pavement watching the car right until I turned the corner at the end of the road.

————

The dinner party was fun.

Lively atmosphere, good food, expensive wine, interesting conversation.

I'd recently returned from a trip into unreality. Earlier that day I'd been to the hospital to receive the results of a laparoscopy. My periods were heavy, cripplingly painful, and because they'd already found I had chlamydia that had been untreated for years, the laparoscopy was the latest investigation to see if it had caused pelvic inflammatory disease. A week earlier they'd sliced into my belly button and inserted a tiny camera inside to see the condition of my reproductive system. Earlier in the day I'd sat in the surgeon's office, having caught him between procedures so he still had his green hat on his head, and heard the findings. They were: blockage of both fallopian tubes, extensive scarring on both ovaries and uterus, nothing we can do at this present time. Permanent infertility. "But there are medical advancements all the time, things may change in the future." All those things I remember because I read them again on the written confirmation. After he told me,

I slipped quietly, gently into shock. Then wandered into a place inside where none of this was happening and none of it mattered. I must have spoken to the surgeon, I must have picked up my bag, I must have gone back to my flat, must have had conversations with people, carried on as usual, but all of it is gone.

The next thing I remembered was sitting in the back of a cab with Gabrielle, being her plus one for a dinner party. She'd mentioned she and her husband, Ted, were going through a hard time so were socializing separately, but I didn't realize what an understatement that had been—they were actually on the last miles of the road to divorce. In the back of the darkened cab, we were both drowning in the reality of our lives, but had no idea we were each suffering as much as the other.

And now I was at a dinner party pretending to be normal. Pretending that I didn't know the exact date when this had begun. I'd always been so serious—paranoid—about safe sex, about becoming accidentally pregnant, that I made sure it was safe every time, so I knew the exact date I'd contracted chlamydia. I had only been stupid the one time; I'd only trusted the wrong person once and . . .

I pushed my chair out. Escaped to the bathroom. I ran the cold tap over my hands, gently patted my neck with cool water. Calming myself down. I forced myself to look at the mirror, to see myself, to look into the depths of my own eyes for more than a few seconds.

You're single, *I reminded myself in the mirror.* It's not like you're trying to have a baby. Or that you've met the man of your dreams and you want a baby. Forget about it for tonight. Do this one day at a time. Think about it one day at a time. It's only because someone's told you that you can't have children that you want them. *I shut off the tap, dried my hands on a towel.* Think about it. What would you do with a child right now anyway?

Back at the table, I took a drink of wine. It slipped down my throat, warming me up inside, and the grip of agony began to subside, loosened its hold on me. I could handle this one day at a time.

"I've got an announcement," our hostess said over the hum of conversation to get our attention. My eyes went to her glass—water. I took in her face: glowing skin tinged ever so slightly with green, gleaming eyes, thick glossy hair. She's pregnant. The thought zipped through my mind. Joy welled up inside, rippled through me until I was overwhelmed with happiness for her. And then it hit me: she was experiencing something I never would. She was going to press a kiss onto the soft head of her newborn baby; she was going to take his or her hand in hers and stare at each crease and line, trying to memorize them; she was going to delight in the soft scent of milk and skin and baby; she was going to gaze at her child and think, "Look what I made." It was like a pillow being pushed over my face, smothering the air out of me. I couldn't take in oxygen, grief was compressing all my internal organs, a vice of loss, twisting tighter and tighter. I hardly knew this friend of Gabrielle's, but I was filled with such happiness and such envy. She was going to have a baby.

"I'm having a baby," she said, and the table became a mass of squeals and women jumping up and running towards her, hugging her, asking about due dates, names, nurseries, schools. I was one of them. I was overjoyed for her, I couldn't help myself feeling that. Just like I couldn't help myself feeling cheated at the same time. I had two strong and conflicting emotions stirring inside me. Over time they became stronger, more polarized.

I saw them everywhere. Mothers. I was probably just more attuned to them because of what I'd been told, but everywhere I went I saw women with abdomens swelled with babies, I saw women pushing infants in prams, I saw women playing with *their children, women shopping with toddlers, women taking their offspring to school, women watching their little ones play, women screaming at their kids, women trying to bear the embarrassment of a full-on tantrum. In shops, in traffic, on trains, on buses, on the street I saw women who, if for this one thing, would be like me. I ached over it. I wouldn't begrudge anyone the right to have children, but it hurt. It hurt more than I could describe. And it was a reminder of that monumental mistake I'd once made.*

I decided to change my life. I decided to start again somewhere else. Australia seemed as good a place as anywhere. I could get a travel visa relatively easily, they spoke English (sort of) and I wouldn't need lots of vaccinations.

Yes, there were children there, but they weren't children I knew. I wouldn't have to see my friends becoming pregnant and starting their families. I wouldn't have to play with my nieces and nephews knowing that they'd never have a blood cousin from me. I wouldn't have to be happy for them and miserable for me. One step removed, one half of the world removed, I could start to rebuild myself in the light of this knowledge.

For months I was so caught in a whirlwind of looking for somewhere to live, looking for work, acquainting myself with the Australian way of life, deciding whether to be sponsored so I could stay in one job for more than three months, eventually starting my new job, that I forgot everything else. It became buried. I could ignore it and move on.

Then I fell in love.

———

I eased the car into the space behind Brockingham High Street, where most days I needed to I managed to get a parking spot, and turned off the engine. I was still a bit disturbed that I'd told Kyle something so private about myself.

I hadn't told anyone else. It's not something I'd ever broadcast and it wasn't as if people ever asked you that sort of thing. *Well*, I decided as I locked the car and put on the alarm, *it's probably a good thing. Now he knows something personal about me, I can try to get him to open up about his wife without feeling as if I'm too much of a trespasser.*

CHAPTER 13

I'd become a little obsessed about what Mrs. Gadsborough's illness could be.

At first, I'd decided it was terminal and being a caring, noble mother, she'd left to spare the children the pain of watching her go. Then I thought it through. No one except eighteenth-century explorers and the elderly Inuit did that. There was also the small matter of wanting the children with her, which was what she and Kyle were constantly arguing about.

My next port of call was Gabrielle, a trained counselor who was studying part-time for her master's degree in the psychology of trauma. We'd talked it through and from the small amount of information I gave her she suggested it could be a form of depression. Bipolar disorder, which could explain the highs and lows. Or, she said, it could be untreated postnatal depression, which often increased in severity if not dealt with properly. That would explain the need to leave as well, to get away for a while. Or it could be just depression, which could cause changes in behavior, especially if she hadn't been given the right medication, wasn't being correctly monitored, or if she did something like drink on certain medication.

All of these theories sounded plausible, and I'd been trying to work out how to bring it up with Kyle most of the evening.

He'd made a spicy lamb stew, which we'd eaten at the kitchen table. I'd washed up, he'd made coffee and we'd settled in the living room. I had draped myself over the armchair, my legs resting over the arms of one side, my head resting over the other, which had amused Kyle.

"You sit like the kids," he'd said.

"So I do," I'd replied innocently. I'd decided it was a good idea not to mention that not only did we often sit like that, we'd also chase each other over the seats of the armchairs and sofas, bouncing and laughing as we ran.

Despite the two sofas, two armchairs and the chairs in the dining room behind us, Kyle chose to sit on the floor. He sat with his long legs pulled up towards his chest, his bare feet flat on the floor, in front of the sofa I'd found him passed out on. He spread his arms out on the seat and rested his head back.

I wondered, briefly, not for the first time, what had happened to all the bottles of alcohol. I'd decided he was either a heavy drinker who'd fallen off the wagon but had pulled himself together or the threat of social services had scared him into sobriety. Either way, he hadn't been drunk as far as I knew. But what he'd done with the alcohol was a mystery.

So far we'd talked a lot about architecture, design and house prices. He'd asked me about my job and told me what Summer and Jaxon were up to at school. All the while, as we talked, as we bonded, I was working my way up to asking about his wife.

True to his word he'd put on Sarah McLachlan. Currently playing was "Fumbling Towards Ecstasy," my favorite of her albums because it was the first one I'd bought. I closed my eyes. I was surprised Kyle liked this music; she sang so often about heartbreak and loss and losing who you are. But the music was perfect, it added to the laid-back, friendly, mellow atmosphere. It set the scene so well that if I asked now, he'd probably tell me. He closed his eyes and I knew this was the moment.

"Erm . . ." I began.

"So . . ." he said at the same time.

"Oh, sorry, go ahead," we both said.

"No, you go," Kyle said, lifting his head.

"No, you," I replied. *Maybe I'll ask later,* I said to myself. *Maybe you're just a big hairy coward,* another part of me replied.

"I was going to ask if you went to the beach a lot in Australia," Kyle said.

"Not really," I said, casting my mind back to the time I'd been there. "I went to the beach a handful of times. I went to Bondi only once—I'm not really into the beach and stuff."

"And yet you moved to Australia, land of beach living."

"What I mean is, I'm not much of a swimmer and not very good at water sports, and if you're not into that, it's mainly about lying around on the beach or playing volley-ball, neither of which I'm much good at. And, if I'm honest, I'm not a fan of swimwear."

"Let me stop you right there," Kyle interrupted. "I don't want to hear any of that women nonsense about you being fat. You're not. I won't have a bit of it."

"I don't think I'm fat. I don't think I'm thin. To be honest, I don't think about myself in those terms at all. Even when I weighed less and wore a size ten I didn't go in for swimwear. I'm not a fan of showing off my body. A slightly above-the-knee skirt is as far as I go. And even that's very rare." My weight fluctuated and it was only partially important to me. I was a curvy woman—I came from curvy genes—and I had larger-than-average breasts, a narrowish waist and slender hips. Someone had once told me I had the most perfect bum he'd ever seen. But my body's weight was not a source of angst for me. I wasn't obese, so I'd found, over the years, there were better, more serious things to worry about.

"You're an unusual woman, not worrying about your weight. Even Ashlyn, who's tiny, used to fret about it. After she had the twins she became obsessed with losing the baby fat. I overheard her telling her mother on the phone that if she didn't get back into shape quickly I might go off her. The woman had just had my children, she'd done this amazing thing making me a father, how could I go off her?" Kyle shook his head. "I could never 'go off her,' not how she meant."

This was the perfect opening. We were on the subject anyway. I opened my mouth to ask him and suddenly Kyle was on his feet, a troubled look on his face. Almost as though talking about his wife had taken him to a place he didn't want to go.

"Another coffee?" he asked.

I glanced down at the undrunk coffee in my hands. "Erm, yeah, thanks." I held out the white mug and he came and took if from me. "Actually, I'll give you a hand," I said. If I went to the kitchen with him, we could carry on the chat and maybe I'd get the courage to bring her up again.

My left leg came off the arm of the sofa fine. My right leg was a little more difficult, protested that it was fused into this position, quite liked being here, and couldn't I just stay put. Kyle saw I was struggling, placed the mugs in his hands on the side table and reached out to me. His large, warm hands closed around mine and he hoisted me up to my feet, bringing me to rest in front of him.

The room stilled for a moment as he looked down at me, stared straight into my eyes. The last time we'd made eye contact for this long we'd been sitting at his kitchen table: I'd been hauling him over the coals for scaring his children and he'd been trying to work out if the black-eyed stranger before him would truly report him for neglect. This stare was softer. Friendlier. We'd come a long way in a short amount of time.

He let go of my hands and I went to smile at him as I turned towards the door. Suddenly his hand came up to my face, he dipped his head and kissed me. His scent filled my nostrils and his other arm circled my body, drew me closer to him, then he ran his hand down my body. His eyes slipped shut, his tongue pushed into my mouth. It happened so quickly, so unexpectedly, it took me a few seconds to react.

My hands went up to his chest and I shoved him as hard as possible away from me.

"WHAT THE HELL ARE YOU DOING?!" I shouted at him as he stumbled back and then stopped. Frantically I used the palm of my hand to rub off the impression his lips had made on mine.

He stood a little distance away, looking at me with genuine confusion. "I—I thought . . ." he stuttered. I was suddenly aware of his physical presence. How much bigger than me he was, how threatening his physique could be in such a situation. I took a step back to put space, a safety zone, between us, to stop myself being in easy reach. I glanced at the door; it would take a few steps to get to it, to escape. I could do it, though, I could make it if I tried. "I . . . I thought," he continued to stutter, bewilderment on his face.

"YOU THOUGHT WHAT?!" I yelled, annoyed by his inability to express what had made him do such a stupid thing. Then I remembered the kids, upstairs asleep. I didn't want to scare them so I lowered my voice. "What did you think? Huh? What?"

"I thought . . . We were having a good time, we were talking . . ."

"Yeah, talking! Not . . ." I rubbed again at my mouth, the

taste of coffee that he'd pressed onto me with his lips was seeping into my mouth. I rubbed hard, trying to get it off. I didn't like coffee. I didn't drink coffee. Yes, I accepted it if it was offered, but I never drank it.

"I don't understand . . . I thought you wanted me to kiss you."

"*What? Why?*"

He said nothing, just frowned his bewilderment at me.

I took a deep breath, calmed my voice. "Seriously, Kyle, what gave you that impression?"

"We were talking . . ."

"Again, as I said, talking not kissing. Do you kiss every woman you talk to? 'Cause if you do, you must have a hard time in the bank or supermarket."

Kyle stepped forward and terror squeezed my heart. "Don't come near me," I said and raised my hands protectively. It had the desired effect: he stopped. Stared at me, perplexed.

"I don't understand," Kyle said. "I thought we had a good vibe going on. You know . . . that maybe . . . I don't understand. I thought you liked me."

I took a step towards the door. "I do like you, Kyle, but I don't kiss every bloke I like. Especially when he's my landlord and all we've done is talk. And I haven't given him even the slightest indication that I'm interested in him in that way."

In the background, Sarah McLachlan's voice dropped a notch and she began to husk her way into the next song, telling us that all the fear had left her, she wasn't frightened any longer. I was still breathing hard, my fear hadn't left me. I was still frightened that I hadn't seen this coming.

Agitated, Kyle rubbed his hand over his head. "I'm sorry. I thought we had something going."

"Something going? Why did you think that?"

"Do I have to spell it out?"

"Yes, I'm afraid you do, Kyle, because I am mystified."

Sarah's voice filled the silence between us as he stared desolately at the carpet. "You've been so supportive. You're always over here—cooking meals, picking up the kids, cleaning up . . ." His voice trailed away and slowly he raised his head. "I thought . . ." His words disappeared again, as though he couldn't explain himself.

"Kyle, I saw you were struggling and I tried to help out, that's all. And, I'm sorry I didn't tell you this before, but I'm in love with someone else." I touched my heart, then indicated to him. "Me and you, it's not going to happen. It's *not* going to happen." He didn't react. He was stuck in confusion, couldn't begin to comprehend why I'd pushed him away.

"I'd better go," I said, gathering up my things: my cardigan and stripy scarf I'd slipped off and chucked over one of the armchairs, my black and red sandals I'd parked beside the sofa, my little bag that held my purse and phone. Had Kyle watched me take these things off, make myself comfortable, thinking I was doing it for him? That I was getting ready for a night of passion?

"I'll see you," I said to him as I left, cradling my belongings in my arms. I didn't even put on my shoes—just padded out of the living room, through the kitchen and into the garden. I took giant steps on tiptoes across the lawn and then into my flat. I locked the front door and then, shaking slightly, I climbed the stairs, dropped my things on the floor and flopped onto the sofa.

I couldn't sit, couldn't rest, and immediately jumped to my feet again.

Still trembling, I paced the floor.

He actually thought . . . Every time I remembered the firm crush of his lips on my mouth and his hand skimming down my body, sickness churned in my stomach. *How could he? How could he?*

I paced my flat, scrubbing at my mouth with the flat of my hand. I could still taste the coffee.

"Don't you ever get frustrated?" whispered the voice in my memory. *"Don't you ever want something so much you'll do anything to get it?"*

I had to get this taste of coffee off me. I went to the bathroom, picked up my toothbrush and squeezed on toothpaste. The bristles moved easily over my teeth, moved over my lips, and then it was mint. Freshmint was filling my mouth. I spat out the foam.

———

He's propped up on one arm, staring down at me as he waits for an answer. I can hear my breathing. That's how I know I'm alive. I'm not moving. I'm staring at the hairline cracks in the ceiling, but I can't move. I can't feel anything. But I can hear my breathing. Short shallow breaths in my ears. I can still breathe so I know I'm alive.

———

I squeezed more toothpaste onto the toothbrush. Cleaned my mouth again. Brushed my gums, my teeth, my tongue, the roof of my mouth, my lips. It wasn't enough. I could still taste it. I could still taste the coffee-flavored kiss. I put down the toothbrush. I had to get this off me.

I took off my cardigan and scarf, threw them onto the tiled floor beside the chrome bin. I quickly stripped off the rest of my clothes, dumped them all beside the bin. Something to deal with later, afterwards.

———

"Aren't you going to say something?" he asks. "Talk to me, Kendra." His long fingers reach out towards my forehead, to maybe brush away a few strands of my hair, to maybe stroke

*my forehead, to maybe just touch me. I flinch. Scared. Terrified
that he's going to hurt me. Again.*

———

The water from the shower spurted out, the warmth hitting my skin, instantly spreading calm through my body. I didn't want calm. I wanted oblivion. Something to remove the memory of his body against mine. My wet fingers slipped over the hot water tap as I turned it up. Steam rose, billowing out of the showerhead as scalding hot water gushed out onto me. It battered against my skin, just the bearable side of scalding. That was better. Cleansing. Soothing. The palms of my hands reddened. My skin started to protest; this hurt. The hot water scorched pain through me. *This* I understood. Physical pain I understood. It took away the agony of everything else. I could concentrate and focus on the pain.

With shaking hands, I picked up the white bar of soap, started to run it over my body, lathering it up, washing away the panic Kyle had caused. This had to work. I had to remove all of it.

In my memory the voice continued to whisper. *I thought that was what you wanted. I thought that was what you wanted.*

CHAPTER 14

*K*yle kissed me last night," I said to Gabrielle.
It'd taken me most of the morning to get up the
courage to say the words and now that it was just the two
of us—Janene had the day off and Teri was out seeing
clients—this had found its way out of my mouth.

What happened the night before weighed heavily on me.
Pushing down on my shoulders, pressing down on my
mind. I turned it over and over, trying, trying, trying . . . I
didn't understand why he'd got it so wrong. On one level I
knew it should have been no big deal, that I'd overreacted,
but then, had I? Wasn't it better to nip this in the bud right
now? I needed to talk it out with someone.

Gabrielle froze at her computer and then slowly spun on
her chair towards me. "I couldn't see that one coming a mile
off," she said.

"What?"

"Divorced man, single attractive woman, sex is generally
quite close behind."

I folded my arms around myself, trying to hold myself together. "Why? Because that's all women think about?
Finding a man?"

"No, not at all."

"Then why did you say that?"

"I suppose I've noticed how much time you've been
spending with Kyle and his family, the pair of you are kind
of close, so I assumed . . ."

"What happened would be like me kissing you."

"That'd be completely different," Gabrielle said.

"What do you mean?"

"I actually fancy you."

She wasn't taking me seriously. I thought she might understand. I don't know why. Gabrielle was rarely serious. All through the period leading up to her husband leaving and then her divorce she'd been telling jokes, poking fun at herself, laughing. In rare moments of honesty I'd notice how much makeup she'd started to wear to give her complexion color, would spot how she had to force her mouth to turn upwards in a smile, would see the sadness carved deep in her eyes. But most of the time she was giggling. Joking. Finding everything hilarious. "If you can't laugh at yourself," she'd often say, "why bother?" But I couldn't bear for her to laugh at this. My body was still tenderized from the heat of the shower last night; my mind still reeling like it'd been sucker punched.

I refocused on my computer screen. "Never mind," I said. "I'm being silly. Shouldn't have said anything."

"I'm sorry, sweetheart," Gabrielle replied. "I didn't realize how shaken up you were. Tell me what happened."

"It's nothing," I said. I shrugged. "I'm just being silly."

"It was only a kiss, right?" she asked, suddenly concerned. "Nothing else?"

"Yeah, it was only a kiss. Look, let's forget it, I'm being silly."

"Is that why you're dressed like that?" she asked.

Dressed like what? I looked down at myself. I was wearing a black vest top, a white cotton shirt, a V-neck lightweight sweater and a black cardigan over the top with black trousers. This was how I always dressed for work, smart but not in a suit. I pulled the cardigan across my chest, folded my arms over the top. "What do you mean?"

"It's one of the hottest days of the year and you're dressed for winter."

I forced a laugh, shrugged, focused on my computer screen. "You know what I'm like, I'm always cold. How many times have I asked you to turn up the heating? I'd forgotten how chilly it got over here, especially after Australia."

"Australia," Gabrielle echoed. "You know, that's the first time you've mentioned it unbidden. I'd love to know about it."

"Australia? I don't want to talk about Australia," I replied. I opened my address book, flipped through its pages looking for a client who could do with a courtesy call—see if I could drum up a couple of assignments or arrange a lunch. I picked up the phone, started to punch out the digits. Gabrielle darted out from behind her desk and was beside my desk in two steps. She pressed down the button to cut the line, took the receiver from my hand and carefully replaced it in its cradle.

"I'm sorry for being glib," she said, her persona completely altered. Now she was serious and concerned. This was probably the person those who went to her for counseling encountered. "Are you worried about going back to the house tonight and seeing him?"

"I told you, I'm being silly."

"You're not. If it's upset you, then it's not silly," she said gently. "Tell me what happened and why it upset you so much."

I hesitated. It'd taken a lot to say anything in the first place and now I wasn't sure if I should continue. But then, I had to live with Kyle. I had to get some perspective on this and the only way to do that would be to talk it out.

Slowly, haltingly, I gave her a brief rundown. "It came from nowhere, truly," I ended. "I've never given him even the slightest indication that I'm interested. Why did he do that?"

"Maybe because he likes you?"

"How can he? He doesn't even know me and it's not as if we've been on a few dates or we've flirted. I don't care what it says in the books or in the films, just because I'm free and he's free and we spend time together, doesn't mean we're going to hook up."

"I'm sure he didn't mean any harm."

"I know, but how can I be normal with him after this? I'll always be wondering if he's going to try it again."

"Ah, sweetheart, we all do stupid things. I'm sure he's probably mortified about it. And you can tell if he's going to do it again by trusting yourself. If he's after something, you'll know. A little voice in your head, your intuition, will tell you not to trust him. We're trained to be polite, to be nice, and we all want people to like us, but if you find yourself having to quash even the slightest feeling of uneasiness about him then you'll know you have to avoid him. Forget politeness, forget all the stuff you were taught about people liking you, listen to yourself. What did you get with Kyle?"

"I didn't hang around long enough afterwards to find out much of anything."

"Well, if you're going to carry on living that closely with him, you're going to have to talk to him to find out."

We heard the chaos coming up the stairs to the office from the high street.

Footsteps, loud chatter, things being dropped and clattering on the wide staircase. With every step the noise got louder and we half expected the door to fly open and a troupe of circus performers to come tumbling in. When the door did open *my* group of circus performers came trouping in: Jaxon arrived first. He was dressed in dark grey trousers, his blue shirt was half tucked in, his striped dark blue, yellow and white tie was askew around the open top button of his shirt, and as usual, one of his socks was pulled up to his knee and had the bottom of his trouser leg half tucked into it, the other sock lounged in rings around his ankle. He had a streak of green felt tip across his cheek and green paint staining his fingers. It always amazed me that such a quiet boy could get so messy in such a few hours.

Behind him was Summer. She was wearing her pleated dark grey school skirt, her blue shirt and the same blue, yellow and white striped tie as Jaxon, but hers was still in place. Overall, she was neater, but her hair, parted and tied in bunches (I'd taught Kyle how to do it properly), had strands escaping at random points all over her head. Her socks were also half and full mast. They'd both clearly had a hard day at the salt mines.

Behind them, a rucksack over one shoulder and another multicolored backpack in his arms along with two navy-blue blazers and two navy-blue jumpers, was Kyle. Perched on top of his pile was a trainer—presumably it had fallen out of the rucksack on his shoulder, since the backpack gaped open and the trainer's twin hung outside the bag by a caught shoelace.

He was pale, hesitant, his features drawn and his eyes darting anxiously around the room. It took a lot longer than it should have done for him to cross the threshold. He clearly thought it was a bad idea coming here.

I stood as soon as Jaxon had pushed open the door and came around my desk to see them.

"KENDIE!" Summer yelled, stepped around Jaxon, ran to me and threw her arms around my waist, slammed her head against my solar plexus, slightly winding me before she squeezed. Anyone would think she hadn't seen me in a year or two, anyone wouldn't think she'd seen me yesterday, just before bedtime. The office was thankfully empty, a slow

Tuesday afternoon. No temps or clients were in and Teri had gone home after her appointments.

"I missed you," she informed me as I peeled her away from me and bent down to her height and allowed her to throw her arms around my neck and squeeze just as hard. Jaxon stood with his father until I looked up at him, a silent invitation to come on over and give me a hug, too. Dragging his feet, as he did when he walked, he came over and looped one arm around my neck and squeezed. Summer had already disentangled herself from me by the time Jaxon arrived. I took a deep breath and inhaled their scent. They smelled of school, of a day painting and running and reading and being outdoors. They smelled of Summer and Jaxon's lives.

Jaxon's hug was brief, just like his speech—rationed because it wasn't necessary to go overboard. I knew he liked me now, he didn't need to make a performance of it. As his arm slid away, I stood up and we both turned to find out what Summer was doing.

She was across the room, sitting in Gabrielle's chair, legs swinging, hands on the arms of the chair, holding court as she discussed the finer points of staplers and whether black ones were better than blue ones. Summer was explaining to Gabrielle that a black stapler would always work better than a blue one because anything black was always better. She spoke as though she couldn't quite believe that someone Gabrielle's age hadn't worked that out yet. Jaxon, as always drawn by whatever his superstar sister did, went over to join them. On his way he picked up the burgundy stapler that perched on the edge of my desk. That effectively left me with Kyle.

My heart had begun to beat in triple time, the blood rushing in my ears like the rapids of a white-water ride, as I turned to him. When I faced him I was doused with a memory of the night before: his tongue pushing into my mouth, his hand on my face, his body too close to mine, the taste of coffee. I shuddered.

Kyle saw my shudder. He knew why I was shuddering. His anxiety, which he already wore in his eyes, on the grim set of his flatline mouth, in his stiff body, increased, began to radiate outwards towards me.

I glanced away, unable to look directly at him. "Um . . . Summer insisted we stop by. She found your watch . . ." He stuttered his way through the words like a schoolboy giving an unscripted talk on something he hadn't studied for. "I think you left it behind last night."

I felt—rather than saw—Gabrielle look up at us. All three adults knew how that sounded—like I'd taken my watch off in his bedroom, not that I'd done the washing up after dinner. *Jeez, what is this man doing to me?*

Kyle's eyes darted to Gabrielle. He met her eye and then paled in horror at how that sounded. His white pallor was swiftly followed by his face exploding with scarlet.

Seriously, what is this man doing to me?

Gabrielle returned her attentions to Summer and Jaxon. "Who wants some lollies?" Gabrielle asked, to cut the tension.

"Ice lollies?" Summer asked.

"No, I mean sweets," Gabrielle replied.

"Then why didn't you say sweets?" Summer replied, indignant. She wasn't a fan of double-talk.

"Lollies is what we Australians call sweets."

In unison Summer and Jaxon's eyes widened and fixed on Gabrielle. "You're from Australia?" Summer asked, her voice loaded with excitement but also the fear that Gabrielle might be having her on. "Like Kendie?"

"No, not like Kendie. Kendie's only a pretend Australian. I'm a real one. I was actually born there and grew up there.

How about I take you both out for some lollies—sweets—
and explain all about it?"

"OK," Jaxon said. "Garvo wants to know about it, too."
The three of us—Summer, Kyle and I—turned and stared at
him. He *never* spoke to strangers. He looked back at us as
though we were the ones who had done something out of
the ordinary.

"That's OK, isn't it?" Gabrielle asked Kyle. "It's only two
shops down. We'll go and come straight back."

Kyle looked over Gabrielle, assessing if it was safe to let
his children go off with her. He must have found her suitable because he replied, "Yeah, sure." He made a move,
jostling the items in his arms as though to get some cash.

"It's OK," Gabrielle said, "this one's on me." She picked up
her fake Louis Vuitton wallet and bustled the children out
the door.

"Not too many sweets," I called after them. Gabrielle
raised her hand in acknowledgement. "Seriously, Gabrielle,
only one bag each. One normal-size bag."

"Yeah, yeah."

Even if I hadn't told her she would have guessed something had happened between Kyle and me—the tension of
it sat in gloops in the air around us. Thick, sticky splodges
that dripped down around and onto us.

As soon as Gabrielle clicked the door shut behind them, I
moved back, behind my desk. Protection. I needed a physical barrier between us, something that would make sure
there was no misunderstanding. At the same instant Kyle
took a step back, emphasizing that he felt the same.

"Kend . . . Miss Tam—" he began. "Look, I'm sorry. I
got . . . I . . . I suppose I was . . . It's no excuse, obviously . . .
I just . . . And it was . . . That's not to say . . ."

I stared at Kyle, wondering if he had any idea that he
hadn't managed to finish a whole sentence yet. And the

words he had spoken, the sentences he had begun made no sense to anyone.

"You do understand, don't you?" he said almost breathlessly to end his soliloquy of unfinished sentences. His eyes were sparkling with the eagerness of wanting to be understood and believed and forgiven.

"To be honest, no, since you haven't actually said anything," I said, my voice so sharp it could slice deep into diamond.

Kyle changed, subtly, but definitely. He stood a little straighter, his eyes became a little harder, his voice was cool and distant as he said, "I misread the situation. It could have happened to anyone. I thought we were both free, we could maybe, you know, we get on . . . We have the kids in common, relationships have been built on less."

"*Relationship?*" I replied, incredulous. "You didn't just want to . . . You wanted a *relationship?*"

He shrugged, deciding suddenly that anything he said would be used against him so best he keep his peace.

"Kyle, you don't think you've got enough problems with your wife, you obviously want to add to it with a new relationship with someone you know absolutely nothing about?" I shook my head in disbelief.

"Look, Kendra," his voice slid effortlessly from cool to hard. "Just because I did something incredibly stupid—and with every passing second I'm realizing exactly how stupid—doesn't mean you have the right to treat me like I'm an idiot."

He had a point. Stupid behavior, stupid acts didn't make someone an idiot. Even perfectly rational, levelheaded individuals were capable of great acts of undeniable stupidity. Like me. Why had I befriended the Gadsboroughs? Summer. Jaxon. My belief that they needed me. My belief that in some way, taking care of them would make up for what I did. Looking out for them would be my redemption, my first step on the path to forgiveness. I'd be making up for the family I helped to wreck. Summer and Jaxon and their well-being would be my salvation. Like I said: stupid.

"I'm sorry," Kyle said softly, almost breathing out the words on a regretful sigh. He moved his shoulders up and down in a helpless shrug. "I'm sorry. It really won't happen again. I like having you around, you know? Not just for the kids. As a friend. I haven't had a female friend in . . . I can't remember when, certainly not since I got married. Colleagues, yes. Friends, not so much. That's why I got it so wrong. But I'd like us to be friends. Nothing more. Do you want to give it a go?"

What Gabrielle said came to mind. Did he make me uneasy? Even a little? I knew firsthand that looks could be deceptive, that what you saw wasn't necessarily what you got. But apart from sharing too much when we first met, he didn't scare me. He didn't raise even the slightest hackle, nor stir even a molecule of uneasiness. I hadn't wanted him to kiss me, but there was no little voice, no funny feeling that I shouldn't trust him.

"No funny business?" I asked, already knowing that I wasn't going to allow myself to be in the position where "funny business" was even a possibility. We'd be just friends, but I was going to avoid being alone with him for a long while.

"Not even a chuckle of one," he replied, and smiled. It was that smile he'd presented to me on the day he returned from holiday, the one that had made me come in for breakfast. The smile that had, effectively, started all this.

"OK," I said. "OK, we can be buddies."

Kyle's smile deepened, and I saw Summer in the wrinkling of his eyes, Jaxon in the curve of his mouth. They must have inherited their face shape from their mother, but in moments like this the imprint of their father was beautifully obvious.

"Are you coming home with us?" Summer said, entering the office seconds later. She hung onto the door handle, swinging the door back and forth. She held an unopened bag of jelly babies in her other hand. Jaxon and Gabrielle sidled in around her. They all wore guilty looks. Gabrielle wouldn't meet my eye. It hadn't been just one bag of sweets. There was pop involved, there was something that had stained Jaxon's tongue blue involved.

"No, I haven't finished work yet." I was going nowhere near them for the next few hours.

Kyle's eyes darted from Summer to Jaxon to Gabrielle who had gone back to her desk and was concentrating very hard on replacing her purse in her bag. It was dawning on Kyle that a wicked thing had been done to him in those ten minutes they'd been away. That he was going to have to deal with the mother of all sugar rushes this afternoon.

"Are you sure you can't come home yet?" Kyle asked, desperately.

"Nope," I replied and stepped forward, picked up one of the blazers that had slipped out of his arms and lay it on top of his pile again. I went to Summer. "I'll see you later," I said, stroked the silky black strands off her face, pressed a kiss onto her clammy forehead. I went to Jaxon. "I'll see you later." I pressed my lips onto his forehead. I turned to Kyle and said, "See you later."

"Are you going to kiss Dad see you later?" Summer asked, causing Kyle to flush a gentle, dark pink.

"No, I don't kiss daddies," I told her, ignoring the silence from the adults.

Gabrielle started coughing, theatrical, loud spluttering with the word *bullshit* woven just audibly among each cough.

"Right, come on you two, we're leaving," Kyle said. The chaos circus began to retreat, with Kyle calling, "Nice to meet you," at Gabrielle. And, "See you soon," at me. The door shut behind them, the clattering that had brought them here, taking them away again.

I remembered ten minutes later that I didn't get my watch back. Which meant that at some point in the near future it would be gracing Summer's wrist.

SOFT-BOILED EGG & SOLDIERS

◆　◆　◆

*W*e are not driving up to central London on a Saturday," I said. "Not when there's a perfectly good train system in operation." I pointed out the front window of the Gadsborough house, vaguely in the direction where I imagined the train station was.

My landlord raised an eyebrow at me.

"All right, not when there's a train system in operation," I corrected. "If we're going to drive into London today we might as well fly to Hamburg because it'll take less time."

"Hamburg?" he replied.

"You know what I mean. I don't know what your problem is with public transport, but it's silly. Especially when we've got to get up to town with the kids. Have you heard of traffic? And have you tried parking up there? You'll have to take out a second mortgage just to be able to afford a couple of hours. Let's just get the train."

Summer and Jaxon were sitting on the sofa, ready for our trip to the British Museum. They each wore their multicolored backpacks, inside which they each had a bottle of water, a piece of fruit, a packet of crisps, scarf, hat, gloves, waterproof mac, coloring books, pens and a reading book. Jaxon had packed Garvo's water bowl, Summer had packed Hoppy. Their denim jackets were done up. I was ready, too, my backpack filled with the essentials. The only person holding up proceedings was their father. The man with the public transport phobia. Well, as I said, driving into the city center wasn't going to happen on my watch.

Kyle looked thoughtfully at his children, his expression anxious, like fingers worrying at a loose piece of thread. It was genuine concern about using public transport, not simple snobbishness or a quirk of his personality. "All right, compromise," he said. "How about I drive us to a train station nearer central London and we get a train from there."

It wasn't perfect, but I had a feeling this was a huge concession on his part; it was the proverbial gift horse and I shouldn't even glance near its mouth area. "Deal."

"Are we going?" Summer said, her face lighting up as though she'd been ready for an adventure before, had been ready and willing and more than able and it'd never materialized.

"Yup, after a fashion, we're going," I replied.

"*Really?*" Jaxon asked cautiously, incredulously.

"Unless you don't want to?" I asked them.

In unison, for that's how Jaxon and Summer seemed to do most things, they leapt off the sofa. "We do!" they cried. "We do!"

"I'll get my coat." Kyle said.

The journey into London was uneventful, of course. Jaxon, who was obsessed with steam trains, was just as excited about going on a modern train. He'd never been on a train before. I'd thought he was going to pass out with excitement the way his little body trembled and he kept bending down to whisper his observations into Garvo's ear. Summer was unbothered by the train ride; she grinned because she was going away from Brockingham.

They sat on seats facing each other and stared out of the window in quiet awe. Kyle stuck his head in an architecture magazine for most of the way.

Once we'd left the house, the kids divvied us up—Jaxon

took me, Summer took Kyle. Jaxon sat next to me and took my hand when we went down into Charing Cross underground to get to Russell Square and didn't let go, Summer did the same with her dad. The four of us walked through the entrance of the British Museum and my heart started to do a little dance of excitement. I loved the museum, loved seeing our history and prehistory unfolded, laid out for us to see. It'd been my idea to come up here instead of doing the shopping on Saturday afternoon because I wanted to take advantage of living in England again. It was to my eternal regret that I didn't get to see Uluru before I left Australia, to see the monolith that held the ancient history of the first Australians up close, and I wasn't making the same mistake again.

An hour or two later and the thrill hadn't worn off for any of us. We wandered from cavernous room to cavernous room, exhibit to exhibit, holding our breath at what we might see next: the proud sarcophagi with their painted faces and bodies, the intricate coins and materials from ancient Africa, the pots and jugs from ancient Greece.

We broke off for lunch and sat outside on the picnic blanket I'd brought in my backpack and ate the chicken salad sandwiches I'd packed. (I knew the kids were hoping for a Smiley Smiler meal because we were up to something different, but just like not driving into town on a Saturday, it wasn't going to happen on my watch.)

As I rifled in my bag for Wet Ones to wipe their faces, Kyle produced a camera from his bag. "OK, photo time," he said and grinned at them. Summer immediately brushed her hands over her hair to smooth it down. Jaxon twisted his lips together to the side and put his head down, showing his father the top of his head as the thing to photograph.

"Come on, Jax, head up," Kyle encouraged.

Slowly he raised his head, allowed his father to see his

eyes. Kyle used his hand to try to hurry me into the frame. I didn't move. "Kendra," he said, exasperated. "Get closer to the kids, you're out of shot."

"No," I replied, "you don't want a picture of me."

"Er, yeah, we do."

"Seriously, you don't. I hate myself. In pictures."

He lowered the camera, his forehead corrugated with a frown. He was trying to work out if there was some story behind my aversion to being in front of the camera and there wasn't. I simply didn't like to see my likeness, not in mirrors, not in photos. In my head, in my imagination, I knew what I looked like. When I saw a reflection or a picture of myself, that image was invariably shot to pieces and as much as possible I liked to keep that image intact. The idea that other people would look at my picture was even worse than me looking at me. I hated the idea of them looking at me when I wasn't there. The thought of them taking a photo and examining the lines and curves, the blemishes and faults that made up who I was without me knowing about it upset me. I hated the idea of someone doing that. *Hated* it.

"How about I take a picture of the three of you?" I said to change the emphasis from me to them. "Camera?" I held out my hand for the slim silver gadget.

He handed it over, shifted to be beside his children. Summer leaned in towards her dad; Jaxon, who suddenly wasn't camera shy, knelt up and then leaned his elbow on his dad's knee. Through the small square viewfinder I stared at them. They looked as though it had only ever been the three of them.

I clicked three pictures of them like that, clicked another one with Summer climbing onto her dad's back and Jaxon lying across his dad's lap. Clicked another one with Jaxon on his dad's shoulders, another with Summer on her dad's shoulders. As I captured them in lots of different freeze-frame moments, I wondered if being edited out was what happened when you went away under a cloud or of your own volition; whether the waters closed quietly behind you, as though you hadn't even made a splash, as though you hadn't been there at all. Because taking photos of the Gadsboroughs now, it was hard to imagine that Ashlyn, their mother and wife, had ever existed.

In Regent's Park, Summer and Jaxon lost their inhibitions and went wild.

They ran over the grass like two caged animals released into their natural environment for the first time. Summer's hair flowed behind her as she ran, a breeze ruffled Jaxon's locks as he chased after his sister. Their legs pumped, their faces glowed, they were unrecognizable. They were different people from the ones I'd been spending time with. These two were free. Free to be children. Free to run and jump and laugh.

Their father, sitting low in his seat beside me on the bench, watched with a grin on his face. A transformation had come over him. His troubles had faded away and watching the kids had replaced his worries with joy.

Summer and Jaxon had taken to racing each other from one tree to the next, even though at their age, with their similarities in weight, height and build, it was a pointless exercise. They were always neck and neck. Kyle laughed out loud when they both reached for the rough brown bark of the latest tree at the same time. It was an easy laugh that would touch and melt even the hardest of hearts. He continued to laugh as they turned around to race the other way. *He should laugh more often,* I thought. The way the lines on his face softened and his eyes lit up took years off his face and posture. He was light and happy and youthful. He, too, was free.

"Remember that time we went to Brighton—" he said, shifting in my direction. He stopped short as soon as his eyes settled on me. We hadn't been to Brighton. Clearly that was a memory from a box he wanted to dust off, open up and explore with his wife. With Ashlyn. He was a little disappointed that it was me instead of her. Kyle's gaze trailed down my face, over my black eyes, my small broad nose, my lips, then back up to my eyes.

His eyes went to my hair, lingered there. "You've got—" He reached out, plucked a piece of grass from my hair, the tips of his fingers briefly brushing my left temple in the process. He showed it to me before letting it float away on the breeze.

"Thanks," I said.

In silence Kyle scanned my face again. For a few moments he didn't seem to know what to say now that he'd remembered who he was with. "Who's this guy you were in love with?" he asked unexpectedly. "Just interested, as a friend." Since the whole unfortunate incident with the kiss we'd avoided all such conversation.

"He's in Australia. It wasn't an ideal situation. The being in love part wasn't a problem; everything else was. Which is why I came back. A little necessary distance, you know."

He nodded, he knew.

This was my chance to ask about Ashlyn—one personal revelation for another.

"You must miss your wife very much," I said to him before I lost my nerve.

He nodded a little, moved his line of sight back to the children. "I suppose I must," he said, an edge of darkness to his tone. He clearly didn't want to talk about his wife.

"The other week, when I was out shopping with the kids, they . . ." I forced myself to keep talking. He may not want to discuss her, but if I didn't ask now, I may never ask. "They mentioned that Ashlyn was ill?"

Every muscle in his body tensed as he jerked himself upright, his features suddenly sharpening, his breathing shallow but quietly heavy in his upper chest.

"They said she was sick and it made both you and her upset?" I pressed on. "Is it, well, serious?"

"Depends what you mean by serious," he said levelly, his body still rigid, his features still set.

I said nothing, waited patiently for clarification.

"Ashlyn's not sick," Kyle eventually continued. "Although, I suppose that depends on who you're talking to. But she's not sick in the sense that you mean." A haze came over his eyes. "The thing of it is . . ." Kyle's voice was as soft as silk, as gentle as the touch of butterfly wings. He seemed to deflate a little, as though finally giving himself up to whatever was burdening him.

"Ashlyn isn't sick," he said quietly. "My wife's an alcoholic."

ORGANIC WHOLE-GRAIN CEREAL & ORGANIC SOY MILK

◆　◆　◆

CHAPTER 16

*T*his is probably the worst idea you've ever had," I said to Gabrielle.

"It will be fun. I read an article that said camping was the new hottest thing to do with your friends," she replied as she turned at the end of Tennant Road.

"And where exactly did you read this article? *Dupe Your Friends into Camping Monthly?*" I replied.

"Listen, you, I need a bonding exercise with my staff and colleagues from other London branches and you need to make more friends over here—ones that aren't six nor a man in the midst of a divorce, this is the answer."

I glowered my dissent in her general direction. It was indeed a very thoughtful thing she was doing, taking me under her wing, but *camping!* A weekend in a luxury hotel being pampered would have the same result.

"I can't wait to be *wo*-man, fighting the elements, hunting our own food, at one with nature," she said. "I love roughing it." In the boot of her car was a luxury hamper with four bottles of Bollinger, two padded sleeping bags and a large tent. Roughing it we were not.

"We're going to Wildberry Woods in Sussex, not the Outback. And hunting—even for survival—is banned."

"You can't spoil my fantasy, Tamale. I am living the dream this weekend. Living the dream."

We hit traffic on our way out of Croydon and the multi-colored stream of cars snaking into the horizon as far as the eye could see put Gabrielle's dream on hold.

"Listen, Kennie," she began, her tone light. She was going to try to wheedle something out of me. I couldn't physically do any more hours at work and I had no money to lend her, so I wasn't sure what she might want from me. "We've got a two-hour—at least—drive ahead of us and I've decided that there are two ways we can use the time. Either you tell me about Australia or we talk about work." She took her eyes off the blue Beetle in front of us to look at me. "And neither of us wants to talk about work, not really, which leaves Australia. And I'm not talking about the country. I want to know why you came back so suddenly. I want to know who he is."

Gabrielle and I worked so well together, we always had, and I didn't want to ruin things by admitting to something that would make her think less of me. Would make me seem a bad person in her eyes. But then, maybe I should tell her. The urge to confess and to have someone remind me how awful I'd been had been swimming around my chest for weeks. I was due a telling off. I'd been having it pretty easy since I got back. So easy I'd almost forgotten what I'd done.

"He was married," I said and braced myself for the gasp, the look of disgust, the setting of the jaw.

"I'm going to need more information than that," she replied when I said nothing else.

I looked at her sideways through slitted, suspicious eyes. I'd expected more of a reaction. OK, so she needed the full story before she berated me and packed my bags and sent me to friendship Siberia.

"I knew he was married and nothing happened the first time I met him. I didn't even remember him that much. The next time I saw him was at a party. I walked into the garden and there he was. It was like a bolt from the blue or Cupid's arrow hit me when I saw him. Pow! Right in the center of my chest. Seriously, I hold my hands up, I don't normally believe in such things. But I can't describe what happened in any other way. It wasn't his looks, it was just him. I did the only thing I could, I turned and ran."

———

I turned and ran. Pushed through the drunken bodies standing in the garden and ran to put myself somewhere else. Somewhere safe and hidden. I ended up in the kitchen. I'd been at Evangeline's house most of the day helping her to set up for her party and now I clattered around, trying to tidy up, trying to quiet the nerves tumbling through me.

He walked into the kitchen and my heart punched me in that space where my ribs were meant to meet at the front. My heart was panicking and it was trying to escape my body. It, and I, was terrified. I'd never felt anything like that bolt from the blue when I saw him in the garden and that was why I'd had to turn and flee. I didn't even know who he was. He was nothing to me, not really. Someone I'd once spent a few hours sitting next to in a bar, talking about nothing I could remember now. Despite that, his presence in my vicinity was making me insane. There was no escape now, either.

His face brightened beatifically as he smiled at me.

I pushed my fear aside, stood on tiptoes to wrap my arms around his neck. "Hello, you," I whispered into his ear as his arms slid around me. He clung onto me, our bodies becoming almost as one as he received and gave his hello. A few seconds passed and I was about to let go when I realized he wasn't going to release me. He was holding on just that bit longer. Clinging to me as though I was his salvation. The smell of him—ck one, his skin, pheromones—filled my senses. I was

about to give in to it, relax and enjoy the closeness when he let
me go and took a step back.

"*How are you?*" *he asked.*

"*I'm fine. How are you?*"

"*Good.*"

"*Are your wife and kids here?*" *I asked, cementing in both*
our minds that nothing was going to happen. He may have
caused all sorts of new and not unpleasant emotions to surge
through me, I may have unintentionally done something to
make him cling to me, but nothing could happen.

"*No,*" *he replied, looking uncomfortable.*

"*Are they in Manly, too?*"

He paused, glanced away for a moment, then back at me.
"*No.*"

"*So, are you staying in Manly overnight or are you going*
back to the bosom of your family?" *I was determined to bring*
up his other life, to keep this block between us, but he was de-
termined, too. Determined not to talk about it.

"*One of my friends lives a few miles away so he's letting me*
stay over."

"*Oh, right,*" *I replied.* "*So, why aren't you—*"

"*What's this?*" *Will cut in to deflect my question. I turned to*
what he was looking at. He took a step towards me, to look at
the pot on the stove.

"*That's my barbecue sauce,*" *I said.* "*I made it from scratch.*"

"*Can I try some?*" *he asked.*

"*Of course,*" *I replied. I reached for a wooden spoon from*
the pot of utensils on the side, scooped some of the thick, red,
onion-speckled sauce from the pan and lifted it to his mouth,
holding my other hand under the spoon so nothing would drip.
He leaned towards me, took my hand to hold it steady, received
the sauce. His eyes held mine, and my heart started that pleas-
ant panic again.

"*Good, isn't it?*" *I said brusquely, pulling away the spoon.*

"The best," he replied with a slow grin.

"It's not like you're going to say it's crap, are you?"

He laughed and the sound sent shards of pleasure through me that pooled in my stomach. I took the spoon to the sink.

As I turned back, a man came towards me. I watched his eyes flick over me, up my legs rarely revealed in a brown suede skirt, over the mounds of my chest under my orange top that kept slipping off my left shoulder. "Are you Kendra?" he asked.

"Yup, I am indeed."

"I was told that you would give me a tour of the house."

My party trick at Evangeline's house was to give a tour of the place. They'd recently finished refurbishing it and she was bored of showing it off so I happily stepped into the fold. I often pretended that I'd designed the place as a favor to Evangeline. "Who told you that?" I asked.

"One of your many admirers," he said with a cheeky smile.

"Oh, stop," I replied.

He grinned, raised an eyebrow at me. "So, about the—"

Will was suddenly beside me. "Actually, mate, she was about to give me one." An uncomfortable beat passed. "Tour, that is. You promised me a private tour ages ago."

"Did I?" I had done no such thing.

"No, you didn't. But seeing as we're old friends, I reckon I should get first dibs on a tour."

"Old friends? We sat next to each other once in a bar."

"But you spent the whole night insulting me; that makes you close to a person."

"No, it means you find many faults in a person."

"Yeah, that, too."

I turned to the other man and found he'd gone. Clearly he knew when he was beaten.

I took Will through the various rooms of the house, aware of his presence beside me all the way. His warm body. His footsteps. His rhythmical breathing. Every step made my mouth dry, my heart beat in triple time. The last place on the walkabout was the conservatory. Evangeline kept it locked at parties but I was allowed to have the key and show people in if I locked it afterwards. I let us into Evangeline's pride and joy, an extension to the house that took advantage of their place on the hill. Three of the walls were glass, the ceiling was glass, and from this room you could see out to the Tasman Sea; beyond that was New Zealand.

I left the door open a crack so I wouldn't have to put on the main light or the sidelights, which would spoil the effect of being in here at night.

"And this is the pièce de résistance," I said. From its place on the hill you could look out into the constant rolling blackness of the sea, but my favorite thing was to look up at the thick blue-black sky speckled with tiny stitches of stars. To look up and see into infinity.

"This room is like London architecture," I said to Will, who was standing a little way behind me to my left, gazing awestruck at the horizon.

"How do you mean?" he asked.

I spun to him as I said, "You see the best things if you look up."

He put his head back, exposing his throat, and I wanted to stroke my fingertips over his smooth white skin. I wanted to climb onto tiptoes and touch my lips at that exact same point, taste the softness where his words were made. Instead, I smiled as delight spread itself over his face when he saw that he was standing outside inside, that he could see to the end of the universe. "It's beautiful," he whispered. He lowered his head, stared at me. "Truly beautiful."

Whoa, I warned myself. Whoa. "So, how come your wife didn't come with you tonight?" I said, placing her firmly between us again. I took a few steps back, perched on the back of the sofa that sat in the middle of the room, the shaft of light from the corridor falling across my legs, my stomach, my chest and my neck.

He lowered his eyes, worried at a spot on the ground with the toe of his shoe. "Do you want the official answer or the complete answer?"

"Whichever you feel most comfortable peddling to a virtual stranger."

"OK, virtual stranger, my wife had a one-night stand four years ago. We've got a three-year-old son, and when he became seriously ill last year we thought he might not make it, so she confessed all to me because she thought it was her punishment for what she'd done. He's definitely my son; even if he wasn't biologically, he'd always be mine. But since then we haven't really been able to be normal with each other. So that's why she's not here. We're struggling."

"Right," I said. "Right."

"Yup, that's what I'd say if I was you, as well."

I stood in silence, his worrying at the spot on the floor slowed, and I was aware that he was staring at me. Peeling back my defenses, trying to get under my skin. It was working. And that wasn't right.

"Why didn't you just say 'my wife doesn't understand me' and be done with it?" I asked.

"Because it's not true. My wife does understand me, I understand my wife. We just can't be normal with each other."

"Is that what this is about?" I asked, pointing at our two bodies across the distance between us. "Revenge?"

"I wish it was," he replied. "If it was, then I'd know how I felt. It'd mean that I'd gone beyond the shock. I've been stuck at shock for about a year now. It'd be good to feel something else. To form enough of another emotion to get a plan together to go out looking for revenge."

He took small steps towards me, and I watched his scuffed brown suede shoes, moving closer and closer until they were *toe to toe with the long, pointy toes of my black boots. My head was scared to look up. Scared of how much my face would betray me. I gripped onto the back of the sofa, holding on for dear life. I didn't know why I wanted him now when the first time I met him I didn't. Why I couldn't stop these feeling gushing through my veins, I never got this crazy about men. I was always in control. Always—unintentionally and intentionally—holding back. This Will person made me feel as though I was behind the wheel of a vehicle I had no license to drive; that at any moment I was going to career over the edge of a cliff into an abyss of pure bliss.*

"After I left that night we met I got to the car," he was saying, "which was parked all the way down on the other side of the city, and decided I had to come back to get your number. I was buzzing after talking to you. I hadn't laughed so much in so long, I wanted to see you again. I got to the top of the stairs, and then realized what I was doing. How I couldn't be doing what I was thinking of doing because I wasn't free, you probably weren't free and I couldn't be your friend. I couldn't be just your friend. So I left again."

In my ears I could hear my breath, soft but ragged. I clung tighter to the sofa, closed my eyes, hoping to hide there. Trying to hide in the dark because this vehicle had gone off the cliff and was clinging on by the caught edge of the number plate. Any sudden movements and I'd be lost.

"When I saw your face earlier, when you walked into the garden and turned around and left, I realized that you felt the same. It wasn't a one-way thing."

He gently rested his forehead on mine. My eyes were still closed but the air went out of my body. "And for the record, this," he whispered, "this is attraction." He lowered his head further, gently brushed his nose against mine. "Pure attraction." I lifted my head and slowly, gently, his lips grazed over mine. I gasped silently. Gradually his lips pressed down onto

mine and his hand came up to my face. I let go. Let go of the
last edge keeping me on the cliff, let go of the sofa and laced my
arms around him, ran my fingers up his neck, over the soft
bristles of hair at the back of his head as I let him kiss me. I
kissed him back. We stood under the stars kissing as though
this was just about me and him.

———

Gabrielle's car was crawling slowly along towards the
A23; we'd been in traffic forever. She hadn't asked much as I
told her about Will. I was a little disorientated—talking and
thinking about Sydney made me forget where I was. In
Sydney that would happen sometimes—I'd be watching a
British soap or film, reading a magazine or book, and then
I'd look up and for a moment think I was in England. In
London. That Sydney was a mirage. I, sometimes in the
midst of the Will thing, would wish Sydney was a mirage.

———

We went back to his friend's place, which was near
Evangeline's house.
   He walked around turning on lights and I sat on the sofa
wondering what had happened to me. I never did this. I never
went back to a virtual stranger's place. I felt so safe with him
though, like I'd known him all my life. He brought me a beer
and asked if I wanted a glass. "Hadn't you noticed, I'm not the
glass type," I said. He laughed.
   He cracked open the cold, condensation-covered can and of-
fered it to me.
   It was such a small, simple thing that changed everything
for me. It was one of the nicest things anyone had ever done for
me. The simple act of opening the can showed that in that mo-
ment, in doing such an insignificant thing, he thought of me.
   We fit together. His body, solid and warm, moved enough

for me to mold myself against him; my upper body slipped per-
fectly into the nook of his arm; his head fit into the once-empty
space between my shoulder and jaw.

We didn't have sex, we didn't make love. We didn't take any
clothes off. We lay on top of the covers, talking. Sometimes giv-
ing each other long, deep kisses, but mostly, just talking.

––––––

"We didn't sleep together any other time we saw each
other. And we didn't really see each other that much—six
times in total," I told Gabrielle. "I tried so hard but I
couldn't just walk away.

"We'd stop contact for months at a stretch and I'd stop
thinking about him every day. And then something would
happen or I'd see a book or watch something or listen to
some music and I'd want to share it with him. I'd write him
an e-mail but never send it." I had hundreds of e-mails that
I'd written to Will and never sent. They were like a diary of
things I'd been up to.

I stared at the open road, the cars rolling in front of us.
"After a few months of no contact one of us would crack. It
was usually me. I'd send a couple of lines and it'd start again.
The daily e-mails, the occasional text. The imagining. The
guilt. The deep, unrelenting guilt. Then, about eighteen
months later, his wife found out."

––––––

She found out from an e-mail.

Not from one of those types of e-mails. We didn't send those
types of e-mails—the ones that dripped in sex and longing and
fantasizing. Not anymore. And he'd deleted all evidence that
we ever had. Only a handful of e-mails had been like that.
Only a few suggested this thing between us was physical. Most
of it was banal and ordinary. Sharing things about our lives,

about everyday things. With us, we had no past together, we had no future together, so we talked about the present we spent apart. We shared what was happening, living for the moment. Besides, we were hardly ever in constant contact. Neither of us could handle it. Not for anything more than a few days. What was the point when we weren't going to be together?

The e-mail she read said:

Sooo, tell me the best thing about your day.

That was all. Those nine words were the ones that revealed she had been sharing her husband's affections. She read that e-mail and she knew. I can't imagine what that felt like. What she did next. If she turned off the computer, if she started screaming inside, if she shouted at the computer screen and burst into tears or if she started plotting the revenge that would come later. I know she didn't call him and demand he come home. She didn't scream at him the second he walked in the door. She waited until they'd eaten dinner, the children had been bathed, read to and put to bed. She waited until they both had a glass of wine in their hands and had collapsed on the sofa before she asked him about it.

Maybe she'd been so numb that she hadn't even thought of it until they sat down together, glasses of expensive wine in their hands, feet up on the table, television carrying on in the background. That was the moment when she could turn to him and reveal that those nine words I'd typed without thinking weeks earlier had told her everything.

Will and his wife (I don't speak her name and I don't think her name, I'm not worthy of using it, of being that intimate with her) hadn't had a proper conversation in weeks, maybe months, possibly years. It'd been months since she had bothered to ask him how his day was, weeks and weeks since he'd asked her, but someone else, a woman he had never mentioned, a woman she'd never met, cared enough about him to ask. Another female had the luxury, the freedom from the day-to-day of running a house, raising a family, being with him through all sorts of daily dramas, to ask him about his day. That's why she knew. There were no other e-mails, no texts, nothing except those nine words that told her part of him was elsewhere, with someone else.

"Are you sleeping with someone else?" she asked him when she turned to him over wine.

He replied without hesitation, "No." It was the truth, he wasn't sleeping with someone else, he hadn't slept with some-one else. "Not at all."

She must have been scared then. Terror must have de-scended upon her—possibly like a heavy stone, possibly like the oppressive fluttering of a tonne of feathers—because she asked the next question: "Are you in love with someone else?" She probably whispered those words, held her breath as she waited for the answer, waited to hear if life as she knew it was over. Waited for a response that was never going to come.

Will didn't want to lie to his wife by saying no, and he didn't want to hurt her by saying yes. Being an expert at ignoring things he didn't want to deal with, Will hadn't yet accepted that he'd committed the ultimate betrayal by opening his heart to someone else. That he'd allowed another woman to slip into the places where his wife used to live. He had done something he could only have done if he was in love. He hadn't admitted that to himself, he wasn't going to wound his wife by making her the first person he acknowledged this to. So he said noth-ing. He looked away and said nothing.

She said, "Can't you get anything right? If you wanted revenge, you're meant to fuck someone else, not fall for them." And then she asked, "How long?"

And he said, "Too long. Even one day is too long. I'm sorry."

"Did you do it to get back at me?" she asked.

"I don't think so," he replied. "I didn't go out looking for someone or something else. After I found out what had happened I couldn't talk to you without wanting to shout at you. I didn't want to shout at you, so it got simpler to keep it all in. And this thing happened because I wasn't paying attention. I wasn't concentrating on making things work with us."

"Do you want to make this work?" she asked.

"More than anything," he replied. He tried to take her hand but she shrank away, didn't want him to touch her. He was upset as he told me this. What did you expect? I wanted to ask him. Did you think she'd throw her arms around you and say it was fine? You've done the worst thing imaginable after hurting one of your children. Did you really think she'd let you touch her?

"You can't see her again," she told him.

"I don't see her. I don't speak to her. We only occasionally e-mail each other."

Will thought saying that was OK. That he'd put his wife's mind to rest about it all. What he'd done was the opposite. What he'd actually said was, "Even though I have no contact with her, she's always on my mind. She's always there with me, she climbs into bed with us at night. She's there when we make love. She's with me in my fantasies." What he should have said was, "It's completely over. I ended it because she wasn't you. I never slept with her and it's over. I don't know why she's e-mailing me." As a woman, his wife would have noticed the absence of this, she would have noticed that he didn't say it was over. She would have noticed and she would have stored it up in her mind, in her heart. It would have been one of the things that motivated her to do what she did.

"We go for counseling," she said. "Emergency counseling. I know you didn't want to before, but now we have to. If you want this to work then you have to be willing to do anything to make that happen."

"Anything," he said.

A week later Will turned up for their first counseling session. They'd slept in the same bed, carried on going through the motions of normal life, had found a counselor and made that emergency appointment. He sat there for twenty minutes before he realized that she wasn't coming. He paid the counselor, he rang his wife and got no answer. Not at the house, not at her work, not on her mobile. He was scared, as he rushed home, that she'd been hurt.

He was right to be scared. She had been hurt. And now she was going to hurt him back.

She had decided to use the time she knew he'd be at the counselor's office to put all his belongings outside. To change the locks. To leave outside the solicitor's letter informing him of her intention to file for divorce exactly one year from the date of the letter, when she was legally able to.

Will's wife couldn't forgive him. He hadn't slept with someone else—she had done that, and she probably would have been able to forgive a physical act. But what he did violated the sanctity of their marriage; it was like a knife driven deep into the heart of what they'd built together. What Will didn't realize was that you didn't admit—even by omission—that you'd fallen in love with someone else and stay married. Love isn't like that.

———

"So, that's Australia. You wanted to know and now you can tell me off. Just like the few friends I had before all of this have done. I'm stupid. I'm selfish. Go ahead, let me have it." I was being flippant because I was steeling myself for the lecture. For being told I was stupid to get involved, that he was a bastard, that I was wasting the best years of my life hanging around waiting for a man who had used me. I'd heard it—and a million other versions of it—all before.

Every time it damaged a friendship and cut me deep inside because no one knew. No one understood what he meant to me, why he was so special. I could never tell them, either.

Gabrielle's eyes checked her rearview mirror, checked her wing mirror and then her long, slender fingers hit the right-hand signal just before she violated several laws to pull across two lanes of traffic, causing a chorus of horns to flare up behind us. She took the exit for the service station we'd just been about to pass.

Oh Jeez, she's really going to let me have it, I thought as I eyed up the soft line of her jaw, which was hard and angular now that it was set with her eyes fixed ahead. She'd been married. She never told me why she and Ted had split and then divorced. Probably because of someone like me. Another woman who had entered their relationship. Maybe she was going to tell me to get out and walk to Sussex or walk home. Either way, I wasn't welcome in her car any-more. *Oh Jeez. Oh Jeez. I can't afford to lose my job,* I thought as she prowled the car park looking for a parking spot. *I'll be hard put to find one with such a senior title, so near to where I live and on the money I'm getting. This is karma: a ruined life for a ruined life.*

Silently and carefully, Gabrielle pulled into a parking space, cut the engine. The sound of her unlocking her seat belt filled the car for a moment, then was replaced by the elastic spring of the belt being snatched backwards. I closed my eyes and counted to ten as I heard her shift in her seat. I braced myself for the sharp sting of a slap on the cheek.

"I'm really hurt that you think I'd ever judge you," Gabrielle said quietly.

Startled by her words and the genuine wounding in her voice, I opened my eyes, stared straight out of the wind-screen. *This* I had not been expecting.

"Kennie, we're friends, which means I know you. I know

how many morals you have, how if there's a cause, hopeless or otherwise, you're going to back it. So I know how much you must have already beat yourself up about this. He must have been so special to make you go against everything you believe in.

"In all the time I've known you I don't recall a single time when you've spoken about a man like you did him. Why would I discount that? Because he's married? What you feel is more important than that.

"And no, I'm not saying it was an ideal situation or that it's a great idea. Or that there aren't some people who go out especially to date married people—you're not one of them. He doesn't sound like a serial cheater from what you said, but even if he was, what good would me telling you off do? It'd just push you closer towards him, make you hide things. And if you can't talk to people, then you start to do crazy things.

"Sweetheart, I've been married, I know how complicated things are, especially when you're going through a hard time. Should he have talked things through with his wife? Yes. Would staying away from him have made it easier for them to talk through things and maybe get things back on track? Yes. But it didn't work out that way. And from how you've been acting since you got back, I'm pretty sure you're in the depths of hell right now. You don't need me to make you feel bad—I'm sure you can do that all by yourself."

I closed my eyes again and braced myself. A tidal wave of everything that I hadn't been able to let out in nearly two years was welling up inside. I couldn't stop myself. I tried, I truly tried, but I couldn't stop it. It all came pouring out in an undignified, uncontrollable torrent. It all came out and suddenly I was sobbing my heart out.

Never underestimate the ability of understanding to make you feel truly awful.

TOAST, BUTTER & GINGER MARMALADE

◆ ◆ ◆

CHAPTER 17

*T*here are many shades of darkness.

Kyle was thinking this as he lay, fully clothed, on his bed in between his daughter and his son. His arms were crossed over his chest, the palms of his hands resting on his shoulders. He used to lie like that when he was boy. He hadn't been a fan of the night. Bad things happened at night, he used to think when he was a boy. In the blackness of his bedroom, he could make out the shapes of the closet door to his right, the doorway to the en suite bathroom ahead of him, the bedside tables on each side of the bed, the folds—thick and thin—in the floor-length curtains at the windows, the smooth lines of the dressing table. His children curled up like warm, living bookends on each side of him.

He wasn't remotely tired, it was only 9 p.m., but he had to stay in bed. They'd refused to sleep without him because Kendra was gone. Only for the night, but they'd been wild-eyed and paranoid that she wasn't coming back. As she was leaving with the Lolly Lady, Summer stood on the doorstep, repeatedly making Kendra promise she was coming back. Jaxon had just sat at the far end of the corridor playing with his steam train pretending that it wasn't happening. When Kendra had tried to talk to him, he'd pretended not to hear. She'd managed to get him to talk to her by talking to Garvo. Then she'd gone outside again to another round of "promise you'll come backs" from Summer. The whole thing had added another fifteen minutes to their departure.

When Summer was in bed earlier she'd asked to call Kendra. He'd reminded her that she was camping, was sleeping under the stars tonight and would be back at some point tomorrow. Summer had looked at him as though he was an idiot. As though she hadn't OK'd that plan and wasn't impressed that Kyle had allowed it to happen.

The only way to appease them both was to suggest they camped out in his bedroom so they could tell Kendra that they'd been camping, too. They'd made a canopy with the sheets and read their stories by flashlight. It'd been a pretty lame attempt since he'd had no time to plan it, but it'd worked and they'd both eventually fallen asleep with Kyle in the middle. The last two times he'd tried to leave the bed he'd looked down to find one or other of them staring at him, silently asking where he thought he was going. They had a tag team system guarding him. He understood what they felt. He felt it himself: a trickle of worry that Kendra would disappear from their lives. It was irrational, but real.

Especially since he hadn't been very pleasant to her in the days after she'd asked about Ashlyn. It wasn't her fault. After saying it to Kendra, Kyle had realized how powerful words could be. How they could set you free, how they could chain you, how they could propel you back to the midst of the place called hell. It was hard to look Kendra in the eye after he admitted his secret. Virtually impossible to talk to her.

He hadn't seen her reaction to the handful of words that explained everything. He'd mumbled them while staring into the middistance. She hadn't gasped dramatically, nor reached out to him in comfort. She'd been silent for a moment then said, "If you want to talk about it, I'm listening. If not, no worries."

Had he been imagining it or had there been a slight Australian inflection in her voice when she'd uttered "no worries"? His mouth had moved upwards with the ghost of a smile.

He'd jumped to his feet and said he was going to play with the kids. "OK," she'd said. He hadn't looked at her for the rest of the day.

Now, a week later, he was lying in the dark, held hostage by his children's fear of abandonment, wondering if she would come back. Kendra. Or Ashlyn. Either one. Both. Except, did he want Ashlyn back? *Really?*

Almost violently he moved his mind away from that train of thought, back to the report he had to write and the presentation he needed to rework. It wasn't the most interesting thing on earth, most of his work wasn't now, but this job paid the bills—just—and allowed him to work from home.

———

She was lying on the sofa when he got in.

Her slender form stretched out, her eyes half closed, staring in the direction of the television but probably taking in very little. He reached down to kiss her and paused as usual as the whiff of alcohol hit him.

She must have just had a couple of glasses with dinner *he told himself, carefully ignoring the fact that, as usual, her dinner plate sat on the floor beside the sofa, still heaped with uneaten, untouched food.*

Kyle dropped a kiss on her forehead and she smiled a languid, dreamy grin.

"Hello lover," she said. Her voice was drowsy with sleep, he reassured himself. She'd dozed off because she'd been waiting up for him, he who was working late in the office as usual. *"I thought you were never coming home."*

"Where else would I go?" he said. He used to say, "I have

*nowhere else I'd rather be" but not anymore. Now it was,
"Where else would I go?"*

*In the kitchen, he hated himself for doing it, but he went to
the large chrome bin, checked how many bottles were in there.
Two. Two bottles of cheap red wine. One on the table, two in
the bin. He stared at the bottles, his foot pressed on the black
pedal, the chrome lid of the bin gaping open to show him what
his wife had been doing while his back was turned. She'd found
a new lover and it was lying amongst the other trash, its white
label and its body's sleek, smooth lines mocking him. It'll pass,
he told himself. It'll be fine. He was ignoring the empty liter
bottle of tonic water also lying in the bin. And he was ignoring
the semicircle of lipstick on her glass on the table. He was pretending he didn't know that she never left the house without
her lipstick, which meant she'd taken the children half a mile
down the road to buy the wine and gin to drink with the tonic
water, or she'd left the children alone. Which she'd never do.
Never.*

*In bed her lover's distinctive scent oozed out of her and
stroked him in persistent, acrid waves. They were on opposite
sides of the bed. He wasn't sure when it'd started to happen but
they'd stopped sleeping spooned up, getting comfort from the
warmth of each other's bodies. Now they were like strangers,
friendly strangers, people who knew each other well enough to
share a bed, but not to lie very close to each other. Not to touch.*

*He lay in the dark, thinking around the problem. Not won-
dering when she'd started drinking this much again. He allowed himself to think how he had always been concerned
about Ashlyn's drinking because she'd always been able to put
away a lot more than most women, than most men—him included. But he stopped short at wondering why she'd started
again.*

Instead of doing that, he decided to focus on the big presen-

tation in the morning. He'd come home at a vaguely decent hour tonight because the presentation, the big unveiling, the one he'd buried himself in for the past six months, was tomorrow. So tonight, he—and everyone else he worked with—was home fairly early so they could all sleep, shave, make themselves presentable for the client.

Kyle closed his eyes. Everything he'd been working towards would come to a head tomorrow. What he'd given his life to, what he'd sacrificed his family time for would all be worth it. And when it was over, when the client had looked over the models, the plans, the blueprints, the graphic presentation, when they'd heard the spiel, he'd be able to relax. Take time off. Talk to Ashlyn.

Talk. To. Ashlyn.

Properly.

Do something about her problem. Their problem. Because he was in it as well. It was their problem. For better or worse, he'd promised her. And while things hadn't exactly been "for worse" they'd definitely been residing in the "not good" area for a long time. But that would change. Now he had time, that would change. It'll work itself out, he told himself. It'll be all right.

———

That denial, ignoring the full extent of what was going on, was what needled him the most.

It ate away at him like bacteria ate at rotting meat; the guilt twisted deep inside him, curling tighter and tighter around his heart like a python squeezed the life out of its prey. He could have done something. If he'd spoken up earlier, confronted his wife, maybe, just maybe, she wouldn't have done what she did to Summer.

"Don't cry, Dad, it's all right." Kyle jumped at Summer's

voice. Her eyes were as large and wise as an owl's in the dark. He hadn't realized she was awake and watching him, nor that he was crying. She patted his arm. "All better now."

"I'm OK," he whispered. He unlaced his arms, rubbed quickly at his eyes. "There's just something in my eye."

"All better, Dad," she mumbled, her eyes falling shut and blinking open. "We'll look after you." Then she was out like a light, probably wouldn't remember this conversation in the morning. He rubbed at his eyes again to make sure they were dry, then crossed his arms over his chest. Protecting his heart from the monsters that lived in the different shades of the night. That was what used to scare him when he was younger. That something would carve open his chest and scoop out his heart. Not that it would kill him, but he'd be left with a huge gaping hole right in the middle of his chest.

CHAPTER 18

*G*abrielle and I were the last to arrive at the campsite, owing to our impromptu rest stop.

It was all too humiliating to think about. Crying in the car, her hand rubbing my back as I sobbed. A few people had walked past our car, saw my tears and Gabrielle's comfort and probably thought she was breaking up with me. I hadn't even told her all of it, why I'd had to leave, why I had severed all contact with Will before I left—hadn't answered his calls, blocked his e-mail address, stayed in a hotel for a few days to avoid him. And I hadn't told her why I hadn't opened his letter, nor why I was terrified of thinking about him. No, I hadn't even gotten to the truly awful bit and I'd *still* cried like that.

We pulled into the car park of Wildberry Woods, the forest campsite. They had individually marked out pitches in certain parts of the woods, each with a stone fireplace and cleared earth for pitching tents. We had maps for nature trail walks. Our campsite was in the far left of the woods. The leaves were like a canopy over the forest and as we set out, I started to feel a bit of excitement. This was something out of the ordinary for me. I hadn't been out at all since I'd come back and Gabrielle was right: apart from work, adult conversation was something that was lacking in my life.

And since Kyle had told me about Ashlyn, he hadn't exactly been falling over himself to be friendly. I completely understood. When people found things out about me, I usually unhooked myself from their company rather quickly. He hadn't wanted to tell me about it, but had. He probably hated the idea of me knowing.

We found the others deep in the woods. They had already set up their tents. Like Gabrielle and me, the three others were in jeans or combats, T-shirts and zip-up fleeces. The two women I didn't know were the heads of the branches of Office Wonders in Middlesex and southwest London. Both of them were in their thirties, one with red hair, the other with blond hair. Gabrielle introduced them as Moira and Lindsay. Moira had a dazzling smile, her red hair haphazardly pulled back into a ponytail. Lindsay was petite, very pretty, with smiley eyes and her blond hair styled into a straight bob. The other camper was Janene. Teri was meant to be coming but one of her kids had picked up a stomach bug and she couldn't get overnight babysitting on such short notice so couldn't make it. (Pretty convenient, I thought, since she'd confessed to me at lunch last week that she'd rather change dirty nappies for twenty-four hours straight than go camping.)

Lindsay, an expert camper, helped us set up the tent. In theory it was easy to do. In theory Gabrielle had done it several times before. In reality it took ages. All the while Janene and Moira oohed and ahhhed over the contents of Gabrielle's hamper, because we were roughing it of course.

"OK," Gabrielle said after we'd laid out our luxury sleeping bags at the bottom of our tent. "I need two volunteers to go to the campsite office on the other side of the wood to register that we're here and collect our allocation of firewood." She let a second pass before she said, "Kendra and Janene, that's so lovely of you to offer. Here you go, here's my booking confirmation, here's the map, one of you can pretend to be me, off you go."

I didn't even get a chance to say, "Pardon?" before her

strong hands had settled on both our backs and were firmly shoving us in the direction of the campsite office. Janene looked as pleased with the arrangement as I did.

"Bitch," I mouthed at Gabrielle over my shoulder.

She blew me a kiss.

We traipsed through the woods, following the map in what looked like a straight line. It was beautiful out here. Through the gaps in the trees you could see the cerulean shade of the sky, kissed here and there by the bundles of candy-floss clouds.

"So, are you from Brockingham?" I asked Janene. Gabrielle wanted us to bond, so I was going to do my level best.

"Er, don't think so," she sneered. "I'm from west London."

"Oh, really? Me, too," I said. "I grew up in Ealing and went to college in Leeds. Whereabouts are you from?"

"I mean proper west London," she said with another sneer. "West Ken."

OK, strike one, I thought.

The silence in the wood was calming and unnerving at the same time. The only sounds were from us trampling twigs and fallen leaves under foot, the occasional bird call.

"Are you seeing anyone right now?" I asked.

"I'm going out with my boyfriend from college. He's more serious about it than me. He wants us to get married and I probably will marry him but I'm sure I can do better. He's a nice enough guy and he's totally in love with me, but we'll see."

OK, strike two.

"Going anywhere nice on your holidays this year?" I asked in desperation.

"Yeah, yeah, just because you lived in Australia, don't

think you can rub my face in it. I wouldn't go over there if you paid me."

Strike three and you're out.

We got to the campsite office, registered and collected our wood then made our way back without saying another word to each other.

"How was that, my lovelies?" Gabrielle, plastic champagne flute in hand, asked from her place lounging on her tartan blanket beside the empty stone belly where the fire was going to be built.

Janene gave her a wan smile.

"I found it a real team-building experience," I said to Gabrielle. Janene rolled her eyes and sloped off to her tent, probably to fix her makeup.

"Me and Janene," I held up the middle fingers of both hands and moved them as far apart as my arms would go, "we're like that."

CHAPTER 19

With thoughts of tomorrow's big presentation and how afterwards he would have the chance to rebuild his family circling his head, Kyle started to let go of consciousness. Started to leave it all behind him when he heard the hush of the bedroom door being pushed open and tiny footsteps entering the room.

He opened his eyes, saw the outline of Summer in the doorway. She clutched her rag doll she'd named Winter in her arms, clinging to it like a lifebuoy. She stared at her parents, obviously waiting for one of them to wake up.

Kyle pushed himself up on his elbows. Ashlyn, curled up in the fetal position, was turned away from him, facing the window, oblivious to anything and everything.

"Sum?" Kyle whispered. "What's the matter?"

"There's a monster in my bed, Daddy," Summer said with quiet certainty.

There's one in mine, too, Kyle thought before he could stop himself.

"I bet there isn't," Kyle replied. He hadn't done this before. It was Ashlyn who got up in the night. It was Ashlyn who talked the three-year-old twins back into bed. Kyle usually slept through it all.

Summer's eyes set in her head—who was this man to tell her what was and wasn't in her bed? Of course there was a monster in her room, she'd heard it. She'd felt it. She would have seen it if she'd dared turn around and look at it; if she hadn't closed her eyes before she leapt off the bed and ran for the safety of her parents' room, it might have grabbed her.

"Daddy," Summer said, summoning up all the patience she had for adults, "there is." She fixed her father with her navy-green eyes and the line of her determined mouth. She nodded and reassured, "There is. Promise."

Kyle was looking into the face of his wife, he realized. That grim certainty that descended upon her face and her posture in those days when they used to talk and he dared disagree. Her face would become a mask of stone, her navy-green eyes like twin emeralds that merely tolerated but didn't condone his dissent. Summer was doing the same. Kyle would be an idiot to argue, he realized. What did he know?

He sighed, threw back the covers. "OK," he moved to climb out, "I'll come get rid of it."

"No, it OK," Summer said, moving towards her father. "I sleep in your bed, Daddy. Naughty monster go away tomorrow."

Kyle went to protest, then stopped. Looked at her, the little girl in a pink Care Bears T-shirt that reached her knees. The little girl who he hadn't spent much time with in the past few weeks—months—actually. Working on the project also had the unpleasant side effect in that he was rarely around for the kids. He'd almost forgotten what their voices sounded like, how dimples formed on Summer's face when she smiled, how Jaxon's eyes seemed to change color as he stared intently, waiting for the answer to a question.

Besides, his three-year-old had decided she was going to sleep in his bed so the decision was made. There was no discussing it. Even if he did climb out of bed, go fight the monster, go check that everything was safe in her room, she'd still want to sleep in their bed. That was her way. When she got the idea she wanted to sleep here, here was where she'd sleep. Jaxon, although quieter than Summer, rarely came to their bed. He was *independent. Even as a baby that'd been the difference between them. How anyone could tell the bald, wrinkled newborns apart—Jaxon would sleep anywhere, in anyone's arms, in the crib or car seat; Summer would protest loudly if her mother, and then eventually her father, wasn't cuddling her. She refused to settle until she knew one of her parents was close.*

He swung his legs out of bed and stood up a little unsteadily—he'd been more asleep than he thought, his limbs numbed by slumber. He picked up Summer under the arms, marveling that someone who had so easily hustled her way into his bed could be so easy to lift, so light to carry. He placed her in the middle of the bed, beside Ashlyn, who only stirred a couple of times to cough.

He settled down beside her, pulling the covers back up, making sure she had half of his pillow.

"Now," Kyle said softly to his daughter, "Daddy's got to get up really early in the morning so we need to go straight to sleep, OK?"

Summer grinned, Summer nodded. " 'K," she said. "I saw a fairy, Daddy."

"Really?" Kyle mumbled, sleep tugging at his senses. He really needed to go to sleep. And soon. His mind was buzzing with what he had to say in tomorrow's presentation. And he had to be first in line at the copy shop to get extra poster-size plans made up.

"She's orange," Summer explained. "Her hair is blue and orange. And dress is orange dress. And shoes orange. And wings orange."

"That's a lot of orange." Kyle's voice was a sleep-tinged murmur.

"Daddy can't see her." Summer explained, regret swirled with pride in her voice. "Only me. And Jaxon. Not Daddy."

"That's a shame," Kyle replied.

"I sleep now, Daddy," Summer said as though Kyle had been trying to keep her up.

"Right, honey," Kyle said, feeling chastised.

Summer closed her eyes and instinctively, it seemed, she shifted away from Kyle, turned towards her mother. When she was asleep, she wanted to be as close as possible to Ashlyn. Kyle watched her nestle herself on the edge of her mother's pillow, inches from where he had once upon a time ago slept. Ashlyn, as if sensing something had shifted in the world, hiccupped, cleared her throat, then turned over in bed, facing her daughter and husband. She was still buried in her alcohol-induced sleep, but showed the slackness of her sleeping features to them.

Jealousy prickled at Kyle. If he hadn't been there, Summer would still be standing in the doorway waiting for attention.

Kyle closed his eyes. Told himself he didn't have time to be jealous, he needed to sleep. To be as fresh and alert as possible for the presentation.

He heard it as he finally relaxed his grip on consciousness. The rapid, repetitive sound of a person choking. Someone struggling to breathe, struggling to take air in and let air out. The sound was too loud, too deep to be a child. Kyle's eyes flew open and he struggled half upright, just in time to see it happen. Ashlyn choking, her body convulsing with every choke, forced herself upright, trying to breathe, trying to force air into her lungs, trying to dislodge whatever was in her throat. She coughed and choked until she finally succeeded. Until all that she'd drunk and eaten came spewing out. A slimy red, liquid nightmare that exploded all over Summer.

Kyle couldn't stop it. He'd woken up too late, his reflexes were too slow, he hadn't known what was going to happen. Whatever the reason, he didn't protect his daughter from the deluge that rained down on her.

Summer woke up screaming. She didn't know what had

splattered against her skin and slapped against her hair, but it terrified her. Wrenched her from sleep, from dreaming about the orange fairy riding a yellow unicorn. "MUMMA!" she screamed. Her shout woke up Jaxon, who was on the other side of the wall, and he started screaming. While Summer's screams had words, Jaxon's was a long, loud yell of fear, of knowing something bad had happened and being terribly afraid.

It kept coming. The purple-red nightmare continued to be retched out of the yawning hole of Ashlyn's mouth until she clamped her hand over it, the vomit bulging in her cheeks, spewing through her fingers. Summer stared at her mother, her eyes wide in horror, her mouth still making an awful sound.

Numb and impotent, Kyle was unable to move, to do anything. Ashlyn reached down with her free hand, threw back the covers and fled. She ran for the en suite, one hand over her mouth, her thin upper body convulsing under her oversize T-shirt. She slammed the door behind her, no lock was drawn, the toilet lid was slammed up, she continued to retch into the bowl, a loud harrowing sound, a sound that echoed of true agony. It mingled with the sounds of Summer and Jaxon. Summer's screams of horror, Jaxon's loud sobs, his worry and confusion at the screaming, at why no one had come to him.

Kyle moved then. Like a man possessed he moved, he reached out, pulled Summer into his arms, held her, despite the putrid stench of fermented red wine, stomach acid and shock that stained his daughter's skin and hair and filled the room. "It's OK, Summer," Kyle hushed against her ear, running his hand over her sticky, vomit-stained hair, most of which was flattened against her face. "It's OK." He rocked her in his arms, holding her close, trying to soothe her before he moved her to the bathroom. Before he went to calm Jaxon. "It's OK," he said, rocking her. "It's OK, Daddy's got you. I've got you."

Her screams slowly subsided to an unrelenting whimper.

In the en suite there was silence. Ashlyn had finished throwing up, but she hadn't returned to the scene of her crime. She was hiding. She was passed out. She was choking on her own vomit. Kyle didn't know, he didn't care, either. Right then, if he never had to see her again it would be too soon.

The stench, which grew more putrid with every passing second, which seemed to seep into him through his skin, was unbearable. He had to get Summer into the bath, had to wash this off her. Cleanse her of this act. His eyes strayed to the bed sheets, stained red, an almost bloody reminder of what Ashlyn had done. Of what she'd been doing for far too long.

Moving slowly, so as not to further traumatize the trembling, whimpering child in his arms, he slid off the bed. Cradling Summer, he moved out of the room, whispering to her that she was safe, that she didn't need to be scared. In the corridor he stopped. Didn't know what to do. Go to Jaxon, or whether the state of Summer, stained with red and limp in his arms, would further terrify him. Loud sobbing was coming from his room; he was probably pinned by fear in his bed. He needed someone to go to him, to comfort him as well.

Fuck! was Kyle's only thought.

He moved to Jaxon's room, used the tip of his bare foot to gently kick open the white door, stepped over the threshold. Jaxon's small body was cowering in the corner of his bed, his eyes wide with horror, his face drenched in tears. "Hey, buddy, it's OK, it's Dad," Kyle said softly, using the volume and tone of his voice to try to calm his frightened son. "It's OK, I'm here. OK? I'm here." Kyle took a couple of steps forwards; Jaxon was still crying. "We've got to go to the bathroom right now. So, you gonna come with us?" Jaxon took a huge ragged breath, his cries subsiding. "Yeah?"

Jaxon nodded.

"OK, good. Come on then." Kyle shifted Summer in his

arms, moved her over his shoulder so he could hold out his hand. Before offering it to his son, he wiped off the red slime on his pajama leg. The smell still clung to them, it still turned his stomach, but he masked it. If he showed his disgust it would further upset his son. "Come on, mate, let's go for a bath." Carefully, cautiously, Jaxon got off his bed and slipped his hand in his dad's. In the bathroom, just across the corridor, Kyle had to let go of Jaxon's hand to tug on the light. Jaxon rubbed at his eyes from the sudden brightness. With one arm still cradling Summer, Kyle used his free hand to push the plug into the bath, turned on the taps. The sound of gushing water filled the room.

Jaxon moved across the bathroom, molded himself to his dad's leg. He didn't want to be away from him. He didn't understand what was happening. Why Summer was red. Why they were having a bath in the middle of the night. Why he'd been woken up by the terrible noise. But he did understand his dad. His dad was solid, calm, there. He needed to stay right beside him.

When the bath was half full, Kyle shut off the taps and, gently, with one hand, took off Summer's T-shirt, left it in a reeking heap on the ground. Took off her night nappy, then checked the temperature of the water before he lowered her into it. She struggled a little when he tried to loosen her grip on his neck, so he had to stay like that, leaning over the bath, Summer's arms clamped around his neck, her terror not allowing her to let him go, and Jaxon sitting on the floor, wedged beside him, his thumb in his mouth and his other hand rubbing at his eyes.

Kyle didn't know how long they stayed like that, but the water had cooled by the time tiredness made Summer go limp, releasing him. Jaxon was asleep, leaning on him. Quickly, so he could get her out of the cool water, Kyle cleaned the slime off his daughter, cleansed her skin of the red vileness, washed it out of her hair. He pulled the towel from the rail above the *bath, coaxed Summer to stand up and enveloped her in its soft white folds. He scooped her up in one arm, weighted her so she was in a secure position, then he gently woke up Jaxon and scooped him up in the other arm.*

Walking slowly, he moved out of the bathroom, leaving the red water in the bath, Summer's stained clothes and dirty nappy on the floor, and went back to Jaxon's room. He rested his son on the bed first, then his daughter. They lay like two little shells on top of the covers. Working on autopilot almost, Kyle rummaged through the drawers until he found another pair of Jaxon's pajamas—Spider-Man. Jaxon wouldn't mind, he decided as he took out another nappy and snapped it on before dressing Summer in the red and blue top and trousers.

He stared at Summer, who was virtually asleep. He had to dry her hair. She couldn't sleep with wet hair. He didn't want to go into the bedroom though. He knew Ashlyn's hair dryer was in their bedroom. Maybe . . . He dashed out into Summer's room, went through all her drawers until he found the small pink, baby hair dryer Ashlyn's mother had bought them. It took nearly ten minutes to get her hair dry. He didn't use a brush or anything, just waved it around her head until her hair went from sticking to her head in shiny black clumps to settling in dry black clumps around her face.

Jaxon, who was out for the count, didn't protest when Kyle pulled back the covers and put him in, didn't protest when Kyle laid Summer beside him. Kyle was tired now. It was flooding every sense, every synapse, every nerve in his body. Rest. He needed rest. Checking that they were both still asleep, he dashed down the stairs, snatched up the pillows and seat cushions from the sofas and armchairs, then got the tartan blanket from the blanket box in the playroom before racing back upstairs.

He lay the cushions on the floor beside the bed, something soft in case Summer rolled over and accidentally fell out of bed.

And then he sat in the easy chair under Jaxon's window, pulled the blanket over himself and tried to sleep.

When Ashlyn finally appeared the next morning, Kyle was on his fifth cup of tarlike black coffee. Despite how exhausted he was, he hadn't been able to sleep. He'd dozed off for a few minutes, but every noise, even the wind moving gently against the window, the creak of the floorboards settling, snapped him awake. So terrified was he that it'd happen again. Something would happen to his daughter or son, right in front of him and he wouldn't be able to stop it.

"What time is it?" she croaked, rubbing at her eyes. She hadn't cleaned herself up properly. She'd changed her clothes, but the scent of vomit still wafted around her, her hair was a matted mess, and she had the flower motif imprint of the floor tiles in their en suite bathroom on her left cheek. She must have passed out in there. Spent the rest of the night. Slept. She was disoriented, bleary eyed, still pissed for all he knew. Kyle surveyed her with disgust. Not for how she looked, but this: showing her face like this with no shame, no regret, no apology on her lips.

He turned his back on her and stalked over to the sink. Once there, he didn't know what he meant to do, so he stood glaring into the white porcelain. They'd chosen the sink together, when they were renovating this place. Before the kids had been born. They'd driven from reclamation yard to reclamation yard until they found it. "Our sink," Ashlyn had declared when she saw it. "Yup, that's our sink." He'd laughed and kissed her on the neck because even though he was the one who built buildings, those things were far more important to her. He stood glaring into the sink now. He'd washed up. Down here and upstairs in the bathroom. He was still in his pj bottoms with the red vomit streak on his right leg, because he hadn't been able to bring himself to go into the bedroom.

"Oh, God, it's nine o'clock. Shouldn't you be at work?" Ashlyn said.

Kyle raised his eyes, stared at the corrugated metal splashback and wondered, quite casually, how much noise the cup would make if he threw it against the wall. Frustration and anger and blind rage were bubbling up inside him; they were going to boil over at any minute, of that he was pretty certain. If he didn't throw the cup, he'd put his fist through the wall, or say something truly nasty to his wife. Something he meant and probably wouldn't take back even if he could.

"Where are the kids?" Finally, number three. Her third question had been about the kids.

He inhaled deeply, exhaled to calm himself. *"They're still asleep. They were up late."*

Silence. A long, drawn-out silence from behind him, then a sharp sucking in of breath as she suddenly remembered. *"Oh, God,"* Ashlyn breathed. *"I wasn't feeling well."*

"You were drunk," Kyle replied.

"I'd had a couple of glasses, which I probably shouldn't have because I wasn't feeling well. Did Summer see me being sick?"

Anger flashed through him. He turned to face her. *"You were pissed out of your mind. And Summer didn't see you, she felt you. You threw up on her. As you well know."*

"I'm sorry," Ashlyn said. She had *felt* unwell. Her stomach had been playing up all day, meaning she shouldn't have had those three or four drinks. But sometimes a few drinks made it better. She often didn't feel ill if she had a few drinks.

Kyle shook his head. *"It's not me you should be apologizing to."*

"She probably won't even remember," Ashlyn reasoned. *"She's only three."*

"Are you for real? She won't remember so you don't have to apologize? She was terrified, Ashlyn. And her screaming woke up Jaxon, who was terrified. The pair of them woke up a cou-

ple of times during the night in a cold sweat, crying. They didn't even know why. So, maybe they won't remember what happened exactly, but they'll never forget the terror." Kyle stalked past her, deciding to leave the room—he couldn't stomach sharing the same space as her a moment longer. "Oh, and the reason I'm not at work? I couldn't risk leaving the kids here with you—I didn't know what sort of state you'd be in. It's the biggest day of my career, the shopping center presentation we've been working on for six months is today and I'm going to miss it. Even though it's my project, someone else is going to present it. Probably get to work on site with it, too."

"I said I'm sorry," Ashlyn repeated, on the verge of tears.

"Yep, you did. But this time, I'm not going to accept your apology." He stalked out of the room, leaving Ashlyn to stand alone in her kitchen.

From that day onwards his life was irrevocably altered in two ways: Kyle was unofficially demoted and was never given another big project to work on even though they won the pitch; the rows began.

CHAPTER 20

The fire was gorgeous.

Lindsay built it, being the camping expert, and we all lay on blankets around it, warmed by it as it cast a warm, flickering orangey glow around us. We'd set up insect repellent lamps around the border of our tents to stop us from being eaten alive by bugs. We'd laughed and talked and played campfire games. I felt comfortable with these other women. Relaxed. For the first time in months, I wasn't worried about something. Anything. The kids did come to mind, but I knew they were fine. Probably didn't even notice I was gone. In this haven in the woods, I felt as though nothing bad existed. Not before, not after. In the here and now, everything was perfect.

Janene ruined it, of course. I lay on my back, staring up at the stars. *I love the stars,* I was thinking. If anyone were to get me my ultimate present it would be to box a star. I wouldn't want one named after me, that'd be too vain, but a beautiful star, in a box, would make me happy.

"We're women, we have choices now," Janene's words cut into my thoughts. We hadn't spoken since our mini field trip earlier even though I had tried. I'd made the effort not only because we worked together, but also because Janene wasn't an evil person, just a stupid one. She believed that owning lots of things made you a better person. She didn't know—possibly didn't want to know—that happiness comes from the inside. Like beauty and wealth, they started at the center of who you are. Reading a million self-help books had taught me that and I was on the road to living it—one monumental mistake at a time. "And because we've got choices, we can't be whining about every little thing that happens to us."

I rolled over onto my front, looked over at Janene illuminated by moonlight and firelight. She'd changed her clothes since we got here. Before she'd been wearing low-rider jeans and a skinny T-shirt and a cropped fleece top. Now she'd changed into silk combat trousers and fleece. The rest of us had come wearing jeans and fleeces and had stayed in them. Would most likely sleep in them. Janene was comfortable with her body, enjoyed showing off her curves in her designer clothes, and that would be commendable if I didn't suspect the reason she spent so much money on clothes and getting her hair done wasn't to raise her self-esteem but to try to lower everyone else's.

Janene's true stupidity came from her ability to pontificate for hours on a subject she knew nothing about. With me she didn't like to speak, with everyone else, she liked to hold center stage.

I could see we were in for one of those talks. Us being women with choices and all. Who talks like that at a camping bonding session? Who wouldn't rather yammer on about crap TV, which book we'd last read and whether astrology predictions were usually accurate? Janene was who.

She lay amongst a group of adults—most of us had many more years of experience in this thing called life than her—but she felt no bashfulness in holding court. In dominating the conversation. "Like my friend who's all, like, crying and stuff after this date with this guy."

"Ah, she liked him, he didn't call," Moira said, bored. She

was married, had two kids and wasn't interested in hearing another tale about what bastards all men were, clearly. None of us was.

"Oh, no, no, nothing like that," Janene said. "That's the stuff she usually comes out with. No, after this date with this guy, who she'd been going on and on about liking and being gorgeous for ages, she starts accusing him of all sorts."

Ice water tumbled over in my stomach. *You're special,* murmured the voice from the past. *Stop fighting, you're special.*

I sat bolt upright, pulled my knees up to my chest, laced my arms around them. I was suddenly cold. The fire didn't seem warm enough, I wasn't wearing enough layers. I was suddenly freezing on the inside. So cold nothing could warm me up.

"How'dya mean?" Lindsay asked.

"Well," Janene stopped to take a dramatic swig of her champagne from her plastic glass, "she says they went back to his place for a coffee, one thing led to another . . . But she said she didn't want to, changed her mind, whatever. I'm, like, what did you expect? It's, like, duh, what else did she go there for in the first place if not for that?"

"To maybe have a coffee?" Gabrielle suggested.

"Yeah, but everyone knows if you go back to someone's house you're going back for sex," Janene said.

"Whoa! That's a news flash to me," Lindsay said. "In all my years of dating I never knew that. As far as I know, I go to someone's house for a coffee, I'm wanting coffee. If he tries it on and it leads to bed, then it leads to bed. If I say no, I mean it."

"You can't lead a bloke on—" Janene asserted, a little put out that this conversation wasn't going her way.

"Hang on there, missy, 'lead a bloke on'?" Gabrielle cut in. "What the hell does that mean? Are we living in the dark ages? He needs to take responsibility for his actions. No one is led on. And, let's just say if that ridiculous notion is true, and he is 'led on,' it still means he should stop when asked to."

Janene rolled her eyes, her face demonically illuminated by the orange and yellow flames. "You're all so politically correct," she said with a sigh.

For a moment I felt like picking up one of the burning logs from the fire and beating her over the head with the flaming end. She was one of those people who reached for those two words when she wanted to say something offensive or indefensible by trying to make you think you were in the wrong.

"But politically correct or not, next time she goes out on a date she'll know what to expect," Janene added.

"She'll expect to never feel safe again." Me. This was me talking. My voice was low but determined. I'd decided not to beat her with a flaming log, but to explain the reality of this to her. "She'll expect to always walk down the road, looking behind her, worried about who's following her. She'll expect to never quite trust another person's motives again—even if they're the nicest person in the world. And, of course, she'll expect to never be able to confide in someone without the reaction she got from you."

Silence descended upon the group; the only noise came from the crackling and snapping of the wood as the fire broke it down into ash and charcoal. Everyone's eyes were fixed on me, all wondering where my reaction, my voice came from. Everyone, except Janene, who couldn't bear not to have the last word. "What you don't seem to understand, Kendra, is that you could ruin a man's life by accusing him of something like that."

My voice remained as hard as concrete. "What you don't seem to understand, *Janene,* is that a woman's life is *always*

ruined when something like that happens to them," I replied. I stopped, aware that I was about to slide into a rant
and this wasn't the arena to get my soapbox out.

I struggled to my feet from the ground, folded my arms
around me so my zip-up fleece hugged my body. Moving
over the food containers, plastic glasses and plastic cutlery, I
passed by the fire. "I'm going for a cigarette," I said.

"But you don't smoke," Gabrielle said.

At the edge of our tarpaulin and tents, where the ring of
citronella lanterns sat and the edge of our pool of light
ended, I stopped, turned as one last thing occurred to me.
Something I meant to say. "I hope nothing ever happens to
you, Janene. That you never know such fear. That you never
experience such contempt afterwards." I picked up a lantern
then marched through a gap in the trees into the heart of
the forest.

Anger thudded and pounded through my veins at the
speed of light. My whole body was on fire with it.

Every time I thought about what Janene had said I
wanted to hit something. Every time I heard that sort of
nonsense it needled me. Prodded at the part of me that believed in causes. I meant what I said to her, I hoped nothing
ever happened to her. I wouldn't wish such a thing on anyone. Maybe it was better for her to think as she did because
she knew no better. She was an innocent. Better an innocent
than an enlightened victim.

As the anger slowed its progress through my body, the
reality of my surroundings came back to me. I was in a forest, at night, with insects licking their mandibles and dreaming of feasting on my flesh, and wild animals whose ears
were pricking up at the sound of a ten-stone-something
steak walking right onto their plates. This wasn't good.

A little farther on, I spotted a fallen tree, its leaves
stripped away, its branches broken. Its bark had been worn

off by the elements over time and the most worn sections glowed white in the full moon. Full moon. Werewolves. Great. I survived living in the land of sharks, crocodiles and poisonous spiders for nearly three years, so obviously I was going to be dismembered by a half-man, half-animal super-natural beast in Sussex.

I sat heavily on the fallen tree, placed the lantern on the ground beside my feet, put my face in my hands then slowly pushed my fingers through my hair. Jeez, it was tiring having strong beliefs. Reacting to the filth people like Janene tried to propagate. Sometimes I wanted to sit back and accept it. To not register anything when the nonsense started. To be morally numb—or even morally corrupt—so I could eat certain brands of chocolate, go into certain stores, wear certain brands, listen to certain theories.

Also at times like this, I wished I did smoke.

Crack! The sound of a snapping twig made me jump and I froze, wondering if I should have paid more attention to those black-and-white Hammer House of Horror movies. How *did* you kill a werewolf? Silver bullets? A silver stake through the heart?

The footsteps continued through the forest but they didn't sound like an animal's, they were soft and light. "Ow, shit," the person cursed softly.

Not a werewolf, more likely the only person who would bother to come after me.

"Despite all the bugs, and scary stuff out here, I had to check to see if you'd really taken up smoking," Gabrielle said, coming to stand in front of me.

I gave her a small smile. She sat down on the fallen tree, on the other side of my lantern. She reached into the left pocket of her navy-blue fleece, pulled out a battered packet of low-tar cigarettes. From her right pocket she pulled a slender, silver lighter. She slipped a cigarette between her pink lips and held up the lighter to the end of the cigarette. "Now," she spoke with the cigarette clamped between her teeth, "I've not smoked in about eight years, but I'm willing to start again just to keep you company."

"Don't do that," I said, taking the cigarette out of her mouth and relieving her of her lighter.

A long silence stretched between us.

"I've never seen you like that," she said. "I've never seen you go for anyone like that. Wanna talk about it?"

"She was talking bullshit," I said, straight back into Soapbox Kennie mode. "She's always talking bullshit but no one ever says anything because 'Janene's young.' 'Janene doesn't know any better.' *Bollocks*. I'm so sick of that excuse. I was young once, I never came out with as much nonsense as she does. And we're worse because we do nothing. We pander to her filth. We excuse it by letting her spout that vile nonsense."

Gabrielle unsheathed another cigarette, held it between her forefinger and middle finger, then started threading it along her fingers by twisting it slowly between each finger. "Wanna talk about it?" Gabrielle repeated.

"It . . . *That* happened to someone I know. A long time ago when we were all in college. And she wasn't asking for it, like Janene was implying, or leading him on. She was really hurt by this man, she trusted him, and he took advantage of that. And you know what kills me? There are so many people—*women*—who think like Janene. It's scary. It's why women keep those things to themselves."

Gabrielle watched her cigarette moving along her fingers and back again. She said nothing for a while, then without looking at me, she asked, "What happened to your friend?"

"She got on with her life. Made sure she never made that mistake again," I explained.

"Really?" Gabrielle asked. I could see from the corner of my eye she was looking at me.

I nodded. "As far as I know. We don't keep in touch, but the last time I heard she was doing well. Really well."

"Yeah?" Gabrielle kept looking at me until I faced her.

"Yeah," I replied.

"Good. I'm glad." Her naked lips slid up into a smile, her gentle blue eyes, which reminded me of the color the sky had been earlier, seemed to see right through me. To understand everything about me. I recoiled a fraction. She was clearly making assumptions that were way off base. "Everyone deserves to do really well. To be happy. Don't you think?"

I nodded and looked away.

"Right, well, I am officially freaked about being out here. Are you going to come back to the safety of the campfire?"

"You mean back to that pool of light that might as well be a beacon for wild animals to find us?"

"Erm, yeah. That."

"No."

Gabrielle stared at me, trying to work out if I was joking or not.

"I can't, Gabs, I can't be around Janene, I won't be responsible for what else I say to her. I'm going to wait until you're all asleep, then come back and go sleep in your car."

"If you slink away it'll seem as if you didn't mean what you said, and that Janene was right."

"Hmmmm . . ."

"And I don't know if you can live with that, but I sure can't. Remember the day you first came to our office? Remember what I said to you?"

" 'Don't pick up that phone unless you mean it'?"

"Oh, maybe I didn't say it? What I meant to say was, 'If

anyone allows a little madam to think they're right in my
lifetime, I'll have them killed.' So, you see, you'll have to
come back. 'Cause, much as I love you, Kendra, I won't
think twice about having you done away with if you allow
an 'I told you so' look to pass Janene's face."

"But I'm scared I'll have a go at her again," I said seriously.

"Sweetie, don't you worry about a thing." Gabrielle stood.
"Believe me, I've got your back."

"Feeling better?" Janene asked as I took my place back by the
campfire. She sounded concerned but there was a streak of
sarcasm in her voice, too.

"I'm good, thanks," I replied, without looking at her.
Instead, I pulled open the bag of marshmallows Jaxon and
Summer had bought me, scooped out a white one and
pushed it onto the forked end of a wooden-handled barbecue skewer, and held it out to the fire.

"Oh, Janene, I forgot to tell you," Gabrielle said, as she
reached for a barbecue skewer and a marshmallow, "you're
on earlies and lates for the next month. And if you're late,
even one time, you'll get a verbal warning."

"But . . . ?" she began in protest.

"Yes, sweetheart?" Gabrielle asked, her smile as glacial as
an Arctic pool.

"Nothing," Janene said, then sunk back into a sulk.

Later, much later, I caught her glowering at me over the
top of her plastic glass, promising to pay me back.

I glared back thinking, *Bring it on.*

CHAPTER 21

$\mathcal{J}$anene's eyes nearly popped out of her head when the door to our office opened and a striking man in his late thirties, with short dark hair, amazing brown eyes and a nervous face stepped into the office. This was what she'd been hoping for, the "I can do better" part of her relationship with her boyfriend. A male temp who would be so grateful to her for finding him work he'd ask her out. Or marry her. Or something equally unlikely.

She was out from behind her desk like a shot, plucking her clingy chocolate-brown cat suit into place over her curves, and drawing herself up to the full height given to her by the spiked heels on her feet. She wasn't as tall as the mystery man, even in heels. "Hi, I'm Janene, how can I help you?" she said.

This was an unusual welcome for a visitor. Most potential candidates usually received a variation on, "You want to sign up here? And that's my problem how?" when they entered. The prettier the candidate, the ruder the greeting.

The man looked panicked, took half a step back. He hadn't been expecting this kind of reception, and quite frankly, it scared him. The way she stuck her chest out and moistened her lips terrified him. It was visible on his face. He hadn't been expecting this at all. The man looked to his right, to Gabrielle, who recognized him and smiled at him. Then he looked straight ahead, at me. He raised his hand, pointed as he took another step away from the scary office assistant. "I'm here to see Kendra," he said.

"You *are?*" Janene replied. "*Why?*" Then she added, "I mean, oh, right. Can I take your name?"

"Why, haven't you got one of your own?" Kyle asked as he stepped around her and came over to my desk. "I was wondering if you were free for lunch?" he asked.

It was after twelve and I had nothing planned except to wander down the high street and look in a few shops. Nothing that couldn't wait. "Yeah, sure." I gathered my belongings and led the way out of the office, ignoring the dagger-filled glares from Janene, and Gabrielle's mentally raised, questioning eyebrow.

Outside it was raining. Light rain leeched the color out of Brockingham and made it seem a greyer place than it was. Kyle turned up the collar on his beige raincoat and I rummaged in my bag for my umbrella before we set off.

"Do you want to go somewhere in particular?" I asked.

"No, not really. Would you mind if we just walked around for a bit?"

"Sure."

We wandered over the slick cobblestones of the pedestrianized high street, heading away from home, out towards the park. Side by side, my umbrella reaching Kyle's head. People ran or walked quickly around us, determined not to get wet, not to give in to the weather. I knew the bottoms of my trousers were probably soaking up rainwater because they were too long for me. It was warm out, despite the rain, but I still felt like huddling up inside my red mac. It seemed appropriate.

"I guess I owe you an explanation," Kyle said as we turned the corner onto the road where the train station and the tram stop were. Up the slight hill and then down the other side we would hit the park. "I've been avoiding you for the past couple of weeks."

"Have you?" I replied. "I hadn't noticed."

I felt his eyes dart to me to see if I was ribbing him, which I was, so I smiled.

"I don't know how to talk about it. I've never done it before. I've only said that Ashlyn's an alcoholic once and that was to Ashlyn. Some things are easier if you don't give them a name."

True. Very true.

"I don't know when it started. It probably wouldn't be helpful if I did. That day you found me drunk on the sofa was the first time I'd had a drink in more than three years. That's probably why it hit me so hard. And those bottles were Ashlyn's. She got clean awhile back, but I knew she hadn't cleared out all her bottles." Kyle started to pick at the nails of his left hand with his right hand. "When I had that row with her on the phone, I was so angry—incensed. I wanted to remind myself why I shouldn't give the kids to her and that I hadn't imagined all that had happened. She's so reasonable now it's hard to remember what she could be like. What a complete hell it was. So I went looking for the bottles she'd hidden around the house. Guess I found the reminder I needed. They were hidden everywhere. Not just full ones, empties as well."

Kyle stopped in the middle of the street, turned to me. He was getting wet so I raised my umbrella, held it over him. "It broke my heart when you said the kids had hidden the bottles in your flat. They must have watched their mother do it. She used to hide the empties rather than throw them in the bin because I'd get mad at her if I saw them. They probably thought you'd get mad at me if you saw what I'd drunk."

We started walking again, Kyle taking the umbrella from me so he could hold it high over both of us. A gentle breeze blew raindrops at us, but in the main it was pleasant. "Her drinking cost us a lot. The reason we had to rent out the flat wasn't because she'd left, it was because she'd stopped working. It was awhile before I realized—she was always over at her studio and I thought she had some projects on the go. I thought she was paying the bills with the money she was earning. Then I discovered she hadn't been. She'd lost most of her clients because her work was so shoddy or late. She'd gone through most of her savings and couldn't hide the extent of our debt anymore. I'd been demoted and when I was given the chance to work from home more I took it and so didn't get as much money as I used to, so I told her that we'd have to rent out the flat. Either that or ask her mother for a loan, which she'd never do.

"The reason I don't want the kids going on public transport is because there was a time when they were being verbally attacked on the way home. Ashlyn was really cagey about the details, had told them not to tell me because it'd upset me. But it turns out that after she got onto the stage at a Christmas play—she was drunk and I was at work so I couldn't stop her—the kids were being bullied a bit. Ashlyn told the girl playing Mary she was a troll compared to Summer. The bullying died down quickly because Summer and Jaxon are always together and stick up for each other—and basically, you don't want to mess with them when they're together. But the girl's mother started following them on the bus home, screaming at them. She didn't take a pop at Ashlyn, just the kids. They had to get the bus because I'd taken Ashlyn's car keys off her awhile back because she was constantly driving drunk. I only found out about the abuse because our neighbor witnessed one of the incidents and dropped it into conversation."

We reached the edge of the park, and started down the path that wound through the blanket of emerald green. We walked slowly, our footsteps moving in time. I tried not to breathe too loudly; sometimes the level of Kyle's voice dipped so low that I had to strain to hear what he was saying.

"I wanted to explain as much as I could to you so that you'd understand why I do a lot of the things I do. And why the kids are so attached to you—they don't have a lot of friends or people they can trust beyond the three of us so they've latched onto you."

"You mean it's not my sparkling wit and incredible personality?"

Kyle's smile lit me up inside. We could still do humor. That was important. "No, unfortunately, not," he said.

"OK, I'll have to work on that."

"The kids adore you and I really am grateful for all you've done."

"It's not hard, you know, they're brilliant kids. And you're a great father."

Kyle said nothing. Instead he looked at me the way he did in Regent's Park, when he'd finally told me about Ashlyn's problem. He scanned my face as though trying to unearth my secrets. I glanced away, scared he might see something.

"Is he good enough for you?" he asked.

"Who's that then?" I asked, a little confused.

"This man in Australia."

I shrugged. "I think so. But then, I would, wouldn't I?" Kyle's wrist was exposed from where he held the umbrella and I caught a look at his watch. "Ah, damn, Kyle, I need to get back, do you mind?"

"Not at all," Kyle said and spun on his heels. He seemed so much lighter now that he'd told me this, as though sharing his secret had halved his burden.

"And Kyle, I want you to know that what you've just told me will go no further."

"I appreciate that," he replied with a grin. "I really do."

♦

I heard more stories about Ashlyn, the beautiful woman with caramel-colored hair, sparkling eyes, artistic talent and a drink problem.

Kyle told me about her vomiting on Summer. About her forgetting a doctor's appointment for Jaxon and remembering at the last minute, deciding to drive even though she'd been drinking, losing control of the car, mounting the curb and clipping a tree. She lied and said someone had crashed into her and sped away—it was Jaxon who told Kyle what really happened. I heard about her passing out one evening and leaving a pan on the stove when the kids were in bed and Kyle was working late. Luckily Kyle had come home before it caught fire. I found out about the many promises she made to take the children to places when she was drunk but completely forgot about when she was sober. I heard about the amount of times the children found her passed out and couldn't wake her.

Once he'd opened the floodgates to the past a deluge of the little slights that had gone on in their home came gushing through. One thing was evident from all of this: she wasn't always falling-down drunk, or always loud and mean, but she was constantly and consistently screwing up.

Kyle also told me how and why she decided to stop drinking.

"Do you want to know what the final straw was? What made me stand up to my wife and tell her enough was enough? It wasn't the crash with Jaxon in the car, it wasn't vomiting over Summer, it wasn't the dancing on the table at my work do. It wasn't falling asleep and leaving a pan on the stove. It wasn't getting a call at work because Ashlyn had passed out at home and had forgotten to collect the kids so I had to go. It was the day I walked into the kitchen and heard her tell Summer to shut up."

Kyle didn't look up from the blade of grass he was shredding between his forefingers and thumbs, his digits making light work of the thick, dark green vegetation. He kept his eyes lowered because he was embarrassed. In his mind it needed to be a dramatic event that made him take a stand. He didn't realize that often it was the smallest gesture, the most subtle look, the simplest words that could change everything. For me and Will it had been him opening a beer before he handed it to me that had made me fall in love with him.

"She was hungover. Had been drinking all the day before, and then when I got back unexpectedly early from a visit to a site she did her usual and switched to cola. Even though she hadn't had a chance to drink her usual amount, Saturday morning she was still very hungover. At eight-thirty she was sobering up and it hurt."

CHAPTER 22

*A*shlyn was sobering up and it hurt.

No one could understand how much it hurt. It was turning her inside out, ripping every nerve from her body, molecule by molecule. Kyle could see her agony. Her face was puffy, her skin an off-key green, her navy-green eyes marbled by encroaching sobriety, her hair, which she hadn't bothered to wash in a few days, hung in greasy clumps around her face. Breakfast had been quiet, Ashlyn's pain subduing everyone. The children, although only five, knew that it was important to be quiet in the mornings. Mumma liked the quiet in the mornings and if she didn't get it, she would be miserable.

Kyle had nothing to say to the mess of a woman in front of him. Ashlyn couldn't have talked if she wanted to. They ate their cereal and toast and drank their orange juice and tea in virtual silence, the only sounds the clink of cutlery against crockery, the slurps of drinks being drunk, the settling of items on the table. After everyone had eaten, Kyle had picked up his mug, which was half full of coffee, and escaped upstairs to his office.

He didn't have a project to work on—ever since the incident with the big project he hadn't been given anything of significance, but he needed to escape. He sat in his leather chair, flicked through a few trade journals, read the paper, listened to the radio. An hour or so later he ventured downstairs, knowing from how quiet the house was that Ashlyn's suffering hadn't ended and the kids were probably keeping out of her way. As he approached the kitchen he heard Summer's bright, lively voice *talking, chatting, questioning. Summer was an exhausting child, there was no mistaking it. She liked to talk. She liked to be answered. The ultimate in torture for Summer was to be ignored.*

Ashlyn stood at the sink, her back to Summer, her hands submerged in soapy water. She was dipping plates, giving them a cursory once-over with the soft yellow pad of the sponge, then dumping the plates on the metal rack with bad grace. *Why she was bothering Kyle didn't know.* Probably finding something else to bitch about, *he thought. Her life was so rotten, after all. That's why she drank. Everything, including him—especially* him—*was so awful she drank. He didn't know then, of course. He just blamed her, blamed himself and then blamed her again for making him blame himself.*

"But Mumma, why is the grass green?" Summer asked.

"Chlorophyll," Ashlyn croaked, harassed by her daughter's constant questioning. "It makes grass green."

"But why green, Mumma? Why not blue like the sky? Or yellow like the sun. Or pink like my party dress?"

Ashlyn inhaled deeply, irritated. "I don't know," she replied, her tone adding, "And I don't care."

"But Mumma . . ."

That was it for Ashlyn. Enough was enough. "Shut up, Summer," she snapped. She threw down the plate she was half-heartedly washing, dirty dishwater splashing out of the sink, slopping onto the kitchen floor, onto Ashlyn's suede skirt and cotton gypsy top, into the toes of her sandals. "Look what you made me do!" She indicated her soggy top and ruined skirt. "Shut up about grass. About the sea. About everything. Just shut up."

She swung her head to her daughter, glared bleary-eyed at the girl sitting at the table, raised a wet hand and moved it in a slight chopping motion to emphasize how serious she was. "Just shut up."

Summer froze. She knew her mother's voice when it was like this. She knew it could go either way right now. At times like this, Mumma would sometimes shout. Would sometimes take her arm and shake her. Would drag her and shut her in her bedroom until she did what she was told. Summer knew when Mumma had that look on her face and that tone in her voice that she had to be very quiet. Very careful. She had to stay away.

Ashlyn glared at her daughter, daring her to disobey.

Summer's bottom lip curled up into her mouth and she bit down on it. She didn't mean to be naughty. She didn't mean to make Mumma mad. She'd only wanted to know about colors. Dad was never there to ask and Mumma knew everything. Jaxon. She decided she needed to talk to Jaxon. To find out what he was doing and to ask him why she always made Mumma cross. He didn't seem to do it as much. She picked up Hoppy, the rabbit that had replaced Winter, her rag doll ruined by red vomit, and slid off her seat. Abandoning her drawing papers, her pens, her books, she wandered out into the garden, the last place she'd seen Jaxon head for. Jaxon would play with her. He'd explain to her why she was so naughty.

Ashlyn watched Summer leave the room and Kyle, who had been lurking unseen in the doorway, watched Ashlyn. A host of emotions was spreading throughout his body. He'd spent his childhood being told to shut up by his father. He'd spent all his youth being afraid to speak up, afraid of incurring wrath with the wrong word. That wasn't going to happen to Summer. No matter how annoying she was, she had the right to speak. Always.

He stepped into the room and the atmosphere became charged the second she saw him. A flicker of anxiety crossed her face, wondering whether he'd heard, and then it was re-placed by indignation: so what if he heard? She hadn't done anything wrong.

"This has got to stop," Kyle said, his voice a low growl. He

didn't know where the children were and he didn't want to scare them by shouting at Ashlyn.

"What?" she sneered, immediately on the defensive.

"Don't act dumb," Kyle said, his voice still low. "All of this has got to stop. You have got to stop doing this."

"Doing what?"

"You've just scared the living daylights out of Summer."

Ashlyn rolled her eyes. "Right, and you know how a five-year-old thinks, do you?"

"I don't need to know how a five-year-old thinks to know that you're terrorizing all of us because of your drinking and that I've had enough. This has got to stop."

"I'm terrorizing this family?" Ashlyn slapped her dripping wet hand against her chest, incredulous at what she was hearing. "At least I'm here," she spat. "At least I don't spend every spare second at work or hiding upstairs."

"Yes, at least you're here. You're here to drive the car drunk with our son in the back, and crash it into a tree, and pretend it didn't happen. You're here to throw up on our daughter in the middle of the night because you're so drunk but you don't bother to apologize. You're here to dance on the table at my last work party and then fall off and twist your ankle. You're here to make phone calls in the middle of the night to your mother but leave me to explain what they were about. Yes, you're here, Ashlyn, and aren't we all so grateful for it."

The indignation Ashlyn felt melted away into hard disbelief, made her angry. "I. Said. I. Was. Sorry," she hissed. Her body stiffened, her top lip curled back into a sneer. "Is that how you make yourself feel like a man, Kyle? Remembering every little thing I've ever done wrong?"

Is drinking how you feel like a woman? *Kyle almost spat back at her, but pulled himself up short, stopped himself. "If you were really sorry, Ashlyn, you'd stop drinking."*

Her eyes rolled upwards again and Kyle felt the urge to

shout at her. To tell her to stop acting like an oblivious teen-ager, to take this seriously.

"I don't drink that much," she said. "No more than any other normal person."

"Normal?" Kyle's voice rose a notch. He stepped forward, grabbed Ashlyn's arm. It was the first time he'd ever grabbed her like that. He tugged her towards the kitchen door, not look-ing at her shocked face, not caring that her body had gone stiff under his hold. Kyle wrestled the back door open, dragged her out into the light, not caring that she gasped and cringed at the brightness outside. He pulled her across the path outside their house, onto the lawn, then pulled her left towards Summer's cubby house, the large plywood hut that he'd designed and built. The red roof came off, the back of it had hinges that al-lowed it to be folded back like a concertina. Behind the cubby house was a flower bed that was planted with thick shrubbery and violets.

"That's normal is it?" Kyle spat, letting go of Ashlyn.

Amongst the greenery of the shrubs were five green bottles. Five green beer bottles carefully placed to blend in amongst the leaves. Ashlyn's heartbeat quickened. How had he found them? She'd only put them there temporarily. She couldn't very well put them in the recycling box because Kyle would see. She couldn't put them in the bin for the same reason. He wouldn't understand. He didn't understand. He didn't know what it was like and all he did was look down on her so she had to hide the evidence. And not even in the studio because she suspected he went looking through there, too. This was her temporary hiding place, you couldn't see them unless you were looking. And why was he looking? Why was he always checking up on her? Making her feel bad. It wasn't like she was doing anything wrong.

"Hiding bottles is normal, is it?" Kyle repeated.

"I wouldn't have to hide them if you weren't such a drink

Nazi," Ashlyn accused. *"You're always on my case every time I even look at a drink so I have to hide them. If you didn't do that, I wouldn't have to do that."*

For a moment, Kyle wavered, wondered if she was right. If he didn't always notice when she drank, would she be hiding the bottles and sneaking over to her studio to drink? Would she be that bad if he wasn't that bad? Stop it, *he told himself.* Stop it. She drank too much. Normal people could stop after a couple. Normal people could go for a few days without needing a drink. Normal people didn't* need *a drink. Normal people don't commit so many crimes against their loved ones and their own personal values while under the influence or coming down from the influence* and still go back for more.

Kyle's wife was an alcoholic.

Every time he thought the word, what came to mind was an old man with grime-smeared features, dirt-encrusted clothes, sitting in the gutter, swigging from a can of extra strength. The reality was an alcoholic was his bright, vivacious wife—the woman who could stop a room simply by walking into it, who could walk around the supermarket in jogging bottoms and sloppy T-shirt and blend in, who had given birth to his two children.

The woman Kyle loved was an alcoholic. He had to accept that. After all this time he had to accept that. She had to accept that. He had to force her to accept that. This was the moment he had to step up. Stop pretending the life they'd been living these past few years was fine. He owed it to Jaxon. He owed it to Summer. He owed it to himself. He owed it to Ashlyn.

"It's not my fault," Kyle stated, *steeling himself. "It's not my fault. You're an alcoholic, Ashlyn."*

She rolled her eyes, shook her head.

"You're an alcoholic," he repeated. *"You have to get help."*

"Grow up," she spat and turned on her heels and marched

back into the house, slamming the kitchen door behind her. Kyle stared after her. Not sure of what to do. He didn't want to argue with her, but he'd started on this path. He'd started on this path of honesty so he had to follow it and see what lay at the end.

Her hands were submerged in the washing up again. She lifted a plate, snatched up the sponge and started scrubbing at it.

"Ashlyn—"

"I don't want to talk about this anymore," she interjected. "You've obviously got some sort of problem and you're trying to push it onto me."

"If you don't get help, I want you to leave," Kyle said, only a touch above a whisper. He wanted to know what it sounded like out loud. He'd never said it aloud. It was something that had crossed his mind a few times, but had been fleeting and whimsical. He had never grabbed hold of it and held it, turned it over, run the fingers of his mind over the grooves of the words, examined it and got to know it. Got to know what the meanings behind the words were. What every word would result in.

He said it quietly, but she heard. She heard and she gasped. Ashlyn threw down the plate, not caring this time that water splashed out onto her. She spun to look at her husband. He was standing perfectly still, his feet placed firmly on the varnished wood floor, his arms folded across his chest. He'd lost weight, she realized. She hadn't looked at him properly for months. Why would she look at him when he was always there? He was a presence, one that was part of her life; a shape, a form that answered if she asked a question, who asked questions and waited for a reply, but didn't need close scrutiny. Every day she'd been sleeping beside this man and he'd changed. Kyle had lost weight and she hadn't realized. His face was thinner, he had shadows under his eyes, he'd had his hair cut, not razored *but shorter. And he was missing something. His confidence? His laid-back air? The light in his eyes? Whatever it was that made him Kyle had gone. Had it disappeared overnight, or seeped out over the past few months when she hadn't been looking? A thought niggled at her conscience: maybe it was something to do with her. Maybe she had done it. No, that was nonsense. It wasn't her fault. If Kyle had changed, it was down to him. And she resented him for making her think it could be her fault. Yes, he'd changed, he made her feel rotten. All the time he made her feel rotten. He used to make her feel wonderful, he used to complete her. She used to think she'd die without him. Now he just made her feel awful. Is it any wonder she needed a drink or two? When this man did that to her?*

"What did you say?" she breathed.

"I said . . . ," Kyle hesitated, could he say it again? Could he go through with this? "I said . . . I said . . ." He bit down inside, of course he could go through with it. He had to. "I said if you don't get help I want you to leave. I'm not putting the kids through this anymore. I'm not going through this anymore. Get help or leave."

"You think I'm going to leave the kids here with you? You'd go crazy in a minute."

"We'd work it out. You have to get help, Ashlyn. I don't want you to leave, I want you to get help. But if you don't, then I want you to leave."

"You can't have the kids," she said.

"No one would give you custody, not with all the things you've done while you've been drinking."

"It's called a residency order, actually," she snarled. "It's not called custody, it's called a residency order. How do I know that? Because I wanted to leave you before. When I was doing everything and you were doing nothing, I wondered if it wouldn't be better if you weren't here permanently. So I found out about it. But I'm not like you, I wouldn't go through with

it. Because no matter how much of a shit you are, I wouldn't hurt you like you obviously have no problems hurting me."

Kyle didn't even flinch. He was like a pillar of rock. Nothing she said could penetrate this exterior. Not for the first time she wondered what she had to do to get through to him. He seriously didn't give a damn that she was going to leave him. He didn't give a damn that she decided not to. He didn't give a damn about anything to do with her. Had he ever?

"And they would give them to me, Kyle, because I'm here for them. I work around them, I work half the night so that I can be here during the day. I make their meals, I pick them up when they fall over. I'm always there when they go to bed. I love them. Of course I'll get the kids, because I'm their mother."

"So why don't you try acting like it? Put them first for a change." His arms folded tightly across his chest, Kyle spun on his heels and walked out.

She couldn't know. She couldn't know that he'd almost said he didn't mean it. That he couldn't live without her and the kids. That he was nothing without her. She couldn't know that the idea of her leaving him was something he couldn't bear. Those days when she took Jaxon and Summer to visit her mother he thought he'd go crazy at the quiet in the house, that he'd wander from room to room, sitting on their beds, picking up their toys, hugging their clothes, remembering their conversations. She couldn't know that if she didn't get help, he might not be able to make her leave.

———

"It was OK for a while, after that. Surprisingly. She went to meetings for alcoholics. The very next day. I think I'd scared her as much as she scared me with her admission. She went to meetings every day and stopped drinking. I don't know why, but I thought it'd get magically better. You know, she stops drinking, all our problems go away.

"Not exactly like that. She was in a permanent bad mood, almost like a permanent hangover. But at least she wasn't drinking. We started arguing more, but at least we were communicating." Kyle rolled onto his back, spread himself out on the picnic blanket, stared deep into the sky as though he wanted to be there. As though his place was amongst the clouds rather than here on earth with me and the kids. "Then I messed up." His eyes glazed over as he immersed himself further in the world above us. He sighed.

"Boy did I mess up. She asked me to come to some meetings with her. But . . ." His voice trailed away. I watched him. He was obviously suffering as he remembered. "Couldn't do it, Kendra. The thought of sitting there, listening to people talk about why they drank. Why it was their partner's fault. I didn't want to hear it. I didn't want someone looking at me sitting beside her and judging me."

"I don't think that's how it works," I said. "They don't apportion blame to anyone."

"No, it probably isn't. But I didn't want to find out. I judged myself for not saying something sooner about what she was doing. I judged myself, I didn't need anyone else to do it."

"And it was a way of making sure she got her punishment, making her go to meetings with the threat of losing everything hanging over her," I said.

Kyle turned to me, eyed me with trepidation. Wondering if I was condemning him.

"Not judging you," I added. "I mean, she put you through hell, Kyle, you wouldn't be human if you weren't pissed off with her. And not that keen on helping her out, even if it meant she was getting better. She became an alcoholic alone, why shouldn't she get better alone? And, if you're blaming yourself on top of that, I'm not surprised you didn't want to go along."

"I did want her to get better. And I helped as much as I could—I didn't drink, I asked her how the meetings were going, asked her how she was feeling. But I couldn't do what she wanted. I couldn't help her in that way.

"When I said no, Ashlyn thought I'd betrayed her. That I'd forced her to do this thing and now I wasn't supporting her. We had a few rows about it, nothing over the top, more low-level ones. No real shouting, just sniping. We stopped talking except if it was about the things to do with the kids. Then, one night, she just didn't come to bed. Then another night, and another. I think it was Summer who asked her why she wasn't in the big bed anymore—I sure as hell wasn't going to ask—and she said she'd been working all night and had fallen asleep in the studio. I didn't say anything, and that became the way things were—she basically moved into the studio permanently. That's why the children know how to open the door and to come on over anytime—they started going over there in the mornings to see her. And then one morning she was gone. She'd moved out. Gone in the middle of the night. Except Jaxon had seen her. He'd had a bad dream and was awake when she came in to his room to say good-bye. Summer was asleep in our bed so she didn't say good-bye to her. But Jaxon, who liked to sleep in his own bed, was awake. She told him not to say anything. And he took her literally and stopped talking. Two days later she called wanting to see the kids. Not me, just the kids. So I dropped them off at her mother's place—she wasn't staying there but didn't want me to know where she was staying so asked me to leave them there. The next time I saw her was a few weeks later when we went to New York."

He exhaled deeply. "If I could go back in time, I'd just go to the meetings with her."

"It might not have made any difference," I said.

"But at least then I'd know."

"True. How about the next time she's back you tell her you'll go to meetings with her?"

He turned his head to me. "It's too late now."

"Even if you were divorced it wouldn't be too late—if you wanted it to work out. If you wanted to try anything to make it work."

I could see him thinking it over. As he thought I caught sight of the children running in our direction. Was it my imagination or had they grown several meters in the past few days? All right, maybe not meters, but their bodies looked longer, as though they were both going to take after their father when it came to height. Jaxon arrived first and threw himself bodily onto his father. Kyle, who hadn't been expecting it, was winded by the blow and made an *ouf* sound as he almost doubled up. Seconds later Summer was on top of him as well and he was flailing under his children, all of them laughing. In a few hours, Ashlyn would call. Then they would become transformed, they'd stop laughing and joking, they'd go and hide in their rooms, devastated that their mumma wasn't here, devastated she was another world away.

Kyle owed it to them, really, to try everything. And if that meant going to meetings with his wife then that's what he had to do. Isn't that what for better or worse meant?

SPANISH OMELETTE

◆ ◆ ◆

Oh, Kendra, there's a message for you," Janene said to me. She was using her normal voice. The one with which she spoke to Gabrielle and Teri. It immediately made me suspicious. It'd been an age since we'd gone camping and her silent threat to get me back hadn't materialized.

"Your phones rang when you were in the loo so I took a message. Forgot to give it to you." I'd been to the loo over an hour ago. It was probably an important client who expected to be called back within fifteen minutes. This was her revenge, trying to lose me business.

She came across the office, her flat, beady eyes not receiving the message that her face was "smiling" at me. She handed me the note.

Mrs. Chelner, she'd written, along with a mobile number. She'd also printed URGENT, and carefully scored under it three times. She cocked her eyebrow a fraction as she waited for me to fall apart. To rip the phone from its cradle and dial frantically. Our business worked on maintaining good relationships and running an efficient service. Either this person needed a temp quickly or the temp they had wasn't working out. Whatever the situation, they were not going to be impressed by an unreturned phone call. *Bitch.*

"Thanks for that," I said smiling sweetly and placing the yellow square on the desk. No way was I giving her the satisfaction of being riled about this. I'd probably already lost the business, wasn't going to add to my distress by giving Janene even a splinter of pleasure.

Gritting her teeth, unimpressed—veritably peeved—that she hadn't managed to get a rise out of me, she turned on her LK Bennett heels and stalked back to her desk. Gabrielle was monitoring all of this from her desk, even though to the outside world she was still typing away on her computer. If she was honest—as she had been with me once—she wasn't particularly enamoured with Janene, but she wanted to give the girl a chance. She thought that with understanding and training, she could mold Janene into a decent worker—the irony of course being that Gabrielle thought *I* was queen of the lost cause. Teri was staring open-mouthed at Janene's audacity. She had confessed to me that she didn't like Janene, but did her best to get on with her so as not to upset the office dynamic. We all, in our own ways, pandered to Janene's bad behavior like overindulgent parents pandered to a brat for a quiet life. That annoyed me more than I cared to admit to anyone, myself included. I hated people getting away with bad behavior.

Mrs. Chelner. I groped around my memory to place her. The name seemed familiar, but the company wasn't immediately coming to mind. As I ransacked my brain, what Janene had said replayed itself in my head.

"Did you say my *phones* rang?" I asked her.

"Yeah," Janene said. "Your mobile kept ringing so I turned it off. It's in your top drawer."

I will not let you get to me, I thought at her, *because that is what you want.* I'd sat here for over an hour with my mobile off. That wouldn't be so bad if I'd turned it off, but for someone else to do it . . . I opened the top drawer and picked up my silver phone. Calmly, not revealing even a sliver of the irritation that was building inside me, I turned it on and dialed my answer machine.

I had six messages. Six. They'd obviously been calling and calling and not getting hold of me. Inhaling deeply, taking in tranquillity and exhaling the urge to go slap Janene into April next year, I listened to the first message.

Mrs. Chelner had a very soothing voice. You could tell she was a person who could put "calm under pressure" on her CV or on an application form without feeling guilty that she'd never actually been tested. She *had* been in a highly charged, stressful situation where she needed to keep herself and everyone in her immediate vicinity from coming apart at the seams, and she hadn't even begun to panic. Mrs. Chelner really could be calm under pressure.

Take now, for example: she was calling me, had called me more than eight times, to tell me that Jaxon had had an accident and they were taking him to the hospital. And could I possibly meet them there because they hadn't been able to get hold of Kyle, Ashlyn or their grandmother and I was the fourth person on their contact list.

Well, of course you can't get hold of Kyle, he's at the bank trying to rework his finances and get a loan because he's so broke at the moment. He'll have turned off his mobile, I thought as I hung up the phone and stowed it in the depths of my bag. *And you can't get hold of Ashlyn because she's in New York,* I told the Mrs. Chelner in my mind as I switched off my computer. *And you can't get hold of Naomi because she's on holiday in the Algarve,* I thought as I stood up.

And, I thought as I slipped on my raincoat, *you couldn't get hold of me because someone wanted revenge on me and turned off my mobile and didn't give me your message.*

"Gabrielle," I said, sounding very far away to myself. Far away, and so shocked, so scared, I couldn't engage in any other emotion. "Is it OK if I have the rest of the day off? Jaxon has had an accident and I need to go to the hospital. They didn't say on any of the messages if he was OK or how serious it was, but they can't get hold of Kyle and there's no one else. I suspect Summer will be a bit worried."

My boss, my friend, Gabrielle went white; even her lips lost their color. Teri's face did the exact same thing even though she hadn't met him. I knew what they were both thinking. How scared they both were. They didn't need to be—I had enough of that for all three of us. "Send him my love," Gabrielle whispered.

"I really hope I can do that," I said placidly.

I didn't even look at Janene as I left.

The last time I saw Will he was doing this, I thought as I walked down the high street towards the main road where I could hail a taxi. He was heading for a hospital not knowing what he was going to find.

————

After his wife made him leave, he didn't come running to me. Far from it. I hadn't heard from him for three months, which was nothing new. We were so inconsistent, always trying to stay away from each other, that months without contact was normal. The first I knew that he and his wife weren't together anymore was when I received a white envelope from a solicitor.

Upon unfolding the letter I discovered they were writing to inform me that when Mrs. Craigwood filed for divorce in just under a year, she was going to name me as a corespondent. She was going to tell the world that I was the slut who had slept with her husband and had ruined her marriage and, by default, her life.

This is what being involved with a married person means, *she was telling me in that letter.* This is what you get for sleeping with my husband.

Except, I hadn't slept with her husband. Not in that sense. I'd spent a few hours curled up beside him, but I didn't make love to him nor did I have sex with him. In eighteen months I'd kissed him on three different occasions. We were more friends than anything else.

A few hours later Will showed up at my apartment. He'd never been there before, but he, like his wife, seemed to have found out where I lived. It was far too easy to find someone in Sydney. Far too easy.

"What's going on?" I asked him as he sat on my sofa.

That's when he told me what had happened, that his wife had found an e-mail and that he'd been staying with his sister. He hadn't wanted to come to me because he didn't want to lay this at my door, make it my problem. He'd only come now because his wife had rung him and told him what she'd done. He'd been hoping to get to me and have the chance to explain before I got the letter.

"But why didn't you tell her we weren't sleeping together?" I asked.

"I thought I had," he replied. "I said I wasn't sleeping with anyone else."

"So why did she come after me like this?" I asked, staring at the letter. "She must hate me. All her friends—your friends— are going to hate me. Evangeline's already pissed off like you wouldn't believe; this is going to make her go mental."

"My friends won't hate you. And Sarie doesn't hate you."

"Are you sure about that?" I waved the A4 sheet with two precise, neatly spaced folds in it, at him. "Are you sure about that?"

My whole body seemed to catch fire—the burning sensation was localized in my cheeks and I pressed the palms of my hands on them to try to cool them.

"This is such a nightmare. It's going to be on record what I've done. That I'm 'the other woman.' If anyone ever does a search on me this is what will come up. No one's going to listen

to me when I say we just kissed. They'll think I'm a whore." All I'd done was fall in love and now I was going to be forever marked as a homewrecker. It wouldn't matter that the home was pretty much wrecked before I came along, that I didn't mean for this to happen, that I hadn't had sex with him.

"I'm sorry, Kendra. You don't deserve this."

Will looked so tired: his beautiful face sprinkled with stubble, his hair an ebony mess on his head, his suit crumpled. He must have been going through hell.

My arms slipped around him, took him close to me, stayed still to feel his heart beating against my body. "Don't say sorry. I mean, where was this going to end? I didn't want you to leave your family, you didn't want to leave your family. It's not like we were planning for the future or having sex in the present," I said. "But it wasn't pure friendship so we have to take responsibility for that. We were walking a very precarious line and this is what happens."

His breath fell on my neck as he sighed and I felt my body responding as it always did to him. I was coming alive. My heart starting to race, my breathing deepening, my knees weakening, my core becoming a soft, melting pool of desire. He was the only man who'd ever done this to me. To make my body crave being touched. Most of the time—all of the time—I couldn't bear to be that close to another human being, I couldn't stomach another person's body close to mine, nor hands touching me. If they did I had to hide my revulsion and fake being interested in physical intimacy. It was easier than explaining why I'd rather be left alone.

His body began to respond to mine. I could feel his heart-beat increasing as his hand moved slowly and gently over my curves. I closed my eyes and inhaled him, took him in whole. I was suddenly drunk on him. Intoxicated with longing. I got up, took his hand and led him towards my bedroom. He didn't resist, didn't protest. We could now. He was single. Everyone *thought we had. It would go down on record that we had, so we might as well. Plus, I wanted to. I was aching to. For the first time ever I was desperate to.*

His mouth was on mine, my hands ran over his chest. I slipped off his jacket, he pulled off my top. In between deep, lingering kisses I unbuttoned his shirt, he unhooked my bra. The smell of him filled the room, the taste of wanting him filled my body. And yet . . .

"I can't do it," he said suddenly, stepping away from me.

"Neither can I," I replied. I held my bra over my chest as relief washed through me. I'd been trying to work myself up to it, but I couldn't. It was easy to say we might as well do the crime we were going to do the time for, but the reality was it didn't work like that. I couldn't. Wanted to, longed to, but couldn't. "It feels like you're still married."

"I know," he replied, stepping forwards and lightly running his thumbs along the outline of my jaw. "And I am. But it feels like I'm still with my wife."

"I know, and despite what that piece of paper says, I don't want to sleep with a married man."

"We're a right pair of plonkers, aren't we?" he said.

I laughed, I hadn't heard that in an age. Even British people over here didn't say that.

"I'd say we're more like a pair of wallies," I replied. And he laughed.

We lay on the bed and Will took me in his arms, resting his head on my chest, listening to my heart. "I want to hear you," he said. "I want to hear how you feel." One of the things I loved about him was his ability to be joking one minute and in the next, saying things so emotional. He had no problems with being honest about his feelings with me.

I ran my fingers through the fine black shards of his hair, enjoying this. Sliding easily into this part of just being together.

"I want to hear if your heart starts bitching to your lungs

that you don't eat enough salads because you don't like cold food . . . Oh, I think your lungs are saying you don't get enough fresh air . . . Ah, yes, now your liver's piped up. It's asking your heart how it feels about that British git . . . And hark at your spleen, giving it some. It's saying it reckons that the British git is in love with you."

"Well there you go," I replied. "Of all my organs my spleen has always been the most over-optimistic. Silly thing."

"Nah, I think it's spot on."

"Well you listen to my heart and hear what it has to say on the matter."

Will was silent for a moment, then snatched his head away from my chest as though he'd been burnt. "I regret to inform you, Ms. Tamale, but your heart is filthy! The things it was saying . . ."

I went to laugh, and he stopped me by stroking his thumb over the well of my cheek and the outline of my lips. "I could do this forever," he said seriously. "I could be with you forever."

His mobile broke into the moment, sliced into our intimate circle. He hesitated, toyed with the idea of not answering it. And then he peeled himself away from me, reached off the bed for his jacket and retrieved it. Flipped it open and put it to his ear.

He said hello. And then there was silence. A deathly silence that seemed to stop time.

He cried out. A deep, feral shout that came from a place of pain. It rang through the room, reverberated through my body.

"I'll be there," he said loudly, his voice wild and urgent. "I'll be there." He hung up without saying good-bye. "She tried to kill herself," he said. "Sarie tried to kill herself." He was off the bed, buttoning up his shirt, pulling on his jacket, all the while shaking. "Because of me," he kept saying. "Because of me."

No, I wanted to say to him. In the fifteen years they were together she'd never tried to kill herself; no matter how bad things got, she never tried to kill herself. She didn't do that until he met me. Not because of him. Because of me.

"I'll call you," he said, as he headed for the door.

"No, don't," I said to him. "Just don't. I can't, not after this. Don't get in touch with me again."

He stopped, turned and took my face in his warm, gentle hands. "I'll call you," he repeated, earnestly, looking deep into my eyes. "I'll call you."

The door shut behind him and I knew I couldn't see him again.

Two days later I got the e-mail from Gabrielle asking if I wanted a job back in England.

CHAPTER 24

Summer was sitting beside Mrs. Chelner in the emergency room.

They were in the front row of seats, closest to the reception desk, sitting side by side in silence. Her feet didn't come anywhere near to the ground. She looked tiny, a fragile little doll dressed in a blue and grey school uniform, who seemed incomplete without her blue rabbit in her arms and her brother at her side. She leapt off her seat and came to me as I approached them. Her hand curled into mine and clung on. She didn't say anything, but I was someone she knew in all of this, so she held on for dear life.

She didn't realize I was clinging onto her, too, relieved and grateful she at least was OK.

Mrs. Chelner, an older woman with grey-streaked brown hair secured back in a bun, a blue coat that she wore zipped up and a very matronly manner, stood up. "You must be Kendra Tamale," she said to me.

She didn't smile and I felt my heart dip. A smile would have meant he was OK; a smile would have meant "He's going to be just fine."

"How is he?" I asked, aware of Summer's cold hand trembling in mine, or was it my hand trembling around hers?

"We're waiting to hear," she replied. "They're not willing to release any information to anyone other than a relative, but he was never in any serious danger. I don't think it's going to be anything more serious than a broken arm and concussion."

"Can we see him?" I asked.

She looked uncertain. "You're not a family member are you?" she said gently.

No, I'm not. "In the absence of his father and his mother and his grandmother I'm kind of responsible for him," I said.

She didn't look convinced. "We were just waiting for his father. All we could get out of Summer is that her mother was a long time away, on a plane."

Summer knew where her mother was, but the shock had probably erased the knowledge from her mind. "She's in New York."

Mrs. Chelner nodded.

Despite what she had said about me not being a relative, I decided to try with the receptionist. I didn't want Jaxon to be alone. Not when his sister and I were there. Summer and I walked the short distance to the long reception desk, waited patiently in line to be seen.

"I wanted to see Jaxon Gadsborough." I said. "He was brought in about two hours ago, suspected broken arm and concussion."

She tapped into her keyboard, looked at the computer screen as Jaxon's details came up.

"And you are?" she asked.

"I'm Kendra Tamale," I replied.

"Are you a relative?"

I paused. I didn't want to lie. I tried to avoid lying at all costs, even felt uncomfortable telling so-called "white lies," but the thought of him lying there all alone, scared and in pain . . . "Sort of," I said.

The receptionist's face gave me a closed-lip smile. "Sort

of" wasn't good enough. "Sort of" wasn't going to get me to see him.

"Kendie's my other mumma," Summer piped up suddenly to the receptionist. "She lives in my house and she makes me and Jaxon special Saturday breakfast. It tastes like marshmallows."

"Really?" the receptionist asked Summer. She replied with three short, decisive nods. I could see the receptionist wasn't buying it, but she could see my worry and Summer was Jaxon's relative and I was with Summer. And he was only six. She called a nurse to show us into the back of the emergency room, saying that they wouldn't be able to release any medical information, but if we wanted to wait in the back until Jaxon's parents arrived, then that would be OK.

"What happened?" I asked Summer as we followed the nurse past the empty cubicles and cubicles with drawn curtains. I hadn't found out in all this time. Hadn't thought to ask.

"He fell," she said quietly.

"Off what?"

"He fell. We were climbing and he fell." Her little face crumpled and she stopped walking and I crouched down to her height. She was so incredibly pale, her face streaked with tears. "He fell. He fell." She'd been there, had seen it. Had witnessed the one person who'd always been with her during her mother's drinking and her dad's flakiness being hurt right in front of her. I could imagine it. One moment he was next to her on the climbing frame, the next he wasn't. She must have looked down and seen him lying motionless on the ground. Maybe she called his name but, like her mother on countless occasions, and her father a few months ago, he didn't reply. I scooped Summer up. Held her close. "He fell.

He fell," she kept repeating as I rubbed the center of her back, tried to soothe her. I told her it was OK and we carried on walking towards her little brother.

He was asleep.

He lay flat on his back, a few bruises slowly turning red on the left side of his pale torso from where he'd landed, a graze on his cheek, another on his temple. His left wrist was propped up away from him in a splint and whorls of his dark hair were plastered to his forehead. He looked so peaceful, calm, still. I wanted to touch his face to check that he was warm and still with us. That he was really only sleeping.

Still holding onto Summer, who had buried her face in my neck, we sat down on the chair on his right side. The nurse pulled the curtain around us, shutting out the world and enveloping us in a pale yellow cocoon.

"We're here," I told her. "We're with Jaxon."

Now that we were with her brother, she turned around and sat on my lap, staring at him. I wondered what she thought. If she counted the ribs faintly outlined in his chest, or wanted to touch the bruises on his skin.

"Is Jaxon going to wake up?" she asked me quietly when she'd stared long and hard at him.

"Yes," I replied with conviction. "He just needs to sleep now. Sleeping helps him to get better."

She nodded. Without another word to me, she clambered onto her feet on my lap and I had to steady her as she pulled herself over the rail surrounding Jaxon's bed, curled herself up in the space between his body and the metal bars. "I'm going to sleep," she told me. "So Jaxon can get better." She closed her eyes. Not knowing what else to do, I moved my chair closer to the bed, took Jaxon's limp hand in one hand and Summer's hand in the other.

And sat watching them sleep.

I must have gone into a trance or fallen asleep with my eyes open.

The next thing I remembered, the curtain was being moved aside and Kyle stepped through the gap. He stopped short, shoved his hands into the short curls of his hair. "Ah, mate, mate," he said, quietly, staring at Jaxon's arm, his bruised body, his marked, motionless face. "*Mate.*" I let go of their hands and allowed their father to step into the breach, into his rightful place. He rested his hand on Summer's back and stroked his other hand over Jaxon's forehead. They were both still asleep.

"You know what my tattoos are of?" he asked, even though he hadn't acknowledged my presence at all. "They're Summer and Jaxon's names in binary code. That's why there's one on each arm. If I ever lost either of them, you might as well chop my arm off because I'd be useless without them." He shook his head slightly. "I can't believe I wasn't there when they needed me."

"You weren't to know," I replied.

"This is what I used to panic about. That I'd get the call saying Ashlyn had wrapped the car around a tree or there'd been a fire and that I'd lost them.

"They're all the family I've got," he said. "I don't see much of my brothers. My dad died a decade ago and I never got on with him. And my mum remarried some bastard who was always leching over other women, including Ashlyn. Didn't want him anywhere near me or her or our kids. They're all I've got."

"Well, they're going to be fine," I said, sounding more

positive than I'd felt in all the time since I picked up Mrs. Chelner's message. "Jaxon's going to be fine—I'm sure he'll love having a cast on his arm—and Summer's only sleeping because it'll make Jaxon get better."

"They're all I've got," he repeated, staring at them.

When the doctor arrived to talk about Jaxon's condition, I went to step out, but Kyle asked me to stay. He'd taken Summer off the bed and was holding onto her. While the doctor explained that they'd probably keep Jaxon in for a few more hours because he lost consciousness for a few minutes at the scene of the accident, and that he had a clean break of the wrist and very mild concussion, and could go home after his cast had been set, the pale semicircles of Jaxon's eyelids began to flutter as he started to wake up.

We all stopped and watched him as he slowly felt his way back into the waking world.

His pale lips began moving as he stirred and as his eyes came fully open, he said, "Mumma?"

It was the middle of the night by the time I drove us home.

Kyle sat in the back between the kids, who were both out for the count, and we didn't speak much. He'd rung Ashlyn while we were waiting for Jaxon to be discharged, and they didn't row this time. They couldn't because she became hysterical and was all for jumping on a plane there and then. Kyle had calmed her down and said Jaxon was fine, but if she did want to come back, the kids would love to see her, of course. His phone battery had died halfway through the call and he'd used mine to call her back to say he'd call her when he got home.

I carried Summer and Kyle carried Jaxon up to his bedroom and after carefully changing them into their pjs, we settled them both in the middle of the bed putting them together as they might have slept before birth—facing each other, heads down, knees up.

Kyle stood perfectly still, gazing down at his children, marveling, I think, at how close he came to losing them. How easily this could have ended badly. How he couldn't bear to be without them.

"Don't go back to the flat tonight, Kendra," he said, still staring at his kids. "Stay here. You can sleep on that side of the bed, I'll sleep on this side. I won't touch you or try to touch you, I swear."

It wasn't that that I was worried about. It concerned me a little, obviously, but if I slept here . . . If I stayed with the children this time, in this bed, like it was a normal thing to do, how would I be able to go back to the flat? Back to sleeping alone? I shook my head. "I can't," I said to him. "I'm sorry, but I can't. I'd love to, and I do believe you when you say you won't try anything, but I can't."

He nodded, as though half expecting that answer but hoping he wouldn't get it. "OK."

I touched his arm gently on my way out, accepted his thank-yous and made the long walk across the courtyard.

If I'd stayed, I could have found out. I could have found out, for those short hours, what it felt like to be a wife and mother.

I could have found out what it was like to be the first person a little boy asks for when he wakes up from a long sleep.

EGGS, BACON, TOAST, HASH BROWNS & BLACK PUDDING

◆　◆　◆

CHAPTER 25

As we moved further into summer and the days got longer, the weather grew warmer and the air felt alive with possibilities, my life with the Gadsboroughs seemed to become almost permanent. As though I belonged with them and nowhere else.

I loved it. I loved being with Summer and Jaxon and their father. I'd already started reordering my life to fit in with them, and they made room for me. There was never any question of me slotting into the hole their mother and wife had left. I avoided thinking about Summer calling me her "other mumma" and simply enjoyed the place I had with them.

The arrangement to pick the kids up from school once or twice a week, bring them home, leave them with Kyle and return to work became permanent. On days he was working on-site I'd fix it so I'd go in early and stay late other days, then leave work early and spend the afternoon with them. All calls would be diverted to my mobile, I'd pick up e-mails at home. Gabrielle was understanding that I had to rework my hours to pick up the kids, but that's because I made up the time. In fact, I worked more than the required hours to make up for it. She'd often call, "See you tomorrow, super mum," as I was leaving.

On our afternoons together we'd do their homework, we'd detour via the park and run around, we'd sit and watch after-school television, we'd play computer games, we'd sometimes lie in the middle of their playroom, being starfish and talking. A few times back at my flat we moved the dining table into the kitchen area and we had a campout in my living room.

I started to think about Will again. Only in little moments, when I wanted to tell him something Summer and Jaxon did or said, but he was there in my mind. In my head. I didn't freeze in fear whenever he came to mind. It took a little longer each time for the urge to throw up to overwhelm me whenever I looked at his letter.

Slowly he was allowed into my life again. Very slowly, in the tiniest increments, but I didn't shut down whenever I thought of him. And that was because I was happy. This happiness, this sense of strength and hope I got from being around Summer and Jaxon, meant I was moving ever closer to the time when I could one day possibly even maybe consider opening the letter. Finding out what had happened. Finding out if . . .

Being with the kids was empowering. I was becoming a different person. I was becoming a person who was settled and had found a home. I knew I could never replace Ashlyn. I'd never try. I simply went with the flow of having three new friends. Spending time with them, luxuriating in their company.

It couldn't last.

One June afternoon, the door to the office swung open and Kyle stepped in. His face was pale, his hands were trembling, his jaw was so tightly clenched the muscles in his neck stood out. Janene didn't even have a chance to throw herself across his path because he marched straight over to me. Alarmed, a little scared, I got up from my desk and without saying a word, I led him to the computer room where we held tests. From his jeans back pocket he took out a crumpled piece of paper, thrust it at me in lieu of speech.

Carefully, I smoothed it out, all the while throwing anxious looks at Kyle's face. I looked down, saw a set of solicitors' names on the letterhead on the piece of paper and time stopped. *Not again,* I thought as sickness welled up inside. *Being named in a divorce can't happen to the same person twice in one lifetime let alone happen to me twice in one year.*

The sickness subsided and became transmuted into pure, unadulterated horror by what the letter actually said. My terrified eyes flew up to meet Kyle's.

"She can't do this," he said, finally able to speak.

Ashlyn's solicitor was informing Kyle that she was going to make an application for a residency order if he and she couldn't come to an amicable agreement outside of court. Her son's accident during her absence had confirmed in her mind that the children would be safer with her.

Reading between the lines she was saying: *"One way or another, I'm going to get custody of the children."*

"She can't do this," Kyle repeated, looking to me for reassurance.

Unfortunately, she could.

CHAPTER 26

She's beautiful. Exactly like her pictures. And beautiful.
She was sitting in the back of the large, bright café in Beckenham, three towns away from the flat. It was a stylish café, light wood floors, white walls, chrome fixtures—Ashlyn fitted right in.

In front of her was a squat white cup and a packet of cigarettes, even though it was a no-smoking establishment. I stood at the doorway, pretending to be looking for someone when I knew exactly who I was meeting. I was just holding off the moment of first contact for as long as possible. I was going to have to go over and say hello, introduce myself and tell her that even though her husband had arranged to meet her on this neutral ground, he wasn't coming. He was very sorry, but he'd thrown himself on my mercy and made it abundantly clear he couldn't meet her today to discuss where their children were going to live.

"I can't see her," he'd said as he frantically paced the kitchen floor. "I can't sit down and talk to her." I'd reminded him that he had to because the children had to come first. And he'd explained: "It's not because I don't want to talk to her. It's because I'm afraid I'll beg her to come back to me. Most of the time I don't want her back, but if I see her, I'll probably say anything to get her to come back. I was doing it before. I was using the kids to get her to come home. I'm not doing that anymore and I don't want her back. But, God help me, if I sit opposite her, look at her, I know I'll lose it. I won't remember the hell, I'll remember everything else. I did in New York." Not long after that he'd hit upon the "inspired" idea of me going instead. Despite my protestations, he'd begged. And begged. And begged. I'd agreed to go and listen to what she had to say because he was so sincerely terrified by the prospect and, I have to admit, because I was curious, I wanted to find out for myself what Ashlyn Gadsborough was like.

After Jaxon's accident she'd flown back for a long weekend. She hadn't seen Kyle then, either. Instead she'd picked her kids up from school on a Thursday night and stayed with them over the weekend at her mother's place, let Kyle pick them up on the Sunday afternoon and had flown out on Monday morning.

As I approached her table I noted the differences between the photographic Ashlyn and the real one. She'd had her caramel-colored hair trimmed a couple of inches into long layers that danced around her shoulders. Like any woman our age she had crow's feet around her eyes, but her skin was flawless because of makeup.

For this meeting she'd obviously made an effort with her appearance. She'd blended several shades of pearly green and blue eye shadow around her eyes to make their deep green stand out; she'd curled on black mascara; she'd slicked on a shimmery red-pink lipstick; she was wearing a brown silk camisole top with a small sequin butterfly motif at the heart of the slightly plunging neckline. Her bare shoulders were a smooth, dark cream color.

"Hi," I said to her as I arrived at the table and smiled. "I'm Kendra, you must be Ashlyn."

A confused, cautious smile moved over her face as she looked me over. I'd made an effort with my smart navy-blue jeans, white T-shirt and red corduroy jacket, but it'd taken me awhile to decide on that—it's hard to know what to wear to meet your landlord's estranged wife to discuss how they were going to proceed with custody arrangements for their children.

"Kendra," Ashlyn repeated. "Kendra . . . Kendra . . . Kendra . . . ?" she mumbled over and over as though trying to recall where she'd heard it before. "Kendie?" she asked, catching on. "Are you Kendie?"

I grinned, should have remembered the children didn't call me anything else. "Yes, that's me."

"Ah," she said, spearing me to the spot with a look of understanding, "Kyle's not coming is he?"

"No, I'm afraid not."

Her disappointment was heartbreaking: the light went out of her eyes and her face fell. She'd made such an effort, she'd made herself beautiful to see him and now he wasn't coming. It was for nothing.

"Sit down," she invited. "You might as well." Her thin, white fingers reached for her cigarette packet, unsheathed a cigarette. I noticed the slight tremble in her hands. Nerves, I assumed.

"He hates me that much," she said, tapping her cigarette on the table in a nervous gesture.

"No, not at all. Not at all. He was just nervous about seeing you. He wanted me to talk to you instead."

It wasn't difficult to see how they had once meshed together, how his quiet, barely contained strength fueled her bright exuberance. How her outward joyfulness inspired him. When that had changed was anyone's guess. "I suppose he's told you everything about me," she said, a hopeful note suggesting she didn't want it to be true. That her estranged husband had kept her secret from the lodger.

"He's told me some things," I said diplomatically.

Ashlyn's carefully painted mouth twisted into a bitter

little smile. "You mean he's told you that I used to be a raging alkie."

———

Ashlyn had her first drink at fourteen.

She was with Tessa Brandhope, whose parents were going through a divorce. They were the only parents in the whole school who were splitting up. Ashlyn's parents were never going to get a divorce. Even though Ashlyn's father was always in a bad mood with her mother and her mother suspected he was having an affair, Ashlyn knew that people like them didn't get divorced. They didn't show to the outside world that anything was wrong. They hid their problems, got on with it. Ashlyn got on with it. Ashlyn and Tessa sneaked the alcohol from Ashlyn's parents' drinks cabinet.

They glugged the whiskey into a tall, straight glass almost to the top, then refilled the bottle to the right level with water. Upstairs in Ashlyn's bedroom they drizzled the strong-smelling amber liquid into their half-empty cola cans until the glass was almost empty.

She started coughing after her first gulp. It burnt her throat, made it impossible to breathe, caused an intense bout of spluttering. I don't like this, she thought. It's disgusting.

She pretended to Tessa it was the most delicious thing ever. She pretended she was like all those people on television who knocked back alcohol and loved the taste of it. They spent the afternoon giggling in her room. Tessa passed out. Laughing one minute, then out cold on the bed. Ashlyn tried to wake her, shook and shook her best friend but she'd just flopped around like a rag doll, a silly grin fixed to her face.

When Ashlyn's mother called them for dinner Ashlyn had been giddy. The burning in her throat had become a warm glow in her stomach and a gentle fuzziness in her head. She was happy inside; calm and excited. She could feel the blood flowing through her veins for the very first time. She felt alive. Ashlyn had smiled at her mother from the gap in her bedroom doorway and said they weren't hungry.

She saw her mother's face contract in displeasure; she knew she was in trouble. Her mother didn't argue, she wouldn't raise her voice with a guest in the house, but Ashlyn knew she'd be in trouble the next day. And she didn't care. Everything was soft and fuzzy around the edges; smoothed out and easy. The world was nicer, softer, gentler. Tessa was still snoring in the middle of her bed, saliva dribbling from the side of her mouth, her face flushed. Ashlyn sat on the edge of her bed, draining the last of the cola from her can, and then gulping down Tessa's half-full can. Ashlyn still didn't like the taste. But she was buzzing. She didn't feel sick, out of control or like passing out like Tessa had done. Ashlyn climbed on the bed beside Tessa, a smile spreading across her face. Bliss. This was bliss. This was what it must feel like to be someone other than Ashlyn Clarke-Sellars.

———

I watched Ashlyn raise her cigarette between her forefinger and middle finger. Her nails were long pale ovals that had been manicured awhile ago so were now ragged when the rest of her was polished. "Kyle exaggerates you know," she said. "He exaggerates how bad I was."

———

She woke up fully clothed on her bed. Her eyes were swollen and felt like two gritty tennis balls in her head; her mouth was so dry her tongue hurt. The space where her head used to be was banging like an army of miners who were eking out a very good living. She rolled over onto her side and pain bolted through the left side of her body. She lifted her hand, the mound of the palm and wrist were scraped raw, grit and gravel embedded into the wound. She balked as she stared at it. How did that happen? *she asked herself as she became aware that her knee was throbbing. Looking down, she found her black tights in shreds around her knee, long ladders snaking up and down her leg. Instinctively she touched her face. It was tender. Bruised. Bits of dried blood sticking to her fingers as she took her hand away.* What happened?

Ignoring the pain, Ashlyn lay flat on her back, stared up at the ceiling. The night before she'd been out with Tessa, Audrey Narten and Lesley Trindale. They'd gone down to the swings at the local park—a few of the boys hung out around there. Justin Sharpe hung out around there. Audrey looked oldest out of all of them and she'd managed to steal her older sister's driver's license so she'd bought a couple of bottles of Crazy Cat 40/40 fortified wine and a bottle of whiskey. Crazy Cat was too sweet for Ashlyn—in the past two years she'd grown accustomed to the smoky taste of whiskey and liked the way it spiced up cola, the way it produced quicker results if she drank it neat. They'd changed into short skirts; Ashley hated the mottled skin on her legs so she'd pulled on tights. They'd been playing Bros and Culture Club, Ashlyn remembered that. She remembered that the edges of her day—revising for her mock exams, listening to her mother complain about her father, watching her dad avoid looking at her or her mother once during dinner—had been planed off very quickly by her drinks. Quicker than usual. Lately, she hadn't needed as much for the fuzziness to descend. For the world to be a nicer, brighter place; for her to be pretty, to be good enough to speak to Justin. Or any other boy. Nowadays it didn't take long for the world to become the kind of place where she fitted, felt wanted, felt important.

She remembered them leaving, the four of them with different colored miniskirts, sloppy tops that hung off their shoulders over colored vests, tights, legwarmers, and their hair teased up to be big and bold. They strutted down the street like they owned it. Ashlyn had her black bomber jacket on and in the pocket she'd slipped three miniatures—a bottle of Malibu and a couple of Baileys—she'd found stashed at the back of her parents' drinks cabinet.

The memories started to fade at this point, became ghostly shadows she couldn't quite hold onto. They got to the park. Justin was there. He'd been talking to that idiot Eric. And then . . . nothing. It was gone. No, wait, she had talked to Justin. He'd told her a joke. He must have, because she remembered laughing. Giggling. Throwing her head back and laughing. Was it loud? Did she imagine that she saw Justin give her a strange look? That the others were all looking at her? What happened next? The fingers of her mind groped around, trying to grasp hold of what happened after the laughing. How she hurt herself. How she got home. Wasn't she meant to have stayed at Tessa's? How did she end up here? The blackness was deep and wide, blanketing over the whole of the night before.

The fear of that made her shiver inside. What had happened? Why couldn't she remember? Was it really the drinks she'd had the night before? That hadn't happened before. Not ever. The fear shivered inside again. She pulled her jacket over her chest, turned onto her right side and curled up.

It'd be all right, she told herself. It was only this once. And once she'd spoken to Tessa, she'd know what happened. It'd be all right. Of course it would.

———

I ordered coffee and a glass of water and we sat in silence as we waited for it to arrive. I was struck again by the surrealism of the situation. A needle of doubt was prodding at my conscience. I really shouldn't have come. I should not have gotten involved. I had never been married, I knew nothing of their marriage, I could do so much more harm than good.

The waitress clattered my coffee onto the table, folded the bill and placed it in the middle of the table, then left us alone.

———

Tessa said a lot of things. That Ashlyn had been out of control. She'd been laughing and Justin had looked at her like she was a weirdo. Ashlyn had decided to show them all how high she could go on the swing. And she showed them. Higher and higher she went until she'd lost her grip and had fallen off. Everyone started laughing at her, even though she'd scraped her hand and her face and her knee and there was blood. She'd jumped to her feet and run off. Across the grass and then away out onto the street. Tessa had been calling her, had tried to chase her, but Ashlyn had raced ahead of her, a lightning streak of humiliation. Tessa had also said that she was worried by how much Ashlyn was drinking. She'd seen the bottle Ashlyn kept in her desk at school. She'd noticed how Ashlyn was often pale and quiet and tired in the mornings. She was worried that Ashlyn hadn't been able to remember what had happened.

If you were me, Ashlyn thought, you'd understand why I need a little pick-me-up now and again. It was all right for Tessa: she could talk to boys; her mother wasn't always on her case for every little thing; she was beautiful. Tessa had it all, Ashlyn didn't. She needed a little liquid confidence every now and again, just to get her going. Tessa didn't understand. Ashlyn thought they were friends, but obviously she was wrong. Ashlyn and Tessa stopped hanging around together as much. Ashlyn found new friends. Ones who didn't judge her. Ones who, when she blacked out again, would tell her what had happened and wouldn't give her a lecture. If she wanted a lecture, God, if she wanted to be reminded of every wrong thing she'd ever done, she'd talk to her mother.

CHAPTER 27

"I might have guessed he'd pull something like this," Ashlyn said.

"It wasn't malicious," I said. "He was a bit freaked out by the solicitor's letter."

"We weren't exactly getting anywhere on the phone and I had to let him know I was serious about wanting the kids. It killed me that Jaxon was hurt and I wasn't there. He should have been with me."

"He knows you're serious. He does want to sort things out—I think after New York he was just worried that the pair of you might start rowing again. This way, with someone acting as a bit of a buffer, maybe you can move forwards. Do what's best for the kids."

Mrs. Gadsborough nodded. She was deeply disappointed. She made no secret of it. She stared forlornly at the slip of white paper between us, then looked up at me. Her eyes narrowed a little and she turned her head slightly, exploring me with slightly suspicious eyes. "Kyle's in love with you," Ashlyn stated.

I stared at her, wondering what she expected me to say to that.

"He is," she said, "I know him."

"You've had no meaningful contact with your husband for months, Mrs. Gadsborough," I said, "so forgive me if I don't quite believe that you know what he feels."

Her lips curled up into a smile, not unpleasant, more

self-satisfied, as though I'd proved her point. "See, that's exactly the sort of thing that makes you the type of woman he likes. *Loves.* Straight-talking. Strong. Incredibly sexy. Nothing fazes you."

Bless Mrs. Gadsborough. She'd known me all of ten minutes and she had managed to get every little thing wrong about me.

"That's not me, by the way," she said as she laid her cigarette beside her coffee cup, stroked her finger over the frayed top of the collapsing foam of her cappuccino. "I'm none of those things. That's the sort of woman Kyle used to go out with before me."

————

Ashlyn and Kyle had been in the same group of friends and slowly she'd become closer to him. She'd fallen for him the moment she met him. He was good-looking, quiet and incredibly kind. For years she was in love with him but he didn't know she was alive; she was just another friend in his large collection of friends. She had tried to make him notice her by studying the sort of people he went out with, the women he slept with, the women he casually dated, the ones who became his girlfriends. She kept trying to be like them—changed her hair, changed the way she dressed, even tried to change her personality—so he'd notice her. When trying to be someone else didn't work, when he still just treated her like a friend, she resorted to telling him the truth. She invited him over for dinner, she made fresh pasta with spinach and ricotta sauce, she poured him a glass of expensive white wine and told him she was in love with him. She decided not to hold back—if he knew how deeply she felt he might give her a chance. He was taken aback, had stared at her and said nothing. A little part of her died at that moment because she knew, just knew, he didn't feel the same way.

But Kyle eventually said, "Let's go on a proper date and see what happens." Obviously that made her fall in love with him even more. He didn't have to, but he did. So they went out. And then they went on another date. And another one. And all the while she was thinking, he's just seeing what happens, so she was always on her best behavior. Didn't drink because she could never stop at one and she didn't smoke. She also let him decide when they should go to bed. Because she thought he was testing her. He clearly wasn't that into her because he waited eight weeks before he made a move on her. A few months into their "just seeing what happens" dating, someone asked her out. She thought it would be easier for both of them if she said yes. Then he'd have a way out, she'd be off his hands and maybe this new guy would like her better. When she told him . . .

———

"When I told Kyle that someone had asked me out, he went mental." Ashlyn shook her head before a smile crept onto her face. "I mean completely and utterly lost it. 'My girlfriend,' he said. 'What right has some bloke got to ask out my girlfriend? I'll kill the bastard.'

"I'd never seen him like that before. I've never seen him like that since. Me being so pleased that it seemed Kyle had fallen in love with me at last, ignored the obvious. I was young and naïve and desperately in love, I didn't want to see the obvious. Do you know what the obvious is, Kendie?"

I shook my head. I suspected I knew but I didn't want to interrupt her, to stop her flow, because then I'd be required to speak. And, seriously, what would I say? I'd wanted to know what Ashlyn was like and this was it. She was the type of person who shared things a stranger shouldn't know.

"No, it's not that he wanted me because someone else wanted me. The obvious was that he wasn't in love with me. Kyle always wants to do the right thing. Always. And the right thing was not to reject me out of hand, because that would hurt my feelings. The right thing was not to just let me go when someone else was interested, the right thing was to give me a chance. The right thing was to feel jealous when someone else moved in. That's what motivates Kyle, doing the right thing. And dating me was the right thing. It wasn't love that brought us together—well, not on his part—it was his decency.

"I like to think sometimes that he did fall in love with me. But if he did it wasn't love that made him fall in love, it was his sense of decency. And because of that, I always loved him more than he loved me. And that's why I had a few drinks. After a few drinks I felt good enough to be his wife. After a few drinks I seemed to have it all. I was everything that Kyle wanted."

"I see," I said and trained my line of sight on my coffee.

Had these two people—Kyle Gadsborough and Ashlyn Gadsborough—actually *met*? Were they at all acquainted with the other person, because seriously, the pair of them sounded as though they were married to completely different people. Neither of them ever felt good enough for the other. They were both so desperate to be good enough, they never bothered to find out if they were. Or even what they could do to be good enough. *Is this what marriage does to you?* I wondered. You don't speak to each other, you don't tell each other the truth, try to find a solution to your problem together. Instead you go away and self-destruct: you fall in love with someone else, you sleep with someone else, you drink, you gamble. You do anything except be honest—*talk*—with the person you're meant to spend the rest of your life with.

"Marriage is easy when you drink a little to take the edge off things. My marriage was easy when I could take the edge off things. And when I stopped drinking because Kyle wanted me to it became less easy. The sharp edges and nasty bits came back. It became a nightmare."

The pink tip of her tongue slipped out between her moist lips and she licked the small bubbles of the cappuccino foam off her finger. The move was so breathtakingly erotic, I had to look away in embarrassment. The man at the next table stared at her with his mouth open, his sandwich frozen between his plate and mouth; his male companion nearly fell off his chair. How this woman thought she wasn't good enough for anyone was a mystery. She was so sexual and beautiful. Most women would kill for either of these, let alone both.

"My father was an alcoholic," Ashlyn said matter-of-factly. "That was the big family secret. I didn't even know for years. Not till I left home and my father died. That was why my mother was so controlling—she had no control over his drinking, so she tried to control me.

"At least he was fun sometimes. He might have been falling-down drunk, but all I remember is the fun. The presents he'd buy, the funny stories he'd tell. Mum tried to tell me that he'd get nasty, but I don't remember that. She was the one always being nasty. Trying to make every little thing perfect. Wouldn't you know it, her daughter's not perfect so I paid for that . . ." Her voice and her eyes drifted away for a moment. "Maybe my father was an alcoholic, but it doesn't mean that I am. Kyle knew about my dad, which is why he threw that in my face."

In all the research I'd done since I'd found out about Ashlyn's problem, it constantly said that alcoholism was handed down from generation to generation. Now she had confirmed that it hadn't started with her. Slivers of fear ran through me: Summer or Jaxon or both? Who would it be passed down to? Who would find themselves powerless around alcohol? I'd been looking and looking but hadn't yet found the answer as to whether it was a fait accompli. Were one or both of them going to end up on that path, become like Ashlyn no matter how they were brought up?

"I want my kids back," Ashlyn said to me, as though sensing I was thinking about them—being their mother connected her so closely to them that even when a stranger was thinking of them she could tell.

"That's what I wanted to tell Kyle but instead he sent you. I also wanted to tell him I wasn't that bad," Ashlyn said. "Kyle was always on my case about how much I drank but I wasn't that bad. I bet the way he tells it I was some kind of monster. But if you go to meetings you'll hear far worse stories. You'll see that I'm not so bad.

"My husband thinks I'm the worst person on earth because I liked a drink, but no one got hurt. I think that's why he wouldn't go to meetings with me; he didn't want to know that I wasn't as bad as he made me out to be. In the grand scheme of things, I wasn't like the other people in the rooms.

"The main reason I wanted to meet was to tell him I want the kids. The letter was just a courtesy, a prewarning of my intentions. I was hoping we'd be able talk it through. I can't imagine Kyle's coping very well, and I know from what they say on the phone they miss me as much as I miss them, so, would you tell him that I want my children. I'm fine now and I want my kids."

I couldn't help but think she was talking about Kyle, their father, as though he was a babysitter. She'd stepped out for a while and now that she was back, she wanted him to disappear.

Her eyes met mine, then tried to dig into my head, trying to ferret out my unspoken thoughts and unexpressed feelings. "You don't like me very much, do you," she stated.

"I don't know you, Mrs. Gadsborough, so I can't make any judgements on that. I try not to be judgemental."

"I wouldn't like me if I were you. Here I am, a mother who left her kids. Is there any greater crime?" she said.

"Yeah," I replied mildly, "lots."

That grin, the slow, easy grin that was often captured in the photos on display in her house made its way across her face. I marvelled at how you couldn't tell that she'd once been a drinker. Not from just looking at her. Her skin was flawless under her makeup, her eyes clear. "Kyle must be incapable with you. Smart, sassy, no bullshit . . . Are you two . . . ? Or have you ever . . . ?"

"No," I replied. Just no. I wasn't playing that game, didn't want her to start making up stories, to make suppositions, to try to name me in her divorce. "No."

"That was straightforward. I thought I'd have to coax it out of you or work it out for myself."

"I have nothing to hide, I have no interest in your husband other than as a friend. So, no."

"I didn't want to leave them," she said suddenly. There were tears in her voice, her body deflated a little. For the first time since I sat down at this table, I realized that I was being presented with the real Ashlyn.

"I really didn't." She shook her head slowly, her eyes falling shut. "I couldn't take them with me. I didn't know where I was going . . . I thought about taking them with me but I had nowhere to go. I couldn't go to my mother's. I can't spend more than three hours with her without her driving me crazy. And I couldn't stand that right then."

She stood in the upstairs corridor of her home, her bags sitting by the front door, dressed in her coat, the scarf her babies had bought her for Christmas wrapped around her neck as a reminder of how it felt when they wrapped their arms around her for a hug. She was shaking, tears had been running down her face while she'd been packing. She had to leave. She had to go. She couldn't stay another second here. Everything had gone wrong here and she couldn't stay. She'd just said good-bye to Jaxon. She thought of taking him with her. Of getting him dressed and taking him with her. But she didn't know where she was going. She had enough cash for a taxi to take her to the other side of Brockingham. She had a new, unused credit card stowed safely in her purse. But she had no idea where she was going. And she couldn't take Jaxon and leave Summer—it'd kill them to be apart.

"I'll come back for you," she mouthed at Jaxon's bedroom door. "I promise, I'll come back for you." She turned to her bedroom door where Summer was asleep in the big bed. "I'll come back for you, too," she said to Summer through the door. "I promise you." She almost changed her mind then. Almost decided to go back to the flat and unpack her bags. But she'd been here before. She'd packed to leave before but had decided to stay. And if she kept staying she'd suffocate. She'd die. She couldn't breathe here. She couldn't think, she couldn't feel, she couldn't live. Another day here would kill her. Or she'd kill herself. Alive or dead she had to leave.

The sound of the taxi pulling up outside made up her mind. She'd packed before but hadn't ever called the taxi. Now she had to go. Her escape was all mapped out, the plan was set in motion, she had to go.

Wiping her eyes determinedly, tears soaking into the wool of her gloves, she turned and made her way downstairs. She couldn't look as the taxi pulled away. She couldn't look at the house because if she did, she might just change her mind.

"I couldn't cope. There, I've said it, I couldn't cope." She ground the palms of her hands into her eyes, smudging her carefully applied makeup. "Being a mother is isolating. I found it so hard to say to Kyle that I couldn't handle it all on my own. And I certainly couldn't say it to my mother. I didn't want them to think I wasn't good enough. And all my other friends seemed to be doing it so well. I say friends. I don't really have friends, not anymore.

"There's this idea that you meet lots of women in mothers' groups, at the clinic, at the park. But what happens when you just have nothing in common with them? When you're sitting in a room surrounded by them and you have nothing to say. They all look well put together, their kids are all so cute and happy and get over any illness quickly. And you can't even pull a brush through your hair because one of your kids has colic and won't stop crying while the other has fallen off the sofa and bumped his head.

"Kyle was never there. When he was there his head was at work. And I get it, I really do, he was doing his best to make sure we had a roof over our heads and food on the table.

"So, day after day, I got lonelier and lonelier, I was in this catch-22. If I told people I wasn't coping, I was scared they'd take away my children; I wasn't coping so I needed someone to talk to. I kept thinking it'd get better when they started school. There'd be other mothers there, right? I could try to find some other like-minded people amongst them."

"What, the committee of bitches?" I snorted.

Ashlyn removed her face from her hands. "You know them?"

"Oh yeah. They don't talk to me because they assume I'm the nanny and therefore not worthy of wasting conversation on, but are always asking Summer or Jaxon to give me leaflets to give to 'Mummy or Daddy' to allow them to apply for this committee or that. Even if I'm standing right beside the kids."

Ashlyn's grin was back. I was an outsider, she was an outsider . . . I could see the rivulet of jealousy that I was doing the school run snaking its way through her eyes, but it wasn't there for long. I was speaking her language. She reached for her cigarettes, slipped one between her lips and picked up her lighter. Her long, tapered fingers turned the lighter over and over in her hand. "Even the mothers who hadn't joined the cliques were brainwashed. They wanted to join the cliques so if I befriended them, they didn't seem to have any conversations beyond extracurricular learning. They're flippin' six."

"I know."

"And all this extracurricular learning, is it getting us any-where? Are we producing the next generation of super-brains? I don't think so. We're putting pressure on kids and parents. Things didn't seem so bad when I could have the odd drink but when I stopped . . ." She shook her head, de-feated, frustrated; started worrying at the lighter even harder.

"Have you ever looked into a child's eyes and seen that they're relying on you for . . . for the world? No matter what happens to them, they believe you're going to be there for them. You can make it better, you can make it right, you can hold them until the pain goes away, you can make the sun rise." She slammed the lighter down onto the table with the flat of her hand. "Kids think you're the universe. They trust you with everything, with knowing everything. To them, you're the be-all and end-all. So what do you do when you know you're not worthy? That all that trust they have is mis-placed? You have a drink now and again to take the edge off.

"When I stopped, it all became too much. The loneliness, the pressure of being perfect. I had no escape, the therapy didn't seem to be working fast enough, Kyle and I were barely talking.

"I had to get away. For my sanity. So I wouldn't do some-thing stupid. So I left. I missed Summer and Jaxon so much.

So much. For all the times I'd silently blamed them for what was wrong in my life, every day became so hard without them. I couldn't cope with them, but living without them has become impossible. I thought . . . I suppose I thought Kyle would have gone crazy by now, would be begging me to take the children back. He's more stubborn than I thought."

"Not stubborn, just looking after them. He's actually pretty good at it," I said.

"I'm their mother."

"Kyle's their father."

"Only because he's had to be."

I shrugged in partial agreement. "Maybe. But that doesn't change the fact he's been doing a good job." After a fashion.

Ashlyn resheathed her cigarette, slid her lighter off the table, dropped it into her bag, followed that with her cigarettes. She was back. The Ashlyn I'd sat down at the table with. Her mask had come down over her face, her brick wall had come up around her. "It's been nice meeting you, Kendie," she said, each word lightly frosted. "You're all that Summer and Jaxon talk about." A small smile crossed her lips. "I did want to meet the woman my children were spending so much time with—you're not what I expected." The smile faded. "Please tell Kyle that I'm going to have the children living with me. He's going to have to face me sometime. And if not one-on-one then in court."

She zipped up her bag. Got up and walked away, leaving the scent of orchids and lilies perfume in her wake.

NOTHING

♦ ♦ ♦

CHAPTER 28

*A*re you going to take us to school?" Summer asked.

Three minutes ago I'd been luxuriating in the chance of a weekday lie-in. A weekday when I didn't have to get up and go anywhere in a hurry because I was going to a conference in Yorkshire and I didn't have to check in until the afternoon. Two minutes ago I'd heard the jangling of keys being inserted into the lock of my front door and had managed to get to my bedroom door before the twins had appeared at the top of the stairs.

They were already dressed in their uniforms—Jaxon in grey shorts, blue shirt and navy-blue sweater, Summer in navy-blue pleated skirt, checked blue shirt and navy-blue sweater. Both of their socks were pulled up to their knees, their shoes shiny. Jaxon's cast was still whitish and had a few more stickers on it. Every morning they looked so breathtakingly cute and pristine I was always tempted to take a picture, hold this image of them on film because it wouldn't last. I was never sure at what point during the day buttons became undone on their clothes, when a sweater got turned inside out, when shirts became untucked, when a lone sock ended up lounging around ankles.

"I'm going to the conference, I told you," I replied.

"But you're not going to work," Jaxon said. "So you can take us to school."

This was the first weekday lie-in I'd had in months. Certainly since I'd come home. This was a rare jewel in my life, something I had unearthed and was keen to enjoy. I'd been dreaming of treating myself to turning off the snooze button on my alarm, to having a long bath, to seeing what happened on the small screen after breakfast television. I loved these two, yes, but at this moment in time, I loved my bed a fraction more.

"You're going away for four days," Summer reminded, holding up the number of fingers by turning down her little finger. I smiled to myself, wondering at what age children realized it was easier to hold down the thumb instead of their little finger when doing that. "And you might not come back."

"I'll come back," I reassured them, dressing-gown clad, hair still scraped under my protective night scarf. "Apart from the fact I've got nowhere else to go, don't I always come back?"

"Won't you miss us?" Summer asked.

Ah, she'd dragged out the big guns. Nice, effective tactic.

"We'll miss you," Jaxon added. He paused and looked down at the space on the floor by his right leg, nodded, then looked at me. "Garvo says he'll miss you, too." Manipulation in stereo, excellent. I looked from one earnest face to the other. Now they were backing up their quiet assault with patient, innocent silence.

"I'll go get dressed," I replied. I had no defense against these two hustlers.

Once I'd taken them both inside the gates, hugged them, promised I would indeed return to them and got back to the flat, I was too awake to go back to bed. I showered, got dressed and got into my car.

It was my car now. I'd bought it from Kyle for the same price as I would have bought it secondhand. It'd given him some much-needed cash, and it'd given me another sense of home. I belonged here and I was staying. Every time I got into it, it felt different. Like it was mine now. I'd put new mats on the floor, I'd put pictures of my nieces and nephews on the dashboard, I'd hung a crystal from the rearview mirror. I'd made it my own. Will had a silver car. And it was silly, but every time I got into my car I remembered him driving me back to Sydney city center the morning after we spent the night together. I remembered him reaching out to help me clip in my seat belt, his thumb stroking over the back of my hand as he finished. It was the only time I could think about him nowadays. I'd regressed somewhat in that respect. It was probably Ashlyn's solicitor's letter that did it, but I had big fear now whenever I thought of Will's letter. I couldn't take it out and look at it; I had palpitations if I accidentally came across it when I took underwear from the drawer where I kept it. And if I thought of him too long everything else would fade away and his cry when he heard what she'd done would fill my mind. No, the only way I could safely think of Will was in the moment when I got in the car. Nothing more.

As I steered my car up the M1, I thought again of my meeting with Ashlyn last weekend. Nothing had been resolved. She'd rung the kids and said she was back in England "forever and ever and ever amen," as Summer said, so she'd see them this weekend. She'd told Kyle that she wanted to see the kids and nothing else. No mention of him sending me in his place. No mention of solicitors. I guessed that meant that she was going down the court route. Which would unleash a whole new set of unpleasantness upon the family.

Unpleasantness. Ha! I thought as I moved out of the fast lane. Court was going to unleash a new and previously unexperienced type of hell upon all those concerned. All their dirty little secrets, scurried away into the smallest, remotest spaces of their lives, would become public knowledge. Would become weapons to use against each other.

The thought of this troubled me for most of the journey. What I should have been doing is worrying about how I'd lied to the kids. Despite my best intentions, the Kendra they knew was not going to be coming back.

The conference was being held at a vast country manor estate set in blankets and blankets of Yorkshire greenery. For the next two days delegates from all over the country would hear about all the latest developments in the recruitment industry, changes in employment law and how to increase profits.

I arrived early. Gravel crunched under the wheels of the car as I drew up outside the hotel. The estate had been beautifully and meticulously restored. When I'd showed Kyle the Web site he'd pointed out that wherever possible the original, sand-colored, roughly hewn bricks had been used, the original dark slates had been relaid on the roof, and most of the beams were original or wood from the same period. He'd told me to look for lots of nooks, some of which would be hollow behind because they'd once been entrances to secret passages. He'd also recommended looking down in the cellars if I could get the chance. "I don't think so," I told him. Damp, musty, confined spaces might be for some people, but not me.

I couldn't check into my room until after two, so I gave my car keys to the concierge to park, gave my bags to reception and went for a wander. I wanted to explore the hotel before it became full of noisy, uptight delegates in their pristine suits all gagging to make everyone believe they were confident and successful.

The wide reception squelched with the footsteps of my flat driving shoes as I walked over the polished stone slabs. To the right and opposite of the dark wood desk was a dark wood staircase with ornate banisters that swept up to the first floor. Coming down the stairs were two people. A couple.

They weren't holding hands but had the air of being "together." It was most likely their first holiday together. They'd probably spent the morning breakfasting in bed, and now were going to go for a walk to work up another appetite. I smiled at them. He was telling her a story that involved gesticulating wildly, which made her laugh at every other word. My smile widened. After living in the midst of a divorce, it was nice to see two people at the other end of the spectrum who were doing the good stuff. Dating, holidaying, making love. It did work, it was worth it.

As I continued to openly stare at the happy couple, another person appeared at the top of the staircase.

He seemed to occupy the whole space behind the couple. He seemed to fill up the entire first floor. He seemed to be capable of filling up the entire hotel with his presence.

Him. The man from every one of my nightmares.

———

"I like you, Kendra, I like you a lot, but it's not going to work out between us." Tobey, *my first boyfriend, the first man I'd ever kissed, was finishing with me and part of me didn't quite believe it. We'd been in love these past six months and now he was saying this.*

"But you said you loved me," I whispered, ashamed to be saying the words. I had only just turned twenty, was still in college, and he was my first, but I still noticed how he flinched at my words.

"I did. But I don't anymore."

I wanted to ask him what had changed, what I'd done wrong, if it was because I was inexperienced and I hadn't been good enough. I was also going to say I could change. Ask him to give me another chance. But I kept my peace because the words got stuck in my throat. I had some pride. Even though my heart was breaking, maybe because my heart was breaking, I couldn't do it. I couldn't beg.

"Kennie," he said quietly, "it's not you. It's not you, it's Penny. We're getting back together. I like you, but I love her." I didn't see it coming, didn't know he was still in love with his ex, didn't even know he was still in touch with her. "I'm really sorry," he said to my shock. "I've got to go." He left, never to re-turn a phone call again.

I cried. I wallowed. Emotionally bruised and battered, I ob-sessed about Tobey. Was convinced that he'd see the error of his ways, would remember why he and Penny had broken up in the first place. I found it hard to understand how someone could love you one day and then not the next day. And if they were slowly not loving you, shouldn't you have some idea, an inkling that they were pulling away from you and towards someone else? Shouldn't you know?

When, a month after we finished, I bumped into Lance, Tobey's best friend since childhood, in a bookshop in Leeds city center, I thought fate was rubbing my face in it. "He's gone but here's his friend, make polite chitchat talk with him like a good girl," fate was saying. I turned and ran out of the shop, not wanting to let how badly I was doing get back to Tobey. Lance chased after me, got me to stop by gently touching my arm. They were very different and very similar, Tobey and Lance. Tobey was quiet and reserved until you got to know him, he had the same offbeat sense of humor as I did and he was beau-tiful. He had the most amazing, cocoa-brown skin and big, mahogany eyes, and lips that knew how to weaken legs with a kiss—I couldn't believe it when he'd asked me to dance in the club where we met. Lance was white, was more forthright and gregarious, even with people he didn't know. Lots of women thought he was good looking and in the time I'd been with Tobey we'd gotten on well because he always made the effort to include me in their activities. He was a natural-born socializer.

"I'm really sorry about you and Tobey," Lance said, standing in front of me and looking uncomfortable. "If it makes any difference, I told him I thought he was mad."

"You did?" I asked. I didn't think men said things like that to each other.

"I did. You two were so good together. He was crazy to give you up. And if it makes you feel any better, I don't see much of Tobey and Penny now. I didn't like her before and she hasn't changed." This was what I needed to hear. My flatmates had all been fabulous about it, but to know that other people didn't like Tobey's old new woman and thought he'd made a mistake vindicated me. I wasn't a bad girlfriend, he was simply going through a period of temporary insanity and he'd come to his senses soon. Lance asked for my number, mentioned that he could arrange work experience for me on the paper he worked on if I was still interested in journalism and said he was sorry again before he had to dash off to meet his girlfriend.

When Lance called me a few days later to see how I was I thought nothing of it. We'd met so many times when I was with Tobey, we'd talked, we'd chatted, we'd become friends, so it was sweet of him to care. We even met for a drink a couple of weeks later because he was over in Leeds from Harrogate where he lived.

Every morning I'd wake up wanting to see Tobey, to talk to him, to hold him, to hear him whisper that he loved me. If I couldn't have that, a friendship with Lance would do.

We talked, went to dinner, sometimes he came out clubbing with me and my flatmates. We had fun together. About three months after the breakup with Tobey, Lance and I went for a pizza and he walked me back to my place in Burley Park and we stood on my doorstep for a while finishing our conversation. As it became clear the conversation was winding down, I got my keys out of my pocket and suddenly Lance's lips were on mine and he was pulling me towards him. I was startled. I'd only ever kissed Tobey so this was different. Our lips didn't fit together like mine and Tobey's, he put both his hands on my face instead of around my body, he smelled of aftershave, his blond hair brushed my cheek, his mouth tasted of the coffee he'd drunk earlier. I hesitated at first, then let myself go with it. Kissed him back a little but in the main just didn't resist. Eventually Lance stepped back and said, "I've wanted to do that for ages."

I smiled a closed-mouth smile back, not sure of what to say. I hadn't wanted to do that for ages. I hadn't even thought of him in that way, so to spare us both the awkwardness of me having to say that, I said good night and escaped inside.

The next time I saw him, I went over to Harrogate for an interview for work experience on the newspaper where he was features editor. Afterwards we went for a drink and he walked me back to the train station. As we stood on the concourse I said good-bye quickly, keeping my head lowered and turned to walk away.

He pulled me back, kissed me again. This time I couldn't go with it. I liked Lance, he was a friend I didn't want to alienate, especially when I had to see him every day at the paper, but I couldn't allow this to carry on. I pressed the flat of my hand against his chest and gently yet firmly pushed him back. A physical "let's not." Actions, after all, speak louder than words. He immediately stepped back, understanding straight away what I meant. He smiled at me a little sheepishly. Of course he understood.

———

He didn't see me. I'm sure he didn't see me, I said to myself as I turned on my heels and walked away into the heart of the hotel where the receptionist had told me the restaurant and bar were. On the way, I saw a small discreet sign for the women's toilets. I turned towards it, pushed open the door and walked in.

Large, clean, furnished with brass and marble and clean white towels, it was also empty, all eight stall doors stood open.

———

"I thought that was what you wanted, I've seen you. I know what you're like. I thought that was what you wanted."

———

I leaned over the bank of sinks, each carved out of smooth cool stone. I stared down into the bowl at the white plug.

It was heat first of all. A torrent of it lighting up the cells in my body, burning me up from the inside out.

I pressed my palms flat against the stone, steadying myself, allowing the coolness to seep into me.

———

"You're special. Stop fighting, you're special."

———

Air. I couldn't get air into my lungs. I pressed my right hand against my chest, trying to calm my speeding heart, trying to ease my wrung out lungs.

———

"Stop fighting and I won't kill you."

———

I was going to pass out. If I couldn't get air into my lungs, I was going to pass out. It'd happened before. I'd been like this and I couldn't stop it, and then the blackness had come. But not for years. This hadn't happened in years.

The vice around my chest tightened, the beating of my heart sped up, running away from the fear of a memory. I was stuck here. I couldn't stop myself. I was trapped in this moment. The memory was becoming stronger, the words growing louder.

———

"I thought that was what you—"

———

The door to the bathroom opened, swung back on its hinges and banged against the wall. I jumped. Jumped out of the past into the present. Suddenly I was here again. In a hotel bathroom. Not back there. Not back when.

"Oops, sorry," a woman said when she saw me jump, before she went into a stall, slammed and locked the door.

"Don't say sorry," I wanted to tell her. "You just saved me. You just rescued me from that place."

CHAPTER 29

$\mathcal{T}$he auditorium could seat three hundred people. The original outbuildings of the manor house had been converted into a conference center with meeting rooms, business communications center and the auditorium.

The lights were lowered and at the front a spotlight was on the guest speaker; the screen behind her was lit up with graphs and figures. She was lecturing on the changes in recruitment practices. I knew that because it was written on the sheet in front of me. The sheet that was part of my delegates' pack. I knew because my eyes had scanned the front page of my delegates' pack and had read those words. Hadn't taken them in, hadn't digested them, but like the good girl I was, I had read them. Nothing had registered since the moment beside the stairs. Since I glanced up and saw him.

He hadn't seen me, I was sure of that. As sure as I could be. I'd stayed in a locked stall in the bathroom for an hour before I ventured out, finished checking in and went upstairs to my room on the fourth floor. All the while I'd been on the lookout, in case I bumped into him. In case I had to see him up close and act normal and say hello.

As I sat in the auditorium, I knew I wasn't completely safe. Proximity wasn't an issue now, unless you counted the space in my head. That area he prowled around, baring his teeth, growling like a bloodthirsty animal.

Weeks after I finished my work experience at the Harrogate
Local & International Chronicle, *when I'd spent a fortnight
making tea, photocopying and transcribing interviews, when
I'd been totally enamored with the whole process and decided
it was for me, Lance asked me to come to a party at the paper.*

*"Nothing fancy," he said. "But it's a good way to get your
face known. If they see you again they'll remember how good
you were. There may be a job in it for you when you finish
college."*

*Since I'd been a little girl noting down my stories and pieces
of my imagination, writing had been my passion. What he was
saying meant my dream could come true, I could become a
journalist.*

*It was a quiet party, held upstairs at a pub in Harrogate.
The air was heavy with cigarette smoke, and the smell of beer
and cheap wine clung to the smoke. I sat in a corner, not really
a mover and shaker, far too shy to just go and talk to the editor
or the deputy editor. Or, indeed, anyone with the word editor
in their title apart from Lance.*

*Being there was enough. Lance spent a lot of time at my
side, getting me drinks, introducing me to people, and as a result a few people said to give them a call if I wanted to come
back to do work experience again. I was made.*

*I wasn't drinking much. Had managed to choke down a
half and was struggling through a pint. Since the split with
Tobey, anything more than three drinks transported me to a
bad place, where I felt sorry for myself. Where I wanted to re-
make myself in Penny's image, in anyone's image if it would
get my wonderful boyfriend back. I hated feeling like that. I
didn't understand how I could let a man do that to me. Make
me feel like that but I did.*

*It was getting late and I had to get the train back to Leeds. I
had three-quarters of a pint sitting on the table so decided*

I'd finish it before I left. I went to the loo and lingered there, looking at myself in the mirror. I wasn't always staring at myself in shiny surfaces but I was fascinated. What was it about me that had sent Tobey back to his ex? Did she have longer, more feminine hair than me? Mine was halfway between my shoulders and my chin. Did she have more beautiful eyes? Mine were such a deep dark brown they looked black, as though I had two large pupils. Did she have a smaller mouth? Because my lips were pretty full-on. Did she have a nicer nose? What was it? Oh stop it, I told myself. You should be over this by now, it's been five months. He isn't coming back to you.

I washed my hands in the little sink, went back to the table. As I returned to the bar, I saw Lance and three men from the sports desk crowded around the table where our drinks were. They were snickering, one of them using his body to hide the glasses on the table from the rest of the bar, the other two men I didn't really know watching, egging him on with their whispers. Through the slender gap between their bodies I saw they were pouring a glass of vodka into my drink. Right, so that's how you get your laughs, is it? *I thought.*

I wandered over and when they saw me they all straightened up. Lance looked a little guilty; the others could hardly hide their amusement. Clearly they wanted to see me a stumbling, drunken mess. If I hadn't caught you, you'd have been in for a shock, *I thought.* I'd have just sat here and bored you stupid about my wonderful ex-boyfriend. "All right, lads?" *I asked, as I took my seat at the table again.*

"Yeah, yeah," *they said in unison, two of them snickering slightly.*

"Cool," *I said and reached for my drink. My fingers grazed the fat, sweating body of the glass, but fumbled and the glass toppled over, the liquid glugging out onto the dark wood table, dribbling down onto the floor.*

"Ah, damn!" I said regretfully as I looked into their faces. "That was almost a full pint, as well."

Lance guessed that I'd seen them. He knew that I wouldn't make a fuss but I wouldn't drink the spiked drink. I wish I was the type to make a fuss, to draw attention to myself when I'd been wronged. I wasn't. Lance knew that. Lance counted on that, I realized later.

To avoid any more of their nonsense, I decided to leave, to get the train home and to remember not to drink with them again. Lance offered to walk me to the station.

As we wandered through the dark streets of Harrogate towards the train station, I gulped in the fresh night air. I loved the cleansing feel of it after the fug of the pub. Halfway to the station, Lance stopped in the middle of the pavement.

"I'm worried about you getting the train back so late on your own," he said.

"I'll be fine," I said.

"No, really, I'd hate myself if something happened to you."

"Seriously, I'll be fine."

"Look, my flatmate's away, she won't mind you staying in her room."

His concern was real, I could feel it, but I wanted to get home. To sleep in my own bed. And I still felt a little uneasy about the drink thing in the pub. It hadn't been him, but he hadn't stopped them. It was a joke, but trying to get me drunk, spiking my drink, wasn't funny.

"I'll drive you back to Leeds first thing in the morning," he said.

It was a long way back home and I had stayed at Lance's place a few times when I was going out with Tobey. It was quite a big house arranged over three floors and because they all worked, it wasn't a scuzzy student place. He lived there with three other people and they were all friendly. I still hesitated. I really did want to go back home; I was meant to be going for a *pub lunch with my flatmates tomorrow. And also, there was that other issue. It still hovered around us, still concerned me a little.*

"Look, Lance, I really like having you as a friend," I said, feeling uncomfortable bringing it up but emphasizing the word friend. *I didn't want him to think I thought I was extra-special, that I thought I was something special so he was harboring feelings for me, but I wanted to say something to make it clear that I didn't want to kiss him again.*

"Yeah, I know," he said, looking a bit put out. "I haven't tried anything, have I?"

Embarrassment washed through me. That *had* sounded arrogant. God, what an idiot. He must think the worst of me. What am I like? Of course he doesn't fancy me. If he did, he'd have tried to kiss me again, which he hasn't.

If I didn't stay over, I realized, he'd think I had a big head or something.

"OK, I will stay over," I said. "Thanks so much."

He smiled. *"Come on. And if you're really good, I'll buy you a bag of chips on the way back."*

I thought that was it. The matter was closed. Over. And it was. Until a few hours later. Around the time he said to me, "Don't you ever get frustrated?"

———

"Oi, come on," someone said as they nudged me. "We're supposed to convene down here again in forty minutes for the group exercises."

I twisted to the woman beside me. She was a shapely woman, who, like me, shouldn't wear button-up blouses— the top buttons of her white shirt were straining against her well-stacked chest. She had a friendly face, an easy smile and kind eyes. "We've got yellow lines on our name badges, which means, apparently, that we're in the same group," she continued to my blank expression. "Which also means we're pretty much screwed because I fell asleep, too."

My face offered her a wan smile as I gathered my folder, bottle of water, pen and pad and shoved them all into my large cloth delegates' bags we'd been given.

I have to leave this place, I decided.

I would go upstairs, shower, get changed and then drive over to Leeds to see my former flatmates as planned. They wouldn't mind me turning up two days early. I hadn't seen them in years so they'd probably be overjoyed to see me even earlier.

"I might see you later," I said to the woman.

"If you don't come back, I'll tell on ya," she warned with another of her easy smiles. She had a soft Welsh accent that purred gently under her words. "Ah, go on, come back. You look like the most interesting person in here. And I know, just know, that everyone else will have done their work." She grinned at me again.

I can't leave, I realized. Gabrielle had spent her own money to send me here. Leaving would be a slap in her face, telling her that I had no respect for all that she was working for. I couldn't do that to Gabrielle. And what would I tell her? I saw someone I haven't seen in years and I freaked out? Even if she understood, she'd probably ask me why I freaked out. What it was about him that made me do that to her. I'd have to tell her the truth. Which was never going to happen. I couldn't talk about him. Not to anyone. I didn't even think about him, let alone talk about him. What would that, my refusal to tell her the truth, do to mine and Gabrielle's relationship?

I had three options as far as I could see: I waste her money and refuse to explain why; or I waste her money and tell her why; or I don't waste her money and don't have to get into the telling or not telling.

Out of those three options, what was the easiest one? Really, what was the easiest one?

"All right," I replied to my yellow group partner. "I'll see you outside in twenty minutes."

"Great!" she said. "I'm nipping outside for a fag or five. I'm gasping."

Summer and Jaxon rang just before seven o'clock to tell me about their days and to say their dad had burnt dinner so they had to order a pizza. And their mumma had called them again and she was really excited about seeing them on Saturday. And their dad was trying to make a new house but he kept saying he couldn't concentrate because they were making too much noise and did I think they made too much noise? Talking to them gave me a sense of peace. Reminded me I wasn't twenty, alone, frightened. I was nearly thirty-three with a different life and responsibilities.

I had moved on.

⌒he second day of the conference got under way early. It
⌐was a bright, sunny day, with a wonderfully deep blue
sky and very few clouds.

By 8 a.m. we'd all breakfasted and were sitting in our
well-upholstered seats listening to whatever it was we were
meant to be listening to. I wasn't paying much attention. My
Welsh friend was called Billie, and she was staying two
rooms down from me. She was funny and we behaved like
naughty schoolchildren most of the time, giggling in the
back, talking about TV programs whenever we had a spare
moment, and only doing our work under duress. I was always aware of the monster in the hotel, but after I finished at
the conference I was going over to Leeds to see a couple of
my old flatmates for two nights and I'd be back down south
by Sunday afternoon. I could avoid him for that long because he hadn't seen me. I hadn't seen him—even though I
kept a very close lookout—since the other morning and he
hadn't seen me. All I had to do was avoid him and then leave
and put this whole experience behind me.

At dinner that night I sat with Billie and we pretended to
listen to a pompous man from London expound on his theories on recruiting young women. In reality we were both
giggling into our chocolate puddings, wishing he'd shut up.
Like a lot of other people in the room, I had one eye on the
clock because I was going to call my kids at seven o'clock.

I missed them. Genuinely missed them. I'd probably seen

them almost every day for the past few months and I missed their smiles, and nonsensical conversation, and running around on the sofas, and hearing their keys in my lock. I missed eating dinner with them. I missed talking Summer down from a tantrum and coaxing words out of Jaxon when he was cross.

When Billie got up to go to the loo I got up, too. I wasn't going to be left with the idiot in front of us. And it was six-forty. They would have finished dinner by now; Kyle wouldn't mind their routine being put out by fifteen minutes. Billie and I parted ways at the lift. I called it and felt mildly anxious as I waited. I knew there was a monster around, I had to get to safety. Absently I jiggled my legs, watching the number lights falling from six to five to four to three to two to one to ground.

My leg jiggling got worse. The doors took an age to open, but eventually, softly, they parted. I stepped into the wood-paneled box and pressed the button for the fourth floor.

As I waited for the doors to slide shut again, I heard heavy footsteps heading my way. Probably male footsteps. I willed the doors to close, to let me get away from here. The metal doors began to slide together, when a large hand sliced between them, causing them to clunk to a halt then open again.

My heart sank, my breath caught. I ducked my head, hiding behind my hair as the man who'd stopped the lift stepped in. He had on shiny black shoes. He moved near to me and I jumped back. "Sorry," he said, "didn't mean to startle you. I just need to press three." It wasn't his voice. This one was Scottish. I dared a look at him and he was blithely reading the fire notice on the wall of the lift. I exhaled and told myself to calm down.

The lift delivered him to his floor and he got out with a brief nod. I pushed the arrow to shut the door and relaxed a

little. The lift went up again. "Suspicious Minds" popped
into my head. I started humming it as I wondered how long
it took to go up one more floor.

I was examining the black strip on my swipe card as the
doors finally opened. *At last!* I thought as I stepped forwards.

Someone had been waiting for the lift and he appeared in
the gap between the doors as they opened to free me. He
smiled at me, and I offered a small smile without eye contact. He stood aside to let me past. I rushed down the corridor, turned the corner to my room, which was almost like
walking back towards the lift. A couple was wandering
down the corridor, and the man stepped aside to let me
pass. I smiled a thank-you.

The smooth flatness of my key card slipped in my hands.
I was excited. Pathetic as it was, I was going to talk to
Summer and Jaxon and that made me so happy. At the next
turn another guest left his room, shutting his door behind
him, checked the handle. Turned in the direction of the lift.

He seemed to take up all of the corridor all at once. He
seemed to grow seven feet tall. A smile crawled its way
across his face. "Aren't you going to say hello?" he said.

———

*When I was packing to leave Australia, I sold almost every-
thing. I didn't have time to organize shipping stuff home, so I
kept a handful of my favorite books, my favorite CDs, my
laptop computer and as many of my clothes and shoes as I
could pack. I decided to pay excess fare if I had to, but everything else—from my bed to the teaspoons, my plants to my
reusable shopping bags—I sold. I had an open house afternoon and sold everything. I made about $1,500, which was
about £650. I gave it all to the Samaritans because I wanted
to help them to help other people. I had to make sure that if*

another person ever got to the point where Will's wife had,
they'd reach out for help instead of hitting self-destruct. I know
what it's like to be on that ledge. To want to jump or even to
just let go and fall. I know what it's like, and the thought that
I'd been partially responsible for driving another person to
that point . . . That's why I had to leave. I could never be re-
sponsible for doing to another person what someone had done
to me.

I could have run if I hadn't been so scared. I could have
screamed if I wasn't so frightened. I could have scratched his
face as he came towards me and suddenly we were standing
in a nook, hidden and sheltered from the main corridor, but
I was petrified. Fear, true fear, which is thick and deep,
which crushes you slowly but surely one molecule at a time,
which stops time itself, had me. Fear had me and I couldn't
do anything. I knew what it was like to think you're going to
be killed.

I'd never thought about dying before I was twenty. I'd
never had to, not really. And if I did, in those brief moments
where I thought about the end of my life, I was old, I was
frail, I slipped away quietly in my sleep. I never thought it
would be because someone had decided to do it. Someone
else had closed their hand around my neck and was pushing
all life out of me.

I knew what it was like to think you're going to be killed.
And I was afraid of it.

He was staring at me, I knew, because I could feel his eyes
over every line of my face. I wasn't staring back at him. I was
staring through him, seeing the dark wood paneling that
ringed the lower part of the walls like a heavy, pleated skirt.
I saw the tapestry hanging behind him on the flock wallpaper. I saw the low lighting embedded into the wall.

He lowered his head until his lips were a fraction away from my ear. "I thought it was you," he whispered. "I thought it was an amazing stroke of luck—here I am on holiday and there you were at breakfast this morning. I thought I was imagining it, but no. It's you." He came in even closer. "Long time no see."

Two of his fingers stroked across my collarbone and re-vulsion trailed in the wake of their path across my skin, but I didn't react.

What was there to react to? That thing called my body was something separate and far away and I'd lost contact with it.

"Hmmm," he breathed, "you've still got the same smooth skin. I love your skin."

He ran his hands down and over the rest of my body. I didn't feel anything, I simply knew from the disgust that fol-lowed every touch.

He leaned in and put his lips to my ear again. "Talk to me, Kendra," he said. "We used to talk all the time. Talk to me."

"Aren't you going to ask what you had?" I heard my-self say.

"What?"

"Aren't you going to ask if you had a son or daughter?"

"What are you talking about?" His hands stopped and he pulled away slightly as his eyes concentrated on my face. For the first time I looked at him rather than through him. I looked into his face, saw how little he'd aged, how much the same he was. Still blond; those clear, turquoise, violet-flecked eyes, those lips that didn't fit with mine. Nothing had changed about him.

"I'm talking about," I paused, summoning up the courage to go through with this, "the baby."

"Baby? What baby?"

"Think about it."

The penny had dropped awhile back but his mind hadn't picked it up until that moment. "No," he said. His eyes searched my eyes for any hint of a lie. "You didn't have my baby. You did not have my baby."

"Didn't I?" I replied.

"You're lying," he said. "You're lying."

I said nothing.

"You had my baby but didn't tell me? That's not your style. You'd feel duty-bound to tell me."

"I know what you're capable of, why would I expose a child to that?" I replied.

Doubt crossed his face—it occurred to him for the first time that I might not be lying. That maybe I would keep something monumental from him because he was capable of great acts of evil. Because he was evil.

The truth would never occur to him. That if I couldn't fight him physically, I'd stop him another way. I'd do any-thing—say anything—to stop him.

When he didn't speak, I held my breath.

He stepped back a fraction, not far, but enough so my body wouldn't feel the heat of his. I still held my breath.

"Tell me about my child," he said.

I shook my head.

"Please?"

I tried not to lie. In my life, I tried not to lie. I even found it uncomfortable to twist the truth a little. I'd rather keep quiet, hold something in rather than let it out and it not be the truth. But, in the choice between this and lying, *I would lie every single time.*

A click, then the yawn of a door hinge being opened filled the corridor. There were people. Someone was coming. "Step away from me," I said, listening to the footsteps ap-proaching us, hanging onto their sound.

"But I want to know about—"

"Step away from me or I start screaming," I said, raising my voice.

He stepped back.

The loved-up couple I saw descending the stairs yesterday walked past and I moved out into the corridor proper, so I could be seen. The couple was heading in the direction of the lift, away from my room. I could go with them, but he'd follow. I was trapped in this corridor, and once the couple was out of sight he might try to touch me again. I needed help. I needed help so desperately at that moment to get out of this situation. Away from this. And then a miracle happened. The door to his room opened and a woman emerged.

"Oh, honey, I thought you were already downstairs," she said when she saw him. She was tall, slender, redheaded with alabaster skin and clear blue eyes. She didn't notice me; I was simply another guest in the corridor.

"Ah, yeah," he said. "I meant to ask you to bring my mobile down with you. I'm expecting a call from the editor . . . I know, I know we're on holiday—"

I walked by concentrating on putting one foot in front of the other as quickly as I could. I walked by focusing on the safety I'd find behind the door of my room. I walked with my heart pounding in my ears. At my door, I risked a look down the corridor and found it was empty. I pushed my key card into the door, stepped in quickly, slammed the door just as quickly. I dragged a chair from the desk and hooked it under the handle.

I stood in the space between the bed and the door, frozen again. I was cold inside. Burning on the outside, freezing on the inside. I was a human baked Alaska—slice me through and I'd have ice at my core.

Into the silence *brrrrriiiinnnnnnnng!* exploded.

I wasn't startled: I was too cold inside for that. My eyes

went to my mobile sitting on the bedside table. I was drawn to it. I wanted the noise to stop, I needed silence. I needed quiet. To think, I needed quiet. Moving like a robot with fused joints, I went towards the phone, picked it up.

On the screen Summer, Jaxon and Kyle flashed up. A photo from the day we went to the British Museum. Their picture was replaced with their names. Then they were back, grinning at me. Then their names. Their bright faces. Their names.

I couldn't.

Speak to them. I couldn't.

They were part of a different Kendra's life. Not this one. This one was damaged. This one was disgusting. This one could not speak to two children. I pressed the red button to reject the call, then carefully replaced the phone on the bedside table before I went to the bathroom to begin the process of removing him from every single piece of me.

"Kendie, it's Summer. We have to talk to you. We're going to Gra'ma Naomi's house tomorrow and we're going to see Mumma ... Oh, Dad said I told you that already. Mumma called us again today she said she's excited. Here's Jaxon ... It's Jaxon. Garvo chased a cat. It ran under next door's car and wouldn't come out. Dad said that wasn't very nice but it's not Garvo's fault. Call us back ... It's me again. Yeah, call us back ... What? ... Dad said you have to call back tomorrow if it's after eight o'clock ... But, Dad, we'll be at Gra'ma Naomi's house tomorrow ... All right, Dad ... *Call us back*."

I listened to the message over and over.

Lay in the dark listening to their voices. Bright and happy.

On loudspeaker they filled the room; I could close my eyes and pretend they were with me. They were near enough to touch.

I hadn't called them back and now it was the middle of the night. They were safe. Tucked up in bed. Before my eyes their faces as they slept became clear. The eyelash-fringed semicircles of their closed lids, their gently pursed pink lips, the smooth skin of their faces as they dreamed of pleasant things.

I loved them.

I loved them so much, but I couldn't talk to them.

CHAPTER 31

*H*e was waiting for me in reception. I knew he would be.

The hotel was clothed in quiet because it was only 6 a.m. and I did my best not to crease it as I made my way out. But he was sitting on the sofa directly opposite the reception desk. He didn't move until I'd finished checking out, and then he came towards me as I walked towards the exit.

He looked washed out, wrung out, the kind of grey-white that came from lack of sleep and reworking your life. His hair looked as if he'd run his fingers through it more than once, his clothes were crumpled. I stopped, to keep a distance between us and to keep us in the line of sight of the receptionist.

"I knew you'd leave before everyone got up," he said.

I almost screamed in his face to stop it. To stop believing that he knew me, knew how I thought, how I acted; that there was some kind of connection between us.

"Leave me alone," I said quietly.

"But—"

"Leave me alone," I said again.

"We have to talk about our child. He or she must be about twelve? Is he—" he asked.

"I lied," I cut in. "To stop you from doing what you were doing. I didn't have your child. I don't have any children." *I'll never have children.*

I'd realized that last night. I didn't have children. No

matter how hard I wished, no matter how many school runs I did, day trips I planned, stories I read, I did not have children. No matter how many times I told myself I knew they were someone else's kids, I had been fooling myself. I'd become too close to them when they weren't mine. I did not have children.

For a moment I thought he was going to go for me, to close his hand around my throat and squeeze the life out of me and it didn't scare me that much. A little, but not like last night. Not like it had before. He'd already hurt me as much as he could. His face relaxed. He wasn't sure what to believe.

"You lied?"

I nodded. "You were trying . . . I had to stop you."

"I wasn't going to hurt you," he said. "I just wanted you to talk to me. Like we used to."

"I have nothing to say to you."

He looked disappointed, as though he couldn't understand why I was being like this. Why I wasn't pleased to see him. We were friends, after all, why didn't I want to talk to him? The silence stretched like loosened elastic between us; it could go on and on and still not be pulled back. He didn't know what to say to get me to act like his friend again; I had nothing to say to him—not now, not ever. It was time for me to leave. To put him behind me like I had done all these years. It was time for me to walk away.

I walked down the stairs. In the car park I threw my bags onto the passenger seat and slammed and locked the door. I shoved the key into the ignition, put on my seat belt. I started the car, put it in gear and took the hand brake off.

Lance was standing on the steps watching me as I began to crawl out of the car park. I was driving slowly enough to see him do it. To see him glance in the back window and see Jaxon and Summer's booster seats.

SLICE OF COLD PIZZA

♦ ♦ ♦

CHAPTER 32

Is there something that you can do when it feels as though your head is caving in and your chest is being crushed?

It hadn't stopped since I left the conference. I'd forgotten what it was like to live without the pain and the feeling of being compressed from the inside out.

Saturday afternoon, knowing the kids were with their mother and Kyle would be out shopping, I left a message on their home phone saying I'd be back on Monday instead of Sunday and turned off my phone. I didn't go to Leeds, I'd just driven back to Kent. Then I'd parked the car three streets away and crept into my flat.

I didn't bother to take off my clothes—instead I kicked off my shoes, climbed under the covers and hid. I was safe under the covers, protected and safe. No one knew I was here. I lay huddled under there, and slept in fits and starts. Slept and woke. Would open my eyes and stare at nothing. Trying not to collapse into the knot of what had happened at the hotel. What had happened all those years ago. If I fell back there, even for a moment, I'd be tangled; caught and trapped.

Monday I got up early. Showered with blistering hot water and left at 5:45 a.m., before the children got up. I missed them. I wanted to see them, to listen to what they'd done in the time I'd been away. I wanted to see the light in their eyes, the smile on their lips, to hear their voices excitedly unraveling the mysteries of our time apart. The agony inside my head hadn't gone away, the pressure on my chest was increasing not decreasing, the bruise on my heart was spreading. I couldn't pass that on to them. Not even for a few minutes. And after the revelation I'd had, the reminder that I did not and would not have kids, I knew I had to pull back from them.

I beat Gabrielle to work for the first time ever in us working together. She raised her eyebrows in surprise when she saw me at my desk as she arrived, but made no comment. Instead we just talked about the conference and what I'd learned. "I learned I'm never going to have children," I almost said. "That's what I learned."

I knew what this was. It was bereavement. It was losing something precious. It was losing a part of myself I'd never gotten to know. I hadn't gone through the bereavement process like I should have done three years ago when I found out. I'd simply stayed in shock, maybe even denial, pretended it wasn't happening. Pretended I could hide from it by moving to Australia. As a result, I was nowhere near acceptance, the part of the process where you assimilate the knowledge and move on with your life. I was somewhere along that process of loss and grief. I knew that. Intellectually I knew that. Emotionally was something else completely. Emotionally a simple look would ignite enough pain to knock me out.

The day inched by. I looked up at lunchtime to find it was only ten-thirty and I still had hours before I could go to lunch and walk around the streets, get outside in the fresh air, unnoticed and anonymous.

My skin doesn't fit.

I felt uncomfortable. I wanted to bury my fingernails into the flesh of my inner arm and claw away the skin. I wanted to dig my nails into the softest, tenderest part of my cheek and strip it of everything. I wanted to hurt physically so the rest of it would go away.

"Kendra, for God's sake!" Janene's frustrated voice called across the office and broke into my trance.

My eyes stopped staring at the swirls of words on the newspaper in front of me and moved up to seek out the office assistant.

"Are you back on planet earth?" she asked, each word coated in sarcasm. "Or shall I page you on whichever crazy world you're visiting today?"

Gabrielle was out of the office, so was Teri. It was only the two of us, which was why she was using this tone. Since the incident with the phone message where Gabrielle had given her a written warning, she had been very careful to hide her dislike of me. As soon as we were alone, the razor-blade studded politeness with which she dealt with me fell away, and who she was would appear.

"How can I help you, Janene?" I asked evenly. I didn't want to fight Janene. I didn't want to fight anyone.

"Did you sign those temp invoices?" she asked.

"Not yet," I replied. I'd meant to, but hadn't. They'd actually left my mind.

Her hazel eyes rolled up at the ceiling as she heaved a frustrated sigh. "What *have* you been doing?"

"I'll sign them when I'm ready," I said.

"You do that," she said with a slight snarl. "And if anyone calls because they haven't been paid, I'll be putting them through to you. I won't be taking the blame because you're not doing your job."

"You know what I love most about you, Janene?" I said, my voice as calm and serene as a sea before a violent storm. "Despite every piece of evidence to the contrary, you still think you're the boss. And, despite the fact I have a better title, and I have a better pay structure and I pretty much have a better job, you go on day after day, laboring under this delusion that you can tell me what to do. It's incredible. I applaud your delusionary abilities."

While Janene tried to shift out the insult amongst what I said, my eyes returned to the newspaper in front of me. I raised my pen, went back to the top of the want ads because I hadn't taken in one word that I'd read.

"If ever there was a woman in need of a good seeing to, it's you," Janene said. "What's the matter, Kendra, not getting any?"

I continued to stare at my newspaper, the nib of my pen pressed hard enough into the newsprint to make it snap.

"Do us all a favor and go get laid, Kendra . . . Oh, yes, I forgot, you don't like sex, so afterwards you make things up and call the cops to have the man arrested, don't you? But I suppose it's only fair—sleeping with you is a crime, isn't it?"

If I hadn't just come back from the conference, if I hadn't been missing the kids, if I'd had more sleep in the past few days, what happened next may not have. I may have just calmly removed my diary from my desk, written down in detail what Janene had said to me and reported her to Gabrielle upon her return. I may have gotten up, left the room and walked around the block until I could sit calmly in the office with Janene. I may have ignored her. I'll never know. In the seconds after she spoke, my eyes closed and then opened to glare at her. I took in her straight, gold-blond hair that fell in expensively styled sheets to her shoulders. I took in her mean eyes, her vicious mouth, her nasty nose, the base cut of her jaw, her expensive black suit. All money and no class. I took it all in. And then I opened my mouth. "If you speak to me again, Janene, I will hurt you."

"As if," she scoffed.

"You just spoke to me." I felt my mouth twist into a bitter, humorless smile. "Obviously you didn't understand what I said." I spread my hands out in front of me, leaned forwards. "I mean, if you *ever* speak to me again; if you even utter a simple hello or good-bye, tell me there's a call for me, or say 'excuse me' if we pass in the corridor, I will wait for you someplace and I will *hurt* you. Now, just nod if you understand."

Janene nodded.

"Good." I lowered my eyes to the newspaper in front of me. Shaking. I was shaking. I couldn't read, couldn't move, in fact. Had those words just come out of my mouth. *My* mouth? Did *I* say that? I had left my body for a few moments, had watched myself from a distance. Now I was back and I was horrified. That was not me. I did not do things like that.

"So, now that it's clear that Janene is never to speak to Kendra again, does anyone want to tell me what's going on?" Gabrielle asked.

Mrs. Traveno stood in the doorway, her black leather briefcase in one hand, her square, flat cardboard box of Office Wonders mugs, magnets and mouse mats balanced on the palm of the other. Her eyes were fixed on me. They burnt into me with the same intensity and heat that a branding machine scorched the flesh of an animal.

When neither Janene nor I spoke, she moved stiffly across the office to her desk beside the large sash window, placed the box on her desk, dropped her briefcase on the floor, threw her handbag onto her chair. She seemed to do it all without taking her eyes off me. Without turning even a fraction, she opened her red lipsticked mouth. "Janene.

Leave." Janene didn't need to be told twice. She didn't even look triumphant as she gathered her bag and coat and left. As soon as the door shut behind her, my boss, dressed in a navy-blue skirt suit, went and flipped the lock. No one was coming in or leaving without her say-so. She folded her arms across her chest, planted her feet in the middle of the floor and glared at me.

Under her gaze, with every passing minute, I crumbled a little more. I shouldn't have said what I said. I couldn't believe I'd said what I said.

"What happened?" she eventually asked, her voice soft enough to be kind.

I tried to breathe but I couldn't, not fully. I tried to moisten my lips but my mouth was dry. "I can't tell you," I replied.

Her chest moved up and down in controlled breaths, she was struggling to keep calm. To remain professional. "Anyone could have walked in like I did. A potential employee, Teri, a client. They would have had to witness what I did. I know you wouldn't have said what you said without good reason. But I can't help you if you won't tell me. I'd like you to think very carefully before you answer me this time. Kendra, what did she say to you?"

I knew I should say, should explain it all. Let her know that what Janene had said was too close to home. I knew I should tell her because if there was one person on the earth I was sure would understand it was Gabrielle. But I couldn't, *wouldn't* repeat it. Not even in abstract. "I can't tell you," I replied.

"Are you sure?" She was offering me one last chance to save myself.

I nodded.

"OK." She nodded. "Kendra Tamale, I am placing you on suspension from your position as head of temp recruitment with basic pay until you can give me a proper reason for your behavior today. This suspension is effective immediately."

As she spoke my teeth gritted together, clenching into each other until my jaw hurt. Tears built up behind the lump, which worked like a dam in my throat.

I mumbled, "Thank you," got up, turned off my computer, dropped my mobile and diary into my bag, picked up my coat and left without another word being said between us.

CHAPTER 33

*G*abrielle and I sat in the corner of a pub, nearer to my flat than to the office.

It was a proper British pub with dark wood, paisley carpet and wallpaper. We had a little table, where we sat opposite each other. A large glass of white wine sat in front of her, a glass of cranberry and soda waited in front of me.

I'd got there first and found the table through the throng of bodies. More than once during the time I sat there, I'd been tempted to text Gabrielle and tell her something had come up and I couldn't make it. I didn't want to see her. Not after what had happened. I was desperately ashamed of myself and didn't want to face anyone. That's why I hadn't been in touch with her for the whole week. But she'd called me yesterday, asked if I would meet her for a drink after she'd finished work and I'd hesitated.

"As your friend, not your boss," she'd said to my pause. "We won't talk about work."

I'd still hesitated.

"Don't make me beg," she'd said quietly. "I'm your friend, don't make me beg." I'd agreed.

Kyle and the kids didn't know about my suspension. I left extra early every morning and came back very late every night. During the day I took a train to central London, walked around, sat in the library near Leicester Square and read books and newspapers. One day I caught the tube out to west London and walked past the house where I grew up. None of my family had lived there in years, but I'd wanted to see it now that I was back in England. Another day I went to the flat in north London where I'd lived when I returned to London from university in Leeds. Visiting them was a way of reminding myself where I'd come from. How far I'd come. How far I'd gone just to come back.

Part of being suspended probably meant I was supposed to sit in my house and reflect upon my actions, but then the Gadsboroughs would know and I didn't want them to know. I didn't want anyone to know. I was so ashamed.

Gabrielle took a drink of her wine, put her glass down on the table and looked up at me. I was probably radiating "leave me alone" vibes. And not because I was cross with her for suspending me, but because I was mortified that she'd had to. That wasn't who I was. I wasn't someone who caused trouble. I wasn't someone who threatened people. I didn't want to talk to Gabrielle because I'd let her down.

She looked tired. Her wavy black hair was shiny and glossy as it framed her face, but her complexion was the grey of the sea after a storm, dark shadows haunted the areas under her eyes, her features were pinched and drawn, as though simply looking normal was an effort. "We miss you," Gabrielle said.

Involuntarily the muscles in my body stiffened and recoiled slightly from her.

"I know I said no work, but I miss you."

"I miss you, too."

"So, are you going to come back?"

"We said no work talk," I replied.

"Yeah, we did."

Gabrielle knocked back half her wine in one go, then put

her glass down on the table with a forcefulness that said she'd made an important decision.

"I was raped when I was twenty-five," she said, staring straight into my eyes.

My body snapped back in my seat, recoiling from her again.

"I knew him. He was a friend of the family. Our parents knew each other—they'd all come over from Australia around the same time when I was sixteen and we moved to Cornwall. He was slightly older than me so I didn't see much of him, but when I came up to London to work he kind of took me under his wing, you know, as a favor to my parents. He took me out a few times, showed me a few places, introduced me to his friends. He was nice, fun, like an older brother, almost. Nothing like that ever happened between us until one day, we're meant to be meeting some friends down the pub for Sunday lunch. He comes over . . . We don't get to Sunday lunch. Well, I didn't. He did. As far as he was concerned nothing important happened that day."

She sat scrunched up in the hallway, holding herself, shaking, staring blankly at the wall opposite. What happened? *She kept asking herself.* What happened? *The door had clicked shut a few minutes ago. Or was it seconds ago? Or was it hours ago? The door had clicked shut and she was alone. She couldn't move and she couldn't talk.* What happened?

The door opened again and she scrunched herself up tighter, afraid he was back. But it was a woman's voice, asking her what had happened. I don't know, Gabrielle wanted to say, but she couldn't speak. She looked up at the woman with the voice and it was her flatmate. And then there were police, asking her questions. And then she was in the hospital. More questions. She answered them. But all the while, in her mind, she was asking, What happened? *All the while, in her mind, she knew she wasn't going to get an answer.*

———

"He was arrested and, long story short, all hell broke loose. My parents fell out with his parents. My parents tried to get me to move back to Cornwall. Our relationship went through a nosedive. My brothers went after him—thankfully, they never found him. It went to court, he was found guilty, but got a suspended sentence because the judge said he hadn't hurt me that badly. I had to move out of my flat, I slept with the lights on, I lived in the shower but he hadn't hurt me, right?

"I'm thirty-nine now and that's about how long it's taken me to get to this point. Where I can talk about it. I don't talk to many people about it, obviously, only the ones I know will understand, but before I didn't talk about it at all. Even though everyone knew, I kept my true feelings to myself because most people thought I should get over it. That a bit of counseling and a bit of positive thinking would 'sort me out.'

"And it kind of became this unspoken thing lurking in the background of our family closet. I always think that somewhere in the future someone will come searching for stuff about our family history and they'll discover there's a hideous secret. And that secret is me. And what I let happen to me." Gabrielle smiled with the lights put out in her eyes. "Don't get me wrong, my family never blamed me; it's taken me this long to realize that they didn't understand. They were doing the best they could. I mean this huge thing had been dumped on them—what happened to me affected them, too. They had their lives upended, too. Course they never blamed me.

"Anyways, we all moved on. I had that bit of counseling,

got on with my life. Or so I told myself and everyone else. I even got married. Which is a very strange thing to do when you have a pathological fear of trusting people." She took another gulp of wine. "I reached a turning point about seven years ago when I went to see *Thelma & Louise* at a movie retrospective down at the National. I must have been the only woman over thirty who hadn't seen it, didn't know what it was about. Didn't realize about *that* scene.

"When it started, I lost it. Ran out of the cinema, threw up outside, spent the night crying. That's when I realized I had to get help. Properly this time. I called a help line. Then I went to see a counselor and then I went to see the chiropractor I recommended to you that you didn't go to see.

"He doesn't just adjust your back, he helps to release all the memories that are physically trapped in your body, the ones that keep you stuck in a situation. He'd explain it better if you went to see him, but everything that ever happens to you is trapped in your body and when you talk it through with him and he adjusts your spine it releases the memory from your body. Helps you to let that physical part of it go.

"If it wasn't for them, I wouldn't be talking to you like this. I wouldn't be feeling as comfortable with myself as I am now. I'm not saying I'm 'over it.' I still see my counselor every so often, and I became a counselor and I'm doing my master's in trauma psychology because I want a better understanding of what happened to me, but I've learned to deal with it.

"I'm back. Well, I'm Gabrielle again. The Gabrielle before what happened is gone forever, and I'll never 'get over it.' I'm just in a different place. I don't let it define me any longer. I'm not the scared woman trapped in that moment— unable to move forwards, unable to go back to who she was. Stuck in this never-ending loop of terror . . . You know what I mean, don't you?"

Gabrielle changed her line of sight from her wineglass to me as she repeated, "Don't you?"

I said nothing, did nothing. I hadn't been prepared for this, for this horror, this exercise in butchery. How do you respond when someone slices open their heart and gives you a guided tour of their pain? Now I knew why she looked at me like that back in the woods, now I knew virtually everything about Gabrielle and I had no idea what to say. What she expected me to say.

Her eyes searched mine. "Now, Kennie, I've just told you all that about me for one reason. I want you to tell me what Janene said to you. I have a pretty good idea what it was, which is why I can understand your reaction. I've told her that the second you tell me what she said I'm going to sack her. Tell me, I need an official explanation, and then I can help you."

I looked down at my hands, clinging to each other in my lap. "It was nothing," I said. It was everything. Words are sometimes everything. And those ones would not come out of my mouth. Especially not after what Gabrielle had just shared. I wasn't going to do that to her.

"I can't let you come back to work until you give me a good reason for what I witnessed," Gabrielle said.

"I can't come back to work, then," I said.

"*Kendra,*" Gabrielle said, frustrated. "Why are you fighting me? Do you want to lose your job?"

"No, but I'm not repeating what she said. Not for you, not to save my job."

Gabrielle gritted her teeth, inhaled deeply through her nose, exhaled deeply. "OK, tell me what happened to you," she said. "Why have you come back from the conference a different person? I saw it on your face when I walked in on Monday. Something happened."

I stared off across the bar, watched a man in dirty jeans

and a hoodie feed coin after coin into a fruit machine. The lights flashed as he slipped in money and pushed the colored buttons. I grabbed my glass intending to drink, but my hand, trembling and unsteady, shook half its contents all over the table. I put the glass down and hunted around my bag for a tissue. I was breathing hard. If I didn't, if I didn't take in as much oxygen as possible, I'd lose my grip. This state I was in, the one where I could talk to someone else, was fragile. Any more pressure and it would crack; I would shatter.

"Sweetheart, talk to me."

"What about?" I wiped off my hand.

"About what happened to you," she said.

———————

"Your skin is still as smooth as silk. I love your skin."

———————

"There's nothing to tell," I said to Gabrielle.

"I'd believe that if you weren't the poster child for post-traumatic stress disorder," Gabrielle replied. "For as long as I've known you you've exhibited all the classic symptoms—jumpiness, isolation, the ability to talk about what happened to you as though it happened to someone else but still react like it happened to you. The way you always dress down or wear multiple layers. And you have flashbacks, don't you? Feeling as though you're reliving the event over and over? It's all normal. And it'll get easier to handle if you talk about it. Let me in, tell me about it."

"Please stop this, Gabrielle. I can't . . ." That was all I could manage, my surface was thinning out like the overstretched plastic of an overinflated balloon. Another press or two and it would come apart.

"Did you see him? Is that it?" she asked.

I closed my eyes. I was so tired. Suddenly very, very tired. I couldn't stay any longer. I slipped my bag strap over my shoulder, moved to get up.

"Don't go, Kennie," she said desperately, reaching out to stop me. "I'm sorry, we'll talk about something else. OK? Don't go."

I stayed in my seat, slipped my bag handle off my shoulder, resettled myself on the seat and the bag in my lap.

"I can't cope at the moment without you, so you can come back to work on Monday, but I'll have to give you a verbal warning. It'll go on your record," Gabrielle said.

I nodded. That sounded more than fair. I'd behaved badly and I deserved to be punished.

"Consider yourself warned. But what I said to Janene still stands: if you tell me what she said I'll sack her."

"So," I said, using every last molecule of strength to inject sunshine into my tone, "I'll get the next round in, shall I? Same again?"

"Yes, Kendra, same again," she said. And I pretended I thought she was talking about the drinks.

CHAPTER 34

*U*ou're doing it wrong!" Summer proclaimed. She stared with despair, genuine, deep despair at her plate. It was all wrong. It was just a bowl of cornflakes.

"What do you mean?" Kyle asked.

"You're doing it wrong!" she shrieked in reply.

That sound, the shriek, cut through Kyle's head, set his teeth on edge and ignited his temper. He looked at Jaxon. He was staring at his plate with an identical look of despair.

This is Kendra's fault, Kyle thought. He didn't know how or why, but he knew she was behind this.

"How can I be doing it wrong. It's cornflakes."

"It's Saturday," Jaxon said quietly.

"I'm well aware that it's Saturday. What does that have to do with anything?"

"You're doing it wrong!" his daughter repeated. "I want Kendie to do it."

I knew it! Kyle thought.

"Kendie does it properly. Kendie makes Saturday break-fast properly. You're doing it wrong."

Kendra. What had life been like before Kendra?

The woman coaxed out new behaviors in both his kids. They'd latched onto her and hadn't let go. At first he'd thought it was the novelty factor, the fact there was some-one new to play with, then he realized that it was because Kendra was constant. They knew she'd always be there. In the midst of Ashlyn's drinking, none of them had known whom they would be dealing with from one day to the next. Sometimes she was fun and buoyant, other days she wouldn't stop crying. Some days she would love them all, other days she'd tell them they'd ruined her life.

She would say unbelievable things to him. None of it she remembered. He'd thought, at first, that it was shame and regret that made her act as if nothing had happened; then he discovered she genuinely didn't remember. She didn't remember saying he was the worst lover she'd ever had. She didn't recall telling him it was a good thing they had two children at once because even the thought of having him rutting on top her was more than she could stomach. She didn't remember crying in his arms saying she'd kill herself if he ever left her. He dreaded to think what she said to the twins when he wasn't there. When Ashlyn was drinking, they never knew who was going to walk through the door in the morning.

It wasn't simply life with Ashlyn that made the kids cling to Kendra, Kyle knew, it was him, too. He'd been at work. Always. He'd hidden from the problem in his technical drawings and models and projects, subconsciously telling himself that the children were too young to understand. Subconsciously telling himself there was no problem to understand.

It took him nearly ten years to confront the situation, five of which his children were around to witness—Kendra had done it within minutes of meeting them. Gave his kids breakfast, read him the riot act. And with the kids, when they asked her to jump, she generally asked them how high. Kendra didn't spoil them, didn't give in to their demands, she simply put them first. Always. They'd never had that so unconditionally before. No wonder they dug the hooks of their lives deeply into her and had no intention of letting go.

For some reason, for the past seven days, she'd fallen off

the face of the earth. She'd become the lodger he'd *originally* thought he'd end up with: someone who kept to themselves who paid the rent on time, who never got involved. She left for work extra early, and always returned in the dark, her head down as though if she didn't look up she'd be invisible, that those in the house wouldn't be able to see her. The kids kept asking where she was, why she wasn't in the flat. Why she hadn't picked them up from school that week. If she didn't call them every night they would have thought she, too, had left them.

She was avoiding them.

Him. He suspected it was him.

Kyle had been trying to work out what had caused it. He'd wondered if it was because she knew. She had looked into his eyes in an unguarded moment and she'd seen the truth.

Goddamnit! Kyle slammed the milk carton down on the table, splashing milk all over his hand and the table.

Summer and Jaxon both jumped, stared at their father. He was rigid with anger, his face on the edge of a snarl, his eyes narrowed and fierce. And his hand was covered in milk. They both knew anger from their mother, they both knew this was how the shouting started. No one had shouted at them in so long they'd begun to believe it wouldn't happen again.

Summer wanted Kendie so much at that moment. Her mumma or Kendie. Mumma was with Gra'ma Naomi and Kendie was here. And Kendie made a special breakfast. And when she made breakfast it was lovely. And it made her smile in her tummy. And now Dad was cross because he was doing it wrong. "I want Kendie," she whispered.

"Well you can't have her," Kyle snapped. "I'm all you've got."

Kyle watched as things disintegrated before his eyes. Summer's face crumpled and then the high-pitched wail followed as her mouth became a cavernous wound in her face. Her face filled with scarlet as the tears started. Kyle slapped his milk-splattered hand against his forehead. *Stupid.*

As Summer wailed, Jaxon decided to hide. If he kept his head down and wished hard enough, no one would see him. No one would know he was there until Kendie came over and she asked Garvo where he was. And sometimes Kendie could understand Garvo's language. And Kendie would find him. And she would make Saturday breakfast. For now, he was hiding.

Kyle turned away from a wailing Summer to Jaxon. His son had his head buried in the nook of his arms, his grubby cast on the table, his free arm on top, his shoulders shaking. *Bloody stupid.*

"OK," Kyle said, trying to appease his children. "OK, I'm sorry. I'm sorry. Tell me how to do it properly. OK, pumpkin? Tell me how to do it properly."

"I want Kendie," Summer wailed. Long rivulets of hurt rained down her bright red face and her whole body quaked with tears. Each wail was like a nail in his forehead. It was getting louder, more fervent.

"OK," he said, crouching down to his daughter, while drying his milk-soaked hand on his trousers. "I'll get Kendie. OK? I'll get Kendie. But please stop crying. OK? Please stop crying." Summer's howling subsided as she realized Kendie was coming. "See?" Kyle picked up his mobile, shook off a few droplets of milk, flipped it open and dialed. "See, I'm calling her."

Summer looked at him with deep suspicion but her wailing had stopped. He had a small window of time before the lamentations started again. The phone rang and rang, then the answer machine kicked in.

Great. She was screening. He knew she was screening

because a light in her house had come on at around 2 a.m. last night but he hadn't heard her leave this morning. And he'd been listening for her because he'd unintentionally been keeping track of her. Making sure she came back at night. Was safely in her home.

Kyle and Summer locked eyes, a look of understanding passing between them. They'd had an agreement, he'd re-neged on that agreement, her part of the deal was to start screaming if he let her down. Summer's face crumpled as she got ready to start screeching again; it was only fair.

"I'll go get her," Kyle said, desperately trying to stop her. "I'll go get her."

Barefoot, his shirt half tucked in, Kyle raced out the back door, the change in his pockets jingling as he ran over the flagstones that framed the square of grass, over the flag-stones on the other side, then he was at her door.

Kyle was pretty sure Kendra was avoiding him—and as a consequence the kids —because she knew how he felt about her and wanted nothing to do with him. He didn't want to feel like that about another woman. It was wrong, somehow.

He'd always thought he'd be in love with Ashlyn and only Ashlyn for the rest of his life. He'd willingly signed up to spend forever with her. The night she'd told him she was in love with him, he'd been speechless. He'd never thought he had a chance with her. He'd noticed her amongst the group of friends they shared and was always looking for an excuse to talk to her, never dreamed . . . She was incredible. Vivacious, talented, devastatingly beautiful. She had a sparkle in her eye that always held his attention. The soft twist of her mouth made him want to kiss her over and over. He longed to run his fingers through her hair. He'd been si-lent when she told him how she felt. As the silence swelled between them, he became suspicious. Wondered who had put her up to it. But, his desire for her had outweighed his worry about being made to look like a fool.

Still, he took it slowly. When they'd first started dating, he'd been cautious. Waiting for the other shoe to drop, waiting for her to yell, "April fool! Loser!" at him. He hadn't dared touch her for two months in case she told him to get lost. Being with her was never difficult; it opened up a part of life that he never knew existed. He used to feel his heart expand every time she looked at him; he used to thank God every morning he woke up to find she was still there beside him. Kyle had wanted to give Ashlyn the world. Designing her studio had been the most important project of his life. Every idea created with the need to make life easy, perfect, for his wife-to-be; every line drawn with love. When they'd exchanged vows it had been forever.

And then it wasn't. Then he couldn't look at her without seeing an out-of-control, mean, lying drunk. Couldn't talk to her without it becoming a row. Then he was having to take the kids out in the car to get away from one of her tantrums. And, making love . . . ? Nearly two years had passed since that had happened. In all that time he still had urges, still wanted to have sex with his wife, but after the last time . . .

———

She came to bed late, much later than him. He wasn't asleep because even after all this time he found it hard to sleep without her in the bed. They may not have slept spooned up together anymore, but that didn't mean he could sleep without her. Kyle responded almost immediately to her soft hands running over him, erupting desire with every caress. Then her mouth was kissing him, her lips fervent and eager on his. He'd reeled a little at the smell of her other lover on her breath, but it'd been so long since he'd held her, felt her against him, been a part of her body, that he shoved aside his disgust.

He kissed her back, lifted himself up as she sat astride him, helped her to tug her vest over her head, watching with mounting lust as her hair cascaded back into place. He reached up to unclasp her black bra when she suddenly ripped herself away from him, leapt off the bed, her hand over her mouth, as she ran into the en suite, slamming the door shut behind her and retching into the toilet basin.

For a brief, terror-loaded moment he thought she might be pregnant. Then dismissed it, of course she wasn't pregnant, just drunk. Just drunk.

As he lay in the darkened room, the sheets bunched around his waist, his eyes focused on the ceiling, listening to her cough up, it occurred to him that if she was consistently hungover she might not remember to take the pill. And even if she did remember, would they be getting the full contraceptive protection if she was constantly throwing up?

They were playing Russian roulette every time they slept together, he realized. And the simple fact was he didn't want to have another child with Ashlyn. He couldn't bring another soul into this mess.

That was the last time he attempted to have sex with his wife or responded to any of her attempts, drunk or otherwise.

If he thought of the Ashlyn he loved, he remembered the woman with the pale, sweaty face and straggly hair, sitting in a hospital bed holding his newborn son, while he held their newborn daughter. He remembered the woman who sat up with him every single night during his exams and still went to work the next day. He thought of the woman who convinced him to have sex in his parents' backyard. She didn't exist anymore.

Kendra did. Kendra did and Kyle wanted her. And that made him feel guilty, as though he was cheating on his wife. Kendra brought out something in his kids. In him . . . She made him talk. It wasn't that she encouraged him to do it; it was more that he couldn't help himself. Kyle, who'd spent a lifetime keeping most things to himself, bottling up almost all of his emotions, often told Kendra everything.

She was beautiful in a subtle, understated way compared to Ashlyn. He liked the way Kendra sometimes pulled back her hair into a ponytail, showing all the smooth outlines of her striking face. The warmth and quiet strength that swirled in her large black eyes, the firm fragility that came over her lips when she smiled, and the rarely glimpsed curves of her gorgeous body. He wanted to lose himself in her. To unravel the core of who he was inside her, to become a part of her mind and her body. He longed to hear everything about her. To feel her unspooling her secrets into the depths of his heart.

Kyle hadn't felt even a fraction of all this when he'd kissed her. That moment had been so mortifying he'd erased it from his mind almost immediately. Now that all these longings and desires had blossomed for her, he wanted to remember how her lips felt under his, the scent of her hair up close, how soft her skin was, how their bodies blended together—and he couldn't. He'd tried, but it was gone. The memory of being physically close to Kendra had vanished and because he knew it had once been a reality he found it impossible to create a false memory.

Kyle had fallen for her. For weeks he suspected he had, but it wasn't until Jaxon's accident, when she was there when the kids needed her, when he needed her, that he realized.

She was The One. He loved a past Ashlyn. He loved a present Kendra. That was why he'd asked her to stay with them. With him. He was in love with her.

That was most likely why she was avoiding him. She knew; she was not interested. She'd made that abundantly clear. She just didn't think of him, feel for him, in that way.

So, right now, Kyle had to put those thoughts, those longings, out of his head. He had his kids to sort out. To make happy. Kyle raised his hand and rapped on the door. Nothing. There was movement, footsteps upstairs. She was definitely in. But the footsteps weren't coming towards the door. Kyle knocked again, louder this time. Eventually he heard footsteps coming down the steps and slowly the door opened.

Kyle drew back a little as he looked into the face of a complete stranger.

CHAPTER 35

*E*r, hi," Kyle said to me.

I hadn't seen him since I left for the conference and I'd almost forgotten he was real. I had the photo on my phone, but he was different in the flesh. Warmer, solid, human. Needing to be communicated with.

He was taken aback when he saw me. I wasn't looking my best, I knew that. I was dressed—jeans, T-shirt and sweater— because I was on my way out, but I knew my shoulder-length hair combed into a side parting so it hid most of my face was a dull, flat black; I knew my eyes were threaded with red veins because I didn't sleep for more than three hours a night; I knew dark shadows had ingrained themselves under my eyes; and I knew my mouth was a permanent flatline. Not even makeup, which I rarely wore, could hide how awful I looked.

"I need your help," he said.

"Why, what's happened?" I asked, alarmed at his urgency.

"I've left the kids alone, I need you. Summer is going mental because I've done breakfast wrong or something. Jaxon's going mental as well, but quietly. You know, like he does. They want you. The only way to get them to stop crying was to say I'd get you to do it. Will you come?"

"Course," I replied. "I'll be over soon. Just let me get dressed."

"You are dressed," Kyle replied.

I knew I was, I wasn't that far gone. I just needed time to prepare to see them. I'd spoken to them on the phone but

328 ♦ DOROTHY KOOMSON

hadn't seen them since the conference and needed time to prepare for that torture. "So I am," I said with a hollow, short laugh.

His face creased with concern. "Are you all right?" he asked softly.

"Me? Fine. Just suffering the aftereffects of long hours. Let's go."

The kids were in their differing states of distress when I entered the kitchen behind Kyle. Summer was taking small gulps of air that shook her entire body in short, hiccupy movements. Her little oval face was red, her rounded cheeks streaked with tears. Jaxon had his head resting on his folded arms and his shoulders were moving up and down in heavy, sighlike jerks. Surely they couldn't be this upset over breakfast. Surely? I turned to Kyle, wondering what he'd done to them.

Kyle's face flamed up with indignation. "I was just trying to give them their breakfast, like I do every other day of the week," he said in answer to my silent accusation.

"But it's Saturday," I stated.

He threw his hands open. "Why does everyone keep saying that?"

"He was doing it all wrong," Summer declared between her gulps, obviously having no problems about telling on her dad.

"Could someone explain to me how I could be doing cereal wrong?" Kyle growled between gritted teeth.

He doesn't know, I realized. I cast my mind back. Since I'd moved in they'd pretty much had breakfast with me either over here or over at the flat every Saturday, apart from the odd weekends when they stayed over at their grandmother's place or last weekend when I was away, which meant they'd made breakfast themselves.

This was important to them. This breakfast ritual I'd conjured up out of thin air and desperation was important to them. It was something special the three of us shared. I had something amazing with these two. I'd never be a mother. Never be *their* mother, but I had something wonderful. Especially considering how insular they were. After all their experiences, they rarely let anyone in, but they'd welcomed me. If I wanted, I could ask Hoppy to sleep in my flat for the whole night; with Jaxon's coaching I was starting to understand Garvo's language. We had a breakfast ritual.

What I'd been doing, shutting myself away from them because I was in agony, wasn't fair to them. Hadn't I started this as a way to atone for what I did in Sydney? It wasn't about me, it was about them. I couldn't just shut down from these two, I had to be with them. I could grieve in the spaces in between.

I reached for the cereal box. "OK, we're going to have to teach your dad how to make breakfast on Saturdays," I said. "But only if you both stop crying." Summer rallied first, sniffed back her tears, gripped the bottom of her pink T-shirt and wiped her face clean, leaving a trail of red streaks from how hard she rubbed. "And you sit up," I said to no one in particular. Jaxon realized I was talking to him and sat up. He used the sleeve of his long-sleeve top to scrub away his tears.

Over breakfast? I thought again, although I didn't look at Kyle this time, didn't want to upset him as well.

"OK, Kyle, could you get us four bowls please?" I said.

For a moment, Kyle went to say there were bowls on the table but then ran the wisdom of doing that through his mind.

"Any in particular?" he asked.

"Nope, not as long as they match."

He looked at the white bowl, the bowl with blue stripes around its rim and the bowl that was red in the middle that currently sat on the table.

"Ah, right."

Once he'd retrieved a new set of plates from the cupboard, ones that matched this time, and laid them in front of each place setting at the table, we started to teach him how to make Saturday breakfast properly.

PORRIDGE & THICK, GLOOPY CREAM

◆ ◆ ◆

CHAPTER **36**

*G*ood things come in threes.
Bad things also happen in threes. I forgot that.

CHAPTER 37

*E*louise, one of my former flatmates from college who lived in Leeds, came down to London for a few days on business. She called me, told me off for not turning up in Leeds the other weekend to meet her and our other flatmate, Meg, said I *had* to come up to London to meet her. We could do the whole London thing like tourists: dinner, a show, drinks back in her hotel.

It was the start of the summer holidays so Kyle was going to take the kids on a surprise trip to Brighton. He'd managed to scrape together enough to afford two nights at a B&B. He'd asked if I wanted to come, but I'd declined—I hadn't seen Elouise in four years and felt guilty about blowing her out that time.

Elouise and I had dinner—Thai—in Soho, we went to a show on Shaftesbury Avenue, and we went back to Elouise's hotel and sat up talking. We fell asleep and I woke up in the early hours of Saturday feeling sorry for myself. I hated sleeping in my clothes; I had to go all the way back to Kent and I'd be lucky if the taxi driver didn't ask for my cash card and PIN just for the pleasure of listening to where I wanted him to take me. Besides, the walk of shame would feel the same whether I'd spent five hours sleeping in my clothes or eight. I rolled over and went back to sleep.

Saturday, with nothing to rush back for, we mooched around the shops on Oxford Street. (I'd had a shower and borrowed some of Elouise's clothes.) We went to dinner again, I fell asleep again, this time in Elouise's clothes. Enough was enough, I decided at 3 a.m.—I had to go home. I changed back into my clothes, slung my bag across my body and left her room.

The concierge called me a cab and when it arrived, I sat in the back, valiantly ignoring the digital figures that told me I'd be eating tinned soup for the next month.

I opened my side gate and, feeling scrunchy and in need of my pajamas and bed, I rounded the corner into the courtyard.

On the step outside my flat, where the kids usually sat when they were waiting for me to come home, was a figure, hunched over its knees, its face hidden in the blackness of 4 a.m.

My heart leapt into my throat and I stopped short. The figure, which was definitely a man's, hadn't seen me—I could still turn and run. I thought this as the figure looked up and saw me. The familiarity of the movement and my eyes becoming accustomed to the dark allowed me to see it was Kyle.

"Jeez, Kyle, you gave me such a fright," I whispered because of the hour. I pressed my hand over my chest to still my leapfrogging heart.

He clambered to his feet and seemed to deflate in relief when he saw me. I moved slowly forwards but he crossed the distance between us in three strides, threw his arms around me. Automatically my body stiffened, uncomfortable, edgy; scared, almost.

"Oh, thank God," he said as he clung to me, oblivious to the fact I wanted him to let me go. "Oh, thank God," he said again, then slackened his hold a little, looked into my face, his eyes running over my features as though desperate to confirm I was real. His hand moved towards my face and I jerked my head away before he made contact, pushed out from his hold.

"What's going on?" I asked. It took me a moment to remember, he wasn't supposed to be here. *They* weren't supposed to be here.

"I've been ringing your mobile for the past couple of days. Gabrielle's been calling you as well."

"It ran out of battery and I was meant to be home Friday night so I didn't take my charger. But that's not important. Why are you here, why aren't you in Brighton?"

"I thought something had happened to you, too," he said, ignoring my question.

"Too?" I asked cautiously.

"It's the kids," he said, his face crumpling as he said it. "They're gone."

"Gone?" I asked. "What do you mean, 'gone'?"

"Ashlyn's taken them and I don't know where."

Kyle paced my living room floor as he told the tale. I, meanwhile, having left my body, hovered a little distance away watching myself sitting, stiff and openly incredulous, on the sofa listening to him.

At lunchtime on Friday afternoon he'd gone to collect the kids as usual. As soon as they got home, they'd pack and set off. They'd planned to go straight from school, but they'd taken so long over breakfast and Kyle had a meeting so they didn't have time to pack their things nor tidy the house before they left.

They weren't at school. Mrs. Chelner was confused. Had scrunched her face up as she told him their mother had picked them up. She was on the list, her picture was there on the consent form along with Kyle's.

Ashlyn picking them up wasn't even that unusual. When she'd first moved out she did it all the time; would take them for dinner, spend time with them at her flat and drop them home before bedtime. They even had spare clothes and toys at her place. When she went to America, Kyle assumed those belongings she had kept at her flat had gone to her mother's place, but no, Ashlyn had put them in storage. Apparently, ready for a time like this. She usually called when she was picking them up. Let him know so he wouldn't worry. This time she hadn't called. It'd been two days and she hadn't called.

Kyle found out where she'd been staying in England this time around from her mother and he'd gone there, but the place was packed up. Her neighbor said that she had moved out a few days earlier—Ashlyn had said she had worked out an arrangement with her husband and she was leaving London with her children. Her mobile was off, Naomi didn't know where they were and hadn't heard from her.

Naomi had been distraught, Kyle said. She said they should call the police and track them down, but Kyle had said no. To give them a few more days before they went down that route. Kyle knew how much animosity there was between Naomi and Ashlyn. They had a complex relation-ship—even though Ashlyn loved her mother, they had so many unresolved issues and unspoken resentments that they limited the time they spent together. Of course Naomi didn't know that Ashlyn was an alcoholic and if they went to the police, he'd have to tell them and Naomi would find out. And if, as he suspected, they were going to be back in a few days, that would be one of the worst things he'd ever done to Ashlyn.

He knew she hadn't left the country because he still had their passports and birth certificates but she had planned it with them. He knew because Hoppy, Roald Dahl's *Fantastic*

Mr. Fox and Summer's eye mask/tiara were gone; Garvo's food and water bowls, Ashlyn's sunglasses and Jaxon's favorite steam train were gone. The last weekend they'd spent with her she must have told them to bring the important things to school and not to tell Kyle.

I listened patiently for the part of the story where he said, "And then I called the police and they're combing every inch of the country to find them." Obviously "And then I woke up and found it was all an awful dream" would have been better, but, "And then I called the police and they're combing every inch of the country to find them" would do.

It never came.

While I was sitting in a hotel talking about Elouise's engagement, and how I ended up in Geelong when I'd meant to go to Melbourne, the kids were being moved farther and farther away from home. The kids were being stolen.

Kyle wasn't talking anymore. His large frame stood in the center of the room, very still, as though waiting for me to say something. As though I had an answer.

I was trying to remember the last thing I said to them. "Enjoy your surprise," I think it'd been. I think. But I couldn't be sure.

My mind raced. Did I hug and kiss them? Probably not. I'd had Friday off to spend with Elouise, I'd got that weekday lie-in I'd been craving for so long. I'd only spoken to them on the phone.

What did we talk about the day before? The summer holidays? "My holidays," Summer had called them, believing they'd been named for her. *Maybe. But what did we say we'd do during that time? Did we talk about that at all? What was the last conversation we had? Did Jaxon talk about Garvo? Or am I thinking about every other time?*

I sat staring through Kyle, my mind trying to race through the memories, things we'd talked about, the things we laughed about, the things we'd done in the past few days. Weeks. And then my mind remembered the week I'd spent avoiding them. Those seven days when I squandered precious moments with them.

I didn't know. I didn't know you were meant to savor and hang onto every moment in case it was your last.

CHAPTER 38

$\mathcal{T}$ime passed slowly without the children. Kyle and I spent every free moment together in my flat.

The silence in the house was too big, overwhelming, suffocating. Every time either of us stepped across the threshold it felt like being submerged in a vat of feathers, the softness of the quiet belying the murderous danger that lurked within those walls. The reality of their absence was pressed down our throats, filling up our lungs and deadening our senses. I'd feel the cold of not having Summer run to me as though she hadn't seen me in an age. I'd experience the chill of not having Jaxon drag his feet towards me and throw one arm around my neck before giving me a quick squeeze. Not hearing Summer screaming that she wasn't going to school and no one could make her echoed ghostlike around me; not hearing Jaxon accidentally call me Mumma was a haunting whisper that rang deafeningly in my ears.

Being without them was a wound so deep I didn't know how I'd bear it, if it'd ever heal. The house was a relic to the family we'd created. Kyle hadn't changed a thing since the morning he'd last seen them: their breakfast bowls sat soaking in the sink, where he'd dumped them before corralling them out the door; on the kitchen table the cornflakes box sat, as did the two slices of buttered toast that both of them had only taken three bites from; Jaxon's trainer lay unturned by the front door, having probably fallen from his bag on their way out; Summer's drawing of the plane that took her to America sat on the pouf in the living room with the coloring pencil she'd been using, lying on top of it, where she'd been forced to put it down before they left. Beside the pencil was my turquoise ring, which she hadn't taken with her. I stared at it but I didn't pick it up; I wanted her to give it back to me herself.

Kyle took to sleeping on my sofa, his face unshaved and gaunt, his eyes dull and empty. He ate if I made something; he showered for something to do. Mostly he sat on my sofa clutching the white receiver of the cordless phone from the house, staring into space and praying she'd bring them back. I knew he was praying because I was, too.

I understood why Ashlyn had done it. She must have been feeling this desperate for months. Sober and desperate. Not even being able to drink to dull the pain of not being with her children. I understood why Ashlyn had done it. And I hated her for it.

My hatred of her grew with every minute she had her children. It was the not knowing. Were they OK? Had she had a relapse and done something to put them in danger? Did they mind not being with Kyle? With me? The not knowing was a torture she had no right to put either of us through. They weren't mine, but I loved them. She knew that. Even if she didn't care about that, what about Kyle? He was devastated. She knew he would be; if not, why take them like that?

Often my hatred of her spiraled out of control. I'd think it through, then I'd hate myself. For begrudging a mother being with her children. For not guessing when we met that she was on the verge of doing this. The emotions would spin inside, slipping and twisting over each other like a mass of snakes.

WHY DOESN'T SHE JUST CALL? I'd cry out inside. *Tell us they're OK.* Tell us we'll see them again.

I took to bargaining with God, the universe, whomever: *If we hear they're OK, then that will be OK. We don't even have to live with them again. Just to know they're OK.*

"What you thinking about?" Kyle asked, dragging me out of willing the phone to ring, and hearing Summer say, "Kendie, we're having so much fun." Jaxon mumbling, "Have you got my train set?"

I glanced down at Kyle. It was day ten without the kids. Kyle was stretched out on the sofa, his head resting on my thighs as he stared at the television. Now he'd rolled onto his back, his mussed-up hair flattened against the blue background of my jeans. He'd shaved so looked fresh-faced, more alive than he had in the last ten days. But his sallow cheeks were still sunken, gun-metal grey shadows scored beneath his glazed-over mahogany eyes. Separation had dragged youth out of Kyle's once calm, happy face; separation had aged him.

"Nothing much," I replied to his question. Without thinking I raised my hand, my fingers reaching to stroke the black locks of his hair. It felt so natural, then I remembered, he wasn't Will. We weren't like that. I stopped and lowered my hand.

Kyle's mouth moved upwards, his lips twisting into a small, intimate smile that didn't show his teeth, nor completely eradicate his sadness. He'd seen what I'd almost done and had probably read it wrong.

"I'm glad you're here," he said, his voice hoarse with emotion. "Don't know what I'd have done . . ." He lifted his hand; his fingers with their short, bitten nails came towards my face. His palm rested on my cheek, and slowly his thumb stroked across my cheekbone. He hadn't even attempted to touch me like that in an age. My instincts told me to pull away, to stop this. But I fought myself, allowed him to touch me. I stared down at him, our eyes linked like our hearts had been linked by this loss.

Kiss him. The thought blossomed in my mind. *Kiss him and be done with it.* He was a nice guy. One of the good guys. We both felt from the same place, this place of pain. This land of unending agony. We could do this. *I* could do this. It didn't matter that I didn't feel that way about him, that I wasn't attracted to him. It'd just be a thing to do. A way to get from here to there without feeling all of this in-between. Because it was all of this in-between that was killing me. Killing him. Killing us. We needed a way to forget about all of this for a while. To think about something else. *Kiss him and see what happens.*

"You're special, you know that?" Kyle whispered.

———

"You're special. Stop fighting, you're special."

———

My body jackknifed away from him before I could stop myself. I was suddenly aflame, the memory wending across my skin, burning into my mind, tugging me back. *No,* I decided, *I'm not going there. I'm staying here. I'm staying. I'm not going back to that night, I'm staying here. With Kyle. In the present.*

I reached up, covered Kyle's hand with mine, warmth flowing from me to him, him to me. The bond between us was incredibly strong, possibly unbreakable. But it wasn't this.

I worked my fingers between his and, smiling sadly at him, focusing on him, I gently pulled his hand away, returned it to his chest.

"Kendra," Kyle whispered. "Why . . . ?" He closed his eyes,

shook his head, confused. I continued to stare at him. Had to. He was my anchor. My focus. My root to now. If I lost this connection I'd end up back there. Back when.

Kyle opened his eyes. "You know how much you mean to me, yeah?"

I nodded. I did. I knew. He meant a lot to me, too. He was the father of my children.

"We'll always be friends," I said.

Misery at this new rejection slotted snugly beside the agony that already sat in his eyes. He didn't bother to hide it. *What's the point? Why bother to hide anything?* Kyle's eyes said. *Everything is futile.* He rolled onto his side, hugged the phone to his chest and went back to staring at the television.

Day nineteen.

I was going insane; slowly but surely unraveling from the inside out.

Everywhere I went I saw a flash of jet black hair, caught a glimpse of orange, would hear a giggle, and I'd think it was Summer.

Whenever I'd feel eyes resting on me, experience a presence tapping me on the back, hear a small chuckle I would feel it was Jaxon. They were haunting me. It was making me mentally unstable.

Every moment was filled with the void of their absence. Nothing seemed important. Work certainly wasn't. Gabrielle and I hadn't gotten back to normal yet; I wasn't sure we ever would.

I should have told her what she wanted to hear. I couldn't. She didn't understand why I couldn't repeat what Janene had said. She'd laid herself bare, exposed the very core of who she was, to get me to speak to her and I couldn't. Wouldn't. Such vileness would not come out of my mouth. If I wasn't living in this childless hell, I don't know how our friendship would have progressed. As it was, we worked together and we left it at that. Janene kept her distance, too. Even if she hadn't it wouldn't have mattered. Nothing mattered. Summer and Jaxon were gone.

Every time I thought I saw them, every time I had an urge to chase after their apparitions, I felt the hope that I would see them again die a little more. I began to believe they were ghosts. That they were gone permanently. She'd driven them into a wall. She'd fallen asleep with a pan on and there'd been a fire. She'd taken them somewhere and forgotten them. I was never going to see them again. They were gone.

I started to dread going home. I would turn into Tennant Road and I would see the cloud of grief that hung low and threatening over number thirty-four. My footsteps would slow, my limbs would become anvils I had to drag towards my destination. Sometimes I wanted to turn on my heels and run. To flee the sadness. Sometimes I'd walk around the block five or six times, my footsteps echoing in my ears, my heart heavy and slow in my chest, simply to delay having to go home. To delay having to wander back into the nightmare that was life without the kids.

Things became so bad, so bleak, I came close to opening Will's letter a few times. I actually slipped my finger under the flap on one occasion. If it was bad news, the worst news, it would simply add to the grief I was feeling. It'd complete my misery. Would speed up the insanity process. I didn't do it in the end, but I knew that much longer and I would.

Kyle moved in with me. He didn't ask if I minded—I don't think it occurred to him to ask—he simply did it.

I came back from work one day and found he'd brought over the models and drawings for his latest project, his drawing table and his seat. He set himself up in the dead space between where the dining area ended and before the living area began. A small suitcase with his clothes lived between the arm of the sofa and the wall, his shaver and toothbrush and aftershave and deodorant found a new place in my bathroom. Every evening I'd come back and find him sitting there, hunched over his drawing table rather than his computer, his ruler pressed against the blue and white graph paper, his retractable pencil against it, drawing lines. The television would be a low hum in the background, the air would be heavy with the fresh, bitter smell of real coffee. He lived on coffee. Didn't eat until I came home, looked more aged with every passing day. Hopelessness had scored wrinkles into his forehead, worry had all but darkened the area under his eyes, bereavement had shed pounds from his frame.

He'd barely raise his head when I walked in of a night. We'd say hi without even looking at each other let alone making eye contact. I'd change into jeans and a sweater, I'd make food, something simple—rice and Ghanaian stew, chickpea and kidney bean salad, pasta and tomato sauce— and we'd eat on the sofa, sitting side by side but in different worlds, staring at the television. Afterwards I'd wash up and say good night and would go to bed, lie on top of the covers, the mugginess of the summer night making it impossible to sleep even if I could. I'd lie with my eyes wide open, wakedreaming about seeing the kids again. Knowing in the pit of my stomach, at the root of who I was, I wouldn't. We wouldn't.

Kyle and I hardly spoke because he'd also accepted he wasn't going to see them again. I knew he accepted that because the other day, I noticed he'd tacked the picture

Summer hadn't finished drawing onto the edge of his drawing table, and Jaxon's errant trainer sat underneath it. I noticed a few days later, when I braved the house to get Kyle's post and few other bits and pieces, that he'd washed up and tidied away their breakfast things.

CHAPTER **39**

You have to call the police," I said to Kyle on day thirty-seven.

I'd had enough. I'd held my tongue, but no more. He had to do something. We couldn't sit passively by and let this thing happen to us. We couldn't accept this situation. We had to do something.

Kyle paused in what he was sketching out, but didn't glance up in my direction. He stared unseeingly at the paper in front of him, listening but not looking.

"We've got to accept that she's not going to bring them back on her own; you have to call the police."

"She's their mother," he said and lowered his head to start drawing again.

"I know, but this is hell, Kyle. This is hell and we have to do something."

"Not that."

"Why not?"

"She's their mother."

My eyes flew around the room, looking for something to throw at him. Something that would glance off the back of his head, knock some sense into him but not actually kill him. I couldn't explain a dead body to the police. But then, maybe they'd understand. They'd understand the pure frustration of this situation. The kids were gone and their father wouldn't do anything about it.

"I know she's their mother, I know she loves them, but

she's an alcoholic. She might hurt them without even realizing."

"She's their mother," he said, his voice dangerously low. "STOP SAYING THAT!"

He spun on his chair. "No. I have to keep saying it because I need to remember it."

"*You* need to remember it?"

"I lived with Ashlyn, I remember what she was like. I remember the things she did but I know she's sober. And that she wouldn't hurt them when she's sober. And that's what's going to keep her sober. She's their mother and she won't do a thing to hurt them. If I thought for one minute she would, I'd call the police in a heartbeat."

"You're deluding yourself, Kyle. No one else keeps an alcoholic sober. They keep themselves sober. They can't do it for anyone else. If they could, do you think they'd be alcoholics? They'd be able to stop drinking when someone they love asks them to. They can't. They have a disease and it's all-consuming. That's why it's so destructive, nothing else is as important as the next drink. So what happens if that urge overwhelms Ashlyn? What happens if she slips? What happens to the kids then? You have to call the police."

"No."

"If you don't, I will."

He stood, pulled himself up to his full height. I wasn't sure if he was aware that he was trying to intimidate me, trying to get me to do what he wanted with his physicality.

In response I stood up to my full height, planted my feet firmly on the floor, folded my arms defensively across my chest. This was far too important to be scared by him. Nothing mattered but the kids' safety.

"No you won't. They're my kids. They're Ashlyn's kids and I won't get her into trouble by calling the police. She's going to bring them back."

"Then why hasn't she even called to tell you that they're OK? Or dropped you an e-mail? Or even sent a carrier pigeon? Because maybe they're not. Maybe they're not OK and she doesn't know how to tell you."

Kyle paused, the many scenarios playing out across his mind. He knew, he'd been on the front line, he knew better than me what could happen to them. What more could happen to them. He buried his hand in his thick black hair, dragged it backwards.

"I wished for this so many times," Kyle said, his voice loaded with emotion. "When Summer was complaining about going to school, when Jaxon wouldn't tell me what was wrong with him, when I wasn't given a great assignment—I wished that I wasn't tied down. It wasn't anything that I played out or that I meant, it just crossed my mind. I feel so guilty about even thinking it. And now they're gone and it's all my fault.

"If I'd been more reasonable about visitation, hadn't used them as pawns to get her to come home, she wouldn't have felt cornered into doing this. This is all my fault and I know exactly how she felt. And why she did it."

"The difference being you'd let her know they're OK. You wouldn't torture her like this. You never have, you never would."

"You think I should call the police?" he asked after a pause.

"Yes," I breathed. "Not to get her into trouble. If you call the police, they can get the message out there. Somebody might get in touch if they've seen the kids. We'd at least know that they're all right. It can't be doing her any good, either, living like this, always looking over her shoulder. They could be constantly on the move for all we know, sleeping in different places every few days. And that's not good for kids, is it? Especially not kids who've been through a whole load of disruptions in the past eighteen months."

"I don't want to get her into trouble," he said, looking defeated.

"Neither do I. Look . . ." I dashed into my bedroom, dashed back with a folder I'd compiled. "I found this thing on the Internet for help to get your children back if they've been taken by another parent." I held out the folder to him. "I filled in as much as I could from what I know, I've put in the most recent pictures I could find. You have to fill in the rest and then give it to the police and a solicitor."

"How did I get here? My wife's kidnapped my children and I have to report her to the police. When did my life become a made-for-TV drama?"

I put the folder on the coffee table and went towards him, rested my hand on his forearm, tried to reassure him with a touch. "We both know that Ashlyn loves the kids. They're a part of her. They're her life. But we have to make sure they're safe. Surfing the Web and waiting for that knock on the door that says something has happened is no way to live. And it's not fair to them to have this happen to them twice. First Ashlyn just disappears and then you, essentially, disappear. It's not right."

For long moments Kyle stared into the middistance. I could see him working it out, turning it over slowly and carefully in his mind.

I went to take my hand away: I'd said my piece, it was up to him now. Of course I wouldn't call the police, it wasn't my place. But I wish Kyle would see it was the right thing to do. We had to find them. We had to do something to find them. Kyle's hand covered mine and then slowly moved it off his forearm, then his fingers linked into mine. Our hands fit together. The spaces between our fingers became filled, whole and complete. We stood facing each other, holding hands. He was clinging onto me, as if trying to draw the strength from me to do this. To start this process of revealing to the world how far apart he and Ashlyn were; how fractured their family was. To start the process of accepting that he might not see the kids again. I suppose the police were the last hope—if they didn't find the kids, then we might not ever find them. Knowing for sure that they weren't coming back was something that had to be dealt with slowly. This reality had to creep up on us, not slap us in the face. By inviting the police into this we'd be putting our faces forward to be slapped. I was pretty sure I was ready for that mental slap, had braced myself for it.

He came back to the present from wherever he'd been and stared at me. He inhaled, his chest expanding as he breathed deeply, then it fell, hopelessly. "I can't do it," he whispered. "I can't. She's going to bring them back. I know she will."

Kyle wasn't ready for that mental slap—was he ready for a real one? Because I was three seconds away from delivering a real one right onto his denial-ridden cheek. To slap some sense into him.

I ripped my hand free and tightly folded my arms across my chest. Holding myself together.

This man was an expert at denial, I'd forgotten that. He'd lived with an alcoholic for more than a decade and he'd managed to pretend it wasn't a problem, he transmuted everything she did into little hiccups in behavior so he wouldn't have to accept the reality of his situation. He'd refused to accept that Ashlyn was going to fight him legally for his children, so sent me in his place. He disavowed the fact she'd done something so heinous to him so he did nothing to find the children. Denial made up most of who Kyle was. Denial defined his life. Why would anything change?

I'd become a part of that, I realized as I turned away and moved to the far end of the sofa, sank down and pressed my forehead to my knees. I'd become caught up in the sphere of denial that encompassed this family. I'd been submerged in it. And as a result I accepted his way of doing things.

"I don't know how you can bear it," I said through my knees. The weight of it grinding down into the very cells of my body, crushing me. "I don't know how you can bear being without them."

"I can't," Kyle replied.

"Then why won't you do everything possible to get them back?"

"You don't understand, when I make that call, that's it. I can't unmake it. I can't tell the police she didn't mean it. And mean what, exactly? There's no residency order in place. If anything, it's Ashlyn who's got something in writing that she intended to get the kids to live with her. I never made a formal application. I just assumed, just left it as it was because she'd left them with me. I never put it in writing."

"Then why don't you apply for a custody order now? You can do that. She hasn't applied for one because she'd have to contact you. So you do it, and then you can do something. Then you can call the police and have them find her. But I'm sure if you explained Ashlyn's history they'd do something now. You need to do anything possible to find them."

"I don't know if I can do that to Ashlyn. I can't tell anyone what happened, what she did. She's not like that anymore, I don't want people to think she is."

Every muscle in my body snapped to attention, wrenching my body upwards so I sat bolt upright. "WHEN ARE YOU GOING TO STOP PROTECTING HER?" I screamed at him. "WHEN ARE YOU GOING TO STOP PUTTING HER BEFORE EVERYONE ELSE INCLUDING YOUR KIDS?"

His ever-diminishing frame, clothed in a white T-shirt and baggy blue jeans, drew back, surprised. "You don't understand—" he began.

"NO YOU'RE RIGHT, I DON'T," I continued to shout, cutting him off. "I DON'T UNDERSTAND AND I DON'T WANT TO FOR AS LONG AS YOU PUT SOMEONE ELSE BEFORE YOUR KIDS, I WON'T UNDERSTAND AND I WON'T EVEN TRY."

I struggled to my feet.

"Kendra—"

"I DON'T WANT TO HEAR IT!" I screamed. I wasn't a shouter, wasn't the type to cause this much fuss, but I'd reached the end of my tether. I couldn't take this anymore. This grief, this insurmountable grief was too much to bear. Especially, *especially* when Kyle could end the suffering. We didn't even have to get them back, we just had to find out that they were safe and well and alive. *Alive.* "UNTIL YOU PUT YOUR KIDS FIRST, I DON'T WANT TO HEAR IT." I stepped out from beside the sofa, went towards my bedroom, to hide from him. To seek refuge, even a temporary one from the man who was driving me crazy.

"It's not that simple," Kyle protested to my retreating back.

The words stopped me, but didn't force me to turn around. "Yes," I said with a frustrated sigh, "it is."

"Don't hate me," he said, quietly. "I can't take you hating me on top of everything else."

"I don't," I replied. "Of course I don't, Kyle. But I'm not going to condone this passivity. Not when it comes to this. Even if you're scared to try to get them back, don't you at least want to know they're safe and healthy and happy? You can start the process of that with one phone call."

"I can't do it," he said.

"Then we have nothing to talk about."

Brriinnngggg! The ring of the phone, the white phone from the main house that sat on Kyle's drawing table, made us both jump.

My heart leapt to my throat as hope exploded inside me. Both of us turned to it, stared at it as it continued to ring. It'd rung before, of course, but not that often. Most people were in the habit of calling him on the flat's phone because he'd told them he was staying there for the time the kids were on holiday with their mother. His hand shook as he reached out for the receiver, picked it up, clicked the green answer button and put it to his ear. "Hello?" His voice wavered as he spoke. He said nothing for the few seconds that he listened to the other person speak, and then his face began to tremble, he closed his eyes and sank to his knees on the floor beside his drawing table, the receiver slipping from his limp fingers as he went. He pushed his forehead against the ground and began to rock back and forth, back and forth.

Oh, God, no. No, please, no.

Moving like I was walking towards my death, I went to him, bent and picked up the receiver. I put my hand on his shoulder, steadying myself as I tried to offer him comfort. Pausing for a moment, wanting to delay what I was going to hear for as long as possible, I pressed the phone to my ear.

CHAPTER 40

The sun had set a few hours earlier and I was driving in a blanket of indigo blackness by the time we turned down the semiprivate road that led to the cottage where Ashlyn and the kids were. A cottage in Penzance. Hundreds of miles away.

We'd driven most of the way in our own worlds—not speaking, not really acknowledging each other. I'd had to do the driving because, between the two of us, I was the most composed.

After I'd picked up the phone and pressed it to my ear, I'd heard a woman's voice. "Kyle, are you there?" she said. "Did you hear me? I need you to come and get the kids."

When Ashlyn had given me the address and I'd hung up without speaking to the children, he'd swamped me. His arms enveloping my body, pulling me into him, his face buried against my neck as he cried. A true grief letting. All his composure, all his terror being released in a torrent. I'd realized as I fought my urge to break free, as I stroked the soothing point in the middle of his back, absorbed his tears into my body, that despite all he'd said, he'd thought he wouldn't see them again. That he hadn't been able to face the possibility of not seeing them again, or that she'd hurt them, so had decided not to find out. He'd been locked into a cycle of fear of not knowing, which was awful, and fearing that knowing would have been worse. I knew how it was to be locked into that cycle, to not know which fear—knowing or not knowing—was worse.

Once he'd stopped, we'd broken apart, stared into each other's eyes, understanding each other far more than we had even fifteen minutes earlier. With my thumbs, I wiped away his tears, then gently pressed my lips onto his forehead. He'd closed his eyes as he received my kiss. Then we got to our feet, he'd gone to the bathroom and I'd printed out a route map from the Internet. I'd blanked out. Didn't think about anything apart from the driving I had to do. If I'd stopped to consider it, to take note of the fact we were only hours instead of days, weeks or months away from seeing them, I might have fallen apart like Kyle and we wouldn't have been able to get there as soon as possible.

As I drove, all that motivated me, pushed me, was the thought of Summer's little face, grinning because she had a secret she was probably going to share, and Jaxon's big eyes as he explained to me what Garvo was doing.

My muscles ached, my eyes were dry and tight behind my driving glasses as I concentrated on the house in the distance. It was a yellowish-stone building with a slate roof and three windows at the top, and two large windows at the bottom. The light spilling out from the bottom windows glowed orange, drawing us closer. I slowed to double-check the white sign that stood on the edge of the property: Agateaen Field Cottage.

"This is it," I said to Kyle, my excitement muted by my tiredness. I hadn't stopped the whole way. Nearly seven hours I'd been driving; the only real rests were the snarl-ups in traffic when we waited sometimes twenty minutes to get moving.

Kyle, who'd been wide awake, his head resting on the window, his eyes staring unblinkingly ahead, sat up. His face, which had been mottled red and white from his crying, and his eyes, which had ballooned red and sore once he'd stopped crying, had both calmed down. He looked normal again. The nearness of his family had injected the spark of life into him again. I crawled the car up the wide gravel drive with green grass on either side, up towards another car sitting beside the entrance.

The front door swung open. Before I'd even had a chance to fully stop, Kyle had unlocked his seat belt, clicked open his door and he was out of the car. I slammed on the brakes, although I was nearly at a virtual stop.

Jaxon came running out first. And then Summer. Both in their nightclothes: Jaxon in his Superman pajamas, Summer in her Spider-Man knee-length T-shirt. Both had socks on.

"DAD!" They both screamed at the top of their voices. "DAD!"

Kyle threw himself onto his knees in the headlights of the car. Jaxon leapt on him first, flung his arm around his dad's neck. Then Summer, her arms linking around his neck. His arms looped around them. The kids were talking. Both of them gabbling, telling their father everything they'd done in the past few weeks. Everything, at once. I stared at them, my eyes running over every inch of them, checking. Double-checking. They were fine. They were fine and safe and happy.

The relief hit me like a fist driven into the deepest, softest part of my stomach. I folded forwards, holding my stomach over the epicenter of the relief. The sweet relief. It hurt and it made me feel good. It was OK. They really were OK. I hadn't felt this in a lifetime. Too many things hadn't turned out OK, too many things had gone the bad way. I hadn't been sure this wouldn't go the same way. My body started to heave, the tears I hadn't shed in all the time we were apart rushing up to the surface, fighting to be free, struggling to be released.

Rap-rap on the window made my heart leap. Wiping at my misty eyes, I sat up. "KENDIE!" Jaxon shouted, his face grinning at me through the glass. "KENDIE!" Summer echoed.

Kyle pulled them back as I opened the door and then they were in my arms, their warm bodies pressed against me, the smell of their freshly washed skin filling my nostrils, their hair tickling my cheeks, their arms squeezing the life out of me.

"KendieKendieKendieKendieKendie," they kept repeating. It was only my name, but it was the sweetest thing I'd ever heard.

Ashlyn was standing in front of the big, stone fireplace that had no fire in its belly. She looked as though she'd been pacing, her face a mask of anxiety, her green eyes wide and frightened as she stared at the door. She was thinner than she had been the last time I saw her, but she looked well. Far better than Kyle did. Far better than I did. There were a few dark wisps under her eyes, her hair was pulled back into a sloppy ponytail, her body dressed in unbelted blue jeans and long-sleeved T-shirt, big fluffy slippers on her feet. Four steps over the threshold was all Kyle got before Ashlyn threw herself at him.

She clutched the front of his T-shirt, buried her face in it, as though she might find comfort and absolution in the thick material covering his heart. Burst into noisy tears as she held onto her husband. Kyle's entire body stiffened the moment they made bodily contact and he stared over her head, towards the back of the cottage, towards the doorway that led into the huge kitchen-diner.

I had a twin's hand in each of my hands, small and perfectly formed, warm and beautiful. I had to remind myself not to cling on too tight, had to remind myself letting go wouldn't result in them disappearing again. I guided them towards the cream sofa. Under the sofa lay a huge Oriental rug, its intricate pattern worn in places from the length of time it had been there. The cottage was cozy, homely. The kids must have loved it here. It was the perfect place to spend the school holidays, which is probably what they thought their time away had been. A holiday. Not a slow, winding road through every level of hell that Kyle and I had thought it was.

I sat in the middle of the sofa, and the kids sank down beside me, watching their mother and father. Kyle wasn't engaging with Ashlyn. He hadn't called the police, but that didn't mean he didn't hate her for what she'd done, for dropping him off at the gates of Hades without even a map to help him get to the other side.

Her sobs decreased as she began to talk. "I'm sorry," she said tearfully into his chest. "I wanted to be with them. I missed them so much. I just wanted to be with them. I'm sorry. I'm sorry." She kept repeating her sorries into his chest, until slowly, like an ice block in weak sunlight, he melted, relented. He stopped staring over her head, and shaking his head slightly, he looked down at his wife, gently raised his arms and folded them around her. "Shhh," he hushed as he lowered his head to hers, started to stroke his hand over her hair, soothing her. "Shhh . . . We'll talk about it later. We'll talk about it later." His comfort spread throughout the room, his hushing moving gently over all of us.

The kids and I watched them. The amount of affection between the two of them was palpable. Their bodies fit together, he knew how to offer her comfort, their hearts probably beat in time. How Kyle and Ashlyn fit together took me back briefly to the night Will and I spent together, lying on the bed, our bodies so close it was impossible to believe we hadn't always been like that, hadn't always been so close we couldn't function without the other one. What I would do to be back with Will . . . To have the chance to hold him like that . . . These two had it. How come they were the only two people in the world who could not see that they were meant to be together?

Summer got up on her knees, put her hand on my cheek and twisted my head towards her. "Are Mumma and Dad friends again?" she asked eagerly. Her bright eyes smiled at me, waiting for me to say yes. I couldn't say it. Of course I couldn't say it. Jaxon got up on his knees as well, and I turned to look at him. The same eyes, waiting for the same answer.

I looked at Kyle and Ashlyn, became lost for a moment in the smooth beautiful lines their bodies made as they stood together—it was impossible to tell where she began and he ended.

I returned my attention to the kids. Looked at Jaxon, then rested my gaze back on Summer because she had asked the question. "I hope so," I replied. It was the most honest answer I could give them. They may be friends, but not in the way Summer and Jaxon wanted. Because of their inability to talk to each other, to tell each other the truth, they'd probably never be friends like Summer and Jaxon wanted.

CHAPTER 41

I lay on the sofa under the spare duvet with its white and blue cornflower cover, propped up by three soft, squashy pillows, wide awake in the darkness. I hated the darkness. Darkness was suffocating. When my eyes couldn't focus on a shape, couldn't anchor myself to a point, I feared I'd drown in darkness.

It's dark, an endless pitch. The weight crushes my body. Blackness is creeping in at the sides of my sight as the hand around my throat takes away the air and consciousness. I try to fight it. Try to stop it. But the blackness is still coming. "You're special," the voice whispers. "Stop fighting, you're special. Stop fighting and I won't kill you."

I sat bolt upright. *No. Not now. I'm not going there now*, I decided. If I did something else it would stop. If I moved, it wouldn't keep a hold. I threw back the covers, got off the sofa. I picked up the small fleece blanket that was draped over the back of sofa. I needed to get outside, to the air. I could breathe out there. Theoretically it was probably safer inside the house than outside, but I knew that danger didn't always come from the outside, from strangers.

If I thought about it rationally, the biggest danger to me was in this house. And she was called Ashlyn. The way she had looked at me earlier . . . She'd speared me to the spot with her glacial green eyes and had tried to remove me from her life with all the hatred she felt for me focused into one look.

It was nothing personal, I knew that. Ashlyn hated my presence in her life, my role in her family's life. *Why don't you just disappear?* her look had asked me. Her body language, the slight push with which she'd given me the duvet and pillows, had added: *Why don't you just get out of our lives for good?*

Yes, in the whole of Cornwall she was the most clear and present danger to me. I crept through the kitchen to the patio doors. I eased open the locks and then softly pulled the doors open before I stepped out into the night. Outside was chilly. The end of August meant cold nights, a bite that brushed over the skin, causing goose bumps to clamber upright and the body to curl a little into itself. I crept over the lawn to the twin swings that stood outside in the large back garden.

From the flaking green paint and rust, it was obvious it had been here for a few years. Maybe that was why Ashlyn had rented it: she saw the double swings, it was only a twenty-minute walk from the seafront, it was perfect for the kids.

I sat on the green swing and, thankfully, despite its age, it didn't creak. Didn't alert anyone in the house that I was awake and walking around. I moved the swing gently back and forth, trailing the tips of my trainers in the cork on the ground beneath the swings.

I closed my eyes, remembering the look on Jaxon's face when he'd come running out the front door. The unsuppressed delight that came over him as he ran to his dad. I felt the smile take over my face. The smile became a grin as I remembered Summer circling her arms around my neck. A lump formed in my throat. A lump from remembering how desolate my life had been without them. The thought of living without them . . . The panic rose quickly, fluttering to my throat, forming a lump that I couldn't swallow away. A lump that I could only cry away. I felt the tears coming up behind my eyes. How could I live without them? I needed Summer's constant chatter, Jaxon's oblique observations. I needed the children. At one point I thought they needed me. And maybe they did. But that was only while their mother was gone. Now she was back. I almost doubled over at this new torture. Now she was back she'd take back what was rightfully hers. Yes, they'd probably want to see me still. But as a friend. Not as the person they came to with a homework problem, not as the woman they drove crazy with their questions, not as their "other mumma."

I didn't look up when I heard the door open and someone step quietly out of the house. I knew who it was. The only person it could be.

Ashlyn sat down beside me on the swing. A brief glance from the corner of my eye revealed she was dressed as unsensibly as I was. She had on her calf-length satin nightdress, the T-shirt Kyle had been wearing and a pair of thick, royal blue socks pulled up as far as they would go. I could smell Kyle from her. Sandalwood and citrus, his vaguely sweet masculine scent. That was probably how I smelled—of the man I'd spent nearly six weeks living with. I hoped she smelled of him because they'd got back together. That they'd talked themselves out and made love. It'd be disastrous for me and my relationship with the kids, but it was what this family needed. They needed to be put back together again.

She swung out of time with me, the chains on our individual swings rasping like quietly expiring asthmatics with each movement back and forward. Back and forth we went, moving in uneven time, sounding out an unsynchronized symphony. I wasn't sure if she was expecting me to speak first, but I had nothing to say to her. I wanted their family knitted back together, I wanted them sewn back into a happy patchwork but I was angry. My anger was raging like an undammed river below the surface. I could reach out and claw out a handful of her hair and slap her from left to right, right to left and not break a sweat. I could hurt Ashlyn for the hell she'd put Kyle and me through. I had nothing to say to her. And there was nothing she could say that would make me speak to her.

"I started drinking again." Her voice was only a fraction above a whisper. So quiet, so devastating I wondered if I'd conjured up those words to further demonize her.

When she stilled her swing by putting her feet down and twisted to face me, I realized she'd said it. And it was the only thing she could say that would make me speak to her.

"I'm listening," I said to Ashlyn.

"I haven't told anyone else," she said, her voice barely above a fragile whisper. She spoke carefully, as though she might shatter with every word and not be able to continue. She looked down, away, at her satin-covered lap, her hands still gripping onto the chairs. "Jaxon knows. He found me passed out on the sofa. Summer doesn't know. Or maybe she does—she's started having nightmares, I think because she can smell the alcohol on me and it reminds her . . . Of this one time. She doesn't sleep through the night any-more . . ." Ashlyn's voice trailed away. "I stopped going to meetings," she said. "It was too hard when I . . . When we first came here, I wasn't sure if he'd called the police, if he'd called my sponsor or if he was out looking for me. I didn't want to associate too much with people in case he found out so it was easier not to go. I had the kids to focus on.

"I'd forgotten how much work they were. All the atten-tion they need. I'd only seen them for a few days at a time here and there over the past six months or so. And before that . . . I'd been getting sober. Or so I told myself. I can see now that I was just a nondrinking alcoholic. I wasn't trying to stop being an alcoholic. I went to meetings but I wasn't doing the steps. I just stopped drinking and was miserable with it. I wasn't working towards anything, I was just not drinking and wearing it like a badge: 'Look what a good girl I am, I'm not drinking.'

"I loved having Jaxon and Summer back. It felt as though a part of me had been returned. I didn't realize how numb, how dead inside I'd felt without them. And then my mother came to stay for a week."

Her mother? The bitch. The lying bitch. She did know where they were and she'd tortured Kyle like that. She had bluffed him with that thing of calling the police. The bitch. I hope I never meet her. Never. I really will hurt her. If not physically, then verbally.

"I could get out of the house, so for something to do, I decided to go to a few meetings," Ashlyn was saying.

———

Ashlyn could get out of the house, so for something to do, she decided to go to a few meetings. She hadn't told her mother about her problem; of course she hadn't. Instead she said she was meeting a few friends. Walking into the rooms was worse after the break from the meetings. She hadn't been drinking but it was awful. She said hello to a few people, got herself a cup of coffee and sat at the back in the corner on a fold-out chair. She was self-conscious this time around. Anxious. Probably because she hadn't been for so long. Or maybe because of what happened over the next hour. For the first time it really hit her what this meant.

She was like them. In the past, she'd sat there and listened and thought, I'm not like them. I'm not that bad. *Despite* what Kyle thinks, I'm not as bad as them. *Now she realized that she was. Maybe it was having the kids on her own. Maybe it was knowing that she couldn't talk to anyone else afterwards. But it was sinking in. She'd hurt her family. She'd repeatedly insulted her husband. She'd all but ruined her career.*

The worst thing for her, though, was that she realized she could never have another drink.

Not ever. If she was an alcoholic, she could never drink again. Not to celebrate a birthday, not at a party, not to relax at night, not to take the edge off if the world felt prickly and unsafe.

It's not true, *she told herself. It couldn't be true. Maybe she was different. Maybe she was the alcoholic who could just control her drinking. She'd stopped for so long and hadn't really been to meetings, which showed that maybe she was different. She could just give it a go. Have one glass and prove to herself, prove to Kyle, prove to the rest of the world that she was better. She was cured of her alcoholism.*

When her mother left she decided to give controlled drinking a try. She'd have one glass and that was it. She was better, she wasn't an alcoholic anymore, so she could do that. She'd never been able to have one drink in her life, not ever, but she could do it now. Just to prove a point.

She didn't drink the night she made her decision. She wanted it so badly so she stopped herself. Reminded herself that the craving would pass in a few hours. And it did. This was the reasonable side of her at work, the side that knew she wasn't an alcoholic. She had a problem if she was craving the drink, which would make her experiment fail. She'd wait until the craving passed and then have a drink. That would be how this would work out—she'd only drink when she didn't want it and she'd be able to stop. Who on earth would be able to stop once they gave in to a craving?

Two days later she bought a bottle of wine. Then a second

one because she was going to prove that she didn't need it. She could drink one glass and have another bottle in the house and not even touch it. It was part of the experiment. Proving the point she was cured.

That first taste of wine was so clear in her mind, even now, two weeks later. How wonderful it felt in her mouth, sliding down her throat. The second mouthful was almost as delicious, her head swooned and she felt the first wave of that familiar warmth moving gently through her. She hadn't felt that free in what felt like a lifetime. She smiled. A grin that came from doing something she loved. This was what life was about. Not all that stuff, not all that needing to do things and think about things. You needed to relax sometimes, you owed it to yourself. The third taste sent her back to happier times.

She didn't remember the fourth taste. Nor the fifth or sixth. The next thing she did remember was waking up on the sofa. Jaxon was on the floor in front of the television with the sound turned down (because that's what she used to make them do when she had a hangover) and racing his car around one of the two empty wine bottles. She had one arm stuffed into her coat, the rest of her coat hanging off the end of the sofa, and her car keys were in her hand. She felt a thin thread of shame slither down her spine—she'd obviously wanted to get some more wine but had passed out first.

Her experiment hadn't worked. But that was because she hadn't tried hard enough. She bought more wine—four bottles instead of two. If she had more wine she wouldn't be tempted to drink and drive if the experiment failed again.

After a fortnight of trying and failing to prove she was normal, that she was cured, Ashlyn woke up again on the sofa. This time Jaxon was standing over her, desperately shaking her. His face was twisted with worry, his eyes wide and frightened. He'd obviously been trying to wake her for a while. It was pitch black outside; the only light in the room came from

the television. "Summer's sick," Jaxon said. Even through the
fuzz of alcohol she could see how scared he was, then she heard
Summer's screams from upstairs.

Oh God, oh no. *Ashlyn struggled to her feet, but she*
couldn't remember how her legs worked. They wobbled under
her and she collapsed back onto the sofa. Jaxon was moving
from one foot to the other, wringing his hands and constantly
looking up to where his sister was screaming. Ashlyn pulled
herself up again and, walking on legs of rubber and through a
dense fug of sleep and wine, she managed to stumble up the
stairs after her son.

"Summer was still asleep. She was covered in sweat, and
thrashing about in the bed, screaming. I managed to wake
her up and she started burbling about the goo. The goo was
trying to get her. I couldn't even comfort her properly because I could hardly speak, could hardly hold her. In the end
it was Jaxon who got on the bed and told her it'd be OK.
'Don't worry Summer,' he said, 'I won't let it get you. Me and
Garvo will protect you.' And he hugged her. Patted her head.
My six-year-old son was being mother to my daughter because I couldn't.

"I sat and watched while Jaxon comforted her. He ended
up sleeping in her bed and I went to the other room and
passed out again. I called Kyle the next day. I had a moment
of clarity and I realized they had to be with Kyle right now.
They need stability."

I was stunned. Ashlyn had done this to her children. For
real. Her voice had been full of sorrow as she talked, she had
to keep stopping to take deep breaths, to pull herself together. But she had done this to her children. She had done
this to herself and to other people.

"I know that one day I'll be able to give the kids stability," she was saying. "One day soon. I have to get sober properly, though. I have to get sober for my kids."

"What about getting sober for you?" I asked.

Ashlyn glared at me with eyes slick with tears. "Summer and Jaxon are the two most important things in my life."

"I know. But you didn't drink for your kids, you drank for you. Because you've got this sickness. So maybe getting sober should be about doing it for you, so you can be in good shape for them, rather than pinning success or failure on them. I'm always hearing that you have to take care of you first before you try to take care of anyone else."

Even in the darkness I saw her cheeks flame up as fury spiraled into her eyes and embedded on her expression. She was angry. She hadn't heard what I said, she had heard me criticizing her love of her children. Which I hadn't. I was pointing out that "doing it for her kids" was a fast track to unhappiness. Because if she did slip again she would tell herself it was because she didn't love her kids enough, she would tell herself that she was a bad person, she would tell herself there was no point trying to stay sober. She had to do it for her.

"I'm sorry," I said. "I shouldn't have said anything, you obviously know what you're doing."

"I'm telling you this," she was struggling—and spectacularly failing—to keep anger out of her voice, "because I love my children. More than anything. I'll do anything for them. Being around me at the moment is not good for them. They need Kyle. He's steady and stable . . ." Her voice cracked. "I don't want to do this," her words came out in a teary rush. "I want to be with them. I want to hold them every day in a bear hug. I want to watch Summer dance to TV theme music and Jaxon talk to his imaginary dog. I want to wake up every morning and know that they're going to say or do something different from yesterday." Tears were dripping off the end of her pert nose but she didn't wipe them away. "But that's all about me. They want a normal life. With me and Kyle back together, I know it. And that can't happen right now. Maybe in the future but not now.

"You have to decide what you're going to do." Ashlyn was talking about me now. About me, to me.

"What do you mean?" I asked.

"You have to decide if you're going to stick around or not. Summer and Jaxon love you. It tears me up inside to say that." She put her hand over her heart, to show where it hurt. "They were constantly accidentally calling me Kendie, which reminds me how much you must be around them." Her thin hand pressed harder on her heart. "I won't let them be hurt anymore. If you aren't going to be around for the foreseeable future, until the time when they don't need you, then you leave now. You go now. Don't let them fall even more in love with you and then you go off, decide to live your life somewhere else. If you stay in their lives now, you're in their lives forever. If you can't commit to that, then you leave."

She slid off her swing, stood in front of me with her arms folded. Maybe against the cold, maybe to put the frighteners on me.

"I've been a terrible mother, and I'm going to stop anyone else doing that to them again. You stay for good or you leave."

Just to be dramatic, I think, she turned and walked away.

I watched her leave as what she said sunk in. What she'd asked of me was the equivalent of me taking a pregnancy test and discovering that I was pregnant. Realizing I had to make a choice: keep the baby or not; stay with Jaxon and Summer or leave; say good-bye to the possibility of happiness and marriage and adoption with someone I hadn't met yet or stay forever where I'd always be second-best.

Being with them was fantastic now, being apart from them was a hell I never wanted to live through again, but could I do this? Could I commit to a forever with two children who'd never be mine?

CHAPTER 42

*A*t around ten o'clock the next morning, after showers and breakfast and a cup of tea for the road, Kyle and I started to take Summer and Jaxon's belongings to the car. They'd accumulated quite a lot in the past six weeks—more clothes and toys and books and DVDs—and it took a lot to pack them into their bags. We resorted to shopping bags and when they ran out, it was armfuls, pushed on the top of the neatly packed stuff in the back of the car. Summer and Jaxon sat on the sofa with their mother, going through the map of how we were going to get back to Kent.

Ashlyn was still in her nightdress, although she'd returned Kyle's T-shirt to him and replaced it with an oversized cream cardie with chunky ribbing. After stuffing the last load in the car, we returned to the living room. Summer looked up from the sofa at Kyle and me as we hung around the doorway, waiting for the good-byes to begin. She turned to her nightdressed mother, patted her hand and said, "Mumma, you have to put on proper clothes. Dad won't let you wear your nightdress in the car."

Each adult drew back a little, surprised. We'd all assumed one of the others had explained. No one had actually told the kids Ashlyn wasn't coming back with us. No one had actually told the kids that they wouldn't be seeing their mother for a while. Ashlyn looked up and locked eyes with Kyle. He closed his eyes in silent agony. In the excitement of being reunited with them, we hadn't taken the time to explain the situation to the kids.

Summer noticed the pause that followed her statement. She cocked her head, narrowed her eyes at her mother.

She didn't resist when Ashlyn's thin, reedlike fingers with their long oval nails took her hand. She didn't move as Ashlyn's other hand took hold of Jaxon's hand. "Summer," Ashlyn said. "Jaxon." She paused to look at each of her children. She was taking a mental picture of them. I could tell from the way her eyes hungrily devoured each line and curve of their faces, their hair, their bodies.

"I'm not coming back with you. Not yet, anyway. Not for a while. I have to get better."

"Why not?" Summer asked. Her voice was quiet, small, but on the knife-edge of a scream.

"I have to get better," Ashlyn said. "There are things I need to do. I haven't been feeling too good for a while and I need to be well so I can come back to you. I'll see you really soon, though. I promise."

Summer tugged her hand free from her mother, the hackles of her body visibly rising, the rage swirling with incomprehension taking over. She came apart piece by piece, moment by moment. The betrayal she wore on her face; the agony escaped as she crumpled forwards and, in short little hiccups, started to cry. Her tiny sobs became a high-pitched whine, and then loud sobs. "Why not, Mumma?" she asked through her sobs. "Why not?" She began rocking backwards and forwards. "Come home, Mumma, come home." This wasn't about this time. It wasn't simply about us leaving Ashlyn behind this time—it was about all the time her mother had lived away from them. It was the months and months of her not having her mother.

And after the reunion yesterday, seeing Ashlyn and Kyle hugging, why wouldn't Summer and Jaxon expect Ashlyn to come back? For their family, imperfect as it had been, to be rebuilt?

"Come home, Mumma. Come home." Summer's ragged, breathy sobs tore through me. Kyle folded his arms tightly against him, trying to hide how much each sob slashed at him. Jaxon slid out of his seat beside his mother and went silently across the room, sat down on the floor by the kitchen door, pulled his knees up to his chest and then put his head on his knees.

"I'll be good. I promise. I'll be good," Summer wailed, her cries louder and more distressing with each word. "I'll be a good girl, Mumma. I promise. I promise."

"Oh, Sum, it's not you," Ashlyn scooped her daughter up in her arms. "It's not you. You're a good girl. You're always a good girl. It's me. It's Mumma. I have to stay here until I get better."

"Come HOME!" Summer screamed over her mother's comfort. "PLEASE! MUMMA, PLEASE! PLEASE! MUMMA, PLEASE!"

"Summer, darling," Ashlyn said, barely audible above Summer's constant screams. "Oh Summer, I'm sorry. I'm sorry." Ashlyn's words had no volume, muted by tears. "I'm sorry. I'm sorry."

Kyle moved. I thought he was going to Summer, but he moved towards the kitchen. To Jaxon. To his son, the quiet wheel, the little bundle in the corner whose heart was breaking just as much as his sister's but who wouldn't do what Summer was doing. It wasn't in his nature. He was like his father, came apart from the inside out, but quietly. Absolute agony dressed up in a hush. Kyle crouched by his son, took him in his arms and picked him up. "You all right, mate?" Kyle said as he pulled Jaxon towards him. Jaxon wrapped his legs around his dad's waist, buried his face in his dad's neck, linked his arms around him. Clung to his dad and allowed himself to be carried into the kitchen, away from the pain.

I should leave. I should let Ashlyn calm her daughter in her own way, in her own time, I thought. But I couldn't. I couldn't walk out on Summer while she was falling apart. She was in agony. And I hurt. Like Ashlyn and Kyle must, when she hurt I hurt, too. There was no denying it, I was linked to Summer. I was tied to Jaxon. Anything that affected them affected me.

Summer started to fight her mother, twisting and turning in her mother's hold, fighting because she wasn't hearing what she wanted to hear. "MUMMA COME HOME! COME HOME!" She wasn't asking for much, didn't think it was too much for her mother to do this one thing for her. For them. Without thinking, I moved nearer to the sofa, towards them. I wanted to hold Summer, to soothe her.

"It's OK, Summer," I said before I could stop myself. "Your Mumma is going to come home, just not yet."

Summer escaped her mother's hold, ran the short distance and threw herself against me, flung her arms around my waist and buried her face in my solar plexus. She was still crying, still screaming, but the words had gone. It was just sound. Just a harrowing lament, a constant howling at the pain this was inflicting upon her. For the first time she'd realized her mother wasn't coming back. She wouldn't have her mother and father together again. This, literally, was as good as it got. They'd be in the same room, they'd talk, but they weren't going to be home together. They weren't going to be a family. It was over. Her family was over. And it wasn't fair. It wasn't fair. *It wasn't fair.*

I crouched myself down to Summer's height, enveloped her in my arms, took every cry and wail as it hammered against my body. Took it, absorbed it, accepted it. I stroked my fingers through the smooth locks of her onyx-black hair, held her, tried to soothe her. Summer's cries subsided as she wore herself out. They fell and fell until she was simply quivering in my arms, hiccupping back her distress. "Make her come home, Kendie," she whispered against my cheek. "Make my mumma come home."

I pressed the flat of my hand against her back, held her close. "She will one day," I replied. "Just not yet."

Pale, trembling and her face wet with tears, Ashlyn came to us. When I looked into her eyes I saw grief. Deep, heart-wrenching grief. She didn't want this, either. *"Why don't you just come home?"* I wanted to ask her. *"You can get help at home. You don't need to do this."*

"Can I talk to Summer, please?" she asked stiffly. As though she needed my permission to get an audience with her own child.

"Of course," I said. "Of course." I gently unwrapped Summer from me, although it wasn't easy. Summer clung to me, didn't want to face her mother. If she faced her mother, it'd be real. She'd have to accept that her family was finally over.

Reluctantly, she turned to her mother. Faced her with mottled skin, puffy eyes and a quivering body. She looked defeated and broken. The light of hope had gone out of her eyes. It was an expression that shouldn't ever be seen on a six-year-old face. It was an expression that shouldn't ever be seen on anyone's face.

I left them to it. Opened the front door and escaped out to the car. I opened the door and sat in the passenger seat. I hadn't slept much last night after my "chat" with Ashlyn. I lay down across the passenger and driver's seats, covered my eyes with my hands and listened to the silence. Listened to the sound of my heart, beating loudly and rapidly in the hush of Kyle's car. Filling the space with the agony of what had just happened.

I hadn't thought of this. That getting the kids back would mean breaking their hearts.

Lying back in the car, I took my mobile out of my jeans pocket and looked at the screen. There was something I had to do. I brought up the number, stared at it, my eyes boring into the number and the name above it until it blurred into a mass of black as the screen went dark.

I hit the green call button before I could talk myself out of it.

"Hey-lo," she purred into the phone.

"It's me," I said.

"Oh. Hello, Me. How are you? Why are you calling me, Me? What's happened?"

"I'm in Cornwall. Penzance."

Gabrielle lowered her voice. "OK, I get the picture, you've been kidnapped by the Pasty Patrol, I'll send help ASAP. They'll be wearing balaclavas and carrying bangers and mash, eel pies and a canister of smog."

I smiled into the phone. "Hold on there, I'm leaving in a minute. I've only been here a night—"

"A NIGHT?!" she broke in. "It's too late. I can hear it in your voice. You've got an accent. You'll be spending weekends down there next and then you'll want to do a sea change. You'll be moving down there. Oh God, why? Why do the good Pastify so young? *Why?*"

"Gabrielle, stop," I whispered into the phone. I didn't want to start laughing. Not with all that was going on in the house. "I'm ringing to tell you we've found the kids."

"Oh thank God," Gabrielle breathed into the receiver. "Thank God. I was starting to think . . . That doesn't matter, thank God you've found them. And they're safe? They're OK?"

"Yeah, they're OK, mostly. It's hard for them to leave Ashlyn again, but they'll be fine."

"As long as they're all right, that's all that matters. Thanks for letting me know. I know you've all been going through hell. It was hell for me, too, so thanks for letting me know."

"I also rang to say I'm sorry for what happened in the pub."

"Sweetie, you don't have to say sorry."

"Yes, I do. Just because we're friends, doesn't mean I shouldn't have to say sorry. You deserve that respect."

"You don't have to say sorry because I don't think you did anything wrong. If someone had pushed me like I pushed you, I would have gone carnival freakshow crazy on them. If you'd asked, that'd be one thing, but you didn't. And it wasn't my place. So don't say sorry. If anything, I should say sorry, not you."

"You were only trying to help."

"OK, let's not get into the cycle of us both trying to take the blame. Let's say we've both said sorry and let's hook up when you get back from," she lowered her voice, "*Cornwall.* Just you and me."

"Cool. Thanks, Gabs."

"Thanks for calling, Kennie. Give my love to Summer and Jaxon."

"I will. See ya."

At the car, Ashlyn hugged her children as though she might never see them again. Summer was now defeated instead of calm. She'd hugged her mother and then climbed onto her booster seat, allowed her mother to strap her in, then sat in silence. It was a silence that was better suited to Jaxon. Even when she wasn't speaking Summer was noisy. Now, she was quiet and still, rested her forehead against the window and stared out of it.

"Take care of your sister," Ashlyn whispered to Jaxon as she helped him into the car and strapped him in.

I looked away when Ashlyn turned to Kyle, busied myself with checking Summer and Jaxon's seat belts, that their booster seats were firmly in place, the food bag was settled securely beneath my seat. I could hear them, of course. Their mumbles, their promises, their chat. When silence fell, I presumed it was safe to sit up and I came upright just in time to see Kyle brush a lock of his wife's hair behind her ear, cup her face in his hand, staring at her as though he didn't know what to say. He had so much to say but none of the words to say it—I knew that look well.

"I love you," Ashlyn's lips said.

Kyle nodded, but said nothing.

Tell her you love her too, I almost screamed. It was painful, knowing that they were still in love with each other but were doing this. Not talking, not being honest. They slid into a hug and Kyle broke away first, pulled Ashlyn away, looking at her. Drinking in her image as though he wanted to remember her forever. As though he knew he wouldn't be seeing her like this again. He opened the car door, got in. Anguish was scored into the grooves of his face, into the lines that had developed in the time Jaxon and Summer were gone. As he buckled himself in, struggling to stop himself from breaking down, Ashlyn came to my side of the car, tapped on my window. I rolled it down, a little afraid of what she might say.

"Bye, Kendie," she said, her eyes searching mine. "Enjoy the trip back, OK?" *Remember what I said about you deciding to stay or go,* she was saying. "I've got a lot of thinking to do.

I need to work out who I'm doing things for," she continued. *I'll think about what you said,* she was saying.

"It was good to see you, Ashlyn," I replied.

She stepped away from the car, her lips pressed together into a brave smile, her eyes wide and terrified. She slowly backed away until she was standing on the doorstep of the cottage. The kids waved out of the back window, Kyle beeped his horn, raised a hand and then began to move out of the driveway.

"Stop the car!" I said urgently, unclipping my seat belt and fumbling for the door handle. "I forgot something."

Kyle hit the brakes, pulled on the hand brake. "What did you forget?" he asked, a small frown creasing his forehead because we didn't bring anything with us. Technically, there wasn't much I could have forgotten.

"Oh, you know . . ." I replied, cracking open the door and clambering out before he could ask me any more questions.

I marched up the path, the gravel crunching under my shoes, making me unsteady on my feet, but not in my purpose. With every step I was more certain of what I was doing. I could see the confusion on Ashlyn's face as I approached.

"Kendie?" she asked.

"Let's go inside," I said, sidling around her into the stone brick cottage. "I forgot something." I didn't want Kyle and the kids to see what happened next. I didn't envisage things getting violent, didn't think she'd be pulling my hair out, nor me taking her down with a rugby tackle, but these things were unpredictable.

She followed me inside, gently pushing the door behind her so it almost shut, but not quite. Light streamed in from the large glass doors at the back of the cottage.

"What did you forget?" she asked cautiously. I was standing in front of her, making no move to search through the chaos and detritus of the kids' exodus for whatever it was I had left behind.

"To give you a piece of my mind," I said, trembling slightly behind my stern words. My purpose was right, of that there was no doubt, but I was terrified.

She took a step back. This was good. She didn't step forwards, a snarl on her face, the sinews in her neck standing up, the muscles in her body tensed and poised for attack.

"You, Ashlyn, are the most selfish person I've ever met," I said, controlling the level of my voice. "I think it's incredible that you've never been called to account for all the things you've done to your family. Maybe I'm out of line, but I don't care, you need to be told.

"How dare you. How dare you do this to them? *How dare you.* I know you're sick, I know alcoholism is a disease, but why do your children have to suffer? OK, you're getting help, but why do you have to do it away from them? There are meetings all over the country, all over the world, why can't you come home?

"You're so lucky you're married to Kyle. 'Cause if it'd been down to me, I would have called the police on you from the moment you took the kids. I'd have gotten social services onto you. But he had faith in you. He's had faith in you all along. All through the summer he believed you were still sober. He didn't think you'd even contemplate drinking when you'd stolen the children. But then he's in denial about your disease and about you. Because it would never occur to him that you'd lie to him. He doesn't realize that nothing comes before your next drink, not even your children.

"You have to tell him the truth, Ashlyn. He needs to know so that he can get his head out of denial and be honest about this situation. He needs to see the reality of it. That you're not 'cured,' that there is no magical cure, and that you might do this again."

"I won't," she said, horrified that I'd even suggest such a thing. That in all the things I could accuse her of, this was the most unjust, the most preposterous.

"How do you know? When I saw you a few months ago you said you weren't that bad. You said you'd stopped drinking, well, what do ya know? You not only start drinking again, you put the kids at risk."

"I told you all that in confidence, not so you could throw it back in my face."

"You told me that so you could manipulate me into playing this stupid game of denial that everyone around you participates in. Well, it's not going to work. I'm all for denial unless it hurts two innocent people who love you more than life itself. They'd do anything for you. Do you know how fortunate you are? Do you? There are people out there who'd give anything to have what you have and, yes, you're sick, but that doesn't mean you can't get better around them. Not when it's for selfish reasons."

The air in the cottage fizzed with my outburst and Ashlyn's resulting shock. No one had done this to her. Kyle had confronted her once, but he'd backed off when he thought she was going to leave him, when he thought she'd gotten help and gotten sober. He didn't understand, didn't know, I suppose, that it wasn't an overnight thing. The drinking could stop, but that wouldn't mean a thing if your reasons for drinking were still there. Despite what Ashlyn thought, she didn't drink because of Kyle, because of not being able to deal with the kids. She drank because she was an alcoholic and that meant she'd find any excuse to drink.

If she wanted help, she could get it, and she could get it with her children. Women did it every day. They dealt with their alcoholism every day with their kids, with their husbands, with their jobs.

"You had no right to make demands of me, to tell me to decide to stay or to leave when you won't do the same. *And they're your children.* I wish all the time they were mine, but they're yours."

Ashlyn's fine-boned features paled, her eyes focused on the thick carpet beside my feet; she seemed to have shrunk in the past few minutes. "Are . . . Are you going to tell Kyle I've been drinking?" she asked, her voice barely breaking a whisper. For a moment I wanted to step forwards, to hug her. To fold her up in my arms and hug her better, just like I did with her daughter. *"I'll be a good girl. I promise. I promise"* rang in my ears.

"No," I replied, steeling myself from crumbling. If I wasn't careful I'd go back on everything I'd just said. "You have to tell him."

Slowly, precisely, she shook her head. "I can't."

I shrugged even though she wasn't looking at me. "OK, don't. Don't tell him, don't come back, do whatever you want, Ashlyn. Just remember, that's part of your disease. Doing whatever you want, always putting yourself first at the cost of everything and everyone else; pleasing yourself first is part of what makes you an addict. By not telling Kyle the truth, every conversation you have with him from here on in will be based upon that lie."

Moving much slower than I entered, I went towards the door. My hand rested on the cast-iron handle. "Don't forget as well, I might not tell Kyle, but you've got no guarantee that Jaxon won't. Who would you rather he heard it from?"

Every crunch of gravel under foot seemed to grind what I'd said into the surface of my soul. I understood Ashlyn. More than she knew. More than I wanted to. My drug of choice was hatred for myself.

"Phew!" I said as I got back into the car, my fingers trembling as I clicked the seat belt into place. "Good thing I decided to go; didn't realize I needed the loo so badly. Imagine getting halfway up the motorway and discovering how desperate I was." I was gabbling, I knew, but couldn't help it. I was anxious about what I'd done. This family seemed to constantly push and pull me to the brink of being firm and vocal. I was constantly having to take a stand, get tough.

I so understood Ashlyn. That was why I could say what I did. But I hadn't said I cared about her, I hadn't said it hurt me that she was hurting herself, I hadn't said I'd always love her but I needed her to get help. I didn't say it because it hadn't been true. Every word out of my mouth had been for Jaxon and Summer. It'd been for the two little kids who'd latched onto a virtual stranger because for so long they had a missing mother and a flaky father.

"I thought you said you'd forgotten something," Kyle replied.

"Oh. Yeah. I did . . ." I tried to think quickly. "I said I'd forgotten to go to the loo."

He shook his head. "You didn't. I distinctly remember you saying you'd forgotten something."

My eyes went to the rearview mirror. Two sets of eyes were focused on me. I curled my lips inwards to moisten them, heat rising from my feet to the top of my head at the speed of light. "Yeah, I forgot to go to the loo."

Kyle started the car again and as he moved forwards, my heart lurched.

Poor Ashlyn. Poor Ashlyn.

"Stop the car!" I said. Kyle slammed his foot on the brake. Turned to me.

"What's the matter now?"

"I, er, I forgot something else." I began unclipping my seat belt, pawed at the door until I got it open.

"What else?"

"I'll be back in a minute."

I stepped out of the car, my footsteps crunching even louder on the gravel as I ran back to the house. Ashlyn was sitting on the sofa, staring at the fireplace, her arms wrapped around herself. She glanced around when I entered the living room. I saw her body tense, bracing herself for another onslaught.

"I'm sorry," I said. "I meant what I said, but I shouldn't have said it like that."

She stared at me, glassy-eyed, disconnected. My eyes moved quickly around the room, looking for her bottle, for the booze it looked like she'd been drinking. Nothing. There was nothing to be seen and no smell of alcohol in the air. She shrugged at me desolately. "I deserved it," she mumbled.

"Ashlyn, I'm sorry. I . . . I shouldn't have torn into you. Well, no, I should have torn into you because of the hell you've put everyone through, but I should have also said it was brave for you to try to get help again. You deserve a lot of respect for that. I should have also said that you're a good person and I'm pretty sure no one could make you feel worse than you already do, I just . . ." I went forwards, perched on edge of the sofa. "I love your kids. I'm so close to them, never as close as they'll be to you, obviously, and I'd never try to be a replacement for you, but you not being around hurts them so much and I want to protect them from anything that hurts them. And, you know, I ache for all that you're missing, too.

"I wish you could see how amazing they are. Summer reads these books that are meant for young teenagers and rewrites the endings. She physically sits down and rewrites the endings if she thinks they're lame. And she writes letters of complaint to people. Proper letters about things she doesn't agree with. Like she wrote to the prime minister because she saw a man who had nowhere to sleep. Jaxon has started to create a city in the playroom. It's incredible. Now he gets Kyle to cut up blocks of wood for him and he paints on windows and doors. There are skyscrapers, and a shopping center and houses. It's the most incredible thing. You're missing all of that and . . ." I flopped my hand up and down. "Ashlyn, come home. I'll move out of the flat; you can live there if you can't live with Kyle, but come home."

She shook her head. "If I could come home don't you think I would?"

"I don't know."

"If I could come home, I would. But I can't."

I had to ask again. Had to ask another member of the Gadsborough family. "How can you bear it? How can you stand to be away from them?"

"The question you should be asking, Kendie, is how can I stand to live with myself after everything I've done to them? What I still might do. How much more I may hurt them if I come back. I don't want them to see me like that."

"But it's in the past, it's not who you'll always be."

"Have you told anyone your deepest, darkest secret?"

I stared at her without expression, thinking, *Of course I haven't. No one can ever know that about me.*

"I doubt it. Because you don't want them to see the worst part of you. My kids have spent all their lives seeing the worst part of me. Living with my deepest, darkest secret, I don't want them to do that anymore."

Nothing I said could convince her to change her mind. To come home and get better. "OK. You know what you're doing. But remember, all your children want from you is you. What they need from you is to set them a good example. The only example they've seen is of you being a drunk and then being a miserable sober person.

"Look, I came back to say I'm sorry. I want you to be OK,

and I'm sorry for how I said what I did to you. I hope you find what you're looking for." Before I could think about what I was doing and who I was doing it to, I threw my arms around Ashlyn and gave her a hug. Tried to show her that while I didn't understand why she wouldn't come home, didn't condone what she'd done under the influence, I still hoped she was OK.

I leapt up and she stood, too. As I raced out to the car, she moved slowly to the door.

"OK," I said, settling myself in the front passenger seat. "All done."

"All done?" Kyle asked. "I thought you'd forgotten something."

"Yeah, to go to the loo."

"You just said you went."

"Did I?"

"Yeah, and you said you'd forgotten something else. You said it like it was an object. You didn't say it like it was a verb, like you were going to do something, but like you were going to pick up something."

"Are you the grammar police or something?" I asked him. "And what difference does it make? Seriously, Kyle, what difference does it make?"

Kyle scrutinized me, a little too closely, as though I was under a microscope. His dark eyes were exploring my face, trying to read me. I felt myself wilting under his examination. If he asked me a direct question I'd crack, I knew I would. Heat started burning up my skin; my face was probably throbbing with the heat of his intense gaze.

"Something's going on, isn't it?" he asked quietly.

"I forgot something," Summer piped up. I felt my body relax, each tensed muscle unfurling as she saved me by drawing focus away from me.

In unison, Kyle and I turned in our seats to look at her.

"I forgot something, too," Jaxon said.

"We are *never* going to leave at this rate," Kyle said, his hand reaching for his seat belt clip.

"I forgot it on purpose," Summer continued.

"Me, too," Jaxon added.

"I forgot Hoppy," Summer said. "I left her behind on purpose. She's gonna look after Mumma. I've got Dad and Jaxon and Kendie to look after me. Mumma hasn't got anybody." Summer nodded at us, certain of what she was saying. "Hoppy will look after Mumma. She can give her hugs when we can't."

"I left Garvo," Jaxon said. "He's gonna look after Mumma, too."

I redirected my gaze to Kyle and our eyes collided. I could almost see his heart throbbing fast in his chest, matching the fast beating of my heart. I did the right thing, Ashlyn needed to be told.

"All right, what are we listening to on the way back?" Kyle asked as he settled himself forwards in his seat.

"Jaxon wants Itsy Bitsy Spider CD," Summer said.

"Summer wants Harry Potter book," he replied.

In the car's side mirror, I saw Ashlyn appear again. She seemed more fragile now. Shaken, weak, scared. For a moment what I'd said to her flashed through my mind. Was I responsible for how she looked? No, I realized. Ashlyn's problems had begun long before I entered her life. An eon before Kyle had entered her life, even.

I hope you get help, I sent a silent message to her. *Your children need you to, you need you to.*

From somewhere inside her, Ashlyn conjured a smile on her face and raised her arm to wave. The kids waved out of the back window, Kyle beeped his horn, lifted a hand and then eased the car out of the gravel driveway.

The last time I saw her, Ashlyn was framed in the side

mirror as Kyle turned left at the end of the driveway: she stood on the doorstep, her slender arms folded across her body, one sock pulled up, the other lounging around her ankle. She crumpled. Obviously she couldn't keep it together long enough for us to get out of range. She crumpled forwards and probably started to scream her heart out.

HOMEMADE MUESLI &
NATURAL YOGURT

◆ ◆ ◆

CHAPTER 43

I want to take Summer and Jaxon up to central London in December to do this," I said to Gabrielle. "But I don't think Kyle would let them out of his sight for more than three minutes, let alone a whole day. He's become incredibly paranoid about them. I understand it, even though Jaxon and Summer just give him this, 'what is your childhood trauma?' look whenever he does it."

My gorgeous boss held onto the edge of the ice rink, her chest heaving and her breath escaping in small, dense white clouds from the exertion of the six laps she'd done in quick succession.

I loved ice-skating. I loved being out on the ice, gliding through the world with nothing to stop me. Nothing to hold me back. I had balance issues in most things, I couldn't roller skate for toffee, but on the ice . . . The chill pulling at my face, the exhilaration, the freedom—I was unchained and comfortable. Relaxed and at peace.

It was a passion Gabrielle and I shared, and for our "hook up" after my return from Cornwall she'd suggested ice-skating. After work we'd gone because the rink was open late for serious skaters and only a couple of other people were moving across the ice. They both had coaches and had staked out their little patch and were practicing jumps and turns and other moves. We had one end of the rink virtually to ourselves.

"How is the delectable Kyle?" Gabrielle asked.

"Paranoid, but fine. They're all fine now that they're back together."

"That's fantastic," Gabrielle said. "I'm so glad your family's back together."

I arched an eyebrow at her but ignored her comment.

She launched herself away from the side of the rink, and glided backwards across the ice, graceful and beautiful, her long, dark ringlets flowing in her face. Once on the other side, she paused there, then came back towards me. She stopped, rather clumsily, by throwing herself against the side, almost tipping herself over the barrier in the process.

"I know we're moving on, but Kennie," she began as she righted herself, "I have to say this one thing; you should have told me what Janene said to you."

"I couldn't," I said simply. "There's already too much vileness in the world, I couldn't repeat it."

"But don't you see, she gets away with it. When we keep silent about these kinds of things the perpetrator gets away with it."

"I didn't keep quiet, I . . . well, you heard most of it."

"You should have told me. When people do those sort of hurtful things, even if it's saying something, if we say nothing, we protect them. It's not easy, speaking up, but you know what? It's one of the most important things. For ourselves. Silence helps the people who hurt us."

"What is this, some kind of public-information movie? I thought it was only me who used her soapbox," I said. She'd once told me that I was probably the only person on earth who'd be given more than one soapbox in her lifetime because her first one had been worn out.

Gabrielle's smile illuminated her face, brought out the black in her blue eyes, the strands of pure black in her hair. "I can't help myself sometimes." She let go of the side, did a little turn and then grabbed the side again. "I get so caught up . . . You know, after . . ." She paused, looked me over, working out whether she could say the word in front of me. I don't know why she thought she had to censor herself now. "After I was *assaulted*." She went for the safer word, the less emotive one, the one that didn't sound as brutal and violent. "It was taken out of my hands, reporting it, but I don't regret it. Not for one minute. I sometimes wish people didn't know, I wish sometimes I wasn't 'the one who was . . . *assaulted*' in my family, but I don't regret going through with it. Not out of revenge, but because it meant I stood up to him. It was after the fact, it was after he'd hurt me, but I still stood up to him. I'll never regret that."

"People believed you; some people aren't that lucky."

Gabrielle's face clouded over. "Not everyone believed me. You'd be surprised how many people didn't believe me—so many people refused to even consider the idea that such a 'good bloke' could do something like that. Others said I was a liar and had mental issues. Some said I was so repressed I couldn't just admit it was sex, but that doesn't matter. None of that mattered in the end because I know the truth. He knows the truth. And he knows that I told everyone I could, that his attempt to silence me didn't work."

"Fair enough."

"Evil grows when good people do and say nothing."

"Public service announcement."

"Sorry," she giggled, hunching her shoulders and wrinkling her nose, looking like the little girl she had been all those years ago. "So, changing the subject, can I ask you a question?"

"Sure. Doesn't mean I'll answer."

"Is Kyle paying for what some bastard did to you?" she asked. "Are you not giving him a chance because of something that happened to you?" I could feel her eyes studying me, watching my reaction carefully.

My reaction was to roll my eyes. I leaned over the wall, let the blood rush to my head—my blue hat didn't fall off but my hair came up to expose my neck. Once I was upright again I could look at Gabrielle to face this head on. "Even if I knew what you were talking about, they'd be two separate issues. Kyle's not paying for anything because Kyle's nothing more than a friend. I wish you'd understand that."

"I do."

"You don't. For you to ask that question, you don't. I adore Kyle, he's an amazing person, he has a special place in my heart, but he's not a man to me. Not in that way. He's a friend. I love him like I love you. I can't get away from that. He's not . . . I still love Will. I can't change that. I know it's not going to happen, I know he's in Australia and I know it's not possible, and I know I won't ever be able to forgive myself for the circumstances of our relationship, but I love him. And, yes, everyone thinks I should let it go. But how? Don't get in touch with him? Tried that. Don't live near him? Couldn't get much farther away from him than England. Don't think about him? I don't on purpose. He just hijacks me. I love Will. And I won't be able to give any-one a real chance until that's over."

I looked at Gabrielle, a little embarrassed at how impassioned I'd become. How strongly I felt. I knew I still felt an immense amount for him, but I'd not admitted the depth of those feelings to anyone, myself included. Mainly because I was too scared to think about him. With him came thoughts of the letter and what it might say. When I thought of him I thought of his wife, desperate, so desperate she'd tried to kill herself. Did kill herself as far as I knew. When I thought of him and for a moment I forgot everything else, I felt lit up from the inside out. Like a Christmas tree with the lights flicked on, like the Eiffel Tower illuminated at night. When I was allowed to think of Will without everything else, my heart came alive.

As I finished talking, I realized Gabrielle was smiling to herself.

"Do I sound like a dickhead?" I asked, feeling embarrassment crawling like a plague over my body.

"No, sweetheart, no. Absolutely no. I'm smiling because you said his name. For the first time you said his name. He stopped being the married man whose life you think you ruined and he became a man. He became Will. A real man who you felt something for. For the first time when you spoke then, you weren't beating yourself up for how you felt. You owned your feelings and you weren't embarrassed about having them."

I looked down. "Yeah."

"I'm not saying that it was an ideal situation, but you can't help who you fall in love with. If you could, who'd be single? Who'd be divorced? Who'd have fallings out with their families? Sometimes I think the best way to let things go and to move on is to play them out. See for yourself whether it's going to work out or not. Get hurt if it's not and then learn to get over it."

"That's not very likely to happen in this case."

"Maybe, maybe not. Did Will pay for what some bastard did to you?"

"Even if I did know what you were talking about," I prefaced my reply, "maybe he would have long term. I don't know. I remember feeling incredibly safe with him almost straight away, though. I didn't worry about . . . about anything. He never pressured me for anything, and never asked me to take on his burdens. Remember how you told me about the intuition? Guilt aside, I never had a moment of uneasiness about him or when I was with him. I found myself relaxing. I was normal. My body felt normal things, I wasn't . . ."

Gabrielle rested her hand on my forearm as my words ran out, my explanation disappearing into the air with my white breath. "I hear you, babe," she reassured. "God, do I hear ya."

"So," I said, brightening up, gearing us up for a subject change. "Do you want to race around the rink or are you too chicken to come up against me?"

"Me scared of racing you, yeah right," she scoffed. "Ted suffered for what happened to me. He suffered so much." She straightened up, turned on the points of her skates and leaned forwards over the wall, staring down at the darkness that lurked beneath the seats. "It wasn't so much what I did so much as him watching me tear myself apart. He wanted to help me, but he couldn't. I couldn't help me so how could he? Then he wanted us to try for a baby. I couldn't do it." She shrugged hopelessly as she redirected her gaze towards the ceiling. "I could never bring a child into the world after what had happened. I thought I could, but when it came down to it, I couldn't. That was hard for him to accept, but only at first. He said for better or worse and he meant it. Me, on the other hand, I couldn't let him make that sacrifice. I asked him to leave and he refused. I kept asking him to leave until one day he heard me. He said he'd only do it if I watched him pack. Because if at any point I changed my mind, he'd stay. I sat there crying my eyes out, watching the one man— the only man—I'd trusted since I was twenty-five leave me. I couldn't bear going home for weeks afterwards. I'd sit in the office after work and cry."

"When did this happen?"

"A few months before you left for Australia."

I was stunned. I had no idea. No idea at all. She never let on that something so monumental was happening to her.

"Is he with someone else now?"

"Nope."

"So, you're still in touch?"

"Yeah, we keep in touch."

"You could get back together?"

She turned on me, her eyes like hard, glittering sapphires in her head, her face wearing a hint of a sneer. "Why would I put him through that again?"

"Isn't that up to him?" I asked. "If Ted wants to come back to you, and you want him back, then why stand in the way?"

"Sometimes, what you want isn't always what's best for you."

For the first time since I'd known her I wondered about Gabrielle's grip on sanity. If Will was single and here and still into me, nothing would stop me. Nothing. "It's not like you're abusive to each other," I said to Gabrielle. "And seriously, if you've got even the smallest chance at happiness then why don't you grab onto it with both hands? It's hard enough finding someone who you're attracted to who is single and at the right time in their lives and feels the same way about you. Why would you fight that? I mean, three years later you're both still single, both still into each other. Do you think, possibly, that the universe is trying to tell you something?"

"Oh, I don't know, Kennie. Is it that easy?"

"Sometimes, yes. Sometimes, no. Sometimes you have to make it that easy. But you'll never know if you don't try. After all, what have you got to lose?"

"My one last hope. Once I know for sure, I know for sure. This way, I can always keep the hope alive that it might have worked out."

"Hope is only useful if you do something with it. Sitting around and hoping something works out, and hoping something works out while doing everything in your power to make sure it does are two completely different things."

"Maybe you're right," she said. "I do know every time we speak I imagine what it'd be like to be his wife again. That's why I never changed my name back, you know? Because I could still pretend . . . Maybe I just need to do it. Just do it so I know for sure." She cocked her head to one side as she grinned gently and affectionately at me. "And what about you, eh? What are we going to do about beautiful Kennie?" She reached out, stroked back a lock of my hair.

I snapped back from her, not comfortable with that kind of contact. Not by anyone, male or female; friend, relative or stranger.

"Sorry, sorry, shouldn't have done that," she said. "OK, watch me." She skated out to the empty expanse in the middle of the rink and skated in a few wide circles and then sped up, faster and faster, threw her arms out, and then she leapt up in the air, spun two and a half times and then landed on the ice, her back leg straight out behind her, arms out to balance her. I spontaneously broke out in applause. She was good at that. She was a bloody show-off, it had to be said, but she was allowed to be.

My one last hope? echoed above the scrapes of her skates as she began her large circles again, faster and faster, quicker and quicker until suddenly she was spinning around on the tips of her skates, her arms went up in the air and she was twirling around and around, a long thin twisting blue and red and purple blur on the ice.

I closed my eyes; behind my eyelids I could still see the whirl of the light catching on her metal zipper.

My one last hope. I thought of Will's unopened letter and the familiar anxiety didn't overwhelm me because talking to Gabrielle had brought up a new line of thought. Maybe finding out that it was too late and that Will's wife had died wasn't the only reason why I'd been scared to open the letter.

Maybe I hadn't opened it because it might also mean knowing if it was all over with the first man I've felt such a strong physical, emotional and mental connection with.

Maybe I hadn't opened it because it would tell me that I'd found true love and I'd lost it.

CHAPTER 44

*W*ill's words lay flat on the page, flat and uniform and blue, but what he'd said was three-dimensional, and had filled up the room, filled up my mind, filled up my heart.

I'd taken several deep breaths and had five or six false starts before I finally tore the envelope open. Another ten minutes of deep, calming breathing passed before I could pull out the two sheets of paper. And then another twenty minutes had ebbed away before I could look down at the words.

———

She's fine. She changed her mind just in time, realized that there was nothing worth leaving the kids for and called her sister. They had to pump her stomach, but luckily she didn't suffer any permanent liver damage. She's fine, much better, and getting help.

———

Those were the words I read over and over, gratitude pouring unchecked and unhindered through my veins. She was fine. She was alive. I hadn't been partially responsible for . . .

They had started the counseling required for getting a divorce, he said, and had discovered that they didn't want to be together anymore. They probably should have split awhile ago, he said, or gone for counseling, but now they wanted to move on. They were learning to be friends again and were still going through with the divorce.

The words that made me run my fingers over the page, as though trying to absorb his sentiments via the blue ink, said:

———

I love you, Kendie. If I could come to England, I would, I hope you know that, but I can't leave my kids. Would you think about coming back? I know it's a lot to ask, but I want to be with you. No matter when you get this letter, I know that won't have changed. Nearly two years I waited to be with you, I don't think how I feel will ever change. So, would you think about it? If you're scared your feelings may not stay the same once you get to know me properly, why don't you come for a holiday? Stay three months, think long term later on.

———

He'd written this letter a lifetime ago, but in the little time I knew him I had discovered a sense of who he was. He wouldn't have written it lightly. He would have taken his time over every word. He would have thought about what he was saying. He would have asked me to come back to him because he meant it.

I knew, as someone who loves another person does, that he wouldn't have changed his mind. Nothing would have changed between now and then. It hadn't for me, it wouldn't have for him.

He'd written this letter months ago so the time until they would be divorced was much nearer. We could be together now. I could go back to Australia, back to those moments of happiness that had been snatched away. I could go back and feel calm again. Safe. That's what I had when I was around

Will. A sense of safety. Normality. I was literally stepping back in time. To a time before I had flashbacks. Before I thought twice about everything people said to me. Before I had to hide huge chunks of myself. With Will, I didn't have to do that. I could tell him anything. Everything. I could go back to that now.

I picked up my mobile. Held it in my hand and then called up a blank text screen. I did a quick calculation as to what time it was over there. It was the middle of the night. He stayed up late, I knew that, but even if he didn't, he'd wake up to a message.

I tried to think of the right thing to say. I had to ask him if he still wanted me to come back. If he thought we still had a future. I wasn't rushing over there, I wasn't saying I'd go, but I had to know if he'd be there if I did.

Do you still want me to come back?

I typed and then sent it before I could think about it. I didn't sign it, didn't need to. Unless of course he had another woman in England whom he wanted to come back, in which case he'd get one hell of a shock at the airport.

Riinnnggg! My mobile intoned less than thirty seconds later. I jumped. Was he calling me back that quickly? I glanced at the screen and found Summer, Jaxon and Kyle grinning at me.

"Hi," I said into the phone, wondering which of the three it was.

"Kendra, it's Kyle." His voice was stiff, formal. Something was wrong.

"Hi," I replied.

"Can you come over? There's a problem with your direct debit; can you come over and discuss it?"

"Why? What's happened?" I asked, panicked. I was sure

there was enough money in my account to cover the rent. It's not like I did anything every month. Had someone stolen my identity and emptied my account?

"I'd rather do it in person. Can you come over now?"

"Yeah, sure," I replied.

"Thanks." He hung up without waiting for me to say good-bye. I stared at the phone, my mouth open in shock. *He seriously did not just hang up on me. How dare he! Who does he think he is?*

I wasn't having that. If there was a problem, I would have literally missed only one payment. *One* payment.

I stomped down the stairs, the keys jangling in one hand, mobile gripped in the other, mouth clenched, eyes narrowed. *I'll give him direct f-ing debit.* I rapped briefly on the kitchen door and then, without waiting for an answer, swung open the door and stomped in.

"SURPRISE!" Kyle, Jaxon and Summer cried as I entered the kitchen.

My heart stopped as my body leapt back in shock. Someone as jumpy as me did not, in the main, go in for surprises. Even pleasant ones.

I looked around at their faces, all smiling, all focused on me. There were red, blue and green balloons tied in clumps of three onto the wall cupboard fronts. A red, white and blue tablecloth covered the wooden table, streamers had been pinned along the edge. In the middle of the table sat a huge—and I did mean huge—cake. It was layer upon layer of chocolate and chocolate wafer and chocolate cream and cream. The top had been customized with pink and white marshmallows, carefully placed on each peak of chocolate icing. In the center was a forest of candles—as many as they could cram onto it—all lit.

My bewildered face, after taking in the party scene in front of me, went to their faces.

"One, two, three . . ." Jaxon counted and then the room was filled with their version of "Happy Birthday." They sang in tune, Kyle's rich, smooth baritone underscoring the younger, higher voices. With every word they sang to me, my eyes pricked with tears. "YEAH!!!" they cried at the end of it and clapped at me. I put a hand on my mouth, swallowing back the emotion that was jammed in my throat.

I shook my head at them. "It's not my birthday," I managed between great gulps of air.

"We know," Kyle said.

"You said it was in August," Jaxon began.

"But we were in Corn'all in August," Summer continued.

"So we're having a party now. It couldn't be a bigger surprise than now," Kyle finished. "Now, blow out the candles on your cake." He waved his hand at the cake with its forest of flames and slowly melting marshmallow topping.

"You couldn't fit any more candles on the cake, no?" I joked.

This was so sweet. Not only because of what they'd done, but it showed so much. It meant they'd finally done it. They were finally a melded family. They worked together to do this. They explained stories together. They felt secure. Jaxon could talk because he wasn't scared that something he said would wreck everything. Summer didn't need to throw tantrums regularly because her normal behavior got her dad to notice her. Kyle was back with his family. Jaxon and Summer had their dad back. In some respects, Ashlyn leaving was the best thing she could have done for Kyle's relationship with his kids.

I stepped forwards, went right up to the table and leaned forwards.

"Make a wish!" Summer reminded.

I looked up, caught Kyle's eye. Our eyes stayed locked together for a few moments. I knew what I had to wish for. I closed my eyes, made my wish, took a deep, deep breath, pursed my lips and blew. Hard. I opened my eyes as the breath came out of me in one long, steady stream and I moved around, making sure to put out all the candles in that one blow. This wish *had* to come true.

"We got presents!" Summer said and dashed out of the room, Jaxon hot on her heels, before I could call out that I didn't need presents as well as the cake.

"She'll like my present better than yours!" Jaxon yelled after her, taking the steps right on her heels from the sounds of it.

"No she won't!" Summer screamed back.

They were arguing. Summer and Jaxon were actually arguing. It was only a little spat, but only a few months ago that would have seemed impossible. They used to cling to each other, desperate, unable to exist without the other one to show the other side of their personality. Now, that twin stranglehold they had on each other had been loosened enough for them to have a little rivalry.

I pulled out a chair, removed a long blue sausage balloon and sat down. Kyle did the same opposite me. He picked up a red cone party hat, played with the thin, stringy white elastic before he handed it over. I put it on without hesitation.

Once his hands were free, he found something else to occupy them by pulling candles off the top of the cake. He focused on his task but I could tell he wanted to say something.

"I . . . erm . . . Ashlyn called me," he said. He began fiddling with the twisted body of a pink candle. "She called me, not the kids. She told me." He looked up into my face—obviously he knew that I knew. "Everything. Is that what you were doing when you kept getting out of the car? Were you making her confess?"

"I told you, I forgot something," I said.

"OK. We had a long talk. We've agreed that I should get custody of the kids. I've applied for the residency order and it'll probably be approved because Ashlyn's not going to contest it. She's accepted that she can't be their main care giver and she doesn't want us to get into that situation again."

"Kyle, I'm really pleased for you," I said.

"Never thought I'd be pleased about it as well, truth be known, but I can't think of anything better.

"I can stop worrying about Ashlyn as well. She's in treatment. It wasn't until she said it to me that I realized that she never actually admitted she had a problem. She started going to meetings because I said she had a problem, not because she admitted it to herself or anyone else. She's admitted that she's got a problem and she's asked for help."

"That's the first step, they say, admitting you've got a problem you're powerless over."

He smiled to himself. "That's what she said."

"She's lucky to have you, you know, Kyle. So many women in her situation are married to good men who wouldn't have a clue where to start if they were thrown into this situation. But you really stepped up to the plate. After a few false starts."

"And with a lot of help from a certain person."

"I'll tell Mrs. Eyebrows next door that you said thanks," I said. I hadn't seen her in a while. Probably because I hadn't screwed up in public for a while.

Kyle laughed. A small laugh that illuminated his face. He was so handsome. A sweet man with a good heart.

"I've got a problem, too. I accept that now," he continued. "I helped her to be an alcoholic. By pretending it wasn't happening for so long, covering for her, getting so mad with her when she screwed up, silently blaming her for ruining my career, it didn't help. If I could do it all over, I'd get help. Talk to someone. Silence wasn't helpful."

"Maybe you could talk to someone now?" I suggested gently.

Still fiddling with the pink candle he smiled at me. "I already do."

"A professional," I said. "Or maybe other people who've lived with alcoholics."

"Maybe . . . We'll see . . . We're still going through with the divorce. Moving forwards, not backwards, you know?"

I nodded.

"We've agreed to try to keep it civil, but we're realistic. Things might get nasty but no matter what, we're not going to use the kids as weapons like we were doing before. It shouldn't take too long for it to be sorted; it's the financial stuff that's going to take the longest to sort out. It's scary, the thought of not being with Ashlyn. I've spent most of my adult life with her. It's hard to imagine being with anyone else."

"Whose present do you want to open first?" Summer yelled as she ran back into the room after Jaxon, interrupting our conversation. The two youngsters both stood to attention in the doorway, hands behind their backs, keeping their presents out of sight.

"Don't make me choose on my pretend birthday," I said, neatly stepping out of the line of fire.

"OK, Dad, you choose," Summer said.

The agony of a parent put in an unenviable position passed over Kyle's features. "Jaxon, you go first. Seeing as Summer was born first, you're the youngest in the room."

Jaxon grinned and stepped forwards, took his present from behind his back. It was in a poster tube, decorated with Jaxon's drawings and scrawls saying "Happy Birthday, Ken."

I uncapped the tube, reached in with my forefinger and thumb to pull out the poster. I unrolled the glossy sheet and held it up. On large, shiny poster paper were some plans for a two-story building. At the top of the page, typed in small letters was: "Kendie's house."

"That's your new house," Jaxon enlightened.

"My new house," I stated, staring at the poster. I examined it carefully. On the first floor was a large living room. Connected to it was a kitchen and then a smaller room that had "Kendie's special room" across its center. At the plan's center was a staircase to the second floor. On the second floor there were four rooms. Bedroom 1, bathroom, then "Jaxon's room" and "Summer's room."

"There's a room for me and a room for Summer for when we come to stay with you," Jaxon said.

"I see."

"Dad helped me to do it on his computer. He said he'd build it for you if you give him lots of hashese."

"Cashese, I think you'll find I said," Kyle corrected quickly. "Cashese, as in money."

The lump of emotion in my throat swelled, almost choking me. I lowered my head, unable to blink back the tears. A couple broke free, dripped onto the poster. I used my sleeve to mop them up, watching the moisture soaking into the white cotton of my top.

"I love it," I said to him, wiping my face dry with the back of my hand. "It's wonderful." I managed to look at him. "And when I get some hashese, I'll get your dad to build it."

Jaxon grinned. Summer stepped forward, presented me with her bundle of paper and ribbon and tape. It was impressively wrapped, and I had no idea what could be in it. I took it carefully, sure that it was fragile, and began the painstaking task of unwrapping it, piece of tape by piece of tape, removing layers of paper here, layers of paper there until in front of me I had a side-plate-sized basket. The base was terra-cotta red, the weaving around the sides was a mixture of red, black, yellow and orange straws. Around the base Summer had written in white paint "For Kendie" but she'd misjudged the space she had to write it all so the *d*, the *i* and the *e* were smaller with the *e* being tiny. The weaving was uneven and imperfect.

"It's for your earrings and your funny rings," Summer explained.

"It's beautiful," I whispered, the emotion welling up through every cell in my body.

"Dad helped with the weaving, but I picked the colors and painted your name on the bottom. Your real name, not the one everyone calls you."

My bottom lip began to tremble. Summer was aghast as tears fell from my eyes. "You mustn't cry at everything," Summer said, patting the back of my hand. "Even Dad doesn't cry that much anymore."

"Excuse me, what?" Kyle said.

I bit my lip and tried not to laugh and cry at the same time.

I opened my arms to them. "This is the best birthday I've had in years," I said. They came and hugged me. They smelled so good, felt so good. It was so easy, so uncomplicated being with these two. It made my heart feel so real being able to hold them, being privileged enough to know them. While they hugged me and I clung to them, simply because I could, I felt the weight of Kyle's attention on me and opened my eyes. Our gazes locked again and his full, soft lips slid upwards into a grin. I grinned back, the wish I made coming to mind. My wish was this: I wished for him to find the right woman to love. I suspected she was Ashlyn, but if not her, someone who could see everything wonderful about him and to love him how he deserved to be loved. If anyone deserved to be held and loved and taken care of, it was Kyle.

This birthday party, these presents were fabulous for more than one reason. They showed that they didn't need an outsider to help keep things on an even keel anymore. They were working—*thriving*—as a family; they didn't need me.

Which meant I could go to Australia if I wanted.

As if on cue, my mobile, which I'd left on the table, bleeped. Summer and Jaxon disentangled themselves from me, went to help their father cut up the cake. I picked up my phone and called up the text message.

I'll always want you back. I'll send you money for the flight. Love you. Will x

They didn't need me, Will did. I could go back to Australia if I wanted.

WATER

◆ ◆ ◆

I'll miss this, I thought as I walked around the supermarket, pushing a trolley that already held kidney beans, chickpeas and stock. I didn't have my helpers with me today. They were staying the night at Ashlyn's place after spending the day with Naomi.

Naomi . . . After what she did, I thought Kyle was an incredibly magnanimous person to forgive her like he did. Me, I would have kicked her arse from here to next Easter, only stopping at Christmas to give my foot a rest. But he didn't want to alienate his family. He really was taking this putting-the-kids-first thing seriously.

As I turned into the soft drinks aisle and headed for the mineral water at the other end, my mobile rang. I rooted it out of my bag and because I didn't recognize the number, I answered it cautiously. "Hello, Ms. Tamale, I'm ringing back with a price on flights to Australia," the pleasant voice on the other end said.

"Oh, hi," I replied. "I haven't got a pen right now, but could you give me an idea of how much it'll cost?"

She read them to me. "Do the prices vary if I go via Hong Kong instead of Singapore?" I asked, leaning against the trolley handle and idly running my eyes over the objects littering the wire bottom. There was tapping on a keyboard on the other end of the phone before she read out some of the figures. I'd never let Will pay for my flight, but I was investigating how much it'd cost me to pay for my own flight and working out how much I'd need to save up before I went.

I couldn't go straight away. I had to save not only for the flight, but also for the time I wouldn't be working while I was over there. I also needed to slowly remove myself from the Gadsboroughs.

In about six months, maybe if I went all out to get new business at work, I'd have the money. And now that Ashlyn was back in Kent and working in London, I reckoned she'd start seeing Kyle again and in about six months she'd be ready to move back home.

In that time I could extricate myself slowly from the family. She really wouldn't want me around all the time, and I'd find it impossible. Despite what I tried to pretend to myself, I'd find it difficult being around Ashlyn, having a reminder twenty-four hours a day that she was their mother. I did know it, but sometimes it was easier to ignore it, to live in a state of make-believe. So, Australia would be a good clean break. Once again not being able to have children would send me there, but this time I knew someone was waiting for me. Will would be there.

Will.

Now that I could think about him without the fear of what might have happened to his wife, I grinned all the time about him. It was a slow grin that grew from the center of my face. Gabrielle was often asking me what I was smiling at, and I'd say nothing. I'd sneak a look at his picture, which I kept on my mobile, and stardust would dance across my stomach. I'd never felt like this about a man before and, yes, we were going to be sensible and take it slowly and not rush into anything when I eventually got there, but I couldn't help myself. He couldn't help himself. We made each other giddy.

"Thanks so much," I said as the woman finished reading

me figures and airlines. "I'll have a think about it and call you back." I cut the line and put the phone back in my bag. I started off towards the bottled water again but was cut off by another trolley moving at a diagonal in front of me and stopping, so it blocked my path. I looked up. Kyle. I grinned at him, but my smile drained away when I saw his face. He didn't look pleased to see me, in fact there seemed to be thunder rolling in his mahogany eyes as he stood staring at me. The smooth lines that molded his features were hard, his jaw stiff as though barely reigning in his anger.

"Hi, Kyle," I said cautiously. He didn't reply, simply glared at me. When a man with his trolley tutted loudly because he couldn't get by, Kyle turned his look on him. The man suddenly realized he really would prefer to go in the other direction, turned his trolley around and left. Quite quickly. Kyle's head swung back to me.

"So," he said, in lieu of a hi, "you're moving back to Australia. When the hell were you going to tell me and the kids?"

My mouth flooded with saline then dried just as quickly. He wasn't meant to find out like this. And certainly not now. I was going to tell him and the kids in a few months, when they were used to me not being around as much.

Stunned by being found out, I said nothing. In response, Kyle flattened his palms on his eyes, ground his fists into his forehead. "Why, *why?*" he said in frustration, his face tipped up into the ether of the supermarket. "Why does this keep happening?" He took his hands away. "Why?"

Up and down the aisle, people were heading our way. I stepped out from behind my trolley, pulled Kyle's to one side and touched him to get him to step aside. He jerked himself away from my touch and moved aside on his own.

The first person to sidle past us, to witness Kyle's very physical reaction to my nearness, was our neighbor with the abused eyebrows. Her eyebrows virtually shot off her face as she looked at Kyle, his face crumpled with anger, his body rigid with fury. She walked on, but then stopped by the pop, started eyeing it up as though she was going to find next week's lottery numbers on the labels.

I moved closer to Kyle, lowered my voice so Mrs. Eyebrows couldn't hear. "It's not like I'm leaving tomorrow."

"Why do you have to leave at all, huh?" he replied, loud enough to be heard in Scotland. "Answer me that. Why do you have to leave?"

I glanced over at Mrs. Eyebrows—her eyes were bulging out of her head as she stared at the fizzy drinks. "Shhh," I hushed. "Keep your voice down."

"No," Kyle replied, even louder. "Tell me why you have to leave."

"I won't tell you anything if you don't quiet down."

Kyle folded his lips into his mouth and nodded his acquiescence.

"Look, like I said, I'm not going tomorrow or anything. Maybe in a few months. The thing is, the three of you don't need me anymore, I can go now."

"*What?*" he almost shouted. I raised my eyebrows—after looking at Mrs. Eyebrows (she was openly staring at us)—and gave him a silent warning. "OK, OK," he said quietly. "What the hell are you talking about?"

"You're all doing so well now and it looks like pretty soon Ashlyn's going to become a bigger part of your lives again, so you don't need me, I can go."

"What the—? Do you think you're some kind of Mary Poppins, dropping in wherever you're needed then off you fly again? Kendra, you're a part of our family. We *want* you around."

I had to tell him, to explain. "I . . . I want to be with Will."
He drew back a little, stared at me in confusion. "Who's
Will?" he asked.

"My . . . The . . ." I motioned vaguely over my shoulder.

"The guy in Australia?" Kyle said, catching on. "You
haven't seen him in, what, eight . . . nine months? How can
you go back to him? What's so special about him?"

"Everything. Nothing. It's not him. It's how I feel when
I'm with him. I feel normal. Like a normal person. Things
like not being able to have kids don't feel as bad. I haven't
felt like an ordinary person in so long, but when I'm with
Will, when I talk to Will, that's how I feel. Like everyone
else."

He stared at me for a moment as though trying to unravel
the knots of secrets that made up who I was, as though if he
looked long enough, he'd find out what was wrong with me.
"Why do you hate yourself?" he asked quietly.

I felt my face do a passable impression of Mrs. Eyebrows
as my eyebrows went up in surprise. "Sorry?" I asked.

"You told me once that you hate yourself. Why?"

I turned around to glare at Mrs. Eyebrows, to make sure
she wasn't overhearing this part of the conversation, which
should have been carried out behind closed doors, if at all,
but she had gone. Obviously our whispering had cut short
her fun. Or maybe she was running off to the manager's office to get them to announce over the loudspeaker: would
the couple quietly rowing in the soft drinks aisle either
move on or speak up so everyone can hear?

"I didn't."

"You did. The day we went to the museum. I tried to take
a picture of you and you said you hate yourself."

"In pictures, I hate myself in pictures."

He shook his head. "No, there was definitely a period in
between saying you hate yourself and in pictures."

"Are you some kind of grammar freak because, seriously—"

"I knew the second you said it you didn't mean only in
photographs. Tell me why you hate yourself."

He'd been holding onto that all this time, waiting for the
perfect moment to bring it up. "It's hard to explain," I said to
Kyle, knowing that trying to fob him off incorrectly would
make him even more curious.

"Try me."

"Pardon me?"

"Try explaining it to me."

"I don't see what difference it'll make," I said. "It's got
nothing to do with me leaving."

"You can tell me anything."

I shrugged at him. "I know, but there's nothing to tell."

His eyes started to bore into me, seeking out the truth in
what I was saying. There really was nothing to tell. Nothing
at all. A woman's arm came between us as she reached for a
bottle of bright red cherryade. She hefted it off the shelf and
removed her arm from between us, but Kyle stared at me as
though we hadn't been interrupted.

"You can tell me anything," he said again. "It'll go no further."

"Thank you," I replied.

"You know everything about me. Everything. Stuff I
haven't even told my wife. I want to do the same for you."

"Like I said, thank you, but seriously, Kyle, there's nothing to tell."

"Kendra, you can tell me anything—I will believe you."

Time stopped for a moment. Just a moment. I had an
out-of-body experience. Like so many I'd had recently. Like
watching as I threatened Janene. Like seeing myself react to
the kids disappearing. Like not being there in the nook in
the hotel as *his* hands ran over my body. Now I watched my-

self as time stopped. Standing in the brightly lit supermarket, with the buzz of Saturday carrying on around me, I could see myself. I looked fragile. Even though I was wearing a fleece, jeans and trainers. Even though my hair was hiding my face, there were hairline cracks covering my body. Touch too hard and I would shatter. Those four words had stopped time. I never knew I needed to hear them. I never knew they would unlock everything. Would unravel the permanent knot that was embedded in my chest.

When time started moving again, I was back inside my body. I couldn't see myself from the outside. "Why would you believe me, Kyle?" I said, shaking my head. "I don't even believe myself."

AIR, JUST AIR

♦ ♦ ♦

I want you to stay in here while you read it. I'll be in the bedroom. I . . . um . . . here." I stuck the sealed white envelope into Kyle's hand, avoiding his eyes all the while. It'd taken me two weeks to do this. To tell him "anything."

In the end I'd gone for the safe option, Plan B. Basically, I chickened out and wrote a letter.

Kyle reached out to touch my face, probably to reassure me, but I flinched away. He held his hand midair for a few seconds then dropped it. "I'll call you when I've finished reading it" was all he said.

I wanted to apologize, to let him touch my face and reassure me. But I couldn't. Everything was about to change between us. And when he found out about my past I knew nothing would ever be the same again. I dragged my feet through my flat to my bedroom. I paced about for a few minutes, then found myself sitting on the bed, staring at the knots blemishing the wood floor, my arms wrapped around myself. I imagined Kyle sitting on the sofa, turning over in his large hands the white envelope I'd written *Kyle* on, his fingers tearing it open. I could imagine him taking out the sheets and sheets of white paper, unfolding them and beginning at the first line.

He'd find no *dear,* no *Kyle,* no date, because it'd taken me so long to write.

I'm going to tell you everything. Everything that has led me from where I was, who I was, to here.
I'm going to tell you everything.
I haven't talked about it before. I rarely even think about it. Only one other person knows what happened. And his account may differ from mine.
When I was twenty a man I trusted forced himself on me. Before you think it was what I wanted, it wasn't. I promise you it wasn't.

CHAPTER 47

I'm going to tell you everything. Everything that has led me from where I was, who I was, to here.

I'm going to tell you everything.

I haven't talked about it before. I rarely even think about it. Only one other person knows what happened. And his account may differ from mine.

When I was twenty a man I trusted forced himself on me. Before you think it was what I wanted, it wasn't. I promise you it wasn't.

It began in the middle of the night, the night I went to Harrogate for his work party.

He'd been the perfect gentleman when we got to his place. He made me coffee and showed me the room I was going to stay in. It wasn't the room I'd stayed in with Tobey, but it was nice. Tidy, clean, bed neatly made, curtains drawn. He put on the bedside lamp for me and we sat on the bed talking. I was a little uneasy, abstractly unsettled. He hadn't mentioned that all his flatmates were away, that it'd be just the two of us in the house. But again, I told myself I was being silly. That I shouldn't think I was so extra-special that he was a good guy and he hadn't tried anything since I'd stopped him kissing me.

I got changed for bed—he'd lent me one of his lumber-jack shirts, which was missing its top button, to sleep in. I was grateful for the loan because I didn't want to sleep in my clothes.

Once my head hit the pillow, I fell asleep. I could do that, then. I could fall asleep at will.

In the middle of the night, when it was dark, when it was pitch black, I went to turn over in bed, but there was a heavy weight on top of me. I tried to turn again, but still this weight . . . It was getting heavier, or maybe I was waking up so I was more aware of it. But it was bearing down on me and making it difficult to breathe.

I opened my eyes as his hand came down on my mouth, shutting off my ability to speak, shout or scream.

For a moment I thought he was playing around, was being silly, trying to scare me maybe. I moved to push him off, but my arms wouldn't work; they were pinned I didn't know how, but I couldn't move. I couldn't move at all. That was when the fear, thick and deep, like a vat of hot tar, started to creep up on me. I started struggling. Trying to get him off me, trying to stop him from doing whatever it was he was doing.

Suddenly one of his hands clamped around my throat. Squeezing, shutting off all air to my lungs. As the fear started to rip me apart molecule by molecule, and blackness started to seep in at the edges of my sight, two thoughts popped into my head at the same time: *He's done this before. He's going to kill me.*

His lips were against my ear. "You're special. Stop fighting, you're special," he whispered. "Stop fighting and I won't kill you." I had to stop. If I didn't stop fighting he was going to squeeze harder. If I didn't stop he was going to . . .

It happened for the first time. I left my body. I was a daydreamer as a child. I could go to places inside my head, I could read a book and explore new worlds, but I'd never done this before. I'd never left my body and found a place to hide. I closed my eyes and curled up inside that darkness, safe from everything else. Disconnected and safe.

Something was happening, I knew that, but I wasn't there.

I heard what he was saying in my ear, but it didn't connect. His scent crawled up my nose and slid down my throat, but I wasn't there. He was moving against my body, inside my body, but it wasn't real. It wasn't happening. It couldn't be happening and I wasn't there to witness it.

Suddenly it was over. It was over and he was lying on me, breathing hard, his chest the only part of him that moved. His chest and his sweat. His sweat. It rolled off him and onto me. Covering me in his scent. Covering me in more of him. I wanted to push him off, to get him away from me, but I didn't move. If I moved, I'd be admitting I was there, I'd be admitting it'd happened.

The rest I remember in snippets. In snapshots and flashes. Like clicks of a camera shutter.

Click. He was talking. He was lying beside me, propped up on one arm and talking. "Don't you ever get frustrated?" he asked after a while. "Haven't you ever wanted something so much you'll do anything to get it?"

He was staring down at me, waiting for an answer. I could hear my breathing. That's how I knew I was alive. I wasn't moving, I was staring at the hairline cracks in the ceiling, but I couldn't move. I couldn't feel anything. But I could hear my breathing. Short shallow breaths in my ears. I could still breathe so I knew I was alive.

"Aren't you going to say something?" he asked. "Talk to me, Kendra." His long fingers reached out towards my forehead, to maybe brush away a few strands of my hair, to maybe just stroke my forehead, to maybe just touch me. I flinched. Scared. Terrified that he was going to hurt me. Again.

"I'm not going to hurt you," he said, horrified by my reaction, but he didn't touch me. "I'd never hurt you. Kendra, you're so special to me. I wouldn't ever hurt you. I thought that was what you wanted."

He'd just said that he was willing to do anything to get what he wanted, and now he was saying it was what I wanted. Which was the truth? Was it him or was it me?

Click. "Thing is, Kendra, I know what you're like. What you're really like. I've seen how you are," he was saying. "I thought that was what you wanted."

I'd pushed him away the last time he kissed me. I'd tried to tell him no this time. I tried to shake my head. I would have said no if he'd let me breathe. But he thought it was what I wanted. *Why? How could he think that?*

"Hey, tomorrow, do you fancy going for lunch in town? I think the market's on. They've got some good stuff, you'd really like it."

He was being so normal. Had I imagined what had happened? Had I gotten it all wrong? Did he say he'd kill me? If he could just be chatting, then maybe I'd got it wrong.

"You think about it, OK? You can bunk off lectures tomorrow, can't you? I'll drive you back in the afternoon." He didn't move towards me again. "OK, I'm going to get some sleep. Night." He rolled away and within minutes he was breathing slowly, deeply, asleep. I moved then. Slowly, carefully, I turned away from him. I couldn't move too much because I didn't want him to wake up. To touch me. To talk to me. If I could, I would have gotten up and got dressed and gone home. But I wasn't sure where the train station was from here. I wasn't sure my legs would work. It was still black outside.

Click. I could smell him. His scent was all over me. The room smelled of him as well. Smelled of him and reeked of it. What he'd done.

Click. I hurt, deep inside. Not just where he'd hurt me but in my throat. He'd crushed my windpipe but it hurt deeper than that. At the center of my throat, right in the middle there was nothing but agony. As though someone had gouged out that area of my soul and left a deep wound that would never heal. I wouldn't ever be able to speak of this. At the center of myself I hurt. I wanted to put my hands over it, to soothe it, to stop the pain but there was no way to touch it. It wasn't a part of me that hurt, it was the very substance of who I was. Shame and disgust ran like rivers through my body. They ran into the hole in me. The hole at the center, the hole I could not soothe and I could not fill.

Click. "Do you want to use the shower first?" he asked.

I started inside at his voice. I hadn't slept. I'd been watching the blackness outside the curtains, waiting for the sun to come up. The hours had crawled by and it didn't seem to get light forever.

I nodded.

"Cool, I'll go put the kettle on." He leapt out of bed and bounded out of the room.

Slowly I got off the bed, gathered my jeans and T-shirt and sweater and jacket into my arms, crept out of the room into the bathroom.

Click. I let the water run over me but couldn't bring myself to touch my body.

Click. He'd changed the sheet and made the bed. The sheet sat in a puffy heap, like a giant meringue, in the corner of the room. He'd opened the curtains and allowed the light into the room.

Click. I left his shirt, which was now missing all its buttons, neatly folded up on top of the sheet.

Click. The house echoed with the quiet. The emptiness. What had happened.

Click. The shower spurted to life as I made my way downstairs to wait.

Click. "Did you sleep OK?" he asked as he went over to the kettle. I kept my eyes on the table, running my sight along the thin lines of the grain in the wood. Like walking a maze, I let my mind follow the lines to where they ended, then found new ones to follow from start to finish. "I slept like a log," he continued to my silence. "Didn't realize Heidi had such a comfy bed. Lucky cow." He got two mugs out of the cupboard. Would Heidi mind that I slept in her bed? Would she guess what went on in her bed? "So, did you decide about lunch?"

He was staring at me, waiting for an answer. I heard the kettle click off, and the room still as he waited for me to speak.

"I . . ." This was the first time I'd used my voice since the middle of the night and talking through a bruised throat, a gouged-out soul, was agony. "I have to get back," I said.

"Oh," he said. Surprised. Genuinely surprised. Like he expected me to stay. Maybe he hadn't tried to kill me. Maybe the others had stayed. Maybe he really thought he'd done nothing wrong. Or was it that I was going crazy? "Are you sure?" he asked.

I nodded. One short movement down, no up.

"OK, if you're sure. I'll drive you to the station after this." He settled a cup of coffee in front of me. White, one sugar.

"Thank you," I said automatically. Because that's what you say when someone does something for you: thank you.

Click. I didn't drink the coffee. Just like I didn't drink last night's coffee. It still sat on the bedside table, cold, with a web of milk skin on top. I didn't drink last night's coffee nor this coffee for the simple reason I didn't like coffee. Last night I'd been too polite to say so. At that moment, not doing something I didn't like seemed very important. Vital. It was the only control I had.

Click. Nausea stirred inside as I sat at the table. I hurt. All over. Inside my skin. Outside my skin. Deep in my head. Deep in my chest. I hurt and I wanted it to stop. I wanted to be away from this place.

♦

Click. I knew he was watching me and I kept my head lowered, my eyes watching the coffee I wasn't going to drink so I wouldn't see what he was really thinking. If I saw triumph, the satisfaction that he'd gotten what he wanted, on his face, I might just possibly die. If I saw nothing, looked into his face and realized that it was just another ordinary morning of another ordinary day to him, I *would* die. I'd lose my mind and I would die.

Click. He stood too close to me as I was buying my ticket back to Leeds. My teeth ached. I'd been unintentionally gritting my teeth, clenching them tight, so I could bear this and my teeth throbbed from the pressure.

Click. I thanked him for inviting me to the party, for the place to stay, for the lift to the station. I was polite, had been brought up properly. He nodded. In the seconds that followed he leaned in to kiss my mouth good-bye and I snatched my head away, jerked my body back. Anger, confusion, upset crossed his face. Acceptance crossed my mind: it *had* happened. My body's instinctive reaction told me so. I wasn't going mad, this wasn't another ordinary day, I had been damaged. "I'll call you," he said as I turned towards the gate. He never did, by the way. But the terror that he would stayed with me until I moved out of that house.

Click. The scenery dashed past the train window, a blur of green and houses. A series of smudges that put distance between me and the middle of the night.

♦

Click. My calmness broke when I shut the front door behind me. The house was empty and I ran to the bathroom. I threw down my bag. I tore at my clothes. Frantically, desperately I ripped at them. I wanted none of them to touch me. I wanted nothing to touch me. My hands slipped over the bath taps. It was a student house, only a bath. It filled so slowly. So slowly. But then it was full enough. I sat in the bath, ran the small white bar of soap over myself. The soap but not my hands. I was too disgusted to touch my skin.

Click. After a few minutes, when it wasn't working, when I could still smell him on me and feel him against and inside me, I dropped the soap, leaned forwards over my knees in the bath. I didn't cry. I sat bent forwards, as much as possible of my curled fist stuffed into my mouth so I could scream and no one would hear. So I wouldn't hear.

Click. We sat in the pub, everyone talking and laughing and joking. The world didn't stop. I don't know why I expected it to, but it didn't. Why would it? Meg and Elouise were on top form, they were like a double act and I couldn't help but laugh. It was there, at the back of my mind. Hovering over my shoulder, dancing on the edge of my consciousness, but I forgot for a while. I didn't think about the jeans, T-shirt, bra, knickers, sweater, and grey and white jacket stuffed into a plastic bag and hidden at the bottom of my wardrobe, waiting to be thrown away when the bin men came next week. I didn't think about the internal bruise on my throat that made it hard to swallow. I didn't think about the agony that circled my lower body. I didn't think about the urge to stand up and scream.

Click. For the first time in my life I prayed for my period to start. I prayed that I wouldn't get pregnant. That I wouldn't have to make that choice. I didn't realize at the time that because of that night I'd never get pregnant.

Click. The nurse who drew my blood for the HIV test had a kind face and cold hands. She was my mother's age, but white with short brown hair. She was gentle when she pricked my skin. She'd been impressed that although I'd told her about my fear of needles I hadn't flinched, I hadn't tensed. She asked me why I wore six layers of clothes when it was summer. When I told her I was always cold, she hadn't looked convinced. She looked like she wasn't convinced by me at all. "If you ever want to talk, I'm always here during surgery hours," she said. "Simply make an appointment." I thanked her and went to leave. At the door, she stopped me from turning the handle. "Kendra, even if you can't talk to me, find someone. A friend, a relative, anyone. Even call a help line. Just talk. It's important."

"That's just it," I replied with a shrug. "I have nothing to say." *I have no words to describe this so I have nothing to say.*

Click. Some days I would tell myself it was just sex. I'd been lucky with Tobey because he was a man who respected me and loved me and treated me as though I was another human being. This time had just been different. It was just sex. Even as I was telling myself that, I knew it wasn't about sex. It was violence. It was hate. It was his rage that he'd pushed onto me and into me. Most days I wouldn't think about it at all. And even as I wasn't thinking about it I knew his rage had infected me.

Click. College became a struggle. Socializing became a struggle. People became worried about me. My grades fell. I went to the doctor and he diagnosed depression. Told me I should drink less alcohol, eat more fruit and vegetables. "Take up exercise, as well, young lady," he said. "Looking better will make you feel better." *Looking better?* I wanted to say to him. *I have no idea how I look because I haven't so much as glanced in a mirror in months. I can't bear to see myself. To see the words* stupid *embroidered into my features and* victim *carved into my eyes.* I bucked up my ideas. Pulled off the biggest acting performance of a lifetime to finish college with a better-than-average degree and to let the world think I was normal.

Click. The flashbacks began almost straight away. They take me back there, and I feel it all over my body. His voice in my head, his body next to mine, the terror in my heart. They haven't gone away but I've found that moving or doing something else or focusing on the present stops them in their tracks. I think—I hope—they'll go away one day.

Click. I did have sex again. It was five years later and he was nobody special or important. He was like every other man since then: I'd date them for a while before things got physical. We'd always go out on dates to public places—never stay in—and I'd always let them know I didn't do sleepovers. I always went home. I'd learned to drive in that time so I didn't drink and always drove home. When we did have sex I'd never remember it. I'd pretend to be there. I'd pretend to enjoy it. But I always switched off, stepped out, removed my mind so my body could go through with it.

Will was different. I liked him. My body and mind responded to him. I wanted to kiss him. I wanted him to kiss me. I didn't do it because I was dating him and that's what you do when you date someone. I wanted him to touch me, to hold me, to kiss me. I wanted to make love to him. To have sex with him. Since I was twenty I hadn't responded to a man like that. Since that night, I hadn't known I was capable of *wanting* my body to be that close to a man's. You can't tell people that, can you? You can't say: "I know that married man is special, that I do have a connection with him because for the last twelve years I've not had a man kiss me without me tuning out and pretending I like it. I know I love him because all of me wants him."

Click. Sometimes I would call the Samaritans and not say a word. I just needed someone to be there. So that I wouldn't go the other way. I wouldn't do it.

Click. You asked me why I hate myself and I told you it's hard to explain. I'd sometimes say it out loud: "I hate myself." I'd hate my body not because it was fat or thin or didn't fit clothes. But because something that had always been mine, something so precious—my body—had once been used by someone else. He'd taken it over and I hadn't been able to stop him. For those minutes it wasn't my body and I hated that. I'd hate myself—who I am—because I hadn't paid attention to all those signs that he was dangerous. I'd had a feeling I should just get the train home. I'd had a feeling that

I should have hooked a chair under the door handle on the nonlocking door because there were only the two of us in the house. I'd had a feeling that someone who could watch my drink being spiked and do nothing wasn't 100 percent trustworthy. But I'd ignored all those feelings. I'd had them for a reason and I'd ignored them because I wanted to be polite. I put what someone else thought of me before what I knew would keep me safe.

I don't hate myself constantly now. It's only every now and again. I don't say out loud that I hate myself anymore. And those feelings only come up every now and again, when I'm reminded of the two big mistakes I made. The second mistake was not asking for help earlier. Because if I had, the condition, which I got from him, might not have developed into PID. I may still have been able to have children.

It's OK, though. I'm OK. I have my rough patches, like the moments when someone says or does something that reminds me of that time, but overall I'm OK.

And that's it. The whole story.

Kendra

CHAPTER 48

After about forty-nine minutes and forty-six seconds, I decided to not give Kyle any longer and moved towards the bedroom door.

He could've read it three times by now. He was obviously hiding from me now that he knew the truth. Now that he knew he'd been hasty in his declaration that he would believe me.

I stood in the doorway and watched Kyle. He was hunched over, his elbows resting on his knees, his face in his hands, his shoulders moving up and down, sobbing. I wanted to comfort him, to pull him close and tell him it would be OK.

But it wouldn't. It couldn't.

I froze as he dragged his hands down his face and ran the palms of his hands across his eyes. Then, slowly, like he was moving with a heavy heart, like he didn't want to do what he was about to do, he stood and turned to the door. He stopped when he saw me. Stopped, stared. His face was a mass of blotches, his eyes shot through with red, the tip of his running nose also a pinker shade of scarlet.

"I, er," he began, wiping his nose on his sleeve. "I was just going to splash some water on my face then come find you."

I said nothing, just moved farther into the room so I could put some distance between us. This was like standing in front of a firing line, waiting to be executed. This was like standing naked in the middle of a stadium under all the floodlights. This was like being a frightened person who had no armor because someone now knew everything there was to know about her.

"I read it," he said.

"So now you know."

Kyle nodded. "I believe you." He even made it sound convincing. "I believe you and the thought that you went through it alone . . ." He shook his head, bit his lower lip. "If you knew how much I care about you . . ."

"Kyle, stop, you don't have to say that."

"I said I believe you."

"Oh, I see. Pity. Seriously, I don't need your pity," I replied.

"No, you need my friendship and understanding and support."

I didn't want him here. I'd been fine all this time on my own, keeping my secret, coping on my own. "I want to be alone."

"Don't try and shut me out, Kendra, it's not going to work. You're my best friend."

"I want to be alone. I'd like you to leave."

"I'm not leaving you, not now, not ever."

"Oh, great, another man who wants to force what he wants on me."

Kyle was stunned, his blotchy face reeled a little, then looked as if it was going to crumple again. I knew he'd leave then. I knew he'd realize that on top of everything I was a psycho. He was silent for a few seconds then said: "Tell me what happened to you. You never said it and we both know you have to fully acknowledge something before you can start to deal with it properly. Tell me what happened to you."

I shook my head in disbelief and looked away.

"Tell me what happened to you," he insisted.

I tutted before looking back at him. "I've told you, or are you getting off on all this?"

Kyle's face hardened, set like stone as he stared at me. "Tell me what happened to you."

"I've told you."

"Tell me what happened to you."

"Why are you doing this to me?"

"Tell me what happened to you."

I ran my hands through my hair. I knew what Kyle wanted me to do. What he wanted me to say. And I couldn't. I just couldn't. If I did, I'd become a victim. In his eyes, in my eyes. The only thing I had left—how I defined myself— would be lost. And that was unacceptable to me.

"Tell me what happened to you."

"I can't."

Kyle took a few steps nearer to me, closed the distance between us. "You can, sweetheart, you can." With him being closer to me I could see tears sitting at the bottom of his eyes. This was hurting him, too. And it hurt him because he believed me. He was the first person to do so without doubt. Sometimes even I didn't believe me. Sometimes I wondered if I'd got it mixed up. But Kyle believed me. Deep down I believed me. Now I had to acknowledge it. Believe *and* acknowledge it. I felt myself give it up. Give myself up to the past, give myself up to what happened.

"Tell me what happened to you," said Kyle gently.

"I was raped."

THE WORKS

♦ ♦ ♦

CHAPTER 49

What you do is you get better bit by bit, little by little, one day at a time.

If you try to do it all at once it won't work. You'll fall back and you'll hate yourself. If you want to change long term, you have to do it slowly.

Slowly I got better.

Hadn't known how sick I was, how much I hurt until I let someone else see my wounds. Someone elses see. Kyle was the first. Gabrielle was the second. Will was the third. They all believed me.

It sounds silly that I thought they might not. But all these years I never thought anyone would believe me. Especially since he wasn't a stranger who leapt out at me on the street. He had no knife or gun. I knew him. He was a friend. I'd let him kiss me once, people had regularly seen us together. How could I be sure that anyone would believe that what happened wasn't what I wanted? How could I be sure that anyone would believe him capable of doing that to me? Those were some of the many things that kept me silent. Kept me from telling anyone what he did to me. Now I discovered they would and did believe me. And I was free.

At first, the others treated me differently, acted as though I would break, as if I needed to be protected from everything wrong in the world. They did it from love, it drove me mad.

Kyle constantly asked me how I felt, Gabrielle rang me at

all hours to chat, Will constantly said he'd use the last of his holiday allowance to come to England for two weeks to be with me. I didn't want them to act as though anything had changed. I was the same person they'd all met. They just knew another part of me.

Summer and Jaxon were the ones who helped the most in the early days of accepting what had happened. The kids didn't know I'd been traumatized when I was younger and I doubt they would have treated me any differently if they had known. They would still have berated me for not letting them get burgers from certain joints; they would have still tried to eke out a few more minutes from bedtime; they would have told me I was silly for not realizing straight away that New Garvo was actually a kangaroo not a dog; they would have asked me why I was laughing when the wolf at the end of *Little Red Riding Hood* wasn't killed but was put in a time-out.

My two children by proxy were like that. They were straightforward, they wanted nothing more than for me to be me.

The others only annoyed me because I was still coming to terms with it myself. I was still accepting what those three words meant. I knew. I'd always known. But it wasn't until I said those three words out loud that I acknowledged what they meant about me. I could stop pretending it hadn't happened but suffering because it had. If there was one person I shouldn't be pretending with it was me. I had to accept everything that had happened to me. I was raped.

Once I could say that to myself, I could admit I was powerless over what had happened to me all those years ago. But I was in absolute control, had absolute power over how I reacted to it. How I built my life around it. How I let it influence my every waking moment.

I went into the pain and tried to get to the other side.

I went to Gabrielle's chiropractor, I went for counseling, I sat staring into space, I curled up in my bed and hid from the world. It wasn't easy.

Sometimes the hole in my throat would open up, the silence that had been stuffed into the core of who I was would expand, would become so large I couldn't breathe. The flashbacks would become so strong I'd panic myself into a near-catatonic state. It was terrifying. It was worth it. Every time it happened I knew I wasn't alone. I knew it was normal. I knew I wasn't the only person in the world to feel like this. I was normal. A bad thing had been done to me, but I was still normal. Kendra Tamale was normal. That was the biggest gift of telling my secret—I discovered I wasn't alone and I was normal.

Will and I spoke or e-mailed every day. I missed him. I wanted to be with him, to lie curled up with him, to kiss him, to see his expression when we were talking about big things and about mundane things. We were still giddy at the thought of being together. He couldn't come to England because of his kids; I couldn't afford to go to Australia yet, but that didn't mean we couldn't do this until we could work out how to be together or it wasn't working anymore, whichever came first. He told me he loved me every day. I was cautious of saying it, but I'd shared something so monumental about me he knew how I felt. We were both free now—he was a single man, I had liberated myself of my secret. We only had to get over this physical distance and considering how far we'd come, what we'd been through to get here, it didn't feel like such an insurmountable hurdle.

Gabrielle and I had a more honest relationship. She cried when I told her, said it wasn't my fault, and that I could talk to her at any time. But we never talked about our experiences. Not ever. We just got on with being friends and colleagues and there was a certain comfort in knowing that someone else knew me like I knew her.

Kyle and I became close. Closer. We'd often meet for lunch on days when I wasn't picking up the kids; we'd sit up and talk late into the night; we planned outings with the children. I'd been wary of friends—*people*—for so many years, now I had a best friend living across the garden. I had my good friend Gabrielle and I had my long-distance love, Will, but because he was the first person to make me open up and to unequivocally believe me, Kyle became the best friend I'd ever had.

TOASTED BAGEL & CREAM CHEESE

♦ ♦ ♦

CHAPTER 50

I was an alcoholic mother. I can't breathe when I think about that.

I can't breathe.

What I put my children through. The amount of times I drove drunk. The amount of times I shouted at them because I was hungover. The amount of times I might have hurt them because I blacked out and my ex-husband told me how nasty I got. I have no memory of those times but they all do. I have committed a mountain of atrocities against my children. Against my family. Against who I am.

It wasn't until I kidnapped my children—yes, I really did that—and I started drinking again that I realized who I was. What I was. I gave in. I stopped fighting. I stopped fighting the truth and hiding from the truth, and I came back here.

I got it. For the first time I realized that I am powerless over alcohol. I am an alcoholic. I am like you. I used to sit in these rooms and think I wasn't like you. I wasn't that bad. I just liked a few drinks; I wasn't that bad. But I was. I am. I am an alcoholic.

When I drank I was funny and pretty and I could talk to anyone, I thought I could cope with anything. That wasn't the reality at all. Everything was always someone else's fault when I was drinking. If my husband would just tell me he loved me more I wouldn't need to drink to boost my self-confidence. If my mother didn't nag I wouldn't have to drink to be able to speak to her. If my kids weren't so energetic I wouldn't need to drink to be able to keep up with them. If the people I worked for weren't so demanding I wouldn't take so long to finish my projects. It never occurred to me that it was the drinking that was stopping me from being able to function properly.

The most important thing I can do now is get sober. Stay sober. That's number one for me at the moment. I've been going to at least one meeting a day every day. At first I thought that would be impossible, then I realized I found the time to drink every day, why shouldn't I be able to go to a meeting every day?

And, when the time is right, and I'm sober, I can be the mother I want to be. But that's future thinking and if there's anything I've learned it's that I've got to do this one day at a time. I never really understood that before. You simply decide to not drink one day at a time. Every day you make that commitment again. Sometimes it's one moment at a time because the urge is so strong. But I try to think, if I can make it through the next hour or next half hour or next minute without a drink I'll be OK. Or I'll call someone. I won't sit there and struggle. I get help. One day at a time.

It's only now that I'm starting to see that I've been grieving these past few months. Grieving for the person I was when I drank. Don't get me wrong, I don't want that back, but I found it hard to know who I was without my liquid self-confidence. But you know what? I remember what my son's imaginary friend is called. I know that my daughter thinks that Weetabix tastes like marshmallows when you have it for breakfast on a Saturday. Not any other day, just Saturday. I know my daughter won't wake up in the middle of the night having nightmares about me throwing up on her because earlier on she got a whiff of alcohol on me. I know my son won't ever have to stand over me, scared because I've passed out and he can't wake me up. I go to work and I don't have to swim through a brain fog to be able to concentrate.

One of the most painful things is that my ex-husband is dating again. Nothing serious, but he's a good man, it won't be long before he meets someone special. I thought he had, but they're just friends. It kills me to think of him with someone else. Kills me. But it's good, too. It hurts, but I'm not using it as an excuse to drink. I have a bad day and I have to live it. I have a good day and I have to live it. I get to experience the world for real. I get to experience the world as me—not hungover me or drunk me. Just plain old Ashlyn.

Today is my first sober birthday. One year without a drink. I thought it'd have got easier by now, but the urge never truly leaves you. My ex-husband wanted to bring the children and come spend the day with me. We'd go out and celebrate, he said. And he'd come to this meeting to be with me. Yes, even though we're divorced. But I said no. Their lives, my children's lives, have been enough about my drinking and my getting sober. The next time I see them I just want to be celebrating being with them. Because I'm their mum. I can't wait until I can go home to them.

My name's Ashlyn and I'm an alcoholic. Thank you for listening.

CHAPTER 51

*L*et me get this straight, Gabrielle. You're the one having the party, but I'm the one you want to stop off on the way and pick up the dips, chips, wine, chocolates, olives, soft drinks, cheese and French bread?" I say. "Have you ever heard the expression 'taking advantage of a friend'?"

I hear her grin down the phone at me. "Oh, sweetie, you don't really mind, do you? It's been so intense getting reacquainted with Ted that I haven't had time."

"You're the one with the day off!" I reply, incredulous.

"Listen, you're my only bridesmaid. Call this one of your duties."

"Like Summer would ever let me be the only bridesmaid."

"Please?" I can hear her batting her eyelashes down the phone at me. "Pretty please?"

"Well, I'm going to want something in return," I say. "You owe me, Traveno."

"Oh, thank you, thank you. Bye, love, bye."

"Hmmm," I say as we both hang up.

Ten seconds later the phone rings again. I snatch it up. "Don't tell me, you need me to buy you the perfect outfit to wear as well," I say.

There's a pause. "I need to see you, we need to talk," the voice on the other end says. I don't register for a moment who it is. "We need to talk about our baby."

The room stills.

This is like the moment between heartbeats. The space

where nothing happens. Where the blood slows in your veins, your breath catches and your mind spins out into that huge blank space of unreality.

I'm talking to him on the phone.

It's him. It's really him.

"We need to talk about our baby," he says.

I would throw down the phone if I could move. If his voice hadn't snaked its way through my body and caused all my muscles to petrify.

"Kendra?" he asks. "Can you hear me?"

The line crackles slightly because he's calling from a mobile, a phone is ringing somewhere across my otherwise empty office but I can hear him. Of course I can hear him. Every word is clear and precise, his low voice is as deep and smooth as a vat of warm syrup. I can hear him and the memory of him flashes through my mind.

———

His large, muscular hand reaches out to stop me from stumbling; his steel-like grip encases my throat. His mouth smiles as he says he'll do anything for me; his breath is against my ear as he promises to kill me.

———

"Kendra, can you hear me?" he repeats to my silence.

"Yes." I push out the words. "Yes, I can hear you."

"We need to talk about our child . . . You need to tell me about him or her." He pauses, sucks in a breath. "I don't even know if it's a boy or a girl. That's not fair. I have a right to know about him or her. I have a right . . . Kendra, you have to talk to me. You owe me that much at least."

I say nothing.

"I'll meet you," he says. "After you've finished work. I'm outside your building now but I'll wait. What time do you finish?"

Like a nest of disturbed bats, panic rises up inside and becomes a blanket of thick, black leathery wings, dampening all other sensations. *He's outside? He's outside—now?*

"I'm busy tonight," I reply, trying to sound normal. Trying not to let my voice expose my fear.

"I don't care if you're busy," he hisses. "Nothing is more important than this. We have to talk."

"I, um, I, erm . . ." I falter. I have to take back control of this situation. He can't do this to me.

"I know where you work, how long do you think it'll be before I find out where you live? I'll show up at your house. I'll come to your work every day and then go to your home. I won't leave you alone until you talk to me. You can avoid all that if you meet me now."

He means it. I know he means it. I know what he does when he doesn't get what he wants.

"I'll meet you outside at quarter to five," I say. "I can give you half an hour."

"Good girl," he purrs, his tone soft, reasonable and calm. "I knew you'd do the right thing. I can't wait—"

"Bye," I blurt out and cut the line, almost throwing the white handset back into its cradle.

Five minutes ago I never thought he'd find me. Five minutes ago it never occurred to me he was looking for me. Five minutes ago the most pressing thing on my mind was about which supermarket to visit for the shopping.

And now this.

———

His hand crushes my throat; his honey voice crawls in my ear.

———

He's really going to kill me this time, isn't he?

♦

I take my time as I leave my desk, then the building. He stands across the street, suitably casual in black jeans, white T-shirt, trainers, and pinstripe suit jacket. His hands are buried in his pockets, his legs are placed wide apart.

I cross the pedestrianized high street slowly, but I can't delay it long enough. Within seconds, I'm in front of him. Suddenly, for the briefest moment, I'm looking up into the eyes of Lance Peters.

"Hi, Kendra," he says, leaning in to kiss my cheek.

I turn my cheek and my whole body away, disgust flooding every nerve. "We can go here," I say, leading the way into a little café four shops down from our office.

The café owner shows us to a quiet little table at the back. I sit with my back to the wall so I can see the door.

He orders coffee, I order a glass of water.

Once we're alone, we sit in silence. Me, staring at the door beyond his shoulder and the world going on outside the window; him, watching the man behind the counter making his coffee. When we have our orders, he still waits in silence. Ten minutes have passed and he still hasn't said a word. So much for all that "I need to see you" urgency. I look from the door to him. Our eyes meet and—I hate myself for this—I look away.

"You've got sixteen minutes left, then I'm going. I don't mind sitting in silence—I have nothing to say to you." I sound cold. Calm and cold. It's a surprise to realize that I sound that way not because I've forced myself to sound that way but because I am. The initial shock and fear have drained away; now I feel nothing. Such a difference from when we accidentally met at the hotel last year. Then, I thought I was going to die just from being in his vicinity.

He clears his throat. "Kendra, I think . . . I've . . ." He smiles, no, grins. "I'm making a mess of this."

I look from the door to him then away again. "Kendra, I've come to apologize for that night."

"What night?" I say as I examine the dimples on the slice of lemon floating in my water.

"You know which night," he sounds confused, "*that* night."

"I have no idea what you're talking about," I say into my water.

"I'm talking about the night we had sex . . ." he begins.

I raise my head, meet his gaze straight on. "But we didn't have sex, Lance. We didn't have sex, we didn't shag, we didn't fuck and we certainly didn't make love." I stare straight at him. "You raped me."

He's taken aback. It shows on his face. I'm probably the first one who's said it to him. It's his turn to look away. First into his coffee, then at the wall behind me. "I'm sorry," he says quietly.

"What for?"

"For that night."

I lower my voice. "Which night? The rape or the sexual assault?"

"Both," he replies without a second thought. Just like what he did to me. He did it without a second thought. He planned the first time, of that I'm sure, but he did it without a second thought. "I really am sorry. What happened was wrong a—"

"And criminal."

He pleads with his eyes, his face, for a break. However, his voice says: "I've, um, been going to anger management classes and I've seen a therapist. I've found myself help to deal with what happened."

"Good for you," I say sarcastically. "It's great that you can deal with what happened."

"I feel so guilty about it. I'm sorry, Kendra. I'm so sorry."

"No, you're not," I reply.

He meets my gaze, surprised. He was probably expecting me to say it was OK, or to accept his apology in gracious silence. He still thinks he knows me. He still thinks I'm the woman who wouldn't dream of causing a fuss. The woman who quietly went home on the train, instead of walking into the nearest police station; the woman who thanked him for the lift and place to stay, instead of screaming in his face that she was going to tell the world what a monster he was. He expects that Kendra to listen while he manipulates her.

"Kendra . . ."

"If you were really sorry you wouldn't be here. If you were truly sorry it would occur to you that maybe I'm happy and that I wouldn't want to think about you. Being sorry doesn't mean asking for forgiveness. It would mean realizing that no matter what, you could never make up for what you did, so you'd leave me alone. Being sorry doesn't mean threatening me so I would come to meet you and then asking for forgiveness with a disingenuous apology. You are not sorry."

"Kendra, I am." His eyes fall shut, he shakes his head. A tiny sob escapes his lips, his voice swells with regret and sorrow. "I am truly, truly sorry." Practiced. All of it practiced.

"What for?"

He opens his eyes, a veneer of surprise and caution covering them. "For what happened, of course."

"What happened or what you did?" I press.

"I . . . I'm sorry."

"What for?"

"Kendra, give me a break. It's taken me a lot to do this."

"I didn't ask you to come here," I say with a shrug. It doesn't occur to him that it might have taken a lot for me to do this. To sit opposite him. To be anywhere near him. It doesn't occur to him that he may turn my stomach in the way rotting meat turns my stomach. I only came because I didn't want him following me home, coming anywhere near the children.

He lapses back into silence and I lapse back into clock-watching.

"Kendra, we're going to have to find a way to get on because I want to see our child. He or she must be, what, twelve, thirteen now? I've missed so much already, but I want to make up for it now. I want to be a part of his or her life. At least tell me if I've got a son or daughter."

I stare into my drink, delaying the moment I have to tell the truth.

"Kendra, are you listening to me?"

I steel myself, raise my head and look him in the eye. I try not to flinch as I flash back to the way his eyes glared into me at the station when I jerked away as he tried to kiss my mouth. "I told you before, you do not have a child with me," I say, my voice strong and even. "I only told you that to stop you trying to rape me again. I knew that was the only way to stop you. I did not have your child."

The hopeful expression drains out of his face as he goes white as alabaster. "I don't believe you. I saw the child seats in your car, I know you've got children and if you lied about that, then you're lying about this."

"I'm physically incapable of having children. I found that out a few years ago. And the car seats? I borrowed someone's car. I did not have your child. I lied about that to stop you from doing what you were doing. I would have said any-thing to stop you."

Silence settles around and over us. He glares at me, I stare back at him. I want him to know he cannot scare me anymore. Now that I've acknowledged what he did, he cannot scare me. He looks down suddenly and I know he believes me. He knows the truth at last and he will leave me alone.

I get to my feet, reach inside my bag and fish out a fiver. As I sling my bag across my body, I drop the note in the space between my glass and his coffee. "This one's on me, since I won't be seeing you again."

I leave the café without looking back but I know he's three steps behind me. I make it to the edge of the pavement then spin to face him.

"I haven't finished with—" he begins.

"I was so scared of you for so long but now I don't know why," I cut in, my voice slightly raised. "You're pathetic. I built you up in my mind to be this powerful man who could crush me, when really, you're pathetic. I know eight-year-olds who are scarier." With every word that comes from my mouth I see his anger rising, his face becoming a mass of red, his hands slowly clenching into fists. I glance down at his fists, huge and fearsome, they could hurt me. I glance back up at him.

"If you hit me I will go to the police," I say evenly, reasonably. "I'll go to the police and I'll tell them why you hit me. I'll tell them what you did to me all those years ago. They may believe me, they may not. But it will go on record, and it will be brought up if there's ever a similar complaint against you. So go ahead and hit me. I'll only feel it for a few seconds. You, on the other hand, I will make suffer for as long as I possibly can."

He does nothing. His body stays rigid, on the cliff-edge of punching me. His turquoise, violet-flecked eyes meet my black eyes. I don't look away.

Slowly, he smiles, no, grins. The sly, evil grin of a predatory animal. "You were asking for it, *bitch*," he snarls through his smile. "And I gave it to you."

"Yeah, and I survived. You tried to destroy me and I survived. How pathetic does that make you?"

Miraculously, slowly, Lance breaks eye contact and turns away. And, just as slowly, he walks away. He doesn't look back, doesn't even acknowledge that he knows I'm standing here. He walks up the cobbled high street and out of my life.

Then I'm shaking. All the terror trembling my body. I did think he was going to hit me. I did think he'd try to kill me. But I wasn't paralyzed by the fear. I could reach out for the switch that would bring the light and make the monster go away.

"All right, darling, come 'ere often?" Kyle says, coming up behind me. I nearly jump out of my skin.

"Sorry, sorry," he says, coming around to stand in front of me. "Sorry, I'm so sorry."

"It's all right, you big silly," I say. My jumpiness will probably never go away, I've accepted that.

"Sure?"

I nod, still watching Lance walk away.

From inside his jacket pocket, Kyle produces a bag of pink and white marshmallows. "The kids wanted me to give this to the Lolly Lady," he says. "In lieu of them not being invited to her party. Why didn't you tell me you hadn't told them where we're going tonight?"

"I didn't tell them, Kyle, because I am not an idiot. I knew they'd go mental. Rather you or her than me."

"They were not happy. They sent these to make her feel guilty, I think."

"Well, it won't work, the woman has no shame. She's making you do all the shopping for her party."

"Me?"

"Yup, she rang earlier with a list that I'm supposed to pass on to you."

"Why me?"

"She likes you, I guess. You'd better be careful, she might try to get you to pay for her wedding."

His eyes widen momentarily and I have to curl my lips inwards to stop myself laughing at his horrified expression. He's so easy to wind up. Kyle gazes down at me, his eyes taking in every inch of my face, and realizing I'm ribbing him, he smiles. The grin envelopes his already beautiful face. I love the way he does that. I love the way my best friend smiles.

I loop my arm through his. "Come on," I say, spinning him towards the direction of the supermarket, "I'll give you a hand with the shopping."

"Hey, who was that good-looking man I saw walking away from you when I turned the corner?" Kyle asks.

I shake my head. "Nobody," I say. "Absolutely nobody."

MARSHMALLOWS

◆ ◆ ◆

*K*endie, when you go to Australia, you have to take us with you," Summer says to me.

We're out buying birthday presents for their parents—their birthdays are three days apart in November. It's late October and cold. I haven't gotten used to the British winter yet. The frost seems to hang in the air and lick at your skin if you stand still for too long; the chill is always looking for a way to sneak inside your clothes and hug you.

So far we've bought Ashlyn a digital picture frame from the pair of them and a pair of killer heels in black satin—one from each of them, which we'll wrap individually. We're heading for an art supplies shop down at the other end of town. I reckon they should buy their dad a drawing table for his nonwork art as well as papers, pencils and drawing pastels. The pair of them hadn't been so sure of the present, but I told them we had to encourage their dad to be as good as they were. They'd agreed with that.

"Yeah," Jaxon says, "if you take us, New Garvo can see his brothers and sisters."

My Australia plans are on hold. I've been saving for a year now and have a decent amount put away. Will and I still speak every day and we saw each other for a whole twelve hours six months ago when he brought his kids over to visit their grandparents. We still want to be together, but . . . but. We're realistic. We've talked through all our options—even the most painful ones—and we still want to be together. But . . . but.

I stop and gently tug them into the rectangle of a shop doorway that's closed on a Saturday, so we can be sheltered from the crowd on the street. "Who said I was going to Australia?" I ask.

"Dad said you might go back," Jaxon tells me. "He said you want to go back to your boyfriend."

"I thought Dad was your boyfriend," Summer admits. "But he said no. He said he wants to be your boyfriend and that he has been in love with you forever and ever and ever amen, but your boyfriend lives in Australia and you want to go there. You have to take us with you. We'll be good."

"Really good. I want to go on the plane," Jaxon explains. "I want to see kangaroos."

My eyes look over Summer. I've plaited her hair with six thick cornrows that lie like smooth, silky lengths of rope away from her face, secured at the ends with different colored elastics. Her hair is mostly hidden under a thick blue woolly hat and she's wearing her black Puffa jacket, which makes her look like a snowman and brings out the freckles scattered across her nose. Her navy-green eyes, flecked and ringed with mahogany brown, watch me closely as she waits for my reply as to whether I'm going to take them with me.

My eyes then take in Jaxon. He has a blue beanie on his head and is wearing his black Puffa jacket. His freckles are scattered across his nose but reach out onto his cheeks. His eyes, identical to his sister's, watch me with the same intensity as hers.

"Listen, first of all, I love your dad, too. But I prefer him as a friend. It's just better that way," I begin. "And, yes, I was thinking about going to Australia, your dad was right about that. And, yes, my sort-of boyfriend is there, but if I was going to go I wouldn't be able to take you with me because your mumma and dad would miss you too much."

Their eyes dart to each other and they both look desperately concerned, their upset palpable.

"But, but . . ." I say to get their attention again. *"But,"* I say when they're both looking at me, apprehension on their faces. "I'd miss you, too, if I went, so I'm not going to go anymore."

They are my two buts. Of course they are. I can't leave them. I love Summer. I love Jaxon. I love Summer and Jaxon. It was meeting them, loving them, that helped to mend my soul, helped to heal my heart. I can't leave them.

Will and I have talked about this option at length—we talk about everything—and he understands. He said he'd wait until I felt I could leave them for an extended period to come be with him. But that's not going to happen. I have to admit that to myself. I have to tell that to Will. It's going to be difficult, but we're going to have to learn to live with the reality that we don't have a future together. We're going to have to let each other go. And I'm going to be single again in the purest sense. That's a terrifying thought, but liberating, too.

I know Ashlyn has her reasons for still not living with them, I know she's doing what she thinks is best for all of them, but I couldn't leave these two. I couldn't leave them and carry on breathing.

"I'm not going to go anywhere, OK?" I tell them. "I'm going to stay with you until you're all grown up."

They both nod and allow a few seconds to pass as they take in this new information, accept what this means about their future.

"But I want to see Australia," Summer protests.

"Me, too," says Jaxon. "And New Garvo."

They have no idea of how momentous my decision has

been, how noble and self-sacrificing. I'm giving up the love of my life for them and they have no idea. That's one of the many things I love about Summer and Jaxon, Jaxon and Summer—they hold no truck with grand gestures of self-sacrifice. Nor should they.

"One day I'm sure you will go there," I say, standing up. I take one of their gloved hands in each of mine and we step out onto the pavement.

"But I want to go now, not one day," Jaxon says.

"And, me," Summer adds.

"Tell you what, when we get back, let's ask your dad—I'm sure he'll be more than pleased to pay for a return trip to Australia for us. And let's say we want to go first class. I'm sure he'll be pleased with that. Really, really pleased."

The pair of them nod in agreement and happily walk beside me as we become part of the stream of people flowing down the high street.